THE JUDAS
ROSE

THE NATIVE TONGUE TRILOGY
by Suzette Haden Elgin

NATIVE TONGUE

THE JUDAS ROSE

EARTHSONG

NATIVE TONGUE 2
THE JUDAS ROSE

Suzette Haden Elgin

Afterword by Susan M. Squier and Julie Vedder

The Feminist Press
at the City University of New York

Published by the Feminist Press at the City University of New York
The Graduate Center, 365 Fifth Avenue, Suite 5406, New York, NY 10016
feministpress.org

First Feminist Press edition, 2002
Originally published in 1987 by DAW Books, Inc., New York

Library of Congress Cataloging-in-Publication Data

Elgin, Suzette Haden.
    Native tongue / Suzette Haden Elgin ; afterword by Susan Squier and Julie Vedder. —1st Feminist Press ed.
        p. cm.
    Originally published: New York: DAW, 1984.
    ISBN 1-55861-255-6 (h.c. : acid-free paper)—ISBN 1-55861-246-7 (pbk : acid-free paper)—ISBN 1-55861-403-6 ; (The judas rose : book 2) (pbk : acid-free paper)—ISBN 1-55861-403-6 ; (Earthsong : book 3) (pbk : acid-free paper)—ISBN 1-55861-404-4
        1. Language and languages—Fiction. 2. Languages, Secret—Fiction. 3. Women—Fiction. I. Title.

PS3555.L42 N38 2000
813'.54—dc2   00-042958

Wild grape vine wreath logo by Randy Farran.

Printed in the United States

THE JUDAS
ROSE

PREFACE

Some years ago, it was our great privilege to publish the novel called *Native Tongue*. So extraordinary did we find that privilege that we published the work as a book in paper, rather than in microfiche or chiplet. The book was more than simply unusual; it brought with it two mysteries. First, we did not know who its author was, only that it had been written by one or more women of Chornyak Household. Second, we did not know the name of the scholar who had safeguarded the manuscript; it was sent to us by messenger, and the brief note of transmittal was unsigned. We have no more information on either of those matters today than we did then. But we have new reason to be grateful to our unknown benefactor, because a second volume of the work has now been made available to us for publication.

Our publishing problems this time at first appeared severe. It had taken us ten years to secure the funds and the skilled workers to produce *Native Tongue*, and we had its uniqueness and its historical significance as forceful arguments of persuasion of its favor. This time our situation was very different. Of course, for those who had enjoyed the first volume, the new book would make pleasant reading—but it could not be said to constitute a historic landmark. How, then, does it happen that once again we are able to put this work into your hands in realbook form?

The answer is another mystery; the only information we have is a few sparse details. Someone—we have no idea who, whether man or woman, linguist or lay—made it possible for the women of the linguist families to open a secret bank account and to contribute to it over the years. This was in the time when Terran women were legally not adults, and were allowed no money of their own except in the most unusual circumstances. Ordinarily they could have only small amounts of what was called "pocket money," doled out to them at the whim of their male guardians, to be spent for a restricted list of personal items such as candy or trinkets or household trivia. We are informed that the women saved tiny sums, perhaps by simply lying about what those personal items cost them, and were permitted to deposit those sums in the secret account through an unidentifed intermediary. The single purpose for which this fund can be used is to pay for the publication, *in realbook form*, of items described to us only as "the works of the women of Lines."

We have been granted no access to the bank records. We do not know whether money continues to go into the account now that the situation of women is different, or what amount might remain as a balance. But even small sums, if left to gather compound interest over many years, can turn into substantial amounts of money, and there was enough to let us offer you this book.

Here, then, is *Native Tongue: Book Two.*

—Patricia Ann Wilkins, Executive Editor

(Native Tongue: Book Two is a joint publication for the following organizations: The Historical Society of Earth; WOMANTALK, Earth Section; The Metaguild of Lay Linguists, Earth Section; The Láadan Group.)

CHAPTER 1

Oh, once again, amazing grace,
abundantly to hand,
for those that journey into space
and those that keep to land.

I am a child of galaxies,
of planets all unknown;
a child of One whose majesty
requires nor sword nor throne.

On other worlds and other seas,
lit by another star,
and hearing other harmonies,
my myriad kindred are.

Oh, as ye sow, so shall ye reap;
the ancient truth lives on—
and I shall guide me by those words
till all my life is gone.

Around me spread the endless skies,
ablaze with star and sun;
no world so small it cannot rise
to greet the Holy One.

(popular hymn, sung to the tune of
            "Amazing Grace")

Heykus Joshua Clete, Chief of the Department of Analysis & Translation of the State Department's Foreign Service, winner of the Reagan Medal for Statesmanship, recipient of dozens of honorary degrees and countless awards and citations, father of three and grandfather of seven, Senior High Deacon of the United Reformed Baptist Church, was a great bulky giant of a man out of rural southern Missouri. His many honors sat easily on his shoulders; he was six feet five inches tall, weighed two hundred seventy pounds, and carried not a single ounce of fat. His silver-white hair was cropped close in almost military fashion, so that his daily hour-long swim could be fit in anywhere, no matter how formal the occasions flanking that hour on either side. He allowed himself an elegant short beard that, like his heavy eyebrows, was gray flecked with silver; it hid a chin that to his mind was just the slightest touch weaker than the chin he would have chosen for himself. His eyes were the classic bright Missouri blue carried by durable inbred Scotch-Irish genes that were not ever going to give up; he was imposing, and distinguished, and in superb health. And he was feared. Not because he was cruel or vicious or wicked but because he applied to everyone the same inflexible ethical standards that he applied to himself. The fact that you were in dire straits when you committed some infraction of the rules would not impress Heykus Clete in any way whatsoever. Your previous flawless record of lifetime service to the government of the United States would not matter either. If you were seen in a bar in New St. Louis with a drink in your hand, and were subsequently seen by reliable witnesses to actually consume some portion of that drink, however small, you no longer worked for the Department of Analysis & Translation. That the D.A.T. regulation was a stupid one, there being no difference between bars on New St. Louis and bars anywhere else, made absolutely no difference to Heykus: a rule was a rule. And you would find yourself both unemployed and saddled with a censure notation in your government file.

Heykus wore glasses because his father and grandfather had worn glasses, because he liked the slight edge of privacy they gave him behind the heavy lenses, and because there were a number of useful clusters of bodyparl that he could carry out with his glasses during language interactions. He didn't need glasses; if he *had* needed them, it had been half a century since the laser surgeons had perfected the techniques that made glasses obsolete. He wore glasses because that was the tradition to which male heads of family in *his* family subscribed. He had not pressured his own son to adhere to that tradition, but he had been serenely confident that when the boy got past the normal state of rebellion against parental values he would take it up of his own accord, and he had been right. At the age of twenty-six Heykus Jr. had appeared at a Sunday family dinner properly bespectacled despite his perfect vision. Heykus had made no comment, nor had anyone else; no comment is necessary when all things are precisely as they should be.

When the computer announced the incoming call from John Bellena of Government Work, Heykus was not seated inside his desk. He was standing in the center of his office at parade rest, glaring at an area of space that displeased him mightily. A map of the known universe took up three walls of the office, floor to ceiling, and it kept him as up to date on interplanetary conditions as it was possible for anyone to be. Every planet, moon, asteroid or other body capable of supporting even one usable installation was shown on the map, with the vast intervening distances collapsed according to a formula about which he knew little and cared less. Heykus was adamantly ignorant about such things as astronomy and astrophysics and space science; that was what his staff of experts was for. What he did understand was the system of lights that he had devised for himself; they told him what he really needed to know.

Heykus had every known usable body in space indicated on his map by a single tiny light. A world lost to the Soviet hordes glowed red; a discovered but as yet unclaimed world—still available for exploration and colonization or other practical use, and still neutral—glowed green. And every world claimed by the Christian nations of Earth, as Heykus defined "Christian," was marked by a light of clear bright yellow. Heykus was much too shrewd to let anyone, be it a member of his private staff or a member of Congress, know that he viewed those lights as golden crosses; he referred to them as "X's" and used the expression "worlds I can cross off my list" as a private joke.

What he was glaring at right now was a nice little cluster of planets that he was accustomed to seeing and had long hankered for. Just the sort of three-cluster that put him in mind of the Holy Trinity and spoke loudly to his esthetic sense, as well as to his experience of the sort of planetary arrangement that was likely to be both efficient and profitable. And he was positive that yesterday all three of those lights had been a steady emerald green. This morning they were neither green nor steady. They were a deep and bloody red, and they were blinking at him.

The blinking meant their status had changed within the previous twenty-four hours; it was intended to get his attention. The red meant they had gone from Status 3 (Unexplored, Uncolonized, Not Off Limits) to Status 7 (Claimed for Exploration by the Soviet Union.) And that galled him. That was bitter. That made his gut twist and his chest ache. Heykus' gestures, like his carefully nurtured country drawl, were smooth and slow; he smacked his right fist into the palm of his left hand and swore softly, calling upon the beards of various prophets to witness his outrage. Three more worlds *gone,* and no way to get them back! Three more opportunities lost. Three more nests of Communists polluting the immensity of space, and only the Almighty knew how many thousands of souls condemned to eternal damnation.

It made Heykus sick. Physically sick. He had to swallow hard, and breathe deeply, for just a minute. As often happened in such situations, he had the feeling that the portrait of Ronald Reagan that hung on the outer wall of his desk behind him was frowning at the back of his head. He was always careful not to look.

"Heykus Joshua Clete," said the computer again in its clear mellow Panglish, as entirely free of regional taint as technology could make it, "you have an incoming call from John Oliver Bellena of Division Twelve, on Line Six." It would give him four chances before it told Bellena that Heykus Joshua Clete was not answering his comset.

Heykus heard it this time, and went straight into his desk, setting aside his fury at the new red cluster of lights. He was always willing and ready to talk to anyone from Division Twelve, which was more generally known as "Government Work"; the projects of GW were dear to his heart. Even today, when a lifespan of one hundred and thirty was not unusual, and vigorous men in their late nineties or early hundreds were no longer a matter for comment in government service, a man of seventy-eight knew the years left to accomplish his goals were beginning to wind down. Heykus was counting on the younger men at GW to carry on when he was gone. Or when he could no longer do more than sit and fidget and polish the voluminous journals that he had kept since his fiftieth birthday for publication after his death.

He touched the stud to complete the circuit for the line, but he didn't bother with any of his scramblers or printers. If the call had been anything rigorously confidential the computer would not have announced it aloud, and it would not have come in on Line Six. He sat down and watched the comset screen, giving it his full attention.

"Heykus? John Bellena here," said the man who appeared on the screen. "Good morning."

"Morning, John," Heykus said easily. He liked and trusted young John Bellena, and expected great things of him. "What can I do for you?"

"We need a favor, Heykus."

"If I can do it, you've got it. What's the problem?"

Bellena cleared his throat. "You're alone?" he asked.

"All secure here, unless you called in on the wrong line."

"Heykus, I had a call yesterday from the orphanage at Arlington."

"Mmhmm."

"Do you remember a baby called Selena Opal Hame, Chief?"

"Should I?"

"It was an awfully long time ago. Long before I went to work for the State Department, and a little while before *you* did, maybe. You would have known about the kid, but it wasn't anything you were personally involved in."

"You'll have to refresh my memory, John. The name doesn't mean anything to me."

"Selena Opal Hame," said Bellena, fixing his eyes on some vague point beyond Clete's massive shoulders so that there'd be no embarrassment, "was one of the infants we Interfaced with the Beta-2 Alien. The time it was the *Alien* who died in the Interface, for once. That would be at least sixty years ago. I was still in school."

Heykus never wasted time beating around bushes unless no other course seemed indicated. He still didn't remember the name, but he was painfully familiar with the records of the incident and the resulting mess. It had taken weeks of negotiations, and a stunning sum of money that had to be hidden from Congress, to keep *that* one quiet. And this Hame had been a womb infant, not a tubie. Tubies didn't have names, they had numbers, and Heykus preferred not to think about them. It was true that nowhere in the Bible was there a command, "Thou shalt not make tubies," but he was much afraid there ought to have been. He had no trouble imagining some translator, back in the dimness of time, looking at whatever strange word the Lord God had then provided for the semantic concept of the infant-conceived-in-a-test-tube-and-brought-to-term-in-a-laboratory-incubator and deciding that some even earlier translator or scribe must have been either drunk or delirious. He could easily see the man deleting the offending piece of nonsense from the Holy Scriptures on the assumption that it was not the inspired word of God but the clerical error of man.

"What does Selena Opal Hame want?" he asked abruptly, to avoid having to consider the theological question further. "Compensation? I wouldn't blame her, and we can certainly provide it. Within reason, of course."

"She's not involved in this directly at all," Bellena answered quickly. "It's nothing like that. As for what she might want, nobody knows. What happened is that a Lingoe doing a routine language check at the orphanage somehow stumbled over Miss Hame—and he didn't like it one damn bit, Heykus."

Heykus frowned. "What was a linguist doing at The Maples, John? That's supposed to be a job for our own people."

"Heykus, if we don't let the linguists in there every once in a while, they get suspicious. That part was routine. The mistake was not keeping him away from Selena Hame, and that happened—I'm going to be frank, Chief—that happened because we'd simply forgotten all about her. But let me tell you, the Lingoe *really* did not like what he saw."

"So? Do we care what a Lingoe does or does not like? Is he threatening a shutdown over one lapse of the federal memory?" The linguists *could* wreak havoc if they chose to do so; they were crucial to dozens of ongoing negotiation sessions at all times. But they had never pulled out yet, and they'd had far more compelling reasons to do so.

"He's a member of the *Lines,* Heykus. From Chornyak Household. You know how they are. He immediately started filling out forms. Rocking boats. Left, right, and center."

"Huh." Heykus considered that, and John Bellena waited courteously for him to go on.

"I don't understand," Heykus said finally, slowly. "Why should a linguist of the Lines, with all the myriad of important things he has to deal with, care about one insignificant woman at a federal orphanage?"

Bellena sighed, and spread his hands wide. "She's all alone out there, Heykus," he explained. "You know what happens to the tubies we use—they all die by the time they're twelve or thirteen, god only knows why. I wish *we* knew why, so we could fix it. But this Hame wasn't a tubie, and she didn't die. And now she's a middle-aged woman in her sixties, still living in that orphanage full of infants and young children. I suppose the Lingoe's right—she probably *is* lonely, and it probably *is* disgraceful."

"Well, what does Chornyak propose that we should do about it, at this late date?"

Bellena shrugged, trim and handsome and larger than life on the comset screen of the desk. And apparently quite comfortable. Heykus knew how much could be learned from the most minute details of a caller's expression and posture and movement; he insisted on the very best, and the largest possible, comset screens. It was not something he was frugal about, and people who called him personally were usually aware of the kind of scrutiny they would be getting. Bellena was sufficiently relaxed, under the circumstances, to give Heykus the impression that he was telling the entire truth as he perceived it. And Heykus wasn't easily fooled. He'd been sitting in on linguistics classes at Georgetown for many years; he'd been a member of the Linguistics Society of America before it changed its name to Language Scientists of America to escape the prejudice against the linguists of the Lines. He was no linguist, but he was as expert in the swift analysis of nonverbal communication as any layman in Washington.

"He wants us to authorize a transfer for her," Bellena said.

"Where?"

"Well, not to another federal installation. He thinks she's had more than her share of that. He wants to move her to Chornyak Barren House—that barn they maintain for their barren women. Hame would have the company of other adult women there. She could do routine housework, help in their effing vegetable gardens, that kind of thing. They'd be kind to her, Heykus."

"Can we risk that?" Clete demanded, and his question was abrupt enough to get past the younger man's polite attempts to avoid causing his superior any loss of face. Bellena looked more than a little surprised, and his voice matched his expression.

"What risk *is* there?" he asked, obviously puzzled. "How could there be any risk? She's just like the tubies we Interfaced, Heykus, except that she survived puberty. She has no language. *None.*"

"None at all? Are you absolutely sure of that?" Heykus was disgusted with himself; he should have kept track of this.

"None whatsoever," Bellena repeated firmly. "Even if she remembered what happened to her—which is impossible, since she was only a baby—even if she did, she couldn't tell anybody about it."

Heykus let his breath out slowly, and sighed. He didn't like this; it was careless, and unnecessary.

"I see," he said. "This is a sad situation, John."

"Yes, it is," Bellena agreed. "And I'm ashamed of it. We just forgot all about her, and there's no excuse for that. We should have taken her out of the federal orphanage forty years ago and made some sort of decent provision for her."

"You're mighty charitable with that 'we,' " Heykus observed, "considering that you had nothing to do with putting her there. It's not something you could be blamed for."

"The information is right there in the GW databanks. I've

reviewed all that data a thousand times. I should have known. I *did* know—that mess was one of the first things I was briefed on when I came aboard here. I forgot, Heykus, just like everybody else did. And I'm not completely heartless; if I'd remembered, *I* would have protested. She's not an animal, she's a human being, and her life must be unspeakably dreary at The Maples. God . . . what an ugly thing.''

Heykus paused a moment, tapping his lower lip gently with one fingertip, watching Bellena. The man's regret seemed genuine, more than just conventional good manners, and that was a little bit unusual. True, Hame was a human being and she'd had a bad time of it. But it wasn't as if she'd ever been deprived of any of the necessities of life. Like every other Terran child, she would always have been provided with ample food and housing and education and medical care, always safeguarded against accident or peril of any kind. Bellena must be a married man, with a satisfactory wife, and children he was fond of.

"John," he said carefully, "I agree with you that this is unfortunate. Like most of what GW has to deal with, it seems to be a mess. It got past us somehow, and it shouldn't have—you're quite right. But I'm not sure that we ought to transfer the woman into a household of linguist females. Isn't that using a hasty wrong to make a very tardy right?''

"Hame's not a child, sir," Bellena pointed out. "It's not as if she were a child, or even a young woman. What harm can they do to a woman her age, who has no language? Heykus, she couldn't live alone, she has to be somewhere where she can be looked after and cared for. And the linguists apparently want her.''

"To experiment on.''

The man from Government Work shook his head sharply.

"That's the first thing we thought of," he said. "And we pinned Chornyak down hard. He reminded us that Selena Hame is long past the age of language acquisition. They might have tried something forty years ago, for all I know, but they wouldn't waste their time that way now. They're too busy, and it's too late.''

"You really feel that it would be a good thing, don't you, John?" Heykus found the young man's concern downright touching. He would make a note of it, just in case.

"Yes, I do. She ought to be out of there. Hell, Heykus, she's never been away from the orphanage, never even been off the grounds. She ought to have *some* life! Now that we've had the situation called to our attention, we have to make some kind of arrangements. We can't pretend we don't know about it. And the linguists know just enough of her history—we won't have to work up a false identity for her, or anything like that. Nobody from outside the Lines ever goes into their houses—no worries there, either. It's an ideal solution under the circumstances. I think we ought to do it."

Heykus could see what he was getting at, but he disliked the idea of giving in to the Lines on an issue like this. It set an undesirable precedent.

"What happens," he asked, "if we *don't* do it?"

"If we don't do it, the Chornyaks are sure to try some kind of publicity tactic to force us to. I suggest we move on this before they start something, but I'd like to do it quietly—without going through forty different bureaus and spreading the word around. That's why I called you."

"*Would* they talk, John? Could they do that without revealing their own participation in the project?"

John Bellena stiffened, and he stared openly right at Heykus Clete. He didn't have a comset image like the one Heykus was looking at, he had the standard fuzzy Civil Service equipment, but he could see his man. "Heykus," he asked deliberately, "do you understand Lingoes?"

"No. Of course I don't." It was a lie Heykus considered justified, and knew to be prudent.

"Well, neither do I. And neither does anybody else I know, including all the world's eggdomes laid end to end. I'm not prepared to say that the Lines couldn't find a way to put out some kind of twisted news story, something that would fry us nicely while it left them clear. That's just *words,* Heykus. That's what they *do.* Better than anybody else alive. If you want to chance it, you just give me the order and I'll say nothing more about it. I'll tell them they can't have Hame, and we'll work out some alternative arrangement for her. But it's not something I'm prepared to do without authority from the top."

Heykus nodded. Slowly and reluctantly, but he nodded. Bellena was right. After you'd had a few chances to experience the obscenely clever ways of linguists, with only language as their implement, you learned that it could be quicker and less painful to just step out an airlock.

"All right," he said, then. "If you don't think they'll make some kind of fuss no matter what we do."

"They were very specific about it. If we let them have the woman to look after, they'll drop the matter. They think we're complete bastards—with good reason, I have to admit—and they just want to get this settled and go on about their business.

"It's not worth fooling around with," Heykus concluded. It was too trivial an issue to challenge the Lines about, precedent or no precedent. Better not to give them the impression that the government saw it as anything more than trivial.

"No, it's not. Not in any way."

"Do it, then," said Heykus, his mind made up. The men of the Lines would make careful notes somewhere in the bowels of their computers; someday in the future a time would come when this knuckling under would be brought out and dangled as a reason for something else that he could not now predict. But he would deal with that when it happened. Or his successor would. It had been many decades since the nonsense about an obligatory retirement age for government employees had been struck down, but Heykus knew he could not go on forever. And the Lingoes had long memories, and an awesome patience.

"Thank you, Heykus. I don't mind telling you I'm relieved."

"Do you need anything official from me?"

"No, we can handle it. We, too, can fill out forms. But I wanted your verbal approval before we bypassed all the usual guardianship protocols."

"You've got it. And I'm glad you called me. How fast can you move on this?"

Bellena smiled for the first time, and Heykus noted that it was one of those smiles usually referred to as boyish; he hadn't been aware of that before. He would send a memo advising the young man to do something about that; it wasn't appropriate to his position.

"We'll have Hame at Chornyak Barren House by tomorrow morning. She has to have a routine medical first, or we'd send her today."

"Good work, John. But use a medrobot. We don't want any live med-Sammys involved in this and asking us strange questions."

"Absolutely. You can count on it."

"Anything else?"

"No, that's it. I'll let you get back to your work."

The screen went dark, and Clete sat quietly, reading the fiz-status display across its base. John Bellena's pulse, heartbeat, blood pressure, electrolyte balance, and both output and composition of sweat, were boringly normal. Which did no more than confirm Clete's expectations. Bellena was a good man, and a loyal one. Not a zealous Christian, but a decent churchgoing man. Heykus remembered now; there *was* a Mrs. Bellena. A dowdy blonde female always acompanied by a pair of pallid little blonde daughters. Bellena was reliable and steady, and the physical status check was superfluous.

But Heykus *never* dispensed with the status check. That was the way careless mistakes were made. That was how people under pressures you knew nothing about were left in place to do mischief. If Bellena called him ten times today, Heykus would read the fiz-display every single time. It was particularly important when the caller was from Government Work. A GW man had a lot more reasons to go round the bend in a basket than your average bureaucrat. Heykus believed in keeping a very close eye on the people from GW.

As for Selena Opal Hame. . . . He thought about it, and then he turned to his keyboard to call up the relevant data. He was still annoyed that he'd forgotten about her; he wouldn't forget again; and he'd flag the file to see that he got regular reports hereafter.

And when he had finished picking the computer's brains for what it knew about Hame, he was going to see what he could find out about how that handsome three-planet cluster had been picked off by the Soviets without so much as a warning note coming through his desk. His staff knew damn well he was especially interested in three-planet clusters. He should have been alerted that the Soviets were poking around, and he was going to find out why he hadn't been. And if somebody had been neglecting his duties, he was going to find himself on Heykus' carpet before the morning was over. There was no room in Heykus' life for incompetence, not his or anybody else's. When the work you do is God's work, you don't have to accept anybody's excuses, and you don't have any for yourself.

Because he was a man of more than average intelligence and good sense, born canny and born wary, Heykus had never been tempted to tell anyone about the angel. He had lived with the secret more than half a century now and intended to live with it till he died. He had never had any desire to spend his life on a short chemical tether through which he could just barely realize that he *was* alive. Sometimes when he was very weary, it would seem to him that all the weariness had settled like a stone into the place in his consciousness occupied by the secret about the angel; at such times Heykus went to the wilderness with a bubble tent and ruffitpack, all alone, and stayed until the fit had passed.

Even then, the temptation he felt was a longing to share the message, not its source. Never its source.

He had been in his third year at the United Reformed Baptist Seminary in Tulsa when the angel appeared to him. He had been the apple of his various professors' eyes. A brilliant young man, personable and charming, devout but in no way womanish, passionate in his fervor for the Savior, with a gift for the pulpit and an effortless knack for power . . . a charismatic young preacher-candidate who would do the seminary and its faculty proud, well into the future; *that* was how they had seen him. They had expected him to be a new Billy Graham, a new Marcus Graynje, a new Clark Ndala; they had expected him to set the Earth afire with love for the Word, and to inspire missionaries who would in their turn set the Earth's colonies afire with that same love. He had been precious to them in every way, and he had returned their regard. He had loved the seminary and everything about it; every last detail had been as pleasing to him as if it had been designed precisely to his specifications.

That was until the angel came. On a night when, praise God, Heykus' roommate had gone home for the weekend and he was alone in his room. He had been studying; he suspected that the roommate's departure had been an attempt to get away from the intolerable *example* of his constant studying, which tended to be so intense that Heykus forgot about both food and sleep.

He could still see that angel after a fashion, in his mind's eye; it was a funny kind of seeing, for which he had no words. That is, although it seemed to him that he could still see it, and that in some portion of his mind he could still gaze at it straight on, there was no way he could have said what it looked like. Not because he didn't have words—Heykus had no patience at all with the claims of "mystics" who pleaded that they saw things for which there were no words—but as if something were wrong with his eyes, or with the connection between his eyes and his brain. As if his eyes somehow could not add up what he was seeing. He thought it must be something like looking at a foreign language written down, and recognizing it as a language but not being able to read it.

He had no such perceptual problems with the angel's voice. To this day, he could hear it as clearly as if it still spoke, and he remembered every word with total fidelity. It was that voice that had sent him home from the seminary with only his Bachelor's in theology, instead of the Professor of Divinity degree that had been planned for him. It was that voice that had sent him into the

State Department and eventually into the Department of Analysis & Translation, instead of into the ministry.

It had broken his mother's heart . . . like so many women, she was overly and blatantly religious, and she had been so childishly proud when she'd thought he would be a great preacher. His father, on the other hand, had been delighted. He would have supported his son's choice of a religious career and had been prepared to do so. But he made no secret of his pleasure when Heykus changed his mind and took the more manly route of diplomacy and administration instead of the church. As for the professors at the seminary—for a while Heykus had thought there would never be an end to their opposition to his change of plans. First there had been the open pleading, and all the out- pouring about the waste of his talents; then there had been more subtle pressures; finally there had been some dirty tricks that had shocked him at the time, in his youthful perception of the clergy as composed entirely of martyrs and saints. The ministry was not the most highly regarded profession in the United States, but neither was it despised, and he learned that influential clergymen had a surprising number of strings they could pull when some- thing mattered to them. But Heykus had ignored it all, and had dealt with the dirty tricks as effortlessly as he had dealt with such frivolities as food and sleep, and in time they had given it up and let him get on with his life. He had never explained to anyone; the angel had forbidden him to.

"Heykus Joshua Clete," the angel had said to him, "hear my words and know that they are the words of Almighty God; know that I am a messenger of the Divine Word, That raised up all the worlds and everything that is within them. *Hear me!*" Heykus had heard most clearly; he had fallen to his knees and listened to every word that came from the glorious unseeable being that he somehow saw nonetheless. Mankind, the angel had said, were being let out of their cradle; not because they were ready for such freedom but because they seemed otherwise determined to destroy themselves and because they had persisted in misinter- preting the Holy Scriptures.

The Second Coming was indeed at hand, the angel had said. But "at hand" meant something quite different to God than it did to man, and there was still time for a great work that had not yet even been begun. There was still time—time before Armaged- don, time before Christ came trailing clouds of glory to gather in His beloved children in the last rapture—there was still time for the new holy work of carrying the Good News out to all *other* worlds. Countless billions of souls beyond this little Earth, the angel said to him, were still condemned to outer darkness because they had not accepted the Good News; there was time, the angel said, to *save* those souls, as many of them as would hear the message and believe and come forward to join the ranks of the blessed! Mankind ought to have started this great work long before, the angel had thundered, making Heykus tremble; but they had persisted instead in the folly of little toy wars on their nursery planet, squandering all their substance on meaningless nonsense instead of moving on to do the holy work that was God's plan.

And thus God had decided in His infinite mercy to intervene, lest man destroy himself and with that destruction condemn most of the universe to everlasting damnation. The means would be provided for men to travel easily to all the outermost limits of space, that they might carry the Good News, and gather in souls for the glory of God, before the Last Days.

"You, Heykus," the angel had said, "shall serve as the chosen instrument of the Heavenly Father. Go forth from this place! Set aside your small and foolish goals, for you are meant for greater things. Find your place among the halls of government, where the plans are made and carried out for adding world upon world to the Universal Congregation."

The angel had gone on to tell him just exactly how he was expected to accomplish this task, so that Heykus had never for one instant had to doubt that the jobs would be given to him, or the promotions awarded, or the projects funded. It was not *his* plan he was carrying out, it was Almighty God's, and what were the whims of a few bureaucrats beside the plans of the Almighty?

The angel had not mentioned the Soviet Union, oddly enough. Heykus did not feel free to call that an oversight—his God did not make mistakes—but he had many times wished that the Lord had seen fit to instruct him in greater detail as to how he was to deal with the USSR. Competing religions were not so serious a challenge; Heykus felt certain that in the fullness of time the battalions of missionaries traveling out to the other worlds would find ways to convince Buddhists and Muslims and Taoists and Free Animists and Shintoists and all the motley rest to change their course and accept the Christ and be born again. Even the religions of Aliens, whatever they might be like, he had no doubt would fall before the soldiers of Christ, if time allowed the missionaries to reach them and if the barriers of language could be overcome. But once the USSR took a planet, the problems *were* serious. The Christian missionaries were refused entry to those worlds, flatly refused; all attempts to send in the Good

News in no matter what medium were stamped out swiftly and relentlessly by censorship at every portal. So that any world, large or small, once claimed by the Soviet Union, was a world seemingly lost to the Almighty . . . what the status of Soviet Christians might be, there was no way of knowing.

For Heykus, the United States and its allies were in a desperate race against the Soviet Union for the staking out of this galaxy and, should it please God to grant them time, all the galaxies beyond. At any moment, *the limits of that time* might be reached, the trumpet might sound, and every soul in the vastness of space not yet reached by the missionaries would be lost for all eternity; this made every planet or asteroid or smallest moon where the cross was raised and Christ's banners flew a beachhead against Hell, an occasion for rejoicing in Heaven, and an occasion for screams of frustration and impotent rage from Satan and all his legions.

"Hear me, Heykus Joshua Clete!" the angel had said again at the very last, when Heykus had been so weak with terror and awe that he had been fighting not to lose consciousness where he knelt on the hard plastic dormitory floor. "Listen well! You will do as you are bid, for you are chosen, and this is your sacred mission! But you will tell no one what you have seen and heard this night! You will guard this as the most holy of secrets, Heykus Joshua Clete, for so long as you shall live!" And then it had gone as suddenly as it had come, and he *had* lost consciousness, not coming to himself until the sun was already beginning to rise over the roof of the building across the courtyard. He had gone shuddering and trembling to bathe himself and change his sweat-drenched clothing, and even to take some nourishment . . . he had not been able to remember when he had last eaten. And everywhere he went that day, the message had roared and surged through him till it seemed to him that people roundabout ought to have been able to hear the pounding of it in his blood.

Heykus had been the Lord's agent all his days, and had kept his secret just as he had been told, although there had been times when it had been a burden of loneliness almost too heavy to bear. He had gloried in every world won for his Lord, and mourned over every world lost to the Antichrist, and kept his own counsel. And he had waited. Waited, and lately begun to wonder. Who had been appointed to carry on the work when he was gone? Or was it up to the missionaries to continue, with no one at the helm? Was there to be no one who would take his place? He kept reminding himself that if there *was* a successor that man, too, would have been sworn to secrecy, so that the fact that Heykus did not know who or where he was meant nothing at all. Still, it seemed to him that he had earned the right to know. That the two of them, he and his successor, sharing their miraculous secret, should have been able to exchange knowing glances over a prayer breakfast some morning.

He kept close watch, hoping. Like Samuel, in the temple. Hoping that before he died he would have reason, as Samuel had had reason, to feel that he could depart in peace.

CHAPTER 2

"Unto the woman he said, I will greatly multiply thy sorrow and thy conception; in sorrow shalt thou bring forth children . . ."

(Genesis 3:16)

It was already day when the woman's labor began, and the nuns were grateful for that. Not that it would be unusual for the screams of a laboring woman to be heard by night from the Convent of Saint Gertrude of the Lambs; any woman pregnant and in disgrace might be sent here by her outraged family, and those screams were as much a part of the convent sounds as the tolling of bells. But what they attracted under usual circumstances were the attentions of a priest, hurrying to be present in case there should be a need for last rites. Which was absurd; no convent of the Sisters Of Genesis had lost a mother in childbirth in more than fifty years. But you could not tell a priest that he was superfluous and a nuisance as well. Ordinarily, the Fathers were given to believe that their attentions were welcome.

This time, however, the nuns were deeply thankful that the sounds of daily life both inside the convent and on the grounds outside would mask the woman's cries. They had taken her down to an old cellar storage room, a full week before the baby was due, and they were reasonably certain that nothing could be heard upstairs. For extra insurance they had set the choir to rehearsing Easter madrigals in the corridor most nearly overhead. If it had been the middle of the night they could not have done that, and they saw the combination of fortuitous circumstances as a mark of the Virgin's favor and offered their devout thanks. Once this was over, and they were less busy, they would elaborate those thanks in the chapel. But not now. Right now, they were occupied with the laboring woman.

The problem was that nothing about this situation was ordinary. The mother was not their usual guest. She wasn't even Catholic, much less the usual terrified and frantic specimen; she was a daughter of the Lines, utterly without religion so far as they could determine (although their discreet inquiries had established that the linguists of her Household usually attended the United Reformed Baptist Church), and she was possessed of an uncanny calm entirely suitable to her godless condition. They resented being in this awkward position, but their vows had not allowed them the option—when she appeared on their doorstep one winter midnight—of ordering her back to her own home or to the charity hospitals or simply closing the door in her wicked face. The Sisters Of Genesis were consecrated to the needs of unmarried pregnant women, women adulterously pregnant in circumstances that made them fear discovery, and so on. Nowhere in their vows was it specified that they might pick and choose among those who asked for their help. Still . . . this seemed to all of them to be exceptionally trying.

"Don't we have to tell the Fathers?" Sister Carapace had asked, clearly distressed at the irregularity.

"No. We do not."

"I don't understand. Surely we *must* tell them!"

"And why 'must' we?" Sister Antonia had demanded, hands on hips and arms akimbo. "Where in our instructions for the succor of these women does it state that we must tell the priests where they come from, Sister Carapace?"

"But a woman of the *Lines!*" the younger nun had protested. "The priests would want to know!"

There were times when the others wondered how Carapace had managed to last out the long extra novitiate for the Sisters Of Genesis. She would have been far better suited to more routine duties; she was excessively emotional, and had an irritating tendency to faint when she was needed most. The Sisters Of Gensis were expected to be an elite group, selected for their unusual qualifications from among the nuns in every convent of the Order. In the case of Sister Carapace, a serious error of judgment had clearly been made somewhere along the way. Now what were they going to say to the fool woman? Sister Antonia knew that the same question was in the minds of everyone present; what she did not know was the *answer* to the question.

Resorting to the most primitive tactics available to her, for want of anything better, she pinned Sister Carapace down with questions fired like springdarts. "Has any one of the Fathers ever ordered you to come tell him the origin of each and every woman tended by the Sisters Of Genesis?"

"No, Sister."

"Have you ever been given that instruction by a Mother Superior? Or a Mistress of Novices? Or even by a senior nun?"

"No, Sister."

"Have you ever *read* such an instruction anywhere, Sister Carapace? Or heard it read aloud? Or heard it mentioned in passing?"

"No, Sister Antonia," said Sister Carapace. "But still—"

"You have simply taken it upon yourself to make it up!" The accusation snapped like a whip, and the younger nun flinched and clutched ridiculously at her throat. "*You*, Sister Carapace, in *your* wisdom, have decided to make a modification in our instructions, based upon your personal perceptions and preferences! *Is that correct?*"

Accused outright of the sin of subjectivity, right out loud and before everyone, Carapace had gone white and trembling and refused to say anything more about it, and Antonia had been sorry that she had to stoop to such bullying. In spite of her pity, however, she had gone on to rub salt in the wounds, because it was her duty.

"Sister Carapace," she had said, the words stern and cold, even their tone a rebuke, "you will give me your word, *now*, on the Blessed Virgin, that you will not speak of this young mother, nor of her origins, nor of her condition, nor of anything else about her whatsoever, without first receiving permission from me or from Mother to do so. *Not even in the confessional*, Sister Carapace."

That had sufficed; the ethical problems it presented had distracted Sister Carapace from her determination to tell everything she knew and much she only suspected, and she had in time come to the end of her drivel and given her word. While Sister Antonia shouldered yet one more sin and was grateful that the Blessed Virgin, being a mother herself, would understand and intercede for her.

The priests would want to know, indeed! They certainly would. And if they had known that a linguist woman was under this roof and pregnant, and here without the knowledge of any male relative, what would they have done? It turned Sister Antonia's stomach just to think of the meetings they would have held, the planning and scheming and wrangling over strategy, the brazen attempts to decide what best use could be made of this tidbit of power to further the ends of Mother Church. Sometimes, disobe-

dient though it might be, Sister Antonia wondered at the extraordinary patience of the Lord, Who tolerated such antics among
men who were allegedly models of holiness. Instead of striking
them all deaf and dumb, or afflicting them with salutary cases of
boils resistant to all current antibiotics, as seemed appropriate to
her. She had absolutely no intention of abandoning the woman in
her care, be she godless linguist or no godless linguist (Sister
Antonia would never have used or even thought the coarse word
"Lingoe"), to the strange proclivities of the priests. They would
have seen her as a pawn, to be put into play in their struggle
against the Protestants, or against the government, or against
whoever happened to be in this week's most prominent oppo-
nent; Sister Antonia saw her as a body and soul in her charge.
She would do right by the woman. And that meant seeing her
through to term, caring for her through labor and its aftermath,
and accepting responsibility for the infant she would leave behind to be raised there at the convent. That done, Antonia could
send the creature packing, and give her an extensive piece of her
mind as she left, and she was looking forward to it. Until then,
she would do the very best she could to nurture and to protect her.

How in the name of the good green Earth an unmarried
linguist woman could have become pregnant, Sister Antonia
absolutely could not imagine. It seemed to her that it ought to
have been impossible. The linguists' children were educated
privately except for their obligatory participation in the two-hour
daily sessions of Homeroom required by law for every American
youngster—except of course when they were excused from Homeroom because they were needed as interpreters—and every moment of Homeroom is spent under the watchful eyes of a teacher.
They had no leisure time; it was not unusual for a child of the
Lines to already be working many hours each day in official
delegations between Earth delegations and Alien delegations by
the age of eight or nine, and that was true six days of the
week. Leftover time went to household duties and to the endless
study of the many languages the poor little things were required
to master . . . and then on Sunday the family went like a platoon
to church and returned like a platoon home. Where, as Antonia
understood it, the children were required to take part in various
sorts of "recreation" rigidly supervised by adults every instant.
They were never, so far as she knew, allowed to simply play;
and although the boys could go about unattended once they were
in their teens, the women were as controlled as any other women.
They went out to the negotiations, certainly; they traveled a great
deal. But they were taken to their destinations by men of their

family and returned home in the same way, and except in their work they probably had *less* freedom than other women. When, and where, could this defiant young woman have found an opportunity for illicit sexual congress? Not in the dormitories where the little girls slept, all in rows, with an adult woman always awake and on duty all night long. Not in an interpreting booth, under the eyes of federal employees and Aliens and heaven only knew what else. Not in the big family flyers, trekking back and forth between government buildings and home. *Where?* And equally as mysterious, with *whom?*

They had asked her, of course, and encouraged her to confess the full details of her sin for the sake of her immortal soul. And for the sake of her mother, who had somehow managed to arrange this daughter's absence and concoct a cover story the males of the house would believe, in itself an extraordinary accomplishment. For the lies she had told, and the punishments she risked, that mother deserved to know who the father was. At least that! But the pregnant girl had looked at them calmly and said that she was grateful for their concern but had no intention of telling them anything at all. And there it had stayed.

Perhaps now, in her agony, she would cry out the man's name. That was common enough, and the nuns were prepared to pay close attention to even fragments of cries. And they might learn *her* real name, perhaps; they doubted very much that it was, as she had told them, just "Jane Jefferson," although she'd answered to that readily enough through the last four months. The linguists were much given to exotic and elaborate names, especially for their women; perhaps because the family customs forbade them any other ornament, they were almost excessively ornamental with their naming. Sister Antonia did not believe in any "just Janes" among the women of the Lines today. "Patagonia Gloriosa" was more likely, or "Autumn Dawn Crocus," or some such awful nonsense.

The girl was healthy, as was any young linguist; the children of the Lines, like expensive race horses (and for similar reasons), followed superb regimens of diet and exercise and health care. Sister Antonia had been sure she would not require much assistance during her labor—thank goodness there'd be no reason to call on Sister Carapace!—and had sent Sisters Claudia and Ruth, both experienced women of even temperament, to see to her. With no expectation that anything more would be needed.

She was therefore much surprised when Sister Ruth arrived red-faced and breathless from running up the stairs and down the corridors, rushing into the room asking for her to come at once.

"Whatever in the world is the matter?" she asked, already on her feet and headed for the cellar room; if the situation had not been serious, she knew Ruth would never have come for her, and in childbed serious situations could turn into disaster while you discussed them. They could settle the details on the way.

"Hemorrhage?" Antonia asked, starting the checklist as they ran for the stairs. "Placenta pr—"

"Sister, forgive me for interrupting you, but it's not that sort of problem."

"No? What, then?"

"Please . . . come and see."

"You're sure you need me, Sister?" Antonia was going to be very annoyed if she'd been called away from her work to tend to a case of ordinary hysterics.

"Quite sure," said Ruth steadily. "This is beyond me, and Claudia is as much at a loss as I am. We've never seen or heard anything like it, not *here!*"

They took the stairs to the basement, and the narrow old stairs to the cellar below, as quickly as the skirts of their habits allowed, and Antonia asked her colleague nothing more. The Sisters Of Genesis worked well together—with a few inexplicable exceptions such as Carapace to prove the rule—and they did not waste time.

Come and see, Sister Ruth had said. Antonia stood now and looked carefully at the room—it was in order—at the birthing bed, which appeared just as it ought to appear, and at the Jefferson woman. She was flushed, of course; as its name indicates, labor is hard work. Her hair was damp, soaked, clinging to her skull; with hard work went copious sweat, and that too was normal. No sign of unusual bleeding; no sign of shock. . . . Sister Antonia turned to look at the other nuns, her eyebrows raised.

"I'm sorry, Sisters," she said gravely. "I don't understand why you've called me."

"Please, Antonia," said Ruth. "It's time for another pain—please watch."

Antonia nodded, and looked again at the woman on the bed. She saw the great belly gather, clench, and ripple under the force of a major contraction; she must be far advanced, the birth near.

"How close together?" she demanded.

"Less than a minute now. And good long ones."

"And she's been like this all along?"

"Exactly like this."

Antonia waited through one more pain, to be sure, and then

she went straight out the door to the staircase and pressed the alarm that would bring the Mother Superior at once. Mother would be a bit startled when her wrist computer told her where the alarm was coming from, but that would not delay her.

"Do you think—" Claudia began, but Sister Antonia shook her head, saying, "We'll wait for Mother, Sisters."

Dorothea Luke, Mother Superior of this convent for forty years and a Sister Of Genesis for nearly sixty, reached them in minutes, and when Sister Antonia had explained she did not wait to verify what she was told. "Sister Ruth! Sister Claudia!" she said. "Leave us at once, both of you!"

They turned startled eyes to her, and she said again only, "At once!", and they hurried away looking troubled, but without offering either objections or questions. Dorothea Luke closed the door after them, sighing heavily, wishing this were not happening under her roof, and she and Antonia went to the bed where the woman lay. They bent over her together, urgently.

"You must scream, my child," said the Mother Superior tenderly. She leaned close, and spoke directly into the young woman's face, because it would not be easy to get her attention at this stage. "Jane! It's Mother Dorothea Luke. Sister Antonia and I are here to help you. Listen to me, child—you must *scream!* For the sake of your immortal soul, my dear child . . . you *must.*"

Not a sound. The fierce contractions, almost continuous now, wracked her body, but except for the rough animal panting she was absolutely silent. According to the other nuns, she had not so much as whimpered, in all this time. Not a word of complaint. She should have been shrieking by now, begging for mercy, begging them to free her from her agony, but she was doing nothing of the kind. She was working; she was laboring; but she made no outcry. She was not even weeping. And that would not do. In the Book of Genesis it was decreed: a woman must bring forth her children in sorrow, that she might be cleansed of the guilt of tempting Adam and causing the Fall of all humankind. This woman knew that, *must* know that; however empty her own faith, she'd spent almost every Sunday morning of her life in a church. There was no chance that she had not heard the verses that applied to her condition.

"*Jane! Jane Jefferson! For your soul's sake, you must scream!*"

Nothing! Nothing but the panting; and now the deeper sounds that meant the moment was upon them.

There was no time for discussion. There was only one thing to be done, and by a quick jerk of her head the Mother Superior

authorized it. They were older women, she and Antonia, but
they were as strong as most men; they had spent their lives
lifting and turning and hauling and tending. Antonia went to the
other side of the bed; and she and Dorothea Luke, moving as
one, threw their bodies with full strength upon Jane's, holding
her thighs tight together in a grip that even the frenzy of birth
would not be able to loose.

"Now," said the Mother Superior, she, too, panting with
effort, "now, my child, we will explain to you. And you will
listen to us, because we will hold you, exactly like this, until you
do. We ask your forgiveness, Jane, for what will seem to you to
be cruelty—we are not cruel, dear child, we are doing what we
must do if you are not to spend all eternity in the depths of
Hell." And she and Antonia together, never for an instant
weakening the hold they had on Jane and on the infant struggling
to come into the world, began murmuring the appropriate verses
of Genesis. Tenderly, with infinite love, they explained the case
to Jane.

She did scream, before they were through. She screamed quite
satisfactorily, bringing smiles of relief and gratitude to the faces
of both the women tending her, before it was over.

The other nuns had no respect for little Sister Carapace, and
she knew that. She was so low in their estimation that she had
nothing to lose; it was an attitude she went to great pains to
cultivate in them. It was Carapace who came into the cellar room
that afternoon, when the dusk had begun to fall and it was easy
to tuck a newborn infant into the bottom of a basket and spread a
light cloth over it to hide the nature of her burden. She went
through the door, and she locked it behind her, which was
strictly forbidden; if she were caught, if she were asked why she
had done that, she would say that she had been confused, and
she would be believed. She was only silly Sister Carapace,
almost always confused.

She went over to the narrow bed, where the young woman lay
with huge eyes in an ashen face, staring at the ceiling in the way
that victims of any torture do stare, and she reached out to gather
the rigid body into her arms. When Jane resisted, Carapace was
prepared for that; she reached into the deepest pocket of her skirt
and took out a small wreath of wild vines no bigger than her
palm, and she laid it in the other woman's hand. She waited until
the tormented face cleared, and understanding showed in the
eyes, and then she tried again. "Dear child," she said softly,
and kissed her forehead, and this time the girl came to her

willingly and let herself be comforted. Carapace set two plump
pillows behind Jane's back and helped her to sit up on them, and
smoothed her wet hair. And then she took the infant from the
basket on the floor and put it to its mother's breast and saw the
tiny mouth first fumble and then grip tightly on the nipple.

No milk there yet, of course, but substances necessary to the
well-being of this baby, made by the mother's body through the
infinite generosity of the Blessed Lord. It never ceased to aston-
ish Carapace—that generosity, embodied in women. Every month
for most of her life, a woman's body prepared wholesome
life-sustaining food. In abundance, always made new each four
weeks, just in case. Just in case! In case some child, male or
female, might have need of it. It was a miracle, though it was a
miracle a woman was obliged to hide away as if it were a mark
of shame instead of a mark of God's grace. And then there were
these substances of birth, first the colostrum with its powerful
medicines against illness, and then the good pure milk . . . more
miracles! It was just such miracles that had drawn Carapace into
the Sisters Of Genesis and sustained her through the rigors of its
novitiate, in spite of every obstacle placed before her; and when
she found herself in a situation like this present one she was very
glad that she had not given up.

"Dear child," she said briskly, because nothing would be
gained by maudlin sympathizing, "it's over. There won't be any
more pain, and no one will torment you any longer, for any
reason. Here's your sweet babe, Jane—such a *lovely* little baby
girl! Look, Jane, look at how beautiful her little face is; look at
the perfect little eyebrows and eyelashes! I don't know how
many newborns I've seen that seemed to have no brows or lashes
at all, but just look at this one! Isn't she beautiful, Jane?" As she
talked, she took the vine wreath gently from the girl's hand and
dropped it back into the depths of her pockets.

She went on like that a while. A flow of the sort of empty
soothing nonsense that was just what was needed right now.
Until the awful rigidity left the pale face, and a shadow of a
smile tugged at the corners of the bloodied lips.

"Who are you, Sister?" It was only a whisper, but it was a
return to the world beyond shock and terror, and it gladdened
Sister Carapace to hear it. "I was told . . . the other nuns told
me I wouldn't be allowed to see my baby, not even once. May I
know your name, Sister?"

"I'm only Sister Carapace," said the nun, who had been born
a Doris and had been "only Doris" until she took her vows.
"And if the other sisters learn that I've brought you your child,

they will expel me from the Order. I'm not afraid of that; there's plenty of work to do out in the world. But if I'm not here, there'll be no one to help when someone like you needs me. And so you will be very careful not to betray me, sweet little Jane of the Lines, won't you?'' She kissed Jane again, and kissed the top of the baby's head where the blood pulsed, and repeated her warning. "There's no one else here, except me, Jane.''

Jane Jefferson's voice was weary, but it was not weak. "Sister Carapace," she said, "they must have told you what happened here—you must know what was done to me.''

"Yes," said the nun, her voice heavy with pity. "Mother told us, and told us why. And it's a very good thing I wasn't here then, because I would have fainted and then I would have been in trouble with Mother. Yes; they told us all.''

"Well, then . . . consider what it took to make me cry out, Sister Carapace. What do you think it would take to make me betray you?''

The nun smiled at her, and laid one hand against her cheek.

"Thank you, Jane," she said. "I always wonder.''

"You don't need to wonder, not this time. And Sister—my name is Aquina. After my great-grandmother Aquina.''

Sister Carapace stayed a few minutes longer, sitting quietly on the bench against the wall that had been brought in for this birthing, watching the mother and baby with silent satisfaction, listening for the rustle of a heavy skirt on the steps outside the door. And then she stood up and said, "I have to take her away now, child. I'm so sorry. But she'll be missed if we stay longer—or I will.''

She thought the mother might plead for just another minute; many would have, and it was natural. But Aquina didn't do that. Without a word, she took her baby gently from her breast and handed her to Sister Carapace to be fit back into the basket. Sound asleep, the baby would be returned with less hazard of discovery than it had been brought.

As she left the room, promising to bring the child again the next day as soon as it could be managed, Sister Carapace blundered into the doorframe. She had reacted instantly to shield the baby from the blow, slight as it was; and she stopped to apologize to the doorframe.

"I am *so* sorry," said foolish Sister Carapace.

Behind her, Aquina laughed in spite of her raw throat.

Later, when she told Nazareth Chornyak Adiness what had happened, the old woman made a soft distressed noise. "I told you to scream, you stubborn foolish child," she fussed. "I *warned* you! Why didn't you? Or at least a few dramatic moans . . . that would have satisfied them, I expect."

"I didn't want to," said Aquina, firming her mouth. "It's nothing to scream about, Nazareth. Such silly ignorant superstition!"

Nazareth turned her head to hide her smile, and murmured that she was her great-grandmother all over again.

Which pleased Aquina mightily.

The baby was named Miriam Rose—a suitably simple name— and she kept that name when she entered the novitiate of the Order of Saint Gertrude of the Lambs at the age of thirteen, becoming Sister Miriam. Still simple. Through those thirteen years she was smuggled out of the building and smuggled back in in a few reliable ways; like her mother, Miriam knew how to keep her mouth shut. It wasn't always easy, but everyone was very busy and nobody paid much attention to what one silly woman did, and Sister Carapace managed. Sometimes it was the mother she smuggled in and out, disguised as a nun heavily veiled or cloaked or hooded. But she managed, always, so that until Miriam entered the novitiate, where close supervision made it truly impossible, she and Aquina had time enough together.

In the care of the good sisters, Miriam began speaking Panglish like any other American child. From her mother, she learned Sign, so that even at the most dangerous of times they could still communicate. From both her mother and Sister Carapace, she learned Láadan, the womanlanguage constructed by the women of the Lines. All of these were valuable to her, and she made good use of them.

But they were not what mattered most, and Aquina and Sister Carapace made sure she understood that. What mattered most, and what she worked at with almost fanatic dedication, was the skill they taught her of using her voice and her body in communication as the linguists did—like exquisitely tuned instruments, responsive to the smallest scrap of data, instantly adjustable to the needs of every language interaction. If she'd had nothing but that skill and Panglish, she could have done what she was in this world to do. The rest was just so much gingerbread, so much trimming, helpful and delightful. But not crucial to her task, which was deception.

Miriam understood that perfectly.

CHAPTER 3

"It was only coincidence that every Alien civilization we encountered was so advanced beyond the civilizations of Earth that we looked like pathetic savages scrabbling in the dirt by comparison. I knew that, of course; I understood the laws of probability. And I knew that in time, of all the inhabited worlds there were, we would begin to come upon the many whose peoples were far behind or at best equal to ours.

"It is impossible for Earth to be the most backward inhabited planet in the known universe, the proof of that being overpoweringly obvious: it is to Earth that God sent His only begotten Son with the gift of eternal life, and it is Earth that God entrusted with the mission of spreading the Good News to every other world. God does not make errors, and I was in no way disturbed as we discovered world upon world with fancier gadgets than ours. However, the average man in the street does not always have my faith, even when he understands the principles of science. And I knew—all of us at the top knew—what would happen if the apparent skew toward Alien "superiority" were to become known to the Terran populations. That way lay hysteria and panic, or worse; that way lay the fate of the dinosaurs, or perhaps the lemmings.

"The holding action we decided upon was therefore absolutely necessary; it was in fact crucial to the survival of our species and to the work of God. The policy of total deception was implemented at the highest levels, with the full understanding that anyone showing the smallest sign of a potential for betraying the situation would be killed at once and without remorse; there would be no exceptions, not even in the White House. That is the sort of killing that God not only permits, but endorses. And it seemed to me that here was the full explanation of the story of

the Tower of Babel. If communication with the Aliens had not been limited by the difficulty of learning their languages—if ordinary citizens could have had casual and unsupervised conversations with Aliens—I doubt very much that we would have been able to restrict the flow of information to just those items it was safe for the general public to know. It was a barrier that gave the linguists an excessive amount of power; on the other hand, it was a barrier that made control of the public's knowledge possible, and was therefore to be welcomed rather than deplored. Like the enmity between the linguists and the pubic—because a careless word let slip to a linguist by an Alien would then be unlikely to go beyond the linguist Households—it was unpleasant, but absolutely essential. I never felt the least twinge of guilt about all this, though I felt deep regret. And I have seen God's divine hand in the convenient fact that the aliens have without exception been as anxious to keep the secret as we have.

"We knew that the situation, infuriating as it was, was temporary, and that our turn would come as surely as the luck of the gambler shifts from player to player when the dice are flung. But in the meantime, we were in unanimous accord. WHATEVER HAD TO BE DONE TO KEEP THE PEOPLE OF EARTH FROM KNOWING, IT WOULD BE DONE. We had no higher human directive than that one."

> *(from the private papers of Heykus Joshua Clete, with instructions that they be made public only "subsequent to the implementation of Condition Golden" . . .)*

Kony had had a number of ideas about the best way to spend the night before the session. He'd made a list. There was the trip to the Ho Do Da Casino Complex, where he would gamble away at least one million credits, awing everyone at the tables with his total disdain for his losses and his indifference to his winnings. There was the one where a dozen expensive go-come girls were delivered to his room and he exhausted the entire dozen, with every sound and movement preserved on holotape, and then had fifty copies made and sent out by special messenger to all his friends. Not that he had fifty friends, but he could have sent some of them a matched set. There was the one where he strolled casually down to the port district and cleaned out bar after bar, systematically, leaving a trail of battered and bleeding males behind him, and not one mark on his brawny brutal self. There was the one with the massive three-horned killer bulls of Planet Blair-Edna, that ended with him swinging a pair of the poisonous

central horns around his head like batons and roaring his laughter
into the respectful crowds that watched him.

It was getting to be a long list. As was reasonable, since what
he actually did before each session was spend the night polishing
and perfecting and expanding the list. In his head, it was titled
"WAYS TO EXHIBIT MY AWESOME PERSONAL POWER";
on the paper, it was titled simply "List."

Antony Fordle, who sat beside Kony in the tiny compartment,
had spent his night the same way, making the same sort of list,
in the same sort of excruciating detail. It was what they had been
trained to do. It was what every one of the D.A.T. Special
Ambassadors had been trained to do, on the careful advice of the
supershrink hired by Government Work to solve the problem.
Who perhaps *had* actually died almost immediately thereafter of
a heart attack, as reported in the tasteful obituary.

None of them would actually do any of the things on the list.
Not before the session; not after. Another of the things they were
trained to do was be inconspicuous. A trail of battered and
bleeding toughs . . . a trail of battered and bleeding three-horned
killer bulls . . . it would not do. Even a trail of glowing satiated
go-come girls would not do. The list wasn't for actual planning
purposes. The list was to pump up your ego to such monstrous
inflated proportions that it would carry you through the session.
The supershrink, like any med-Sammy, had been sure he was
right; he had insisted that it would do that very well.

He had been wrong. The ego jolt never lasted even through
the short flight up to the asteroid's well-camouflaged dock. It
might happen that you'd take your seat thinking serenely, I AM
ONE OF THE MOST POWERFUL MEN IN THE ENTIRE
SOLAR SYSTEM, I HAVE EXTY MILLION MEGACREDITS
IN MY SECRET ACCOUNT, I OWN A PRIVATE ASTEROID
WHERE I AM KING AND POPE AND SULTAN AND MA-
GUS AND THERE IS NO OTHER POWER BEFORE ME.
That could happen. But it leaked out fast. You sat in the cramped
passenger compartment of the tiny automatic Air Force flyer
and watched the digits on the left-to-go spot get smaller and
smaller; and while you watched, your ego got smaller and smaller,
too. Long before the tone sounded to tell you that the flyer had
docked and that you could enter the corridor in the conference
room where the Aliens were waiting, the last of it had evaporated and you were wishing they had chosen you for something
else. *Anything* else. Never mind the exty million megacredits and
all the rest; you would rather have been a servomechanism
supervisor on a tourist asteroid than a member of the elite corps

of seven handpicked men to which you actually belonged. It was only an elite corps while you had your feet firmly on the surface of the Earth, or some colony of Earth, and could revel in the idea that nobody around you knew the wondrous secrets you knew or had all the wondrous goodies you had or had seen all the wondrous sights you'd seen. You were a man who could call up the President of the United States and give him *orders*, for example; that was a tremendous consolation while you were on Earth and made up for many disadvantages. But it was no use to you when you actually set out, twice a year, to do the job for which you had been so painstakingly selected. Kony would have given up making the sillyass list, it was so useless, except then how *would* he have spent the nights before the sessions?

He was always afraid to go to sleep. Even with drugs to make sure the sleep was dreamless, he was afraid. And if you were awake, the seconds crawled toward eternity. So. He kept on making the list called "List." Maybe the shrink had known a little bit more than they gave him credit for? Naah . . . the poor simple bastard. How could he possibly not have realized that once he'd done his task he could not be allowed to keep walking around the world, carrying the information he carried? Heart attack, my sweet ass, Kony thought. Anybody who cared to take a look at the statistics about mental illness, nervous collapse, drug addiction, alcoholism, and general status tapioca-brain and free-flowing mouth among shrinks would have known that a heart attack was the next thing on the poor guy's schedule after he was handed his generous fee for services rendered. Poor simple bastard.

Special Ambassadors, on the other hand, were *safe*. Like the bottoms of chasms. Minds of solid aluminum, plated with platinum, studded with emeralds and rubies and priceless pearls. If Kony hadn't been absolutely sure of that, he would have taken the quitpill he always carried, instantly, without a second's hesitation. If he ever so much as noticed himself getting nervous, he would take that quitpill. Except during the night before a session, when it would have been a hell of a lot more demented to be calm than to be a mass of flinching nerves that had to be soothed with the mindless construction of the List.

The S.A.'s could have handled being hated. That would have been easy. Powerful men had always been hated; they fed on it the way infants fed on mothers' milk. The satisfaction of being surrounded by people who hated you but would have to wait till you were dead to express that hatred was like the satisfaction of sex . . . it was wonderful to watch such people squirm, in all the infinite variety of ways that such squirming could take place, while the slow pleasure spread through your loins. Hatred was an index of your power; the more truly powerful you were, the more intense the hatred. Only women wanted to be "liked."

But the Aliens didn't hate them. Not at all. The Aliens thought they were *cute*.

That was not easy to bear. Cute! It was a word you used for females, and children below a certain age, and small animals with the huge round eyes that human beings are hardwired to find appealing. Knowing that you, an adult human male, were considered "cute" . . . it was impossible to bear. But you didn't have any choice, you had to bear it anyway.

You knew what they were thinking, even when all you faced were their robot extensions and you didn't know where the real Aliens were or what they might look like; among their technological tricks was that of making robot simulacra with magnificently authentic body language. Kony had stopped caring whether the amused tolerance he faced came from one of the Alien species able to function on its own in the asteroid's canned environment or from a simulack—it was the very same amused tolerance, in either case.

And you knew how you were being spoken to, nice little native that you were. "Good fella chop chop him talkee fine fine." That kind of thing. No doubt the Alien went home at night to his spouse, or whatever Aliens had, and said, "Darling, I saw the cutest little Terran today! You wouldn't *believe* how hard he was trying, poor little fellow . . . I had to really fight not to pick him up and cuddle him, just to let him know it was okay." Or maybe, "Terrans are so damn *cute* when they're mad!" That was also possible.

You couldn't speak the Alien languages, of course. You had to search desperately for the words you needed on your ring of phrase-chips, and then you had to key them into the portable speech synthesizer, which pronounced them in a flawless imitation of your own voice. (The idea behind that had been that you would hide the synthy on your person someplace and mouth the words along with it, fooling the Aliens into thinking your mouth was the *source* of the noises.) This had worked very well in the lab, and had seemed entirely convincing to the staff for whom it was demonstrated; the Aliens had thought it cuter than anything else the Terrans did, and Kony had abandoned it instantly when he saw that gleam in their eyes that meant, "Well, will you *look* at that dear little creature trying to play like it speaks Alien!" The experts told the men they were "anthropo-

morphizing'' when they interpreted the Aliens' reactions in that
way; the experts had never *been* there.

If the technique with the speech synthesizer failed you, you
fell back on PanSig, semaphoring and posturing and flashing
color cards and spraying odors . . . . Chop chop. Good fella not
likee likee, too damn bad for good fella.

Some of the Aliens you dealt with were polite; they would
condescend to speak Standard Panglish at you. Flawlessly. Others were arrogant, and would not stoop to such an inadequate
excuse for a language. The polite ones obviously found the
behavior of the arrogant ones distasteful. But it was equally
obvious that even to those whose courtesy was impeccable you
were no more than a posturing child whose little feelings must
never be hurt, lest it lose its little temper, and whose little
sensibilities must never be startled, lest its little personality be
damaged in some way. One must be kind to the natives, old
boy—beneath one to behave otherwise, donchaknow.

Sometimes, when Kony was sitting around, shaking a little,
trying to recover some of his self-respect so he'd be able to go
out again the next time, the grotesque hilarity of it would strike
him. All those years in the past spent dreading the marauders
from outer space, the monsters that would subjugate Terra and
make her peoples their slaves! It *was* funny. Because the Aliens,
no matter which part of the Interstellar Consortium they had
been sent from in their mysterious rotation of duty, had no more
interest in taking over Earth and its colonies than the United
States government would have had in subjugating an Appala-
chian pig farm and persimmon grove. Earth was a reservation planet,
a place where dear little primitives lived in quaint but deplorable
squalor. Earth was not to subjugate; Earth was to *help,* to the
very limited extent that Terrans could be trusted not to hurt
themselves or others with the Alien knowledge and the Alien
gadgets.

Here we come! Kony thought giddily, as they stopped to let
the conference room door recognize them, announce them, and
iris open to let them in. Kony B. Flagg and Antony Quentin
Fordle, Special Ambassadors, Department of Analysis & Translation, Top Secret Section, Foreign Service Division, State Department, Government of the United States of America, Planet
Earth. Here we come! Little naked heathen ignorant savages,
strutting our stuff, rattling our beads . . . . He swallowed bile, as
always, and that meant that he entered the conference room with
foul breath, as always. With Antony Fordle it was sweat; something about the repulsion and degradation he felt would activate

in his metabolism a chemical that turned his otherwise ordinary human perspiration to a musky reek—which would gradually permeate the room in spite of the air exchange system's most valiant efforts. Here we come, Kony thought, with our different but equally appalling primitive stinks! Chop chop. He put on his most icily contemptuous facial expression, for his own benefit—it certainly would not impress the Aliens—and stepped into the room, ready to do his duty.

This time, if the briefing had not been flawed, there'd be one Alien that was the real thing and one that was a robot simulacrum. No way to tell which was which probably, though D.A.T. folklore was that if you were good enough you could spot the simulack by the pupils of its eyes. Kony had never spotted one yet; he waited until he was told. The Aliens were scrupulous about telling you things like that. "I am X, Robot Simulacrum of Y, who speaks for Planet Z." And then you knew where you were, and it didn't matter one diddly anyway.

The real thing turned out to be in the seat on the left, the simulack on the right. And they were both polite versions, able and willing to speak Panglish, which would make this easier. Both nodded genteel appreciation of the ritual greetings and salutations in their respective native languages offered by the speech synthesizers, which had been programmed by the Lingoes. (Who Kony hated more than he hated the Aliens; because the Lingoes were *family* in this context, and when your family turns on you, it's much worse than when strangers do it.) Refreshments emerged from a slot in the wall and floated over the small conference table on a gravytrain; it waited while Kony and Antony made their selections, playing a folktune while it hovered near them. Then national anthems were piped in, and holos of the relevant flags were made to wave at the center of the table; opening speeches, taped for convenience, were played. Every possible effort was made to help the Earthlings feel comfortable, and it was all torture. And when at long last the end of the introductory ceremonies was reached, and the session formally began, it was as abrupt as the preliminaries had been prolonged; the Aliens waved their magic wands, and the new figures appeared on the comscreen.

Kony looked at the data; they weren't interesting. The Soviet Union and its allies had added one new Alien language to their inventory since the last session, and had acquired three new colony planets. The United States and its allies had added three Alien languages but had acquired only two new colony planets. The end result was essentially a draw, give or take a planet, give or take a language. It always was. It was something else the Aliens were scrupulous about. They maintained absolute neutrality toward Earth politics; they saw to it that neither East nor West ever gained any scrap of their knowledge that was not immediately transmitted to the other side. They were simply there to provide information based upon their superior resources for gathering that information.

And of course to announce the new quotas for the Interfaces, where the human infants of the linguist dynasties learned the Alien languages that made all the rest of it possible.

"We want fifty new pairs of Aliens for Interfacing," Director Clete had told them at the briefing, the veins of his neck pulsing with urgency. "*Fifty!*" And when they'd stared blankly at him, he'd narrowed his eyes and told them not to tell him it couldn't be done, and they had gone along with that. Neither of them had said it couldn't be done. Heykus Joshua Clete wanted them to ask for fifty pairs of Aliens, they'd ask for fifty pairs of Aliens. They could ask for fifty, or five thousand, or for any other number he fancied. It would make no difference.

The quota this time, the simulack was saying, would be four pairs for the Soviet Union and two pairs for the United States. The simulack was pleased to be able to tell them that all six *would* be pairs—no singlets. It was always easier when the AIRY's were in pairs, because two Aliens-in-Residence could carry on ordinary natural conversation in the Alien tongue in a way that greatly increased the data from which the human infants acquired the language; a single AIRY was less satisfactory. (Was a single AIRY also lonely? Miserable in its isolation from its own kind? Kony didn't allow himself to think about that.) The simulack was sure that the men from D.A.T. would be equally pleased, and it hastened to assure them that the Soviet Union had been entirely satisfied.

Four for the Soviets. Two for us. If there were no failures, the number of Alien tongues acquired on each side would continue to be equal. For some reason not well understood, the USSR did sometimes have failures in its Interfaces, while the US almost never did; on the other hand, the US had more failures in its attempts at settling planets and establishing colonies than the Soviets did. Also for reasons not well understood. On an interplanetary scale, it was near enough equal, over time, to satisfy almost anyone. It did not satisfy Heykus Clete, who took each and every new Soviet colony, each and every new Soviet exploratory base, as a personal insult. It was an article of faith in D.A.T. that what kept Heykus not just alive but as vigorous as a man half his age was his insatiable drive to beat the USSR to each and every planet, moon, and asteroid in each and every galaxy, till the end of time. It might be enough to make him immortal, space being theoretically supplied with infinite real estate for him to lust after.

Carefully, grateful that this was one of the times when Standard Panglish would be all he needed, Kony switched to his most neutral expression and spoke up. He had seniority; that meant he got to be the first to make a fool of himself.

"There is a problem," he observed, with dignity. Maintaining in his mind's eye his own perception of his own speech, *as* dignified; the linguists claimed that even if the Aliens did consider Panglish a pidgin, it was ignorant to feel degraded by the *speaking* of a pidgin. He didn't believe it, but he clung to it.

"Ah?"

Kony noted the twinkle in the eyes of the simulack making the polite noise of query; how that was accomplished, he had no idea. If he asked, they might very well be willing to tell him. The Aliens had been generous with their technologies, including their FTL travel and their miraculous medicines and their antigravity techniques and any number of other goodies. You asked; they asked you why; you told them; they thought a minute or two; much of the time they said "Yes, of course." And in a few days along would come the official communication stating how much it would cost and how long it would take, when and where the negotiations should be scheduled, what Alien languages would be involved, and so on. Whereupon, D.A.T. called in the linguists of the Lines, to settle the details. Once in a while you asked and were refused, and then you knew that whatever it was you'd asked for, however innocuous it might have seemed to you, was something that children could not be allowed to play with, so sorry. But usually they were indulgent.

"Please state the problem, Special Ambassador Kony," it said.

"The United States regrets that the number of subjects for Interfacing is not adequate," Kony told it.

"Is that true?" Up went the eyebrows, over the twinkle. "How many subjects does the United States consider necessary?"

"One hundred pairs are needed at this time," said Kony, calm as a puddle.

Silence. Then: "One hundred pairs." The lips twitched.

"The United States has a huge population, spread over vast territories. This requires an acceleration of the Interfacing program."

"And of course," put in Antony smoothly, lending a hand, "the more extraterrestrial cultures we are privileged to interact with, the more strongly we forge the ties between your peoples and ours."

"There will be six pairs," said the simulack courteously; at its side, the Alien nodded.

"The United States will be delighted to cut its request by fifty percent!" Kony declared. Flourish of trumpets, stage left.

Gently, the simulack repeated itself. "There will be six pairs."

"It is not satisfactory," said Kony. "Let that be noted, for the record."

They smiled at him, and then looked down at the conference table. More politeness . . . wouldn't do to let the Earthlings see their amusement, donchaknow. And the Terrans shrugged. They were used to this; they knew the orchestration and the choreography, and they had given up trying to do variations.

There had been a time when D.A.T.'s Special Ambassador had genuinely tried to negotiate. Not any more. They all knew now that it made no difference whether they recited nursery rhymes or burst into tears or broke into word salad. The communication of the Consortium's representatives was not a feedback system except in the absolute formal sense in which an utterance by one speaker is followed by an utterance from another speaker. There was no rule demanding a semantic connection among those utterances. The Aliens came in pairs to announce the current statistics for the two major Terran power blocks and the current quota for Interfacing; those predetermined announcements would be made, no matter what was said. That they didn't just send a memo instead of meeting with the Terrans was no doubt just one more example of their determination to be well-bred at all costs.

Kony had explained it to Heykus Clete himself, once. A command performance.

"Say they tell me there'll be ten pairs for the Interfaces this time," he'd told the Director. "And I say we need twenty. The Alien will say, 'There will be ten pairs.' And if I then say, 'Mary had a little lamb,' the same thing will happen. The Alien will say, 'There will be ten pairs.' Politely."

"That doesn't make sense," Clete had objected.

"Why should it make sense? They are *Aliens*. That's what 'Alien' *means*."

Clete had glared fiercely at Kony, and had spoken in a long rush of angry words. "They're technologically centuries beyond us. They have humanoid brains. They speak humanoid languages. I don't *believe* that they don't know when a sequence of utterances is meaningless!''

Kony had sighed, too worn out with it all to care very much.

"Mr. Clete," he'd said, "you think about it. What if we were negotiating, you and I, with some truly primitive tribe. Say we were, out of the goodness of our superior hearts, letting this tribe have two . . . oh, I don't know, make it two laser scalpels a year. For their medical needs. Say they want us to give them fifty, but we don't trust them with fifty. They might cut themselves up at parties or something. We tell 'em they can have two, they ask for fifty, we say they can have two, and they whirl around three times and shout 'Kabbakabba ding dong two three four!' Do you really believe we're going to stop and concern ourselves with that? We're going to think to ourselves, 'Hmmmm . . . some kind of primitive incantation,' and we're going to exchange knowing glances with one another, and then we're going to say again, patiently, that they can have two laser scalpels.''

"It's like that? As bad as that?''

"It's like that. Always. Oh, not at the *real* negotiations, where the linguists are brought in and we're working out details for something they've already agreed to. But in *our* so-called negotiations, Director, it is *exactly* like that.''

Clete had sat there smacking one big fist over and over into his other palm, chewing on his bottom lip, while Kony waited. *You believe you could do better,* Kony thought. *You think you could get through to them, make them understand we're worth the time it would take for them to really work with us. You go right ahead and try it!* But he didn't say any of that. The old man was terrified of spaceflight; everybody knew it, but everybody pretended it was a secret. You'd never get him beyond the toddle-along commercial flightlanes, and rumor had it that Klete even had a tendency to go all white-knuckled anywhere that his own personal flyer couldn't take him. He'd turned D.A.T. down flat when they'd offered to give him a small artificial asteroid for an operations base instead of this creaky old office in Washington.

Eventually the silence broken only by the slow steady thud of his fist had brought Clete out of whatever state he'd drifted into; Kony did not make the mistake of assuming that it was a daydream. When Heykus Clete was thinking, you were respectful, because you could be absolutely sure that he was not thinking idle thoughts.

"Sorry, Special Ambassador Flagg," Clete had said finally. "I'm afraid my mind was wandering.''

"Yes, sir."

"I was wondering. . . . You still haven't been able to get them to tell you how the Aliens-in-Residence are selected? Whether they volunteer, or are drafted, or what?"

"No, sir. And we have tried. They just say not to concern ourselves with such matters, and change the subject."

"I see. That's not good."

"No, sir."

"You know, Flagg, I'm convinced that—even if there's no real diplomatic interaction—it would be best to keep the title you men now use. To avoid causing comment within the Department. But if we'd realized it would be like this, we'd have chosen something that didn't rub your nose in it. Agent. Consultant. Something like that."

"If we had known it would be like this, sir," Kony had asked cautiously, "would we ever have started Interfacing at all?"

Heykus Clete had looked shocked. "We most certainly would have!" he'd said sternly. "We had to get out into space, and we had no time to waste. We couldn't decide we'd go by covered wagon because our feelings were hurt."

"No, sir."

"That's all, then, Flagg."

"Yes, sir."

You had to give the old man one thing (you had to give him a hell of a *lot* of things!); he didn't try any of the crap about how it was going to get better and it couldn't go on like this forever and so on and on and smarmily on. Kony appreciated that, because it was *not* going to get better, and it *was* going to go on like this, and all that Kony prayed for was that they would continue to be able to keep the lid on it. It was random good luck that the Aliens felt the same way about the confidentiality . . . they could just as well have gone on all the comsets of Earth at once, like in the ancient films, and said, "NOW HEAR THIS . . ." and blown the whole thing sky high. They chose not to do so. By random good luck. Kony would settle for that.

He realized, finally, that Antony was discreetly nudging his boot to get his attention; this time he was the one whose mind had wandered. But it didn't matter. It didn't matter at all. If he had fallen out of his chair and lain on the floor laughing, the Aliens would have assumed it was an exotic primitive native custom. It would not have made the least bit of difference.

"Steady, Kony," said his partner clearly, and Kony steadied. It was over again for six months. The national anthem began to play again, and Antony keyed in the parting utterances to the speech synthesizers, and it was time to go home to the reservation.

It occurred to Kony for a few brief seconds then to wonder why, in his making of the list called "List," he had never included a scenario in which he rampaged through *Alien* ports and *Alien* bars, leaving behind him a trail of battered and bleeding *Alien* toughs. The thought wandered through his mind, was firmly stashed under some cognitive bulkhead, and disappeared from his awareness.

Kony would sleep now, all the way back to Earth.

CHAPTER 4

"According to the radical feminologists, men were directly responsible—through negligence, not malice—for the rise of feminism in the epidemic form which it took in the late twentieth century. These so-called scholars acknowledge the magnificent research of Haskyl and Netherland which proved the genetic inferiority of the human female. They admit that it was the prompt and efficient male response to Haskyl and Netherland's work, at every level of government, which brought about the speedy passage in 1991 of the constitutional amendments restoring to women their proper and valuable place in society, and formally imposing upon men the stewardship role so many had neglected for at least the preceding fifty years. But they persist— with an almost feminine disregard for the requirements of scholarship—in their claim that prior to Haskyl and Netherland the twentieth century was a scientific wasteland, in which no research or publication in feminology whatsoever could be found. As if Haskyl and Netherland's discoveries sprang full-blown from the void, owing nothing to the work of others before them!

"This is manifestly absurd. These gentlemen know full well the difficult circumstances in which the early feminologists were obliged to do their work, in a time when the mere statement of the basic principles of the discipline could actually lead to legislative and judicial penalties; they know that the pioneers of the field had no choice but to speak and write in veiled terms. But they were not silent, and their work did not go unnoticed! *Anyone who denies this has failed to examine the history of twentieth-century America with even minimal care; certainly no such individual has taken even the elementary step of viewing the historical collections of commercial advertisements presented in all American media of the period. The most cursory viewing of*

these collections demonstrates that although lip service to 'feminist' views was paid by what might be referred to as the intellectual *media, no such distortion existed elsewhere. Academics, themselves all too frequently effeminate, may indeed have been unaware of the work of the early feminologists; but those with* true *power—for example, those who controlled the advertising industry, the giant corporations, the health care industry, the national defense, and the major churches—were clearly quite free of such ignorance.*

"Any scholar who reads the records of history from about 1940 to 1990 with care *finds an abundance of examples stating both the inferiority of the female and the custodial obligations of the male. This is true even when the curious social customs of the time necessitate various mechanisms for disguising those principles, as opposed to stating them openly. To insist that the twentieth-century preoccupation with high technology and its military applications delayed Haskyl and Netherland's work is more than just a vicious lie. It is a blatant exhibition of ignorance which must no longer be tolerated within our field. It ignores the unobtrusive but superbly effective statesmanship of Ronald Reagan and George Bush; it ignores the equally restrained—and equally effective—statesmanship of Pope John Paul the Second; it ignores all the thousands of wise and capable men who steadfastly kept our nation* on course *through a period of temporary turmoil that would have meant the collapse of Western society had they been less faithful to their principles.*

"There is not sufficient space to name all those men here. Some, like Chodoff, or the great Dobson, need no mention. But the manner in which our stubborn colleagues persist in denying them the honor to which they are entitled shames us all.

"I ask them just one question in closing: how do they explain the fact that Haskyl and Netherland were able to obtain funding for their research into women's cognitive and emotional competence during this period, as well as an immediate forum for the publication of their results? I challenge *them to explain!"*

(from "A Call for an End to Radical Feminology," editorial by Broos W. Clawn, Ph.D., Annals of Patriarchy *37:4, Spring 2207)*

There was no way that Jo-Bethany could keep from hearing her brother-in-law's voice, however much she might have wanted to . . . human beings, by some curious oversight of the Creator, were not equipped with earlids as they are with eyelids and have no way to shut out the sounds coming at them. But she didn't have to look at him, as long as she made some noncommittal noise every once in a while to indicate that she was still there, and so she looked out the window at the yard outside while he talked.

She had been with her sister and her fiancé when they went to order the yard, as chaperone. And she had done what she could to talk them out of it. She had done her best to make a case for something more pleasant to look at, something with grass and a few evergreens and perhaps a white picket fence or a nice low redwood or cedar one. But it hadn't been any use. Ham Klander was absolutely determined to have what she was looking at now. A formal courtyard all the way round the house, laid in burgundy slate, and a wrought-iron fence topped with vicious spikes. Formal granite urns with topiary roses in them, and a formal granite pool with a formal granite boy standing in it holding a formal granite ram's horn from which a stream of water was allowed to fall, formally, into the pool. And that was all. Not a blade of grass, not a daisy, not a tree. . . . Jo-Bethany didn't consider the skinny bile-green ornamental cypresses to be trees, whatever the botany people might say. It looked like the courtyard of a not very flourishing stuffy small hotel, and in the slow steady rain it was a dismal prospect. Just as she had told them it would be.

She had known, even then, that Ham Klander's major concern in life was to avoid any unnecessary labor, and she'd gone out of her way to be sure he knew that the grass which was offered with the more traditional yards was specially bred to stop at one-and a-half velvety inches, and would never have to be cut. "And there's a service contract that comes with it, Mr. Klander," she had added. "When you buy one of those you can forget about maintenance; the company comes around every month or two and does whatever needs doing."

He'd grinned at her and told her to call him Ham, and he'd hugged Melissa to him as if she were already his property. And Melissa hadn't opposed him, of course. She had looked like a terrified scrawny rabbit; she was hugged in under his big arm and clasped to his side so hard that Jo-Bethany was sure it must have hurt her. Nobody had ever held her like that, but she was positive it couldn't be comfortable. And there the yard was, this minute, just as it had been displayed on the comset catalog. Number 171, French Townhouse Courtyard. Jo-Bethany loathed it, and so did Melissa, but if Ham liked it that made no difference at all, and Ham liked it very much. He said it had class, and Ham valued class.

"Hey, Jo?"

She jumped, startled, realizing that she'd let too many minutes of his monologue go by without an encouraging murmur, and she gave him her swift attention.

"Yes, Ham," she said. "I'm sorry. I must have been daydreaming."

"I didn't call you in here to daydream, Jo."

"I know you didn't, Ham.'

"You think you could manage to stay awake for two minutes?"

And then she heard it. What he'd said before. It had taken her brain that long to get over the shock and present it to her awareness.

"Oh!" she said, foolishly.

"Oh? What does that mean . . . *oh?*"

"Ham, you can't be serious," she said slowly, her fists clenching at her sides. It was possible that he was teasing her. He thought it hilariously funny to tease her, or Melissa, or any other woman unfortunate enough to be close at hand; if he could make that woman cry, he was genuinely amused. It was good sport, teasing women.

"Damn right I'm serious," he told her, and he grinned just the way he always had. That grin that says I'm the boss and you're nothing and if you don't like it you can stop breathing.

"Ham, don't tease," she pleaded.

"Hoo baby . . . I'm not teasing. You'd better listen, Jo-Bethany."

She bit her lower lip and watched him. Hating the grin; hating the way he lay there on the couch with his hands clasped behind his thick neck and his shoes making marks on the upholstery that somebody else would have to clean up; hating his expensive suit and his expensive shirt and his immaculate fingernails that Melissa tended; hating everything about him. He was laughing at her.

"Jo-baby," said her brother-in-law, "I've already signed your contract. You start Monday morning . . . and you move Saturday afternoon, so you'll be right there to start in bright and early."

"Ham," she said softly, "I don't believe it. You wouldn't send me to work for—" She paused, because it wasn't a nice word, and then she said it anyway. "You wouldn't send me to work for Lingoes, Ham." *Not even you,* she thought.

"At the salary they're offering?" He made a small circle in the air with the tip of one shoe, admiring its silver gleam. "You can be damn sure I *would* send you, lady! And I *am* sending you. We can use the money . . . I've got big plans for that money. Three hundred credits a month, plus room and board, Jo—that's a good four hundred a month in my pocket. I'd send you to work for the devil himself for that kind of money."

Jo-Bethany reached behind her for a chair that was near the window, not taking her eyes off him, and sat down carefully. He meant it. He really meant it.

"Please, Ham," she said, deadly serious now, and frightened. "Please don't do it."

"I told you. I've *done* it. I've already signed the papers."

"You can't do this. You can't send me to live with linguists."

He didn't bother to answer that. It was his legal right, as her guardian, to send her anywhere he chose, as long as it didn't endanger her physically. She was talking nonsense, and he had no tolerance for women's nonsense.

"Well?" he demanded. "Have you got anything else to say, Sis?"

"Yes."

"Say it, then. I've got things to do."

"Ham, if it's the money, why don't we do something that would bring in *real* money? I don't mean three hundred credits a month, Ham. I mean *real* money!"

"Jo, don't start that shit about going out to the colony planets again. I'm warning you."

"Ham, you're not thinking! They need nurses desperately in the colonies, and they need men like you—strong men, young vigorous men who can get things done! We could have twice the income we have here, Ham . . . and why not? There's nothing here you couldn't have on—"

"Shut up, Jo."

He swung his legs over and sat up straight, slamming the heavy glass he held in his hand down on the tabletop.

"But, Ham—"

"I said shut up."

Jo-Bethany closed her mouth, convinced, and sagged in the chair. She knew why he didn't want to go out to one of the colonies, even those that had been there long enough to be well established and very comfortable. If he did that, he might end up involved in some real work; Hamilton Norse Klander was not about to be involved in real work. Right now he pushed a button all day. Every thirty minutes. The rest of the time, he sat and watched the robots to be sure they didn't stop doing what the pushed button signaled them to do. And that was absolutely the sum total maximum of work that he was willing to do in this world. Jobs like that were rare in the colonies, and they didn't go to able-bodied men.

"Ham," she began, because there wasn't anything to lose, "'I'm not suggesting that we go to a *frontier* colony. I mean some place like—"

"Hey!" he shouted, and she hushed instantly. "If I was going to go anyplace, lady, it would *be* a frontier colony, someplace where men can stretch out and *be* men! I'm not afraid of any goddam thing they've got, and you'd better remember that! But I'm not going anywhere, because I like it right here where I am. *You* are the one going someplace, lady. *You,* day after tomorrow, are going to march your skinny butt over to Chornyak Barren House and move in there to be their live-in nurse. Where I won't have to look at your ugly face or listen to your effing whining and nagging all the time. And I don't want to hear any more out of you about it."

She didn't answer him. There was no point in it. But he wasn't quite through.

"One more thing, Jo-Jo," he said, narrowing his eyes at her. "Just one more thing. Let's say you've got some shitty idea about going over to Family Court and complaining that I'm forcing you to do something you shouldn't have to do, or some shit like that. Let's just say that's occurred to you. I want you to know, dear Jo-Bethany, that if you even *think* about doing that I'll put your sweet little sister into nursing training so fast she won't have time to pack! You got that? You foul this up, Jo-Jo, and I'll see to it that you're *both* out working . . . I could *use* two salaries coming in. You just think about that."

She stared at him, not caring now whether the hate showed or not, and she was taking a deep breath, getting ready to tell him what a despicable excuse for a human being he was, no matter what he did to her for it, but she didn't get a chance. Melissa was there before she could speak, standing in the livingroom door clutching her shoulders in her hands, shivering, huddled into herself. They must have been talking louder than Jo had realized.

Ham Klander looked at his wife, gave one snort of disgust, and lay back down on the couch to watch the fun.

"Oh dear God, no," whimpered Melissa Ann Klander, in the faint thin voice of one about to swoon or flee, "oh dear God, no, Jo-Bethany, please don't let him do that to me! Oh please, Jo, please, you have to go . . . Jo, I couldn't stand it! I couldn't! The baby . . . Jo, I'd have to leave her, if Ham makes me go into nursing training, it would kill me, Jo, I couldn't. . . ."

Jo-Bethany had no earlids, that was true. But thirty years of practice had given her a remarkable skill at tuning out her sister's drivel. Melissa had large breasts and a pretty face and long red hair, which had been enough to get her Hamilton Klander. She had no discernible intelligence or common sense. What passed for communication with Melissa was an almost unbearable confused hodgepodge of silly sentences and parts of sentences strung together any old way, with everything said at least three times, and no sentence said in ten words if fifty would do, and most of it based on the single theme of Poor Little Me. There'd been no money to send either of the Schrafft girls to a marital academy, and Jo-Bethany had not had Melissa's physical advantages, for which blessings and the single state that accompanied them she was profoundly grateful. But there were times when Jo-Bethany wondered if a marital academy would have been able to teach her sister the basic principles of ordinary conversation—if so, it might have been a good investment.

"Jo-Bethany!" Melissa wailed. "You're not listening to me!"

"Of course she isn't," Ham said flatly. "She doesn't care anything about you, sweetheart. She doesn't even *care* if I have to put you in training and send you out to work and the baby has to go to daycare! Why *should* she care? Hell, it's not *her* baby!"

That was worse garbage than Melissa was putting out, thought Jo-Bethany, calm now. In the first place, Ham made good money. This wasn't an elegant or expensive neighborhood; it was a blue collar suburb, but it was comfortable. He had a nice house, he had his French courtyard, he had nice furniture and nice clothes and all the toys a man of his age could yearn for. There was a sporty groundcar, and a pair of flyers—one ordinary and one with several illegal features added, for going out with the boys. There was a comset in every room and a swimming pool in the basement made to look like a tropical lagoon, complete with waterfall. There was a robot Irish setter, well-trained, without the disadvantages of either shedding or shitting. Ham didn't need for Melissa to earn one cent. As for the baby, it was Melissa who needed Flowerette, not the other way around. No baby in the United States was allowed to do without anything it might need, ever, and the daycare centers were absolute Baby Heaven. Flowerette . . . *stupid* name! . . . would be much better off at daycare, where she would be superbly cared for, than she was here at home. With her mother constantly clinging to her and weeping over her and panicking every time she made a noise she hadn't made previously, and teaching her to cower in terror before Ham's every word and gesture.

But Ham knew his prey; garbage or not, drivel or not, Melissa's carryings on had the effect on Jo-Bethany that he'd been aiming at. And Melissa was only just getting started. She had fallen to her knees in the doorway and thrown her hands over her face, and knelt there weeping as if she'd been whipped, swaying back and forth like a mourning bereaved mother of seven. . . . Jo-Bethany's stomach knotted, watching her. And watching Ham, who was beaming at his wife in a positive glow of pleasure. Jo supposed that if Melissa would begin to bleed, there on her knees, in some tasteful way, he would be even more delighted.

Any minute now, Melissa would begin crawling across the room toward her sister, pleading and dithering. She would not plead with Ham, because that might irritate him; she would plead with Jo-Bethany, and if that meant trouble for Jo-Bethany it was a shame, but it couldn't be helped. Just so it didn't irritate Ham.

Jo-Bethany couldn't face it. Suddenly, she had the feeling that however repulsive it might be to live with the Chornyaks it could not possibly be as repulsive as watching Melissa grovel and Ham gloat. And watching Flowerette learning how to grovel just like Mama. It could not possibly be that bad.

While Melissa was still only rocking back and forth on her knees, keening, before she could begin the crawling and begging, Jo-Bethany stood up. "All right!" she said sharply. "Stop it! I'll go, Melissa . . . don't worry about it."

Her sister raised her face from her hands, and Jo-Bethany noted that even with all her hysterics she was still blandly pretty, the reliable cosmetics she wore still unsmudged, the rosy color from the weeping almost becoming. That would not last, she thought; give Melissa ten years, and her performances would make her ugly. Melissa would not find that out in time, of course.

"Oh, Jo-Bethany! Sweet Jo!" she began, and no doubt that would go on for a while, until Ham got bored watching the wife-robot he'd created and pushed some different equivalent of a program button.

Jo-Bethany genuinely loved her sister. She had always loved her, pitiful and pathetic though she might be, since the day their mother had laid her in the older girl's arms and said, "Jo-Beth, this is *your* baby." She had been, too, because Cleo Schrafft had been interested only in her sons. She walked over and drew Melissa to her feet, set her hair to rights with one sure hand, kissed her damp forehead, and went straight on up to her rooms without a word.

Behind her, she could hear Ham laughing. The full robust laugh of a satisfied adult male, rocked in the bosom of his family, content with his world and all things in it.

II

Once she'd made a decision, Jo-Bethany never dawdled. She asked Ham if he could arrange for her to leave at once instead of waiting for the weekend, and he was willing. Having her gone meant one less woman for him to tease and torment, but she was in some ways an annoyance to have around. There were a lot of times when he wasn't sure exactly what she meant by things she said to him, and he didn't like that; and because she wasn't his wife, the means he could use to punish her were restricted in inconvenient ways. He didn't really mind seeing her go, and when the Chornyaks agreed without argument to start her salary at once, it overruled any faint objections he might otherwise have felt. So that Jo-Bethany found herself, late in the afternoon of that same day, being welcomed in out of the cold rain at Chornyak Household by a woman who introduced herself as Dorcas Ndal Chornyak and who rushed her straight down the stairs to be officially welcomed by Jonathan Asher Chornyak in his office.

He was quick and thorough and clear; Jo-Bethany saw that he was extremely busy, and realized that her unexpectedly prompt arrival had forced him to interrupt other business for this interview, but he didn't seem angry about it. He was simply brisk, not wasting any time on social frills or unnecessary details. There were nearly two hundred people at Chornyak Household, he told her, for all of whom she was technically responsible. She would supervise the care of the chronically ill or infirm elderly women, and she would serve as triage nurse for all the rest of the family, deciding when they needed to go to the local clinic or hospital for care rather than seeing to their own needs at home. Ham had not bothered to explain any of that to her, and she didn't blame him.

"It's not as bad as it sounds," Chornyak added. This man, who was Head not just of the Chornyaks but Head of all the other Lines as well. Head of Heads—what a grotesque idea! "Our women are very clever with matters medical," he went on, and she told herself sternly to keep her mind in order and pay attention. "Anything that just means bandages and potions and hygiene, they can handle. Dorcas is infirmarian; she'll show you her supplies and facilities, and your own quarters. If you find anything inadequate, don't hesitate to let her know. You'll have all the help you need with baths and beds and all that sort of thing. But we require someone who can tell us quickly and accurately when our inhouse care isn't enough—we do *not* need our people sitting for hours waiting until some med-Sammy deigns to tell them they shouldn't have bothered to come in because whatever-it-is will go away by itself. We don't have time for that.''

He had looked at her, his hands already taking up a packet of chiplets from his correspondence basket, and asked if that was clear, if she felt capable of handling it, and if she had any other questions that couldn't wait. Jo-Bethany assured him that she could manage, and he dismissed the two women immediately; the interview could not have lasted more than five minutes, she was sure.

"Takes your breath away with his cordiality, doesn't he?" Dorcas said, as they hurried back up the stairs to the ground floor. "'I'd apologize, but he genuinely is busy, and we hadn't expected you to arrive for several days—there was a more seemly chunk of time on his schedule for you on Saturday. He's not busy enough to *excuse* the way he rapid-fired all that at you, but busy enough to provide an explanation. And be glad, my dear. If he'd had time to talk to you at leisure, you'd have been awfully bored before it was over.''

The woman led her through the buildings, all earth-sheltered, all connected by covered walkways above ground and by well-lit and ventilated tunnels below, explaining as they went along. There was the main house, for the married men and the bachelor males and the children; there was Chornyak Barren House, with only women in residence, a number of them bedfast but none acutely ill; and there was Chornyak Womanhouse, which sheltered the wives, and all girls past puberty, and any barren woman who just preferred being there to living at Barren House. Because her regular patients would be the elderly and bedfast women at Barren House, Jo-Bethany's room was in that building, and Dorcas took her there to catch her breath.

The room was small, and had no windows; there was an attached cubicle, hardly bigger than a closet, that was supposed to serve her as an office. Jo-Bethany stood looking around her, shocked, and her distress must have been obvious on her face, because Dorcas Chornyak spoke at once.

"You won't be expected to see people here," she said. "If you're needed, you'll be paged on your wrist computer and arrangements will be made in whatever way is appropriate to the situation. We'll do our best not to have you running back and forth among the buildings, I promise. This space is just somewhere to keep your database and your medical texts and your equipment.''

Jo-Bethany looked at her, and then away, trying to maintain a pleasant expression, wondering what to say. This woman, who seemed genuinely concerned about her comfort and her feelings, was what people like Ham Klander called "a bitch Lingoe." What do you *say* to a nice bitch Lingoe?

Dorcas could apparently read minds as well as faces; she helped her. She said, ''I know what the problem is, Nurse Schrafft, and there's no reason in all this world for you to try to hide it. We know you're used to a very different sort of living arrangement . . . this will be strange to you, and terribly cramped. If you find you can't be comfortable with us, just say so, and you'll be released from your contract—no one wants you miserable, my dear.''

Jo cleared her throat and spoke carefully. "It must seem ridiculous to you. You women living four to a bedroom, and the children all in dormitories, and the women here at Barren House all together in one big room the way they are—''

"And communal baths, which you're not used to. Let's not forget communal baths. And communal diningrooms.''

"That's what I meant. With all of you living like that, it must seem silly that I feel crowded, when you've given me a room all to myself.''

Dorcas looked at her hard, her brows drawn slightly together, and Jo-Bethany felt a flush rise on her cheeks. *Damn*. This was going very badly. "You're used to . . . what?" asked Dorcas. "Precisely.''

Jo thought of her suite in Ham Klander's house. Bedroom, sittingroom, bath, and a tiny enclosed garden all her own. And all of it above ground, with windows for light and air to pour through, instead of these solid walls and the artificial lighting.

"A small suite,'' she managed. "Three rooms. And a little garden.''

"My goodness,'' Dorcas said. "No wonder you're startled at what we're offering you!''

Jo-Bethany wanted to defend herself. To say, we were a blue collar family, the man in our house was a factory worker, we lived in an ordinary working class residential district. But she hadn't been criticized or accused of anything; she had been treated with the most complete courtesy. She had no reason to feel defensive.

And she was confused, because everybody knew that the linguists of the Lines lived in luxury paid for by the honest taxpayers they so shamelessly exploited. But she hadn't seen any luxury. The buildings were clean and well-built, and the one they called Womanhouse was nicely furnished and seemed to have all the necessary comforts. But there was no luxury, and the crowding was awful. She stood there speechless, trying not to do absurd things with her hands, feeling foolish and miserable.

"Miss Schrafft," said Dorcas, when the uncomfortable silence had dragged on too long, "please don't be distressed. It really is all right. I know the sort of thing you've been told. You were expecting sunken marble pools in all the bedrooms, and gold-plated bathroom fixtures, and hothouses full of exotic colonial flowers, and hallways lined with priceless paintings, and all the very latest laser toys. I do know, my dear. You had been thinking, 'Well, if I have to go and live with Lingoes, at least I'll be comfortable.' And instead you find yourself in this spartan place, and underground besides, and not even a bathroom to call your own. It must be awful for you."

Jo-Bethany was a Southern lady; she prided herself on her manners, and felt much contempt for those who had none, like Ham Klander. Now her manners had failed her; she had insulted this woman, who had done her no harm and was in some ways her hostess. She was so dismayed at herself that all she could do was put her hands to her hot cheeks and murmur that she was terribly sorry.

"Don't be sorry. I'm sure you didn't choose to come here. Some man signed you up, because our salary is attractive and he had little trinkets he wanted to buy, isn't that so? Uhuh. I thought so. It isn't what you wanted, and it's even worse than you expected."

"I should not be so . . . obvious."

"Nonsense. You're doing very well, under the circumstances. But Nurse Schrafft, current conditions in this country are *very* recent. Your great-grandmother would have considered the 'small suite' you mentioned to be fairy tale accommodations . . . so would your grandmother, I expect, unless she was a wealthy woman. And there are many of our colonies where the Chornyak buildings would still seem like luxury. The problem, and the essential difference, is that here you don't have that sense of adventure that goes with living in a nine-by-twelve bubble hut on the red barrens outside New St. Louis. There's nothing *exciting* about being here. In a plain old crowded Lingoe den, in the plain old state of Virginia, on plain old Earth. And there's nothing we can do about it, because this *is* the way we live; this is the way all linguists of the thirteen families of the Lines live, no matter what you see on the newspapes. Perhaps you won't mind it as much as you think, once the first shock is over; our last nurse was contented here, I know."

"I'm sure I will be, too," Jo-Bethany stammered.

"And if not, we'll help you find another place. If your male guardian . . . husband? Father?"

"Brother-in-law. My sister's husband."

"If your brother-in-law will allow you to make the change."

"You're very kind, Mrs. Chornyak." It was quite true. She *was* very kind, and Jo-Bethany had been very rude. She could not remember ever having been that rude before in her whole life.

The other woman smiled at her. "Your reaction was expected," she said, and her lips twitched. "It happens every time a new nurse is hired in one of our Households. They always are looking for the sunken marble pools. And except for what our men refer to so tastefully as our 'rendezvous rooms,' there's not even a *hot* tub in any of our buildings, from one end of the Lines to the other."

"Rendezvous rooms?"

"Mmmm. When one of our men wishes to invite his wife to spend an evening, or a night, with him—always supposing he has energy left for that after the sort of days our men put in—he may, if he chooses, reserve one of those rooms instead of just taking her to his bedroom. Shall I show you a rendezvous room, my dear? They're a bit fancier than the rest of our accommodations."

Jo-Bethany shook her head. "No . . . thank you. I understand the concept."

"No marble pools, even there," chuckled Dorcas. "It means fancy bedclothes, and extra pillows. And flowers, sometimes. But I'll tell you what: why don't you try to pretend, just for now, that you're on a frontier planet, facing magnificent adventures. While in reality I take you down to the basement to show you where *I* work. Perhaps it would help."

"I swear," Jo-Bethany blurted, worn out with trying to be polite, "I don't know how you can be so pleasant about all this!"

"Nurse Schrafft, we linguists spend our entire lives interacting with cultures that don't even originate on this planet—*Alien* cultures. Being surprised at what one finds is our most common problem—it would be disgraceful if we couldn't understand it. Now, if you'll follow me, please, we'll finish the tour. Please be prepared for really bare bones surroundings now; we spend very little on decorating basements."

Jo-Bethany followed her silently, down stairs and along corridors painted beige, into a room lined with cupboards and cabinets and shelves. "Potions," her employer had said, and Jo had expected the ordinary household medicines any housewife might keep, and perhaps a few drugs prescribed by physicians. There *were* a few prescriptions, each properly labeled, all the caps glowing to indicate that the substances inside were pure and safe and not too old for usage. But she had not expected what Dorcas showed her, which was in literal truth the stuff of potions in the ancient sense of the word. Herbs. Dried and fresh in hanging bunches and powdered, made into oils and extracts and teas and lozenges and salves. It smelled wonderful, it was magnificently organized, and it scared Jo-Bethany to death. There were sturdy locks everywhere, and the keys were around Dorcas' neck; presumably the palm locks responded only to her touch. But many of the herbs she saw were dangerous; improperly handled, they would be fatal.

She said nothing, because she had made up her mind that she would not criticize anything else in this bizarre place today, no matter what she saw. But she made a mental note to spend plenty of time reviewing her files on poisons and antidotes, and tomorrow she would see what she could find out about Dorcas Chornyak's claim to be "superbly trained" in the preparation and use of all these substances.

By the time she'd finished the tour, and unpacked her things and put them away, the day was gone and she was numb with exhaustion. Too numb to face the diningroom in the main house this first night. She went in search of the backup kitchen she'd been told was on the lower level at Womanhouse; there was hot soup, and a good dark bread, and plenty of fruit and nourishing drinks. She ate quickly, not sure she could even taste what she was swallowing, cleared up the minimal mess she'd made, and headed for her own room feeling desperately sleepy.

And managed to get turned around, of course, in her fog of weariness. The women in the room she blundered into were reciting something or other aloud, and didn't hear her; she hoped that only the one woman standing at the front of the room had seen her. She backed out fast, closing the door as quietly as she could, and stood there trying to get her bearings, looking at the women who were sitting around the single big room they called the "common room." They were all busy, she could see that; she hated to interrupt them.

"I'm sorry," she said finally, to the room at large. "I'm

afraid I've gotten myself lost. Which door goes to Barren House? I was looking for it, and I went in there by mistake . . . ." She gestured vaguely at the door behind her.

"That's the chapel," said a woman sitting nearby with a microfiche reader and a lapful of fiches. "It's all right. They're only practicing, and you're always welcome there."

Jo-Bethany shook her head. "Thank you," she said, "but I just want to go to bed."

"In that case, let me show you," said the woman. "You turned the wrong way at the head of the stairs, that's all. I'll see you home."

"It's not necessary."

"Of course it's not, but it's a terrific excuse to get away from these damn tables of prefixes. You'll be doing me a favor."

She came over to Jo-Bethany and stood facing her, hands clasped in front of her, feet apart, a pair of amazingly long thick braids—some effect of the family potions, no doubt—swinging almost to her waist. She was taller than Jo-Bethany, and that was unusual; most women had to look *up* at the plainer of the two Schrafft girls. This one looked down, and clucked her tongue as if what she saw were deplorable.

"Law, but you're tired!" she said, fussing. "You're worn out . . . too much for one day, and nobody with sense enough to look after you, obviously. You come along with me. I'll see you to your room and I'll tuck you in besides, nurse or no nurse. I'm Belle-Anne Jefferson Chornyak, named after the famous poisoner and lunatic."

It was the very last straw. Jo-Bethany gave up, and let herself be led away to bed, unresisting, one hand firmly gripped by the poisoner-and-lunatic's namesake. If she was about to be poisoned, at least she'd get some rest; as for lunatic behavior, it would have to be spectacular indeed to impress her now.

CHAPTER 5

"Since I've been listening to the thologys, I understand why it is that although the toys and the gadgets change as frequently as they ever did, very little changes on this Earth. I might not understand it if I'd been observing it all along; but looking at a century as a whole piece, I can perceive the explanation. When I was a little girl, people would laugh about the way we were 'trapped in the year 2000,' and it was funny then, almost charming. But now, nearly a hundred years later, when we appear to have advanced no farther than the year 2010, it's not so amusing any more.

"It's also no mystery. Just as a person of enormous wealth, comfortably insulated from life's problems, always was able to grow old without being obliged to change, Earth has been able to molder along undisturbed in its comfortable rut. Pressures that would have meant inevitable change before the colonization of space are siphoned off now—we just export them to the stars. A new political ideology? A revolutionary movement? A radical shift in religion? A potentially disruptive element of any kind? We ship it off to the colonies, which proliferate endlessly. While Earth sits like a pampered old monarch, set in her ways, indulged and humored and surely the source of much nostalgic amusement elsewhere. . . .

"Because our situation was new to human history, we didn't become an empire except on paper. We never had to fight our way out to the frontiers; we never had to starve Earth to support the frontiers, or vice versa. The Aliens handed us space travel for a pittance, for the price of our defense budgets and the cashing in of a few missile systems. They handed us any other technology essential to our needs, at payments we were always able to manage. So that from the beginning the colonies were

*self-supporting. And they were much more than that! They were
our magical solution to every problem. They took the populations of our prisons, they took our slum dwellers and our home-
less; they accepted and welcomed all the enormous populations
of refugees from war and famine and drought and disaster and
poverty. All those hordes, screaming at the gates and demanding
a fair share, went into space; sources of conflict were just
removed, with little effort to us—what it may have meant for*
them, *I don't pretend to know.*

*"The Palestinians, for example . . . given an entire planet of
their own, to be their world, what did they care about a little scrap
of the Middle East? Israel stayed here, and still sits, presiding in
splendor over a desert. Jerusalem, the Holy City over which
three great religions spilled so much blood, was preserved as a
set of holograms before it was swallowed up by the Great
Earthquake of 2009; now each of the faiths has its own Jerusalem, indistinguishable from the original, and where that first
Jerusalem stood is a fissure like the Grand Canyon of the
Colorado. I suppose that when a devout Jew, or Muslim, or
Christian, begins to argue that a hologram of a holy city is not as
holy as the holy city itself was, they just export him. . . ."*

(from the diaries of Nazareth Chornyak Adiness)

"She's asleep, Delina."

"I don't think so, Willow—I think she's just watching the
thologys."

"With her *eyes shut?* She can't see the holos that way—" The
younger child stopped and looked warily at her sister. It seemed
unlikely that Delina would have made a semantic error of that
kind. Unless it was a test. One of Delina's responsibilities as
older sister was the incessant testing of Willow's linguistics
skills; probably it *was* a test. If Willow missed it, poor Delina
would be obliged to spend time explaining the error and providing examples and probing to be certain her little sister was
acquiring the expertise expected of her. Willow spoke swiftly, to
spare Delina all that bother.

"Perhaps, Delina," she said, "there's a better choice for what
Great-Grandmother Nazareth does with the thologys than the
predicate 'watch'. . . . Perhaps something should be chosen that
does not require the use of sight."

Delina smiled and touched Willow's hand, in reassurance.
Yes. It had been a test.

"And the mind's eye?" she asked. "What about the mind's eye?"

"Hmmm." Willow was still so young that she found it difficult to do anything complex without the tip of her tongue creeping out of her mouth, a phenomenon she would have to get under firm control before she could be trusted in the interpreting booths. She concentrated now on keeping the unruly tongue where it belonged, firming her lips as a barrier, keeping the signs of her concentration from showing on her face as best she could. A quick check of Delina's expression showed her that she was doing well, and she dropped her eyes to make the thinking easier.

"You *might* say it," she said slowly. "You *might*. But I think there would have to be one of two things. Either you would have to have a context . . . somebody would already have to have been talking about mind's eyes and so on . . . or you would have to make it open."

"*Overt*, Willow," Delina prompted.

"Or you would have to make it overt. You would have to say 'I think she's just watching the thologys with her mind's eye.' " Then she stopped and looked at her sister. "Or *is* it just one eye, Delina? Why don't people say 'the mind's eyes,' plural?"

"Well, think about it! Think how silly it would be, imagining the mind with a pair of little images side by side, and inverting them and merging them into one, and running all that back through the optic system . . . or maybe forward through the optic system, not that it matters. *Eyes* of the body, you perceive; *eye* of the mind."

"*Thalehal wa!*" *Very nice*. It was Nazareth's voice, her eyes were open, and she was smiling at her great-granddaughters. "*Wil sha*, dearloves. To what do I owe the honor of this visit?"

"To the men, Natha," said Delina. "And to our bad manners, I guess. We've interrupted you."

Nazareth didn't deny that, since it was obvious, but she held out her arms and gathered them both in, to lay her cheek against each small head in turn and to administer a firm welcoming hug.

"I am happy to have you here, nevertheless," she told them. "The thologys will wait, and there are always more of them."

"You *do* . . ." Willow began, and then she stopped again. "Shoot!" she said. "It's a lexical gap, Delina. You can't say it."

"What?"

"You can't say to Great-Grandmother, 'You do watch the thologys with your eyes closed, don't you?' because it's the wrong predicate. And I can't use 'listen' if she's doing it with her mind's eye. Drat! Why hasn't somebody fixed that?''

"I have a suggestion," said Delina.

"What?"

"Say, 'You watch the thologys with your *eyelids* closed,' and bypass the whole mess."

"*No*, Lina! That would still mean 'perceive with the eyes,' plural, to me. It's still wrong."

Nazareth observed them, very pleased. They were going to make fine linguists; they had the necessary interest in the phenomena of speech. They weren't just showing off for her; they had in fact forgotten all about her. "That will demonstrate to you," she said, "one of the reasons why linguists find the predicate 'perceive' so very useful. It doesn't drag in eyes and ears and tongue and nose and skin and so on."

"Still," said Willow, disgusted for the moment with Panglish, "it spoils it all the same. Just listen to this, Natha." She made a very formal prissy face. "Oh, Great-*Grand*mother, you are perceiving the thologys with your *eye*lids closed, *aren't* you?" She made an exasperated noise. "Now that's silly, Natha. It has completely the wrong . . . whatever it is."

"Tone."

"Yes. The wrong tone."

"Did you two come here," asked Nazareth gravely, "to interrupt me for a lecture on subtleties of style? Or are you bringing a message?"

"Oh, goodness," said Delina. "We forgot."

"I thought you might have," Nazareth observed, while the older child fumbled in her smock pocket and found the note she'd been sent to deliver.

"Not for comset, eh? Or for wrist computer, either?"

"No, Great-Grandmother. Hand delivery, they said."

"And-don't-wait-while-she-reads-it," muttered Willow urgently.

Delina nodded. "I remember," she said. "If you'll excuse us, then, Natha, we'll go talk to the aunts a while."

Talk to the aunts. There were not quite so many "aunts" at Chornyak Barren House these days as there used to be, Nazareth thought. They'd lost four of the old women confined to their beds in the past six months. It happened like that . . . one would leave them, and then in swift succession, as if they had all agreed, several more would follow. Still there were some aunts left for the little girls to pet and fuss over, and to practice their languages with. Presumably there always would be at least a few, and no doubt one of these days she herself would be among

them. Although the nineties were treating her gently, and she
had no intention of taking to her bed any time soon.

"Certainly," she said. "You go right on, dearloves, and I'll
deal with this, whatever it is. I'll bet you it could just as well
have come by computer instead of riding over in your pocket."

She was *absolutely* sure of that. Nothing so confidential that it
could not be transmitted by the ordinary household communication systems would be written down on paper and trusted to the
memory of a child. Not even a dependable child like ten-year-
old Delina Meloren Chornyak. The point of the errand had been
to provide the girls with an errand, and nothing more. She
watched them run off toward the aunts' room, loving them with
all her heart, and then she unfolded the note.

And said, "Oh, my goodness!" The note read, "Natha, dear
Natha, why are you keeping us all waiting?" It was signed,
solemnly, with many a formal flourish and curlicue, by the four
other senior women of Barren and Womanhouse—all of whom
knew quite well that she was keeping them waiting because
she'd forgotten. And she had been chiding the children!

Yes, the nineties were treating her gently, but her memory
was definitely not what it once had been. She remembered
calling up the display of her day's schedule when she first woke
up this morning, before she even got out of bed, and she
remembered having seen the meeting listed. But she obviously
had not set the alarm on her wrist computer, or the others would
not be sitting waiting for her, patiently, right this minute. By the
time she turned one hundred she *would* be among the aunts, if
she went on in this fashion, and lucky if they'd have her!

Hurry up, Nazareth, you antiquated old nuisance, she instructed herself sternly, and then almost fell trying to get out of
her chair in a single motion like a girl. "*Idiot!*" she said aloud,
thinking how much nonsense she would have had to put up with
from Michaela if Michaela had been there to watch her deterio-
rate. Instead, it had been Nazareth's dubious privilege to stand
by helpless while Michaela sank ever more deeply into the
drugged darkness prescribed for her at the prison hospital; it had
been a relief to her when Michaela died, and not because—as the
newspapes insisted on putting it—it had been a comfort to see
her father's murderess go at long last to face the justice of the
Lord. Nazareth had no illusions about the debt that she and all
the other women of the Lines owed to Michaela Landry. What
would they have done, if Michaela hadn't killed Nazareth's
father when he discovered the truth about them? Killed him
themselves? Nazareth knew she could not have done that, and

knew Michaela had spared her even the task of having to *consider* it.

She cut straight through the common room in the main house, to make up some of the time she'd lost, her mind occupied with memories and the grim set of her mouth demonstrating that they were not pleasant. A foolhardy young man stood up at the sight of her and took one step in her direction, presumably intending to exercise his rights and demand that she explain her presence there; behind him, someone murmured quietly that if he wanted to be a perfect ass that was okay, but please wait till a larger audience could be brought in for the occasion, and he sat down again and let her pass. With an elaborate air of not having noticed that she was there at all, of course. Nazareth ignored him, because she was in a hurry, and because she was reasonably sure that as soon as she was out of earshot his peers would explain to him about demanding house passes from women who'd been coming and going on Household business for ninety years.

When she got to the parlor, much out of breath, she found the other women seated in their rockers, their fingers moving sedately to the rhythms of needlework they'd been doing so long that it was fully on automatic, with carefully composed faces. Chatting. They were talking about daylilies? Yes . . . daylilies. And Nazareth realized that she'd forgotten her needlework bag, which would have hurt the feelings of the nephews who'd given it to her, but they were all off at negotiations and would never know. And it didn't matter, because she was always prepared. She reached into a deep pocket and pulled out a quarter-skein of yarn and a crochet hook. Her emergency kit. Lavender yarn, suitable for one's nineties.

"I am too sensible to waste your time saying that I'm sorry," Nazareth observed, providing them with the contradictory figure free of charge. "After all, I'm only twenty minutes late. It could have been an hour."

"It could have been a day," agreed Sabyna. "That would have been much worse."

"Or a week." Quilla stared blandly at Nazareth, wisps of hair as always drifting out of her carefully constructed crown of braids in all directions. "In a week, though, we'd all have run out of yarn and given you up."

"I *am* sorry," Nazareth admitted, drawing up another chair, and they all agreed that no doubt she was, not that that made it any better, and she agreed with *that* and made a comment about the daylilies.

The meeting was not about daylilies. It was about the strategy for moving the womanlanguage Láadan out at last to women who were not members of the Lines. It had been Nazareth, just home from the hospital and barely moved in at Barren House, sitting on a plastic crate in the basement, who had first insisted that Láadan was ready to use. Time, she had said, for it to be spoken among the women, and learned by the girlbabies. *Long past* time! She had been furious with them that day, because they were still fooling about, claiming that the language wasn't "finished" yet, making excuses. It had been Nazareth who had known—while the other women were wasting their energies in "contingency plans" against a list of potential reactions from the men, should they discover the existence of Láadan—that there was in fact nothing at all to do except wait and be ready. It had been Nazareth, and only Nazareth, who had truly understood that it wasn't possible to make plans that obliged you to extrapolate from one reality to another. She had been the only one who understood that such planning had to be postponed until after the reality shift brought about by the language had taken hold, and who had stood firm and silent and watchful while they thrashed about, flatly refusing to be drawn into their fretful arguments. Always she had been there, difficult to love but impossible not to respect and rely upon, keeping them from making foolish choices for which they would pay dearly, but otherwise never interfering. Even when they pleaded with her to interfere.

Now that they found themselves at the next step of the plan, they had waited for her. And would indeed have waited a whole day, or a whole week, if that had been necessary. Whether it was genuinely crucial to have her with them for these sessions or not, they didn't feel safe without her. I am a symbol, she thought. A talisman. And what will they do when I am gone?

The youngest of the women there that morning, Quilla Hashihawa Chornyak, was in her seventies. Still she, like every other woman of the Lines, relied on the foolish mantra: *What will we do when Nazareth is gone? Hush—Nazareth will not die till we can spare her*. It made Nazareth cross just thinking about it, and she abandoned the subject of the daylilies and spoke up, to get her mind off her irritation.

"Well, how are we getting along? Do we have a report from everybody now?" The constant fine tremor that she'd had for many years—and that the physicians could certainly have relieved her of, if the grim hatred she felt for all med-Sammys hadn't prevented her from allowing them to do so—in no way interfered with the blinding speed of her crocheting. Her left hand, holding the battered old hook, was almost a blur. "Shall I start a mitten, or is this a light shawl meeting?"

Quilla set an additional skein of lavender in Nazareth's lap, to supplement her supply. "At least *start* the shawl," she advised. "Unless you'd like to make several mittens."

Nazareth suspected that this camouflage of needlework was no longer necessary; since the men of the Lines had built the separate Womanhouses in 2218 and established the custom of summoning their wives to the main house by sending computer messages, men were as rare in the women's buildings as green swans. But if you were a woman who still remembered the days when a man might come stomping into the parlor at any time, with no warning, demanding anything at all and its housecat, the camouflage was a comfort. And although their present plan was a pathetic little thing, the men could have stopped it with a single word if they'd taken it into their heads to do so, and it was the *only* plan they had. They didn't choose to take chances with it. Furthermore, they were so accustomed to holding their meetings in these needlework circles that they would have felt awkward doing it any other way. Like meeting naked. Or under water.

"Everything's in place, ready to go," said Sabyna. "They began last night at Jefferson Household, as we'd agreed, and the report came in this morning as a casserole I wouldn't feed a dog. Everything went smoothly, it said, and so far as anyone could tell, the nurse didn't notice a thing."

"No reason why she should have," Nazareth noted.

"No reason she shouldn't have noticed that she was hearing Láadan instead of Panglish?" snapped Elizabeth, the words muffled by her struggle to sever a strand of yarn with her teeth. "That's absurd!"

"The woman's not a linguist, Beth," said Sabyna. "She knows Panglish, and I suppose she must know half a dozen bits of medical Latin, and that's it. But she *will* notice."

"You're sure of that?"

"Nazareth is sure of that," Sabyna answered.

"And so far, Nazareth has always been right."

"Just so."

They sat there a little space, saying nothing; and Nazareth wondered where the woman was—or better, where the women were, preferably several dozens of them, who would take over this ridiculous role for her, and wished that they would hurry up and volunteer themselves—and then Clea sighed so loudly that they all looked at her in surprise.

"What on earth?" asked Sabyna.

"I was just imagining," Clea said.

"Imagining?"

"Imagining us, as the years go by. And every Thursday night in chapel, in every Womanhouse of the Lines, someone reads aloud the opening and closing pieces in Láadan. And none of the resident nurses *ever* notices. . . . And all the nurses die and are replaced, and *we* all die and are replaced, and nobody ever notices."

"Well, if that happens," Nazareth stated firmly, "it will be time for Plan B."

"There isn't any Plan B!" Clea objected.

"Better work one up then, my dear. Because the idea of generations going by, and Láadan still being known only to the women of the Lines, as if it were an Alien language, distresses me greatly. If the dreary scenario you describe is a likely one, Clea, we *need* a Plan B. And perhaps a Plan C as well. And a D." She looked down carefully at the knot-stitch she was working and added, "I know what—we could make a list."

They had made lists, fifty years ago. Endless lists. Provisions to be stored away in packs, ready to be seized and slung to their backs as they fled from the Households into the wilderness, each woman carrying an infant girl on her hip, with the men in hot pursuit. And similar nonsense.

"Nazareth Joanna Chornyak Adiness," said Sabyna. "For *shame*."

Nazareth grinned, but she said nothing more until they insisted, and then she told them that she'd said it all a dozen times and wasn't about to say it all again, and they sat there some more. Five uneasy women of advanced years, in the midst of a quandary.

"All *right*," said Sabyna at last against the counterpoint of clicking needles, "I surrender. *I* will say it all again. Clea, the nurses will come to care about the readings they hear in Láadan because it is a language worth caring about, and the readings are carefully chosen to seduce the ear. In time, they will notice. And they will ask us about it."

"How can we be sure of that? Never mind Nazareth—how can we be sure it's not just a waste of time?"

Sabyna laughed. "If we were sure of it, would we be sitting here listening to Natha tease us about lists? Of course we're not sure of it, and can't be sure of it, it's just the only thing we've been able to think of to do. There are no other women except the nurses who are able to move freely between our Households and the outside world, to serve as contacts between us and other women—therefore we must work through the nurses. There is no other occasion, except for Thursday Night Devotionals at the Womanhouses, when we linguist women and the nurses are together on any sort of regular and reliable basis—therefore we must work through those chapel services. Those are the *facts*, you perceive. And all we can do, as Natha has so often and so accurately pointed out, is *try* it and see what happens."

"It will take a long time!" Clea stabbed at the embroidery with her needle, fiercely, and jabbed her middle finger instead. "Ouch!"

"Everything does," said Nazareth.

"Well, is that all that was in the casserole recipe?" Clea asked. "Just 'we began last night and the nurse didn't notice'?"

"Even with a casserole," Quilla said, "a recipe doesn't have room for elaborate detail."

"*Seriously!* Is that all it said?"

"Just about." Quilla was in charge of the recipe collections for Chornyak Barren House; she kept them, to the men's great amusement, on file cards. In writing. "They started with the Twenty-third Psalm and ended with a benediction, it said, as agreed. And next Thursday the turn goes to Mbal Household. And that's all there was, and all we could expect. We certainly didn't anticipate that the nurse would leap from her seat in chapel shrieking, 'What *is* that wonderful language, I *have* to *know!*' Eventually, something will happen; eventually one of them will hear more than just noise."

It was to make that more certain that they'd decided to always begin with the Twenty-third Psalm, so that the nurses heard the same sequence over and over again, but to vary the closing selection on the off chance that that was the wrong decision. Hedging their bets. The good old Twenty-third had gone beautifully into Láadan, and had a wonderful sonorous roll to it; either that would cause the nurses to begin loving it and wondering what it was they loved, or it would lull them the way an incantation lulls and they'd never wonder. There was no way to find out which, except to try.

"We're next in line, then?" asked Quilla.

"Yes."

"Can you imagine Jo-Bethany Schrafft finding the Twenty-third Psalm in Láadan seductive?" It wasn't a sarcastic question; she was serious.

"It's hard to say," answered Sabyna. "We don't know her yet. She'll only have been here . . . what, six weeks? Seven, maybe? . . . when it's our turn to begin. But she's a human

being, and she is a woman, and she hears normally; and that is
all we can ask for in any of them.''

"She is also devout," put in Nazareth quietly.

"Devout? Devout what?"

"Baptist, I think; Protestant, certainly. No holy pictures or
statues in her room, and she doesn't cross herself, and if you
come up behind her suddenly and startle her she doesn't say
'Holy Mary!' or anything of that sort.''

"Nazareth, how do you know she's 'devout,' as you put it?
You've barely met her.''

Nazareth looked at them, her eyebrows raised, just for a
moment, and then looked down at her work again, saying, "She
has a Bible beside her bed, my friends." She paused. "A
printed Bible.''

"In realbook? Or just hard copied?''

"It's realbook form," Nazareth said. "And it's not junk; it's
the whole Bible, and ordinary print, and decent paper.''

That was significant. To own a printed Bible, a real book
rather than a microfiche or a chiplet in a velvet case, and to do
that on the money that an unmarried nurse earned—she would
have to be devout. That would mean strenuous economies, over
a long period of time.

"Perhaps it's a family heirloom," Elizabeth suggested.

"No," said Nazareth. "I checked—it's a recent edition.''

"It's a good sign, you think?''

"Maybe. It means she *will* go to Thursday night chapel, even
if it's being held by Lingoe bitches, because not to do so would
worry her. That's a good point. But it also means she may find
the Láadan disturbing. Or worse—she may find it blasphemous.''

"*Bomehelh!*" said Sabyna, quite clearly.

"Mercy. Now *that's blas*phemous!" Quilla chuckled; at their
ages, disrespectful remarks about penises were permissible.

"Is there anything we can do?''

"For instance?''

"Well, is there something perhaps less blasphemous to translate than the Twenty-third Psalm? Something she might be less
sensitive about?''

"And throw a wild variable into the experiment? Really,
Sabyna.''

"I suppose that wouldn't be such a good idea.''

They shook their heads at her, unanimous in their agreement
on that point. The variation was to be at the *end* of the service,
not at the beginning, and weeks had been spent deciding on the
Twenty-third Psalm as the proper opening, and they were not

going to spoil any of that now. Sabyna had always had a weakness for the unscientific method, but they would see that she curbed it; this was no time for impulsive fiddling about.

"We have to get this going," said Clea. "It's awful, hogging Láadan in the Lines the way we do. I don't want to go to my grave still hogging it."

"We're all on the defensive about that," Nazareth said gently. "For centuries we linguists have been hated by all the peoples of Earth and all the peoples of Earth's colonies. For our elitism, and our selfishness, and our shameful wealth, and our hoarded secrets—all of which is the most utter cowflop. Except for Láadan, which we *have* hoarded. It's an awful feeling."

"As if we had food," said Quilla bitterly, "and other women were starving all around us. And we not only didn't share but tried to pretend that we were starving, too. It's shameful."

"My dear, we have been over that and over that—it's not shameful. It's just the way that life is. We can't move any faster than we are moving, and that's all there is to it. It isn't shameful to be human."

Nazareth wondered how many thousands of times that same ground would have to be plowed. Linguists, of all people, should know the perils of making haste. You cannot hurry the acquisition of language. A human child, given nothing in the way of language instruction but the ordinary vagaries of communication in its own home, would begin to speak its native language at about eighteen months and have the system under control by about age five. A human child, given intensive daily lessons in its native language from birth, by the most costly teachers, would begin to speak the language at about eighteen months and have the system under control by about age five. If the teachers were as skilled as they were expensive, the child who had the lessons would have a bigger vocabulary than the other child, but that would be the only significant difference. And it had taken the women of the Lines generations to move from the first resolve that a language for women should be constructed to the stage of beginning to speak it with the infant girls. And *still*, they kept fretting for a way to "speed things up"!

"Do you remember," she asked casually, "how it went when our distinguished scientists found a way to speed up the gestation of the human infant from nine months to five? Do you remember the monsters that came from the wombs of women before they closed that project down?"

They didn't answer her, but she knew they were remembering,

and she drove the point home. "Anything forced to birth before its time will be a monster; and the houses of the Lines have been the womb of Láadan. Suppose we stop trying for a Caesarean, dearloves."

"We do it because we grieve for other women," Clea protested.

"No," said Sabyna, saving Nazareth the trouble, "we do it because we feel guilty. Our own guilt is *not* a sufficient justification for ruining something so important. Nazareth is right."

Nazareth is right. She flinched, but the tremor hid it; only someone watching her with the specific purpose of analyzing her bodyparl would have seen it as flinching rather than tremor. It was tiresome, always being right, even about things that were loathsome. It caused her pain.

Nazareth had been longing for death for ten years now, and would serenely have greeted its arrival. Except for the reluctance she felt at the idea of having it all to do over again. She was tired, she realized, and too cross to be useful.

"Natha? Are you all right?"

She stood up, tucking the strip of shawl into her pocket and handing the unused extra yarn back to its donor. "I'm fine," she said, that being what was expected of her. "But we're through here. There's no reason to spend any more time belaboring the overpoweringly obvious. There wasn't any reason to call a meeting to belabor it, for heaven's sakes. Why didn't you just send me a copy of the casserole recipe?"

"It was only a one-mitten meeting?"

"One *thumb* of one mitten. At the most. You overestimated."

"Are you *sure* we're through?" asked Elizabeth plaintively, and Nazareth gave up being cross and started laughing instead, patting their cheeks all around as she abandoned them. She would, she decided, go back through the main house common room again, even though she wasn't in a hurry this time. As a matter of principle. Perhaps she'd have an opportunity to speak to that young man personally. As a matter of principle.

They let her go without a word of protest. But she knew what they would do now. They'd sit there for two more hours, going over it and over it. Saying the same things thirty-five times, in different ways and different languages. Wringing the last fragment of possible significance from the casserole recipe code message.

She wasn't going to do that with them. She would leave them to their dissecting. It eased their minds, and eased their frustration at not being able to do something more direct and obvious, but it did not ease her in any way at all. She had no tolerance for

it, and only got in their way; better for them if she was gone,
instead of staying there and getting more and more annoyed with
them all the time for things that were in no way their fault or
hers. She would go back to her thologys, to find out what was
going on in the world.

Nazareth knew what the family thought about that, of course.
She was neither deaf nor blind nor numb, and she was well
aware that they considered the time she spent with the comset
news thologys a sign of premature senility. Here she was, surrounded by all the wonders of modern technology, with the
holomagazines at her fingertips; Chornyak Household subscribed
to nearly a dozen of them. Nazareth, they would say to her, you
don't have to tune the holos in the way the children do; you
don't have to bring them in lifesize and at full volume, you have
complete *control* of the display!

For Christmas this year her sons had given her a new receiver
of her own, the very latest thing. So small that she could hold it
in the palm of her hand and watch the holograms present the
news and the features and the dramas and all the rest of it. In
perfect detail, but tiny. Not like inviting an entire troupe of
people into the room to do live theater, the way the kids preferred it. This receiver had separate controls for each sensory
modality; you could turn off the smells and the textures and the
tastes and leave only the eye and ear inputs if you liked. Her
sons were no doubt proud of themselves . . . she could imagine
how they'd decided, over the Sunday morning mantalk; they
would have convinced themselves that this, at last, would wean
Mother from her embarrassing addiction to the primitive. Worth
every credit it cost, she was sure they had said.

They had sent a granddaughter with it to demonstrate all the
new toy's dials and frills and features and whatnots, under strict
orders to be sure that she fully understood every last item,
doddering though she was. And the poor thing had been so sorry
to bother Nazareth that way.

"'Natha, darling,'" Demarest had said, looking at her feet, "I
am *so* sorry—but they insisted."

Nazareth had smiled and told her to go right ahead by all
means and run the silly gadget through its paces so that when she
was called in to the office she could report that yes indeed
Demarest *had* shown her absolutely and to its fullest complexity
how superior this toy was to her thologys.

"I am instructed to say, Natha, that there is now no excuse for
you to sit and listen to a stupid newscaster droning away hour

after hour, with nothing but flat visuals on a screen to back him up. Please be advised that I have quoted *exactly* the statement your sons specified, Grandmother—I have not left out one single word.''

"Duly noted, child," she had replied. "Then what did they say?"

"Next. Nobody in full possession of her faculties would listen to the thologys, which are intended only for the frontier colonies where nothing else is available *but* the thologys. I am so sorry to have to say such a rude thing to you, Grandmother. And there was one more thing, which you will be able to guess without my having to say it."

"Ah, yes," Nazareth had said. "The one more thing was that the only *real* reason I listen to the thologys is to get attention."

"Men," signed her granddaughter. The sign for "male" is a hypothetical tug at the hypothetical bill of a hypothetical cap, but Demarest was inventive; she made it large and elaborate and with overtones of tremendous burdens, so that the only possible image was of these poor creatures hauling about great ponderous penises that hung swollen from their aching foreheads.

Nazareth thought it was hilarious, and Demarest kept it up until they were both weak from laughing. She signed a pitiful man with the recalcitrant phallus straight ahead down his nose, so that his eyes crossed, and another like a deformed rhinoceros, but triumphant at his good management of the appendage, and it was clear to Nazareth that she was only just getting warmed up and must be stopped.

"Demarest, do *please* quit," she begged, wiping her eyes; she had no penis to lug about, and thanks to the economies of her male relatives no breasts either, but her ribs were still with her and they ached even when left entirely alone. Battered with waves of hilarity, they were screaming for mercy.

Demarest stopped instantly; she was a kind young woman, and she would have walked through fire for Nazareth. And Nazareth asked her weakly, "Is that all now, I hope? I can go and turn on the thologys now and listen to them in peace? You've carried out every last instruction?"

"Almost."

"Almost? Whatever more could there be?"

"Grandmother, I am instructed to bring back a complete account of your reaction. 'Exactly what she says—every word,' is the way it was put."

"I perceive. Well, then, please get ready, because here comes my reaction. Are you ready? REACTION: 'How *very* kind and

thoughtful my sons are! How did they ever *guess* that I had been
wanting one of *these!*' There. Do you have it?''

''Every word,'' said Demarest gravely.

''Can you remember it?''

''Oh, yes. But I am shocked to discover that you would
deliberately lie to your own sons.''

''Your delicate sensibilities . . .''

''Yes, Grandmother. After all, you're supposed to set me an
example.''

''But I haven't lied, Demarest, and you needn't be shocked. I
have been wanting one of these.''

''Really?'' Demarest looked at her, astonished, because Nazareth was known to hate gadgets, especially expensive gadgets.

''Oh, yes. You see how beautifully it's made, and how well
balanced? It is just *exactly* what I need, to set my cup of tea
down on so it won't mark the surface of the table. The perfect
size, the perfect shape, and not tippy at all. Perceive!''

She set the receiver down on the table beside her—beautiful
old oak, and something she really did treasure—and set her cup
on it to demonstrate.

''You agree?'' she asked, decorously, and Demarest did, observing that of course she would have been hankering after one
of those for a good long time. And then Demarest went off
laughing to find out if anyone needed her help for Christmas
dinner, leaving Nazareth thinking that probably only a woman
of the Lines, and one who'd lived as a woman of the Lines ninety
years and more, could truly understand why the thologys pleased
her so.

All those years of her life, she'd never had any time to really
find out what was *happening*. First she was a child, and there
was all the predigested pap of Homeroom, and the Department
of Education's carefully assembled mass-ed lessons on the comsets,
and that was all she knew. And then at fifteen she was married,
and at sixteen she was a mother, and from then on she had never
had a moment's leisure. She knew it seemed to people outside
the linguist families that she had lived a life of giddy excitement
and adventure; it *would* seem that way, compared to the life of
most women. Six days a week she'd spent in the interpreting
booths in negotiations between the governments of Earth and a
constantly-changing parade of negotiating Aliens. She'd gone
everywhere, flying from city to city, to Washington and San
Francisco and New Orleans and Paris and Peking and Copenha-
gen and Tokyo. . . . Because she had nine children, she almost
never went offplanet; but still, she was forever rushing from

flyer to government building to flyer again, always traveling, always part of important business. While most women stayed home and awaited their husband's pleasure, she was in almost daily contact with exotic Aliens from all over the known universe. *Such* an exciting life!

Except that it hadn't been like that. Perhaps it was, if you were a *man* of the Lines. But not for the women. Every interpreting booth was just like every other interpreting booth, no matter where it was; because women weren't allowed to go out into the cities unescorted, meals were brought to them in the booths to simplify matters . . . she had never even seen the restaurants or the shops of all those glamorous places she had traveled to. And a good simultaneous interpreter has to be like a conduit. If you actually stop to think about what you are translating you fall behind; it can't be done like that. So that you can spend hours presenting the most intricate business and diplomacy and come away from it with almost no memory of what has been said. She had begun by eight in the morning, spent the day in the booth, and gone home to tend the children and see to Household business and prepare for the following day's negotiations; and then she would fall exhausted into her bed. On Sunday she went to church, and that was a treat because it was at least a change— but you don't hear news in church.

All those years! She supposed she had often been present while history was being *made*. But she'd had no opportunity to take notice of it or be involved in it, any more than a robot would have had.

She'd had no social life. Linguists do not mingle outside the Lines, because it would be awkward for everyone else present and because they don't have time. And within them, the women were sent away when the men began to talk of anything serious, so that their presence wouldn't inhibit the conversation. Even before the Womanhouses were built, when women still not barren lived in the main houses with their husbands, the men never talked to them except of personal and Household matters.

And then, when she was in her seventies and it was decided that she was no longer able to keep up an interpreting schedule, she still had not had a moment to herself. There was the education of the little girls, which had to be left to the women no longer actively at work, because they were the only ones available to do it. You can't hire lay persons to train little girls in how to be linguists. She had had to deal with the constant crises that are part of the life of any woman, be she linguist or lay . . . the problems of daughters and granddaughters and great-granddaughters, and sisters and the offspring of sisters, and dear friends and the offspring of dear friends. . . . The work had been endless. Endless!

So. Now she was past ninety, and *obviously* frail. With twenty more years ahead of her if she wasn't killed in a flyer crash, chances were, but old enough to be able to tell everyone to go find somebody else to do whatever it was, and not to have to feel guilty about it any more. There were so many somebody elses now, and all of them perfectly capable of doing almost every-thing without her assistance. And so at last she had a little time that she could use just as she liked, to do exactly what she wanted.

What Nazareth wanted was to *catch up*. Find out what had happened since she was flung into the whirlwind at the age of six! Other women out there in the world, reading all the latest best sellers with their pretty little microfiche pendants, watching the newspapes on their comsets half a dozen times a day, going out to their social clubs, subscribing to the holomagazines ever since they'd been available and having time to *watch* them, moving in a sea of information—they knew so much. What did Nazareth know? Thousands of verb endings. Tens of thousands of postpositions. She wanted to know what other women knew, and she had set about closing the gap.

The holos had been too much, though. Even the newspapes were too much, except in very small doses. All that data coming at her at once, and she not only didn't recognize the names and the faces and the events, she couldn't put a label to half the objects people were carrying or wearing or using. Her mind wouldn't handle it, and her eyes wouldn't. It blinded her, looking at all that multitude of phenomena while at the same time there was talk and smells and textures, and during the commercials there were even tastes, unless you remembered to turn them off.

Nazareth had gone to her Aunt Clara, bless her dear soul, and how she did miss her now that she was gone, and she'd told her what the trouble was, and Clara had set her right. "Listen to the thologys, Natha dear," she'd said. "You don't have to even look at the screen unless you're especially interested. All you have to do is just listen. And it's one person at a time, just telling you things. No multiple narrators, no 'real life drama.' Just quiet talk, like a friend telling you what she's done that day. They're on all day long, Natha, on one channel or another. All of them taped and then flown straight out to the frontier colonies every day on the mail rockets, so that the people out there can keep up with the worlds. That's what you need."

Clara had been absolutely right; the thologys were perfect. Nazareth had been listening to them for several years now; often she listened to them many hours of the night, because of course in the natural way of things now that she could finally get a good night's sleep whenever she liked, she no longer needed much sleep. And she was beginning—just beginning—to acquire a kind of grasp of the shape of events over the past hundred years. She felt a little less ignorant now, and that was the point.

As for being thought senile, that was just fine, too. The less useful they thought she was, the less they'd bother her with nonsense, and that suited her. She'd been bothered more than long enough, to her way of thinking.

CHAPTER 6

"The New St. Louis Blues"

I hate to see the dawn come up on Mars;
I hate to see the dawn come up on Mars;
'cause the NASA police, they shut down all the bars!
Oh, New St. Louis ain't got no grass or trees
and they pollinate the rosebush with little robot bees;
I get so lonesome, don't know what to do—
guess I'll just sit here and sing the New St. Louis Blues. . . .
  Got the new St. Louis blues, blue as I can be!
  My clones've got hearts like rocks cast in the sea . . .
  or else they'd of shipped out to New St. Louis with me!

If I was a bird, I tell you where I'd be;
if I was a bird, I tell you where I'd be;
I'd be wingin' for home through zero gravity!
Oh, New St. Louis, it's like a red rock jail—
I go from bar to bar, leavin' a red rock trail.
Tweren't for liquor and for my foolish pride,
I'd find a crater and throw myself over the side. . . .
  Got the New St. Louis blues, blue as I can be!
  My clones've got hearts like rocks cast in the sea . . .
  or else they'd of shipped out to New St. Louis with me!

We ain't got no arch, no river flowin' by;
ain't got no arch—no river flowin' by;
you look at New St. Louis, you sit right down and cry!
Well, back on Terra, I'd be in jail right now;
but that sounds better to me than New St. Louis anyhow.
They say in two hundred years, it'll be an Eden here—
well, I'll be dead and gone long before two hundred years. . . .

Got the New St. Louis blues, blue as I can be!
My clones've got hearts like rocks cast in the sea . . .
or else they'd of shipped out to New St. Louis with me!

> (popular song, set to the twentieth-century
> tune, "St. Louis Blues")

"Look. This makes me sick."

Five words of one syllable. Each one dropped into the air like a flat rock. Separate, and square, and hard. Heykus was angry. The way the man from Coast Guard sat there in the desk, carrying his foul news and dumping it into this day that had been a *fine* day until he arrived to ruin it, was making him even angrier. Heykus saw no sign of remorse, or even a decent embarrassment at this newest evidence of incompetence, and he didn't like it. He didn't like it at all. He wished he were a man who smoked cigars; he would have liked to take one and grind it out on the surface of the seeyum, right where the Coast Guard man's glazed eyes seemed to be firmly glued . . . as if there were something significant there to look at. Heykus never allowed clutter on the seeyum of his desk. There was a holo of his family, nicely grouped; there was an antique digital clock, with an American Eagle on it; there was the glass of water that he sometimes needed for a throat that age had made inconveniently dry for extended conversation. That was all. There was no excuse for anything else, in Heykus' opinion.

"Well?" he demanded, impatient with the man's silence and with his staring. "Do you plan to sit there all morning wasting my time and yours, or are you going to explain?"

"Director Clete," the fellow said stiffly, "we *are* sorry, you know."

"You're sorry. The Coast Guard is sorry."

"Certainly. We deeply regret the incident."

"Well, damn it, what do I care if you're sorry? I want to know precisely how it happened, and I don't want any bureaucratic nonsense to wade through while you're telling me about it."

"It was not the Coast Guard's *fault*, Director Clete," said the man stubbornly. He wasn't comfortable, but it was obvious that he wasn't intimidated, either; he looked up from the seeyum and met Heykus's eyes with a determined stolid look that said to get off his back. This was a long-time man, who'd been chewed out by experts and had learned to look them right in the eye and never blink; Heykus realized that to go on leaning on him would mean that they'd sit there all morning demonstrating who was toughest. Heykus had no doubt that *he* was, but he didn't have time to waste that way; he leaned back a bit, loosened his shoulders, unclenched his fists, and asked the man mildly if he'd be so kind as to make his report, adding, "I genuinely thought we had put an end to this kind of thing, Captain Frege. There are laws that *ought* to be enough to guarantee that. And there's staff in ample number, paid to enforce those laws. I'd be pleased to hear how all that was bypassed, Captain."

"The satellite scanner for the sector where we found the women started reporting sentient life about a week ago," Frege said calmly, now that the amenities had been seen to and his status acknowledged. "There wasn't any distress signal, so we just instructed the nearest vessel to swing by there and make sure everything was all right."

"Is that usual?"

The man shrugged, and blew air like a horse. "Director Clete," he said, "this kind of thing usually isn't an emergency. Usually, say you bust your ass to send out a seeker mission on top priority, when you get there you find some old millionaire on safari with his sportjet landed for minor repairs, and the guy isn't grateful, he's furious. You bust your ass to get to him, and he threatens to sue the government for invasion of privacy because his wife thought he was someplace else and so did his mistress. It doesn't pay, usually."

"I see. I wasn't aware of that aspect of the problem. Go on."

"Well, when the vessel sent a landing party down to check matters, they found these eleven women all alone, and busy as clams under a floodlight. Putting in gardens, building a kind of hut—very badly—and clearly intending to stay right where they were. They had a working distress beacon with them, with more than adequate range and power; when the officer in charge asked why they hadn't called for help they told him they didn't *need* any help, thank you. And then they rushed him."

"Rushed him? *Women?*"

"Damn right they rushed him. They had all kinds of tools with them. Old stuff, the kind of thing women like to hang up on walls, god knows why, not stuff anybody would ever use. Except they *were* using it. Building tools. Gardening tools. They did their damndest to stop the three men in the landing party, sir, and they managed to do a respectable amount of damage. The men weren't expecting to be attacked—they'd put their weapons away when they saw it was only women."

"Are they all right?"

Frege shrugged again. "They needed patching and pasting,

and the officer they went for first is still not fit for duty. One of
the bitches tore up his face with the point of a hoe, if you can
believe that.''

"I can believe it," Heykus told him grimly. "When women
go mad they're worse than any animal."

"Yes. I suppose they are. But everyone's going to be all right."

"Good. Maybe next time they find a pack of women alone
they won't be so careless."

"No. I don't expect they will be."

"Go on, please."

"Well, it was obvious then what the situation was. As soon as
the men realized they were under attack, they stopped being
polite and subdued the bitches."

"*Stop calling them bitches.*"

Frege straightened, startled, and opened his mouth to mention
that he wasn't a mail clerk; and then he got a look at the old
man's eyes and he dismissed that idea.

"Sorry, Director Clete," he said. "Subdued the females."

"There were no males on the asteroid?"

"No. The crew took the women aboard, and then they checked
the scanners; there was no sentient life signal from the place
once the women were removed."

Heykus sat there thinking, while Captain Frege waited. He
hadn't expected Heykus to be pleased, and he hadn't expected
the session to be pleasant. But that was all right. Pleasant wasn't
his major interest in life, anyway.

"This asteroid . . ." Clete asked him, slowly. "*Could* the
women have stayed there, if they hadn't been caught? Is it
suitable for settlement?"

"Oh, I guess so. If you were absolutely desperate, I suppose
you could manage to survive. But it wasn't any island paradise.
Just a godforsaken scraggly little bare rock, with maybe enough
tillable land for a carrot patch and some onions. Way off the
shipping lanes, in a zone of rotten weather—what soil there is
probably blows away every couple of cycles. Nobody in his right
mind would have wanted that place. Atmosphere just *barely*
breathable, and the gravity all wrong . . . . Somebody with plenty
of money to spend on terraforming could have made it livable,
sure; but nobody with that much money would have wanted it.
As for being stranded out there the way those bi—those women
were, with antique hand tools and survival packs—shit! In their
place, I'd have been yelling mayday with all the power I had
available.''

Heykus sighed, and rubbed his temples with the base of his

palms. It was not supposed to be possible. Here women were, not even legally adults. They couldn't have any money of their own, they couldn't buy property, they couldn't apply for a passport, they couldn't even get through customs without a male escort. Even women on the most primitive frontier settlements, women who had to do a lot of things that women in more civilized places would never have been allowed to do, were under the legal guardianship of responsible adult males. For a lone woman to stow away in a baggage hold, or sneak out an airlock during a commercial cruise, something like that, was always possible. But a *group* of women? A group of eleven women, off by themselves in the wilderness sectors, playing survival games? It was beyond his comprehension.

"Trying to establish a settlement in space is not *like* just hiking into the woods," he stated, as if that weren't self-evident. "We send out exploring parties of well-trained men, equipped with every one of the newest technological tools—and they still have it damn rough."

"They do," Frege agreed.

"Well, what in blazes could possibly make a bunch of ignorant women, runaways with no skills and no equipment, think they could do such a thing? And what kind of worthless men were in charge of them, that they would even think of trying?"

"I don't know," Frege answered. "I don't understand it any more than you do."

"Didn't you interrogate them? Once you had them aboard?"

"They sent for me, sir, and I did my best. But you know the law. You can't use any of the spilldrugs unless you have the permission of the woman's legal guardian, or her husband, or at least a senior male relative. The courts are extremely touchy about any violation on that."

"I'm touchy about it myself!" snapped Heykus. "I wasn't suggesting that you break any laws. But it seems to me that a man with your experience . . . how long have you been in Coast Guard Security? Twenty-some years now, isn't it? It seems to me you might have known a few ways to persuade the ladies to talk sensibly. In some legal and appropriate manner, Frege."

The captain laughed harshly. "Director Clete," he said, "these were not ladies. I've duly noted that the word 'bitches' offends you, and I won't use it again in your office. But you might want to give a little thought to what kind of female human being tries to tear out a man's eyes with a hoe. These women were not 'persuadable.' Not in any legal manner that *I* know about."

"I see. Well . . . it's an ugly story."

"It is."

"What's the ending like?"

"Attempts to identify male relatives or guardians were unsuccessful—we're still working on that. Out in that neck of space, it could take a while."

"All you had to do was check their armpit tattoos," Heykus noted impatiently. "I don't see the problem."

Frege shook his head, and his lips twitched at the corners. "They'd taken care of that before we got to them, Director."

"Oh, they *had?* And just how did they manage that?"

"Regular sewing needles and indelible ink, from the look of it. They'd really messed it up. *No armpit data*—just blurred black lines. They must have done it before they tackled anything else."

"But that's against the law!"

"I don't think the law was one of their main concerns, sir. Under the circumstances, we waited the regulation seventy-two hours and then we took them to the nearest institutional facility and we turned them over."

"Suitably tranquilized."

"Absolutely."

Heykus sighed again, and his regret was genuine. He knew what would happen to the women now. He even approved of it, because the mind of a madwoman was a sewage pit that had to be cleaned out. But a mind treated in that fashion, however essential the process, was a mind beyond the reach of any ministry. Satan was eleven souls richer, at least for the time being. And that reminded him.

"Reversible procedures only?" he asked.

"Sir?"

"I said, reversible procedures only. You made sure that the women would be administered only reversibles, while we locate the male trash that let them get to such a state."

"Director Clete, this was a particularly nasty kind of incident."

"So? The law says, only reversibles for at least sixty days if you can't locate male guardians. No matter *how* nasty the circumstances."

"True. But scruples were superfluous in this case."

Heykus' eyes narrowed, and he laid both palms flat on the seeyum, fingers spread wide. "Explain that," he ordered.

"Because there was only one way those women could have been where they were, in the condition they were in, and doing what they were doing. And that's for them to have landed along with a party of men—probably criminals, because there've been no missing person reports or any other kind of inquiry—but conceivably just a party of loners and oddballs. They could not possibly have gotten there as a group of eleven women, Director Clete; you're right about that. They had men with them, when they landed."

Heykus frowned. "You mean the men abandoned them there?"

"No, sir."

"I don't understand."

"Sir, the women killed them."

The sound Heykus made was the sound a man makes when a fist takes him in the belly, with no warning. Frege looked politely down at the floor while he recovered his composure.

"You know that to be true?" Heykus said heavily. "Be careful what you say, Captain."

"No, I *don't* know it to be true," answered Frege, his irritation obvious in his voice. "It *could* be that a gender-selective plague wiped out all the men, and the women went crazy with grief. You want to accept something like that, fine. I don't care. But the men were all very, very dead, Director."

"You found them."

"The women had done a pretty good job of cleaning up after themselves," said Frege coldly, "but that asteroid was hard rock, and they hadn't brought anything along that would dig very deep. When we went back with lawprobe lasers, we found the bodies without any trouble."

"Dear Jesus," said Heykus, with complete reverence; he leaned back wearily in his chair and closed his eyes. Women. Women murdering their men, burying their bodies, defacing their tattoos . . . he couldn't imagine it, and he was glad he couldn't.

"I want a full investigation," he said. "I want no murder charges *unless they can be proved,* do you understand me?"

"Certainly."

"Captain, did those women say *any*thing that made sense?"

"Not to me. They quoted that Chaleuvre woman and her sister that were jailed in Paris last February—not jailed fast enough, in my opinion, but I'm glad they're finally off the streets. That kind of filth. And they said they wanted to be free."

"Free. Of *what?* Had somebody abused them?

Frege spoke carefully, and gently; the old man was tough, but he looked heartsick about this situation. "Director Clete," he said, "they were all completely—one hundred percent—insane. *Mad*women, sir. You couldn't expect them to say anything logical."

"Free to starve. Free to die of exposure. Free to choke on foul air. Free to die of diseases no doctor has seen in a century. Free to suffer unspeakably. They want to be *free*, to do all those things?"

Frege didn't say anything. What was there to say?

"I wish I could talk to them myself," Heykus declared. "I'd like to hear them say whatever they have to say. To *me*. To my face."

"Sir . . ." Frege knew that Heykus would resent his showing any concern, but it bothered him to see the old man so upset. He was sure it wasn't good for him. "Director Clete, they said things you wouldn't want to hear, believe me. I'd be just as glad if I hadn't had to listen to them, myself."

"They are not responsible," Heykus told him sternly. "No more than little children! No woman becomes sick like that overnight. Where were their men all this time, while their minds were rotting away? Frege, you tell me—could your wife, or your sister, or your mother, or any other woman in your care, reach a state of deterioration in which she would be capable of ending your life, without you ever noticing that she needed medical attention?"

"Of course not."

"It's awful. It's unspeakable."

"Yes. It is. It was."

"Frege, were all eleven of them killers? Or was there just one ringleader . . . or two or three?"

Before Frege could say anything, Heykus waved him silent. "I'm sorry," he said. "I understand—you don't know anything about what happened. And God forgive me, I'm doing just what I ordered you not to do . . . I'm condemning those poor sick women without a scrap of evidence. I apologize."

Heykus had spoken to one such woman. Just once, nearly ten years ago. She'd been caught almost immediately, had stolen her husband's flyer and been intercepted before she ever made landing anywhere. They'd brought her kicking and biting and shrieking like a rabid animal into the port office where he and the husband were waiting. They'd been prepared to give her a spilldrug; the husband—a pompous bully of a man Heykus had felt no sympathy for—had been perfectly willing. But it hadn't been necessary. The problem with that one had been getting her to shut up.

He'd made a real effort to reach her. He had been careful not to say anything that might sound accusing, or punitive. And he had asked her the question that was every man's question in these cases: *why?* "My dear," he'd said to her gently, "we don't understand. On Earth, and on every colony of Earth, to the very limit of our resources, you women are cherished. Treated tenderly. Indulged in every way. Looked after, deferred to, sheltered. . . . *Why* do you turn to this perversion? What more do you want? What is it that we aren't giving you?"

He had been speaking the truth. No woman had to suffer want. No woman had to work, from the day she was born till the day she died; even those women who chose to be nurses or who followed their men out to the frontiers did not really do *work*. In the colonies a woman might need to spend a little more time looking after home and family than she would have on Earth, but it was strictly temporary; it never took many years for the comforts of the motherworld to begin showing up on those colony worlds where women were permitted to go. No man took a woman to Baron, or to Gehenna. And no man dared mistreat or abuse a woman, any more than he dared abuse a child; one call, and the courts would take her away from him forever. Even a woman whose husband earned very little could spend most of her life shopping in the fembouteeks, and chatting with her friends, and involved with her clubs, and enjoying her hobbies. Looking at the runaway, he had thought of his own mother, adored by her sons till the day she died, petted and cosseted, showered with presents, all her foolishness as gently handled as if it had been a major contribution to civilization; and he had leaned toward the raving creature they were holding for him and pleaded with her to explain to him what was wrong.

She had spat in his face. Literally, she had spat on him. He had gone on talking to her nevertheless, wiping the foul slime off his skin, reminding himself that she was only a woman, only a very sick woman, and not responsible for her behavior, until she had exhausted the stream of almost incomprehensible hysterical gibberish that poured from her.

"You don't know anything about it!" she had screamed, over and over. "you don't know anything about women, not anything at all!" He had understood that much, in among the gibberish. He had had a mother, two beloved grandmothers, three adored great-grandmothers; he had a wife he would have cheerfully died for, and two sisters he doted on, and daughters he loved. As for the granddaughters and great-granddaughters, he was a perfect fool about them. He had never known a woman, even one he disliked, who didn't inspire in him an immediate protective impulse. He had never been able even to begin to understand how men could once have been so weak and so worthless that

they had allowed their women to dirty themselves in the world of
business and politics and all the rest—men knew better than that
now, and Heykus thanked God for it. But it was his own
conviction that *he* would have known better even if he'd lived in
the 1980s, and would have cherished *his* women decently regardless of the social perversities of the time. He, Heykus Joshua
Clete, was an *expert* on women. *How dare this runaway female
tell him that he didn't know anything about women?* He knew
everything there was to know about normal women; it was only a
specimen like this that baffled him.

A sudden thought had struck him that day, and he had turned
to the pompous husband and asked, "Are you a linguist? Of the
Lines?" If the feminist was a woman of the Lines . . . their lives
were hard, they were subject to dangerous stresses and influences that no woman should have to experience. He knew that,
and it was a social evil he deplored and had always wished he
could set right without endangering the Lord's plan for the
universe. If she was a linguist woman, it might go a long way
toward explaining. But the husband had recoiled, insulted; that
hadn't been it. And they'd taken the woman away still cursing
and shrieking, and left Heykus standing there with tears in his
eyes that he was in no way ashamed of. Seeing her . . . it broke
his heart. It still broke his heart, remembering. She couldn't
have been more than twenty years old, and her life was over. As
surely as if she were dead. She would have been better off dead,
if it hadn't been for the fact that death for her meant eternal
damnation. She would spend all the years left to her in a mental
institution; the pompous ass she'd married would divorce her at
once and forget that she ever existed.

Men must do better, Heykus was thinking. Remembering that
terrible mad child. Filthy . . . scratched bloody by her own frantic
nails. Men must learn to look after their women better, with
more wisdom; they must learn to see the first tiniest seeds of
perversion. This blind folly, assuming that it could never happen
in your own family, would always happen to someone else, was
not an adequate excuse.

"Director Clete?"

Heykus was startled, but he didn't allow the Captain to see
that; not a muscle twitched. He had been sitting there, he realized, staring, remembering. Wasting the younger man's time. In
just the way that he'd reproached Frege for at the beginning of
their meeting.

"I'm sorry, Captain," he said forthrightly. "I apologize. I'm
afraid this is something I've never been able to take lightly."

"No decent man can. No need to apologize for decency."

"I'm sorry, nevertheless. My reaction is—excessive. I keep wondering. Is there some needed safeguard in the law that we're overlooking? Is it something in the way they're educated? Are we still asking too much of them, Frege? Perhaps we are wrong to allow them to go beyond the inner colonies? Perhaps we should shelter them more. Women are so frail, Captain, so precious—they are given to us to cherish, not to neglect."

Pierre Frege cleared his throat, speaking carefully. "Your concern does you credit, sir. I think far too many of us forget our responsibilities in these matters. But I would remind you that there haven't been more than a dozen attempts of this kind in the past twenty years, and most have involved only two or three women. These are statistical accidents, Director. Every once in a while someone is killed because he trips stepping out his front door and cracks his skull open—it's that kind of thing. You can't predict it, and you can't prevent it. It's like trying to control lightning."

Heykus chuckled. "We do *that* rather well, Captain. But I understand the figure of speech, and I appreciate your courtesy. I'm getting sentimental in my old age, and you're very tolerant of an old man's foibles."

"My pleasure," said Frege sturdily, thinking that Clete was known to be about as sentimental as a guillotine.

"You'll keep me posted on this, Captain?"

"You'll get full reports—and if anything confidential turns up, I'll come tell you about it myself."

"Do that, please. And perhaps it won't happen again, eh?"

"Perhaps not. I certainly hope not. We *all* hope not."

Heykus watched him leave, nodding a parting gesture—this was a good man, a valued employee—and then ran the fiz-status report; everything normal there. As he would have expected.

He began double-checking then. Making sure that all the steps in the program that would suppress this story completely had been implemented. It was worth taking the trouble, worth being scrupulous. The idea of other women reading about this was not acceptable. There had never been any leaks on these episodes, not one, in his entire career. And there were not ever *going* to be any. And there were not going to be any more episodes like the activities of those two Chaleuvre women in France . . . he was going to make some calls that would guarantee that. Such females should be given expert help immediately, at the first signs of their illness, not allowed to wander around in public with their pathetic condition on view to all the world. Whatever was wrong in France that accounted for their slipshod handling of the Chaleuvre case would have to be rooted out and set right; he intended to see to that personally.

II

"Reverend Pinter?"

The preacher already had his raincape over his arm and his hat in his hand, and was reaching out to palm the latch; he was leaving, and not lingering about it. But he stopped readily enough, and smiled at Jo-Bethany.

"Yes, Mrs. Chornyak," he said politely. "Did you want something?"

She didn't bother explaining about her name. Every woman in the place was addressed by outsiders as either Miss or Mrs. Chornyak, apparently on the basis of age alone. The linguist women let it pass, and she intended to do the same.

"There's something I'm uneasy about, Reverend," she told him. "I wonder if I could have a few minutes of your time to discuss a small problem."

"A spiritual problem, my dear?"

"Yes . . . if you can spare the time. I know you're busy, and you must be tired—it's awfully late—but I'm uncomfortable about this."

She could see the reluctance in his eyes; no doubt he had to listen to amazing amounts of gush and nonsense from women involved in "spiritual" problems. But he looked at her as a man looks who knows his duty and does it, and when he spoke he spoke kindly enough.

"I always have time to tend the sheep," he said. "And of course I have time to speak to you. It's a matter of some urgency to you, I take it."

"I wouldn't bother you if it weren't, Reverend Pinter," she said, feeling absurd, wishing there were someone else a woman *could* speak to in a situation like this. If only there could have been women who were preachers, she thought fretfully, knowing it was a scandalous idea and not caring. It was *degrading*, having to appeal to him to grant her an audience. It was like going to a doctor—degrading, and disgusting. You did not *do* it unless it was urgent.

Reverend Pinter was looking around him at the room of quiet women, seated at their various tasks, and Jo-Bethany knew what he was thinking. A spiritual problem—that meant privacy. She was going to have to clarify her status after all.

"Reverend," she said hastily, "I'm the resident nurse here. A member of the staff. If I may walk with you to your flyer, no one will have any objection. They'll assume that I have a health question of some kind to discuss with you."

His face changed, and his smile became less false; he looked at her as if they were not meeting for the first time, as if they shared some secret, and said, "You're not a Chornyak, then? Not a member of the Lines?"

"No, Reverend. I'm not a linguist. I live here because I work here."

"I *see*." The smile was warm now, and the eyes were smiling, too, and she understood—he was glad to learn that he was no longer slumming. "In that case, of *course*. By all means, walk to the curb with me and let's see if I can be of help to you. It's not Mrs. Chornyak, then."

"No, Reverend Pinter. It's Miss. Miss Schrafft. I am Jo-Bethany Schrafft."

"Jo-Bethany . . . a charming old name, my dear."

"It was my grandmother's name."

He bowed slightly as he opened the door for her, and waited while she stepped outside into the darkness, saying, "I do apologize, Miss Schrafft."

"That's all right," she said, reminding herself that the question she had was one he'd know the answer for, whether he was in fact a godly man or not; it was a technical question. "You couldn't have known."

"No, I couldn't, could I?" He laughed softly. "It's not as if they were all green, or all purple, or all spotted—you can't tell."

Jo-Bethany made a polite vague sound of assent, and looked around to be sure no one was close enough to hear them . . . no, they had the lawn to themselves. He moved straight along the walk toward the curb, where a sedate dark flyer with a narrow white clerical stripe on its door was parked, and she walked at his side, hurrying a little to keep up.

"You say you're *uneasy*, Miss Schrafft. Oops . . . watch out for the lilies, or whatever those are! What is the source of this uneasiness, exactly?"

"It's these Thursday night services."

"Like the one tonight?"

"Yes. This is . . . perhaps the fifth one I've gone to."

"And you're uneasy? Why? Regular worship should be encouraged, Miss Schrafft, no matter where it takes place. I'm more than happy to come here and preach when I'm called on to do so—I certainly don't feel uneasy about it.''

"Reverend Pinter, it's not the regular service that troubles me. It's the rest of it. The other things.''

"Other things?'' He stopped his brisk trek down the long walk and turned to look at her, his eyes twinkling. "What other things, my dear? Do they really sacrifice babies?''

Her shock made her gasp, and she wasn't sorry; she had no desire to hide it. The man apologized immediately, and assured her that it was a very old joke, by which he meant no harm whatsoever. "The sort of joke one makes among men, my dear,'' he added. "Not at all suitable for a woman's ears. It's been a very long day, and you're correct that I'm tired—please forgive me.''

They were at the curb, then, and he opened the flyer door to set his cape and hat and Bible down on the passenger seat, while Jo-Bethany waited silently. He closed the door, turned toward her, leaned against the flyer's gleaming side, and rubbed his hands vigorously together.

"There!'' he said. "Now, you have my full attention, and I promise not to tell any more bad jokes. Please tell me what the 'other things' that concern you so are.''

Jo-Bethany keep her eyes on the grass at her feet; she didn't like this man, and she wished she hadn't started this. "You know we don't usually have a preacher,'' she began. "The women tell me that once a month is all the budget will stretch to.''

The Reverend snorted, making it clear what he thought of that, but he didn't interrupt her, and she went on.

"At all the other services, it's just the women, alone. With one of the older ones leading the service.''

The silence went suddenly thick, almost syrupy; she had to look up at him to find out why, and she saw that his face was stern and his eyes were narrowed.

"Miss Schrafft.'' It was the voice of authority now. "Are those women preaching? If they *are*, you're quite right to tell me, and I'll go to the Head at once and have it stopped.''

"Oh, no!'' Jo-Bethany shook her head, flustered, glad he hadn't been able to read her mind when she was longing for a woman to discuss this with. "No, they're just reading aloud from the Bible, and leading the singing. Of *course*, they're not preaching!''

He shrugged his big shoulders and admonished her. "They do go out to work at government negotiations, you know—men's work, Miss Schrafft. They interpret, and they translate. Their judgment is sought. *Most* improper. And one thing leads to another. If there were any group of women in this world sufficiently . . . mmm . . . ill-behaved to try their hand at preaching, it would be the women of the Lines."

"They don't preach, Reverend Pinter," she said wearily. "I'm sure no such idea ever crossed their minds. They're good, decent women."

"'Well, then, my dear—what *is* the problem?"

"Reverend, what worries me is the language that they use sometimes. I don't know about it. I don't know if it's *right*." There. She'd said it. If he thought she was foolish, so be it.

He frowned at her, obviously thinking hard, and then his face cleared and the snap of his fingers was so loud in the darkness that she jumped. "Aha!" he said. "Like the language they were using just as I came in this evening? Is that what you're getting yourself all upset over?"

Silently, Jo-Bethany cursed Panglish. What she had had to say had been simple. A simple moral question. And it was taking *forever*, and she couldn't find the right words, and she was keeping him standing here while she struggled to find some way to explain; and now he was of course treating her like a child. She wished she had never brought it up at all. *Damn* language, anyway!

"It is the shepherd's charge to know everything there is to know about his sheep, my dear," he was saying. "And I do know about the language these silly women use. What I don't know is why it worries you."

"It's very *strange*," she told him, stubbornly. Doggedly. "It's not Greek. It's not Latin. It's certainly not anything American."

"My dear child, what a very scrupulous conscience you have!"

"Yes. I do." And I intend to go on having one, she thought, even if you are laughing at me.

"Miss Schrafft, it's only their 'Langlish'; sometimes they call it 'Lahadan,' something like that. There's absolutely no harm in it. It's a language these women made up as a kind of hobby— after all, they're linguists! If they were farm women they might have houseplants, or pets; since they spend all their lives working with incomprehensible languages, they made up another one of those. The men of the Lines have always approved. I understand it's called 'The Encoding Project,' and the women actually have a kind of mass get-together once a year, to fool with it. An excuse for a holiday for them, poor things! It's a harmless pastime."

"But to use it for *worship?* Is that all right? I mean—"

The preacher laughed heartily, from the belly, and she stepped back, sure he was going to reach over and chuck her under the chin. "All they do, dear, is translate parts of the King James Bible into the stuff. There's no harm in that. It's not as if they were writing things on their own. There's no difference that I can see between saying the Lord's Prayer from the good old King James in French or in Chinese or saying it in 'Langlish.' After *all*, dear child—our Savior didn't say it in Standard American Panglish, either."

Jo-Bethany had never thought of that before; it was almost shocking. But it was true, of course it was; Jesus had said the Lord's Prayer in some other language. Greek? Egyptian? She had no idea. But not Panglish!

"Oh, my," she said, almost whispering. "I'm afraid I've been ridiculous, Reverend Pinter. I've wasted your time."

"Not at all, Miss Schrafft! Not at all!"

He went around to the driver's side of the flyer as he spoke, letting her know that he did feel it was time he left, and opened the door, holding its edge as he talked. "You seem to be a very sensible woman, Miss Schrafft, and I'm going to share a confidence with you. The first time I ever heard them jabbering that stuff, just as I came in for a service, I thought I was hearing voodoo, or some such thing. I don't mind telling you—although I'll ask you not to let it go any farther—I went straight to Jonathan Asher Chornyak and I demanded a full explanation. I reacted very much as you've reacted, my dear, and I don't think either of us was being ridiculous. But it was explained to me, as I've just explained it to you; the women have as a hobby the translating of Bible passages into this invented language they amuse themselves with. It must be like having a secret code, when you're a kid, don't you see. The men keep an eye on it, and are more than willing to humor them—as they pointed out to me, the women might well have taken up translating trashy love stories, or worse. Translating the Bible is actually a rather *wholesome* hobby, as hobbies go. And if they want to show off a bit and read their little translations aloud in their own home worship services . . . well. It's childish, of course, and woman-ish, but it's certainly innocent. My dear, please set your mind at rest and don't fret about it any more."

He took no chances that she wouldn't be satisfied with that; he stepped into the flyer and closed the door firmly behind him, leaving her with a few parting words about being careful not to become more intimate with the linguist women than was necessary, and keeping her distance and simply carrying out her duties, and how hard it was to walk the line sometimes, and then he was gone.

Jo-Bethany *was* satisfied. He was a poor excuse for a man of God, but he had known the answer to her question. A technical question; a technical answer. It was a relief to her, knowing she needn't worry about the language mixed into the services; now that she could be sure nothing about it conflicted with the practices of the United Reformed Baptist Church she was willing to admit to herself that she loved the sound of it. It soothed her, somehow. Rested her. She was *glad* she could relax and enjoy it, the way she enjoyed the singing.

She went back into the house, stopping on her way to touch the soft folded tops of the daylilies that bordered the walk. They were glorious in the daytime, every color of gold and yellow, many of them spotted and flecked.

"The men hate them," Belle-Anne had told her. "They say they stink, and they call them weeds, and they're always suggesting that we pull them up and put in a nice pink rosebush."

"And will you?" Jo-Bethany had asked. "Rosebushes are so pretty."

Belle-Anne laughed. "Just so," she said. "Pretty, and sweet. But not glorious the way the daylilies are. Every little rose, just like every other little rose. And it's so funny—the women used to beg for rosebushes, and the men wouldn't let us have them. We got those huge beds of crazy lilies because they *were* weeds, and we could get them without spending money, and then they just spread and spread all for free. Now the men are sorry they didn't let us have the roses, and we've come to love the lilies."

"You won't pull them up, then?"

"Not in a million years."

"What if the men just go ahead and do it?"

"I don't think they would," said Belle-Anne seriously. "It would be very rude of them, and they have no reason to be rude. But if they did, it wouldn't matter. The lilies would come back, you perceive. They're like any weed—they're not easy to get rid of. And then we'd have both roses *and* lilies."

"No problem?"

"None at all."

CHAPTER 7

"There once was a linguist most eerie,
whose papers made everyone weary;
but when we called them twaddle
he roared, "It's a MODEL!
I never once called it a theory!"

(from *Cautionary Limericks for the Downtrodden,* annual publication of the graduate students of the Department of Language Sciences of California Multiversity)

Jonathan Asher Chornyak was deeply curious this morning; he'd been curious ever since the request for this appointment had appeared on his comscreen four days ago. What in the world did a college professor, with an international reputation already assured and an interplanetary one probable, want with the Head of the Lines? There hadn't been a college professor under the roof of Chornyak Household in Jonathan's lifetime, he was quite sure; he doubted there'd been one here in this century.

Because although the formal split between the Lines and the academic world had involved only Departments of Linguistics, it had spread—slowly, but inexorably—to include not just closely related fields like psychology and anthropology but the entire academic community. Other professors were fully capable of imagining what it was like for their colleagues in linguistics to have the youngsters from the linguist families in their classrooms. With every single one of those kids having native fluency in three human languages, including American Sign Language, plus one Alien language, plus a respectable fluency in perhaps another half dozen languages of Earth, *plus* PanSig! The young of the Lines had not only been far ahead of their fellow students;

they'd been well ahead of their professors as well. The problem was not that they were multilingual; linguistics profs would have enjoyed having multilingual students who were naive about linguistics itself. The problem was that they were experts in what the professors were expected to teach them.

In the same way that a child from one of the great circus families like the Canestrellis would quite naturally know how to walk a tightrope and do a backflip, children of the Lines as young as nine or ten knew how to do formal linguistic analysis. It *was* natural; the adults around them were constantly involved in such analyses. But that made it no less a source of frustration for the profs. It made no difference whether you taught linguistics or the tuba—you could imagine what it would be like, and shudder at the prospect; and you could understand why an absolute split, with associated fervent hatred, had been inevitable.

And now here was a supernova college professor, not only seeking an appointment with a filthy Lingoe but requesting it inside a filthy Lingoe den! Normal procedure would have been to try to summon the filthy Lingoe to the campus, and to be outraged if he wasn't grateful for the privilege. Jonathan was fascinated.

When he saw the man come through his door he became even more curious, because there were things about him that were distinctly not typical. His clothes, for example; and his shaved head. That he could look the way he looked, and still be on the faculty of a great university, vouched for his brilliance in a way that no stack of diplomachips and awards could have done. Had he not been genuinely a superstar among academics, he would not have been allowed to *visit* the campus of Massachusetts Multiversity, much less teach in its sedate, tradition-crusted buildings. Jonathan hadn't had time to read any of the man's work prior to the meeting, and was sure he wouldn't have understood it anyway, but the brief biography he'd pulled from the comset's whozis database was impressive. There were few prestigious mathematics journals in which Professor Macabee Dow had not published, and there were no major awards in his discipline that he had not received except those for which he was ineligible by reason of his youth. But nowhere in the bio had there been even a hint that the man was a flamboy; not even the semantically bleached out word "radical" had appeared there to indicate that this was an eccentric professor in the classical style. Looking at him, Jonathan knew it could only mean that the fellow had tremendous status; nothing else could have kept that information out of the bio. The head was not just shaved, it was stained indigo and waxed to a gleaming fare-thee-well; Jonathan could almost see his reflection in the polished flesh.

Interesting. Definitely interesting. A militant eggdome, sitting in his office, by god! Of his own free will.

He leaned toward the man just enough to signal attention, keeping his facial expression carefully neutral, and bypassed all the formalities. He said, "Let's get at it, Professor, shall we? What do you want from Chornyak Household?"

He hadn't misjudged his man; there was no flicker of surprise in the pale blue eyes that stood out so astonishingly against the indigo skin. Just as there had been no trace of surprise on his face when he came through the door and discovered that the Head of the Lines had no real desk in which to work but sat at the same narrow table-like piece of furniture that had served the Heads of the Lines a hundred years ago. He had simply sat down in the chair across from Jonathan and made himself comfortable; if he'd expected baronial splendor and the latest technology and been startled not to find it here, he was hiding it superbly well.

"I have a two-week-old son," said Macabee Dow. "I want permission to Interface him with your current Alien-in-Residence . . . your current AIRY." Just like that, without preamble. He didn't even say hello first.

Jonathan was stunned. No doubt there'd been a good deal more than a trace of shock on *his* face. One point to Macabee Dow, and he'd only been here ninety seconds.

"Are you serious?"

"Absolutely serious."

Jonathan stared at him, bearing down on the full eye contact, adding a reliable set of bodyparl flourishes guaranteed to shake anyone with reason to be uneasy, and waited. No reactions. Nothing.

"Just a minute," he said. No point in wasting time. He turned to his comset, punched a red stud on the left, and was pleased to see the Ready signal come up immediately. "Grandfather," he said, speaking directly to the set despite the fact that the old man had it blanked as always and there was nothing to be seen on the screen, "there's an eggdome flamboy down here in my office, wearing a dress shirt and a sarong, with his effing skull shaved bare and stained blue—wanting to put his baby in our Interface. I'd appreciate it if you'd come down here and give me a hand."

He kept an eye on his guest as he talked, watching for any sign of resentment at the deliberate rudeness; there was none. Either Macabee Dow was indifferent to such things, or he'd been thoroughly briefed on what to expect and was determined not to be led down any linguistic lanes, or both. Or perhaps something else was going on. The ethic of the broad-chested square-shouldered reaganic American male obligated the professor absolutely, intellectual or no intellectual, sarong or no sarong, to object to the blatant insults or to make an aggressive countermove of his own, but Macabee Dow was doing nothing of the kind. His face was as blank as Jonathan's comset screen, and he sat there in what looked to Jonathan's expert eye like a state of comfortable relaxation. Amazing.

"On my way!" said the old man's voice, the touch of glee obvious if you knew him as well as Jonathan knew him. "Give me three minutes for the stairs, and don't say anything important before I get there."

The light went off, and Jonathan turned to look at Dow again.

"Do you have the baby with you?" he asked him bluntly.

Dow raised both hands, high and open. "No baby," he said.

"Not stashed outside the office with one of the women?"

"Nope. Home with its mother, Chornyak."

"And how does the mother feel about this project of yours?"

"She's having flaming hysterical convulsions, like any decent woman who believes everything she hears on the popnews. That has no bearing on this matter whatsoever."

"No legal bearing," Jonathan agreed. "But perhaps it has an emotional bearing."

Macabee Dow's eyebrows went up a fraction, and the pale blue eyes turned paler. "I don't make jokes, Mr. Chornyak," he said icily. "And I don't say anything I don't mean. The fact that my wife hasn't a brain in her head and is therefore behaving brainlessly has no bearing—of any kind—on this matter. I married her to run my bed and board and bear my children and look decorative; those are the only functions she serves."

"Glad to hear it," said the voice at the door. "Far too many young men let their wives get out of hand early on and then spend the rest of their lives in a futile attempt to regain proper control of the situation. Terrible waste of time, and no excuse for it in this day and age."

"Good morning, Grandfather," said Jonathan. "Thank you for coming down. Professor—my grandfather, James Nathan Chornyak. Grandfather, this is Professor Macabee Dow, Mathematics Department, Massachusetts Multiversity. Here to borrow a cup of Interfacing, so to speak."

James Nathan sat down at Jonathan's side with a polite nod, and the professor across the desk from them said it again. "I am here to request that you allow me to Interface my two-week-old son with your current AIRY, gentlemen. 'Borrowing' is not involved. I am willing to pay any reasonable fee, and to sign whatever legal waivers you require. The boy is a healthy normal infant. Good bones. Like me, he is absolutely bald. Unlike me, his head is not stained indigo—he won't alarm the other babies you have in the Interface."

The old man glanced at his grandson, noted the OVER TO YOU code gesture, and moved on it. "We'll need an explanation," he said sternly, one index finger pointed straight at the professor. "This is completely without precedent, as I'm sure you know. College professors have not mingled with linguists since the year 2050. And nobody, in or out of academe, is willing to have their *infants* mingle with us. State your game, Professor Dow."

Dow narrowed his eyes, and the linguists waited for the resentment to surface, but he was in full control of himself. "I am a man with a great deal of power," he told them flatly. "I intend my son to be a man of at least equal power. If there is a more likely swift route to power than being the first layman to acquire an Alien language natively, I don't know what it is. I'm aware that power of that sort isn't available free of charge, and I'm prepared to pay you handsomely. I am also prepared to provide all the necessary proofs . . . of the child's perfect health, of my own financial position, and whatever else you consider necessary in that line. Whatever you need, my attorneys will get for you. The game, gentlemen, is *power*; there are no other games worth playing."

"And if the answer is no?" Jonathan asked, prepared to hear the man say that in that case he'd go to one of the other linguist Households; but Dow must have been advised that a Chornyak decision would be a decision honored by all thirteen families. He made no such suggestion.

"I'll attempt to convince you that your decision is an error," he answered. "And if I can't convince you, I'll go home and switch to an alternate plan. The boy is only two weeks old; I don't feel cramped for time."

"And you don't think he's a little young for Interfacing."

"You know perfectly well he's not," said Macabee Dow, looking disgusted, "unless you're concerned about feeding and diapering and so on. And I see no reason why the arrangements you make for your own infants can't be extended to mine. If you want a baby nurse on duty to supervise that, I'll pay for one."

It was quiet in the small room; the linguists were thinking. The air exchange was loud enough in the silence to be distracting, and Jonathan tapped a stud to cover the soft hum with a Bach fugue of appropriate tempo and complexity.

"Professor Dow," he asked, "what makes you think this is possible?"

"The fact that I'm able and willing to meet your price," snapped the academic. "You men earn four times my salary, but I'm not dependent on my salary—I know how to make money. The fact that one more little baby won't crowd your Interface. And the fact that there's no reason, other than the irrelevant 'without precedent,' for you to refuse."

"You don't think it's *genetically* impossible, then?" hazarded Jonathan, being exceedingly careful. Dow had made only one error so far, and it was a predictable one: he would have been hearing about the voracious greed of the linguists since he *himself* was an infant; naturally he believed it. But he was a man with plenty of avenues for publicity open to him, who might be capable of doing considerable damage in unanticipated ways. It would not be wise to underestimate him on the basis of a single error.

"I beg your pardon?"

"*Come* now, Professor!" James Nathan's voice flicked the air, a deft cool lash of sound, fitting neatly into the spaces in the fugue. "Don't waste our time, please; we haven't been wasting yours."

"If your reference," Dow answered steadily, "is to the government propaganda that only infants of the Lines are genetically capable of acquiring Alien languages—and I assume that it must be—have the courtesy to remember that I am a scientist. I am quite able to recognize claptrap, even when the motive behind it is a mystery and the source of it is the State Department."

"Then you are an *unusual* scientist, Professor Dow," Jonathan observed, watching, aware that his grandfather was watching as carefully as he was; the professor with his absurd blue-hued hairless skull did not appear to be in any way conscious that the statement he had just made was unusual or remarkable. "We see scientists constantly in our work, and they all seem willing to accept the government's bizarre position. And to give scientific papers in support of the government's position. And to write articles in support of it. And so on."

Macabee Dow sighed. "I'm not responsible for the ignorance of my colleagues," he said. "Nor am I required to share it. And whatever you may encounter when you are involved in government-sponsored activities, gentlemen, I give you my word: there is no such thing as a *competent* scientific scholar who believes that the infants of the Lines are sufficiently different genetically to have unique language acquisition skills. We know what that would

mean, gentlemen. A radically different *brain*, just for starters. . . . It's nonsense. *No* one takes it seriously."

"Well, I'll be damned," breathed James Nathan. "Does this
mean that we should now expect a long line of enlightened
scientists on our doorstep demanding to share our Interface?"

"I have no idea," stated Dow. "Probably not."

"Why not?"

"Because I rarely find myself part of a herd, Mr. Chornyak.
This may be an exception, of course—but I did not reach my
present position by doing things that everyone else does."

"But it *could* happen? Mathematically speaking? Things have
actually changed that much?"

"*Look,* Chornyak—both of you Chornyaks!" Macabee Dow
said harshly. "There hasn't been a child of the Lines educated
other than privately for generations. How the hell would you
know what's going on in the scientific community? In the *real*
scientific community, that is, not the community of federal
toadies? You people sit around on your isolated butts, going
nowhere except these houses buried in the ground like gopher
burrows, and the government facilities where you work, and you
take it for granted that you have your fingers right on the pulse
of contemporary science! Shit! Where do you *get* that kind of
arrogance?"

A more normal male display, Jonathan noted with satisfaction.
Delayed a bit, showing fine control, but normal. Very good.

"I'm sure you're absolutely correct," he said courteously, at
ease now. "We're frequently as astonished by our own ignorance as you are, if that's any consolation."

"I do not require consolation," said Macabee. "And my son
would be Interfacing with an Alien-in-Residence, not a Terran
linguist, thank god!"

James Nathan folded his arms over his chest, clearing his
throat, and grinned at his guest. "Your contemporary sophistica-
tion does not quite stretch to an absence of prejudice toward
nasty Lingoes, then?"

"I can respect those against whom I am prejudiced," Dow
answered. "My prejudices are like anyone else's—irrational.
They are not involved in this transaction any more than my wife
is."

"Very logical," said the Head. "Admirable in every way. By
all means, let us have scientific objectivity, even about our own
corruption. Let's hear your proposal, then. Specifically."

"I have a normal healthy infant son. I wish him to acquire an
Alien language as one of his native languages. The only way to

accomplish this—since you people have somehow managed to establish a total monopoly on the process—is for him to go into an Interface along with an infant or infants of the Lines. And I am prepared to pay for the privilege. That's it. *Specifically.*"

"And you are ready to sign waivers of responsibility?"

"Certainly."

James Nathan Chornyak shrugged his shoulders, and scowled thoughtfully down at his folded arms. While Jonathan waited for a cue, and Macabee Dow—at last—fidgeted. And then, to Jonathan's astonishment, he looked up and said, "Well, why not? The Interfaces are large. We could get another dozen infants in there at a time. The women in charge are perfectly capable of handling the needs of one more baby. I can't imagine that it would make any difference to our AIRYs. I have no objection to at least giving it a trial."

His grandson said nothing at all; this was no time to interfere with whatever James Nathan was up to, however much he disliked it. Not before a stranger, and especially not before this particular stranger. The phrase "a trial" must be the key. An *hour* could be considered a "trial."

"Good," said Macabee Dow. "Glad to hear it. Name your price, then."

"No price," said the old man. "Why should we charge you? One baby doesn't use very much air. However, there are some conditions." His voice changed abruptly, losing the casual tone, and he laid down the prerequisites with the measured snap of a drill instructor. "The baby will be brought here each day promptly at six A.M. and picked up just as promptly at nine A.M., by an individual in your employ. It will spend the period from six to nine in the Interface, although of course those of our women supervising will remove the child at once if it requires attention, just as they would one of our own infants. It will not participate in any other activity of this Household, and we will have no responsibility for it other than as part of the Interfacing proper. We do not Interface our infants on Sundays; we will not Interface yours. Should the child be ill in any way, however minor, you will keep it at home. If you know it to have been exposed to any sort of illness, you will keep it at home. The child's mother will not be permitted to observe the Interfacing or to interfere in the procedure—we have no time for the sort of emotional extravagance you describe and do not wish our own women exposed to it. We will set up this agreement for a trial period of three months, to be renegotiated at the end of that time and each six months thereafter; under no circumstances will it be continued beyond the child's fifth birthday; continuing practice with the language thereafter will be your responsibility, and I advise you to begin considering that aspect immediately—it won't be a simple arrangement. Any questions?''

Dow had stopped fidgeting, and was warily alert; Jonathan would have laid quite a large wager that he hadn't been spoken to in that fashion since he was a teenager. He narrowed his eyes again, and Jonathan saw a pulse beating at his temple.

"No questions," he said. "Not at the moment. I'll want it all in writing, of course, but it seems satisfactory. However, I would prefer to pay you a fee. I assure you I can afford to.''

"Absolutely not," snapped James Nathan. "We are unimpressed by your 'financial standing.' We have no interest in any monetary transaction with you. Not now; not any time in the future. We perceive this as a scientific experiment—even privately educated as we are, without the advantage of the rarified intellectual atmosphere within what you refer to as the real scientific community, we remain interested in science. We agree to participate. Our attorneys will draw up the necessary documents and forward them to your attorneys for examination and—if you find them in proper order—for your signature. We will not negotiate the terms stated. We will expect the infant one week from today at six A.M., or we will expect a communication from your attorneys stating that you have decided not to proceed. And that will suffice. Good day, Professor Dow; the stairs are straight ahead at the end of the corridor.''

Jonathan continued to be impressed with the eggdome; most men would have been distracted from their resolve by his grandfather's skilled tonguelashing, and by the heavy freight of contempt it carried in intonation and other bodyparl. This man merely nodded, handed over his attorneys' card, announced that they'd be hearing from him, and left. If he was typical of the "real" scientific community, Jonathan was encouraged. Someone had obviously told Dow that no matter what happened he must not let the linguists get him rattled, and he'd put on a remarkable display. There might be some hope for the old profs after all, if Dow was even approximately representative. It was time somebody sat in on a few classes and got a more current perspective on the situation, that was clear. He made a brief note to send some suitably ordinary-looking young males with gaps in their schedules over to Georgetown as soon as possible.

And then he leaned back in his chair, turned off the Bach, folded *his* arms over his chest, and stared coldly at James Nathan Chornyak. "All right, Grandfather," he said heavily. "That was

my fault—I invited you to join this meeting. And I didn't
interfere, because your judgment has never failed us yet.''

"That is *why* you invited me to join you," his grandfather
pointed out.

"Correct. That and the fact that I didn't want you to miss the
fun.''

"You're too kind to a useless old man, Jonathan. Try to curb
your mawkish sentimentality, will you?"

"Mawkish sentimentality, my rosy *butt!*"

"Is it? Rosy?"

"Grandfather, I don't have time for this crap."

"In that case, do not refer to business as 'fun'; the semantics
is too intricate for me. Please get on with it.''

"I'll be happy to. But I'm not sure where to begin, because
I'm completely baffled.''

"Well, Jonathan, my boy, if we had let him pay us—"

"Grandfather," Jonathan interrupted, grimly, "cut it out. Of
course we don't want his money. The last thing we want is to be
involved with him in an employee relationship . . . or, sweet
suffering Christ, to have him perceive himself as 'renting' our
Interface. I understand that, and I am in full agreement with
you—furthermore, you know that. What I don't understand is
why you agreed to do it on *any* terms.''

"As I said at the time, Jonathan, why not?"

"Grandfather, I don't need to remind you that the livelihood
of all thirteen of the Lines rests upon the maintenance of our
monopoly. Do you have some kind of job training plan in mind
for us, once you've handed over the only kind of work any of us
knows how to do? I agree that Dow is likely to do unusual
things; but when the word gets out on this—and I didn't hear you
adding any requirement of confidentiality to your list of
conditions—you can't tell me we won't have dozens more
eggdomes wanting to copy him and get *their* kiddies a piece of
the power, too. We only have thirteen Interfaces, but we could
add four or five lay infants to each of them without any strain.
And then you're talking about fifty lay linguists in competition
with the Lines! I realize that we're always being pushed to do
more work than we can keep up with, but I don't think that
turning over the Alien language business to the general public is
a solution to that problem.''

James Nathan had listened to all this with an infuriating grin
on his face, and it was still there after Jonathan stopped talking,
so that he found himself adding stiffly that he would appreciate
less humor and more information.

"I'm a little surprised," said the old man. "I always thought you were a man who saw straight to the heart of a situation. That's why we made you Head."

"BEM-dung. I was made Head because I had sense enough to make use of the wisdom to be found all around me instead of trying to be an effing Emperor. I remember very well being told that we'd had too many Emperor types in a row and it was time for a correction in the curve. Now *share* your wisdom—and it had better be top grade."

James Nathan chuckled, and Jonathan ignored that.

"*Now*, please, Grandfather," he said. "I'm a busy man."

James Nathan liked the Bach fugues, and considered it cheap of his grandson to save them for visitors; he reached over and flipped them on to provide an accompaniment. And he proceeded to explain the situation. "Let me tell you what's going to happen, Johnny," he said indulgently, "so that you can stop fretting. And then you have my permission to apologize to me for being so goddamn slow to perceive the overpoweringly obvious."

And after a while, as the overpoweringly obvious took on a delightful clarity for him, it was Jonathan who was chuckling.

CHAPTER 8

"I sat there and I stared at that lovely child; Aquina's descendant—named for her, and so like her in character that it made me doubt the principles of genetics. And I wondered. She had come so willingly, almost eagerly. I wondered if there were anything at all I could have asked her to do for the sake of Láadan that she would have said no to. If I had said, 'Aquina, find a cliff and jump off, for the sake of Láadan,' would she even have stopped to ask me why? I doubted it. I thought she would have just said, 'Yes, Nazareth!', and taken off at a run in search of an appropriate precipice. I remember that it was storming outside; that would not have slowed Aquina down at all.

"She had exactly the set of characteristics I always looked for, and so very rarely found, in every girlchild of the Lines past puberty. She was the daughter of a widow not remarried, and was therefore free of a male parent's close surveillance; she was herself both unmarried and unbetrothed, and seemed contented to be without a man's attentions; she was intelligent and industrious and brave; she had the troublesome but absolutely crucial sense of mission that was required. And she had a mother I could manage with ease; without that, all of the rest would have been useless to me.

"I sat there, studying her, thinking that fierce and passionate as she was, at seventeen she had more common sense than her great-grandmother had ever had. Still . . . that Aquina had grown up in a very different time. Before we began to speak Láadan. Before the building of the Womanhouses, when we still lived much of our lives with the men. Perhaps she would have been different, too, in different circumstances. Remembering how miserable her life had been, and how wasted, hardened my resolve. I ignored the reflex the girl provoked in me, that made

111

*me want to protect and shelter her, and I took the syringe from
my needlework bag and laid it on the table between us.*

*" 'Aquina,' I said, 'you'll want to play close attention now to
what I tell you. It isn't complicated, but if it's done wrong, it
might as well not be done at all.'*

*"She laughed at me, and at my serious face, and asked me,
'What could go wrong? I wait outside the rendezvous room for
Lara's husband to leave her alone, I go into the room, I—'*

*" 'Listen carefully all the same!' I said sharply. 'There are
things that matter, names and addresses and facts that you must
remember. That you must not write down, even in code.' "*

*"She hushed at that, and I warned her again, before I went
on. I have warned each one of the nine, and not one has let the
warning hold her back, but there could always be a first time. I
said, 'Aquina, dearlove, stop and think. This will be very unpleasant and difficult and dangerous. It has consequences that
will go on for all the rest of your life. Are you absolutely sure
you want to go on with it?"*

" 'It's for Láadan, isn't it?'

" 'Yes. Of course.'

*" 'Then I don't care about any of that,' she said. As calm and
confident as if all she had to do was go get me a cup of tea.*

*"They've all been like that—so calm, so serene, so sure of
themselves. I am still waiting for the first one to fail."*

(from the diaries of Nazareth Chornyak Adiness)

The tour of the Chornyak Household, with every last closet
and cranny opened for her inspection except the bachelor bedrooms, had clarified one thing for Jo-Bethany absolutely: the
idea that the linguists of the Lines lived in luxury was a myth.
Unless the Chornyaks were lying to her, and among the thirteen
families there were exceptions, the linguists lived in a manner
that most Americans would have considered appropriate only for
the poor. It was a very *elegant* poverty, to be sure, and a poverty
that was a matter of choice rather than necessity. But it was a
lifestyle so different from the one portrayed for the Lines by the
media that it was bewildering. Why would they want to distort
the truth that way? Jo-Bethany had no idea, and she preferred not
to think about it; the linguists themselves had proposed no
explanation. And she had seen that although nothing in the
Chornyak dwellings was luxurious, everything was sturdy and
durable and in decent taste—clearly, they were *not* poor. It was
odd, and baffling, and she had tried one very tentative question.

"At first," Dorcas Chornyak had answered, "during the time of the anti-linguist riots, we lived very simply as a way of demonstrating to people outside the Lines that they had no *reason* to consider us some sort of robber barons. It was an important matter, for us."

"But it didn't help!" Jo-Bethany had objected.

"You don't think so?"

"No, I don't. You might just as well have gone ahead and installed the marble pools and diamond chandeliers and all the rest of it, so far as I can see. Because after all these years, all this deliberate low-budget living of yours, the public image is precisely what it always was. I can understand why you might have gone on as you did for a while, thinking that eventually things would change and people would come to realize the truth. But after you saw it wasn't working, why didn't you give it up?"

Dorcas had smiled at her and said, "I suppose by then we'd lost our taste for luxury," and Jo-Bethany could see that she didn't intend to say anything more.

Everyone was so busy that opportunities to explore the subject further didn't present themselves naturally, and Jo-Bethany wasn't sure she could have brought herself to try it even if they had. It was rude, somehow, and childish. Asking people: "But why do you do *this?* But why do you do *that?*" They might well have told her it was none of her business, and they would have been right. Still, it was irritating to live with so many puzzles. So irritating that Jo—to her amazement—found herself wishing she had Melissa there to talk to about it. It was an indication of the disorganized state of her mind; she could have talked more productively to a philodendron than to Melissa. And so she held her peace, and paid attention, and waited for revelation to dawn.

Where the "potions" were concerned, it came swiftly; the concoctions of herbs that Dorcas produced were eccentric, but they were also helpful. The linguists raised their own herbs, free of chemicals and pollutants, with the children doing the gardening because it was good for their health; what would not grow in the climate of one Household was exchanged for what would grow in another, so that herbs from Africa went to Switzerland, and herbs from California went to Arkansas, and so on, with everything necessary being available to all thirteen families. The database on herbal medicine in the computers at Chornyak Barren House was awe-inspiring, and the women who put the potions together knew exactly what they were doing. In fact, Jo-Bethany envied them their skill, and intended to acquire it as a fringe benefit of her employment. She was shrewd enough to realize that the knowledge was valuable, and that training as a herbalist might one day be her ticket to some genuinely interesting nursing position.

She also understood why the linguists had no medical pods. A patient sick enough to need a pod really should be in a hospital, and half a dozen superb facilities were within ten minutes of the Chornyaks by flyer. She would have been somewhat embarrassed to have to admit to Dorcas that in Ham Klander's house, along with the robot Irish setter and the array of multipurpose servomechanisms, there had been one medpod for each member of the family and two spares for the use of guests. *That,* she realized, *was* ostentatious extravagance, as much as marble hot tubs would have been.

But there were other things that bothered her. The chronic ward, for example . . . let them tell her all they liked that it was just a communal bedroom, she knew a chronic ward when she saw one. And the chronic ward at Chornyak Barren House was set up with nothing but beds and screens. On her first day on duty, with Dorcas still at her side to help her get her bearings in the job, she'd been taken to see those patients. Lying there like that, without even bedside healthies! It had been too much for her. She *had* asked: "*Why do you do this?*"

"There are healthies in the storage room," Dorcas had said. "If we had a guest in the house who got sick and asked for a healthy, we could provide one right away. If there should be a . . . oh, an epidemic, something that overwhelmed our usual medical regime . . . we could put the healthies into service on a moment's notice. We have six, Nurse Schrafft, and we can certainly order more if six strikes you as inadequate emergency backup."

Jo-Bethany hadn't known what to say. Even for new colonies, where the standard of living was necessarily nothing like that of Earth, one of the very first things shipped out was a cargo of healthies, along with the solar power units and the hydroponics equipment and the enzyme banks. To see patients without healthies was so strange that she hadn't been able to think of a neutral comment to make—her instinct, as nurse in residence, had been to demand that every bed in the room be equipped with its own healthy before dinnertime, that the same thing be done for the beds in the isolation infirmaries, and that there be six spare units in the storage room to supplement *those.* And even that would have been a primitive arrangement, with nearly two hundred potential patients for her to look after! "I'm sorry. I really can't

approve of this," she had said finally, hearing the hesitation
obvious in her voice and hating it.

Anywhere else she would not have hesitated. But one thing
about the linguists that had turned out not to be a myth was their
magnificent physical condition. When you were one of only
three people on the planet who could speak some particular Alien
language fluently, and that language was needed for a negotiation that had taken months to arrange and could not be postponed
without serious consequences, it was literally a matter of planetary security for you to be in superb health. You had to always
be able to go to the interpreting booth and carry out your duties;
something as otherwise trivial as a cough ceased to be trivial
when the import contracts for an essential mineral couldn't be
drawn up because you weren't able to provide the simultaneous
interpreting necessary to settle its terms. Every linguist child
followed a diet and exercise regime tailored specifically to that
child by experts that the Lines had on permanent retainer; every
linguist still active in negotiations had a complete medical examination every six months, and the children were checked even
more often. It didn't make *sense*, under the circumstances, for
them not to have healthies in this room!

She had stood there, staring at the double row of beds, thinking that not to have healthies was barbaric, still hesitant; and
then suddenly she had remembered something and her hesitation
had vanished.

"Oh, *I* understand!" she had declared then, making a contemptuous announcement out of it, folding her arms tightly
across her chest, hugging her outrage to her. "It's because they
are *old!*"

She had expected Dorcas Chornyak to be taken aback, and she
wasn't disappointed; the woman's eyes widened and her mouth
parted in astonishment. The two of them stood staring at one
another, Jo-Bethany fuming with righteous indignation, and Dorcas looking ridiculous with sheer surprise. But then Dorcas had
begun to laugh, instead of looking ashamed as Jo-Bethany had
expected her to do, and that had been the last straw.

"I don't find it amusing!" she had blurted out. "And I think
it's disgusting! And completely inexcusable!"

That scene had gotten much worse before it got any better.
She'd gone on with her speech for quite a while. "The public
knows that long before you people put all your women except the
little girls into separate houses you used to *banish* any woman
past childbearing age, or any woman who couldn't have children
for some other reason! We remember you doing that, you know

. . . and calling the place you sent them to 'Barren House' to rub their noses in it! And now *these* women—" She had gestured dramatically toward the beds where the elderly women lay, with no privacy at all, hearing every word . . . "—they're not just barren, they're no use in your precious economy at all! So you just. . . ." She had struggled for the exact word, absolutely furious, out of control. "You just *dump* them here, without even minimal facilities, and you hire one licensed nurse to keep the authorities from coming along and taking them somewhere where they could be decently looked after! Well, I won't stand for that, Miss Chornyak—I won't stand for it one *minute,* and you might as well know it right now!" She had been shaking with rage before she got to the end of her oration.

One of the old ladies in the two facing rows of beds had spoken up then in the silence, sharply. "Dorcas," she'd said, her voice thin but strong, "you ought to be ashamed of yourself! That poor child!"

"What poor child?" Jo-Bethany had demanded. "Do you have children in here, *too?*"

"*You,* my dear," the old one had answered. "*You* are the poor child in question! Being given the tour of the back wards, and no preparation whatsoever for the horrors therein. What you'll say when you see our snakepits, I can't imagine."

And that had sent everyone awake into gales of laughter, including the woman standing beside her, and had waked up those who'd been asleep. Dorcas had spoken through the laughter, chiding, "Benita, how can you be so wicked? You stop laughing and set this right, or I'll send for . . . let's see, which of the teenage males would you find most irritating?"

The old lady's hands had gone up instantly in a gesture of mock surrender, and the others had made an effort to get their hilarity under control, and Dorcas had touched Jo-Bethany's hand, gently.

"You're trembling, Miss Schrafft," she'd said, "and I'm sorry. Furthermore, Benita is right, though there's no excuse for the way she chose to express herself. I should never have brought you here without first explaining it to you, so that you'd understand the situation. Please forgive me, if you can—it's been so long since we had a new nurse that I'd forgotten how strange it all would seem to you. Like not having running water, I suppose. . . . Miss Schrafft, the reason we don't have healthies at every bed—or at *any* bed—is not that we don't care about these women, or that they're old, or that they're useless. We'd be in serious difficulties here at Chornyak Household without

their expert services—you'll see that for yourself before this
week is over. But right now I want to make sure you understand
one thing very clearly: the reason that we don't have healthies in
this room is because we don't approve of them.''

"You don't approve of them,'' Jo-Bethany had echoed stupidly. It was *like* not approving of running water! Not approving of
soap.

"That's right. If we'd been given the chance to name them,
Miss Schrafft, we would have called them *un*healthies. And any
woman here who wants one may have one, of course.'' She
turned to the women in the beds and asked them, "Anybody
here want a healthy installed at your bed?''

There was no ambiguity about the resounding chorus of refus-
als. Or about the laughter that accompanied the chorus. Jo-
Bethany, confused past bearing, humiliated, sure she was in the
right, with everyone laughing at her, had burst into tears. To her
absolute horror. As if she had been Melissa!

The reaction to her distress had amazed her. She had stood
with her hands over her face, tears dripping through her fingers,
expecting to be ordered to leave at once and not return until she
could behave decently—in their place, that is what she would
have considered proper. She would not have been surprised to
hear herself told to report to the Head, or to pack her things and
go home in disgrace, permanently discharged without a recom-
mendation. Instead, women had materialized out of nowhere,
half a dozen of them, as if they'd sprung from the floor beneath
her feet. Three had gone swiftly to soothe the elderly women,
and to settle back on their pillows a few who had apparently
decided they had to get up and go to Jo-Bethany's rescue themselves. Dorcas and another three had bustled Jo-Bethany off to a
small empty bedroom on the floor below, installed her in a
comfortable chair, and settled themselves on the floor around her
feet as if to wait for wisdom to drop from her lips. And someone
else had brought strong hot tea and fresh-baked spice bread
almost instantly. Not until she'd had the tea and the spice bread
and the combined soothing and stroking of all five women
present (who certainly had had much more important things to
do!) had they allowed her to try to talk about the matter that had
set her off. And then they had listened to her with their whole
attention, nodding once in a while to encourage her, never once
interrupting, until she'd said every single narrow-minded bigoted
word she had to say. Only when they were sure she'd spoken
what passed for her mind did they begin to explain.

The linguists didn't use healthies, they told her then, because they were convinced that the touch of human hands, the nonverbal communication of live hands doing the tending, was absolutely essential to the care of the sick. They were willing to pay what it cost to have that tending done by human hands, and to provide much of it themselves, with their *own* hands. Only when there was no human being available to tend a patient, or when the only human being available would have been unkind or uncaring, did they consider healthies appropriate, and within the Lines those situations did not exist. They might have been wrong in their belief that the mechanical nursing was bad for the patient—certainly the physicians who had taught Jo's class at nursing school would have considered that not only scientifically incorrect but superstitious, and the evidence for the medical position was overwhelming. But the women of Chornyak Barren House were *not* without healthies because they were old, or because they were not loved. The women had made sure Jo-Bethany understood that, and they had done it without shaming her.

"How could you have known?" they had asked her. "There was no way you could have known."

"And, Miss Schrafft," one said to her firmly, "we think it's very important for you to know that women were never 'banished' to the Barren Houses."

"Everyone knows they were," Jo-Bethany had heard herself say, almost in a whisper, as if she had not learned anything at all that day. "The mass-ed computers, in the lessons about the linguists. . . ." She stopped, finally remembering some of the other things she'd heard in those lessons, that had turned out to be nonsense.

"Everyone 'knows' all sorts of things, Miss Schrafft. Everyone knows that the world holds still beneath their feet except during earthquakes; that does not keep it from turning around, or from traveling through space at many thousands of miles an hour. Everyone knows a great deal of *garbage,* my dear. And that banishing business . . . that's garbage. It's possible that some of the men did think they were 'banishing' women to the Barren Houses—that is possible. But the women themselves . . . they did not feel banished. The women could hardly wait."

"Being sent out of their home? Being—"

"Miss Schrafft . . . Jo-Bethany . . . please. Look at me."

It was Dorcas, and Jo-Bethany did look, obediently responding to the tone of voice in spite of her reluctance to look anywhere but at the floor.

"Jo-Bethany, have you lived in a house with a man recently? Just one man?"

"Yes. My brother-in-law. The man who sent me here."

"Well, did you enjoy it?"

She found herself looking straight into the other woman's eyes, and those eyes were dancing with amusement, as if Dorcas knew all about what it had been like to live with Ham Klander.

"Oh . . ." she had said weakly. "No. No, not very much."

"Then would you please try to imagine what it would be like to live in a house with dozens of men? With fifty men, or more?"

The expression on her face must have been eloquent; and what she had said had been the perfect thing to say. She had heard her mother say it so many times. She had said, "A hill is to climb. A man is to pick up after." Talking to herself, really. And all of the other women had begun to laugh, laughing till there were tears in her eyes; laughing *for* her, not at her.

"It was such a blessed *relief,* moving over to Barren House!" Dorcas had managed at last, wiping her eyes with her hands. "I agree with you that the name of the place left a lot to be desired—but then, my dear, it was the men who did the naming. It wouldn't have been at all tactful for the women to ask them to change it to something like 'Paradise On Earth House,' would it?"

And Jo had joined in the laughter, then, because she couldn't help it.

She still had her doubts about the merits of human tending versus the sterile services of the machines, nevertheless. She understood how they felt about it, and that was a help, but she still fretted. Right now, for instance, as she rubbed a scented cream into Letha Shannontry Chornyak's skin, so that it wouldn't be dry and flaking and itching because one hundred and three years of life had robbed it of the oils that had protected it in the past. Jo-Bethany felt squeamish, awkward. She had scrubbed her hands thoroughly before she began the task, twice. But she had seen the electronic microscope threedys of the surface of a well-scrubbed human hand . . . crawling with organisms, that looked like the holograms of nonhumanoid aliens you could buy in museum gift shops. No matter how hard you scrubbed, no matter how powerful the substance you scrubbed with! Suppose you did, by really working at it, manage to get every last little critter off without removing your skin along with them; by the time you walked the few yards between yourself and your patient, you would be alive with creepy-crawlies again. Jo-Bethany knew all about that, and had had nightmares about it at nursing school.

There was no such problem with the mechanical hands of the healthies, bathed constantly by ultrasonic cleaners; there were no bacteria or viruses on *those* hands! Clean—they were truly clean. All five of them. While her own two hands, now rubbing the balm into Letha's thin shoulders. . . . Jo-Bethany touched the fragile bones, that felt as if they could be effortlessly crushed, and the delicate thin skin over them, and it seemed to her that she was rubbing in filth right along with the cream. The stuff smelled faintly of almonds, and she was reminded of the mass-ed history lessons, the way ancient kings had poured perfume over the roast meats at their tables to hide the fact that they were rotten. It was Letha's preference that she do this; it was her *job* to do this; she would go right on doing it, in spite of the image in her mind of hordes of creatures crawling from her hands into the crevices of the old woman's skin. . . .

Jo-Bethany Schrafft, if you go on thinking like this there will be trouble! she admonished herself. These women had spent their lives attending to the communication of others, even Alien others; they instantly sensed the least sign of unease or discomfort. She could just imagine trying to explain what she'd been thinking. She was not going to let it happen. To prevent it, and to provide a plausible excuse for the agitation that she knew would have become apparent to Letha Chornyak by now, she substituted a less serious concern.

"Mrs. Chornyak," she began—and then stopped short as the old woman reached up and laid a finger over her lips. What in the world?

"Please, child, call me Letha . . . or Aunt Letha, if it suits you better! Everybody in this room, practically, is a 'Mrs. Chornyak.' It gets tiresome hearing it. And I've asked you twice before. My dear, I will give you three chances, but that is as high as I propose to go."

"Oh, dear . . . I'm sorry," Jo answered, awkward and embarrassed because she *knew* she'd been asked before. "I keep forgetting. I'll remember now. *Letha.*" She was not about to call a linguist "Aunt."

"Much better. Thank you. Now, please go on. What were you going to say to me? And why are you all adither like you are?"

"I have a problem. I need some advice. I wonder if you'd be willing to tell me what I should do."

"Try me. There are few things I like better than giving advice."

"It's the Thursday Night Devotional Meetings."

"Something wrong with them?"

"No. Not at all." Jo-Bethany shifted the old lady on the pillows gently, unbuttoned the plain cotton gown, and began rubbing the cream over her chest and throat. "No, I enjoy them very much. In fact, I enjoy them so much that I wanted to share them with some people I'm fond of—my sister, and a few nurses who are friends of mine."

"They'd be very welcome, child, I'm sure," said Letha. "If you're afraid young Johnny would be a wart about it, ask Dorcas to arrange it for you."

It took Jo-Bethany a moment to realize that "young Johnny" would be Jonathan Asher Chornyak, Head of all the Lines, and she had to cough to cover her amusement at that; of course, this woman had probably changed the diapers of the Head of Heads, and saw him more as the Bottom of Bottoms. "The problem," she said hastily, "is that their husbands won't let them come."

"Ah, I perceive! No slumming about in the nasty Lingoe dens, eh? *That* sort of problem!"

"Something like that," Jo said, not meeting the brown eyes, that were so uncomfortably piercing in spite of their setting of fine skin fallen into folds of wrinkled crepe. "I know it's ridiculous."

"It's not your fault, dear," the old lady said comfortingly. "You mustn't worry about it. Heaven knows we're used to it—we old Lingoe bitches!" And she chuckled the wise wicked chuckle of the very old, while Jo-Bethany felt pale red flare on her own cheeks. "Don't you apologize, Jo-Bethany! After a person listens to such stuff for a hundred years, I assure you she gets used to it!"

Jo-Bethany didn't believe that; she was sure she couldn't have joked about such a thing, not if she'd been listening to it for *two* hundred years. But perhaps she was wrong. Again. Perhaps when she was a hundred years old she'd find *many* things less worth worrying about than she found them now.

"It seems like such a shame," she murmured, moving carefully on to Letha's arms and hands. "I know they would enjoy it, and I do wish they could be there just once. It's such a beautiful service."

"Especially on sermon night." Letha puckered up her mouth, and pinched her nostrils in. "Beautiful, my eye."

"But that's only one Thursday a month. And the sermons aren't *that* bad."

"Huh!" Letha made her back poker rigid and spread all the fingers of both hands wide and high, and proceeded to flabbergast Jo-Bethany with a flawless imitation of a Neo-Presbyterian hellfire-and-brimstone man in full spate.

"My goodness!" she said, for want of anything better, and she rubbed the last of the pleasant cream into her own hands. Rubbing little filthy critters into her *own* skin, she realized.

"That's beautiful, is it?" Letha challenged her. "That ranting?"

"No, it's not beautiful. Good for us, I'm sure, but not beautiful. But the rest of it . . . the music, and the readings, and the other parts . . . all of that is beautiful."

"You mean the Láadan parts, don't you?"

"Láadan?"

"Langlish, child. Láadan is the word for Langlish, *in* Láadan."

"I didn't know that," said Jo-Bethany. "But yes, that's what I mean. I love the sound of it . . . it eases me, somehow. But it's hard to describe it to people who haven't heard it for themselves."

"And the husbands are all dead set against it? What if one of our men asked? A formal invitation, on your behalf, from one of the senior Chornyak men? Would that help?"

"I don't think so," said Jo-Bethany slowly. "All the husbands are—stubborn."

"All bigots."

"Perhaps. I hope not."

"It used to be so much worse, dear child. There used to be crowds of nincompoops out in the front yard throwing rocks at our windows. No need for you to be distressed, child—it's getting better! Why, there was a time when no amount of money would have been enough to hire a 'decent' woman to come take the job of nurse at Chornyak Household, but here *you* are. With some man's approval."

"My brother-in-law."

"Well, then! You perceive, he's not all that much of a bigot. Just a *smidgen* of a bigot, on the upward road. He'll risk the contamination of his sister-in-law, even if not his wife. That's progress, my dear."

"Is it?"

"Oh, yes, indeed! And you," she added, "you're getting less prejudiced against us yourself. I've noticed it."

Jo-Bethany had almost dropped the vial of skin cream, she was so startled. What could she have said, or done, to make these women aware of her prejudice? She was ashamed of it; and it wasn't in her mind, it was in her nasty *gut*, where she couldn't get at it. She would have sworn that never, not by look or word or deed, had she betrayed that anything so foul lurked in her! But Letha Chornyak didn't seem the least bit disturbed.

"I am so sorry," Jo whispered. "I didn't think it showed.

And it *is* going away, ma'am. It's just—it's the way I was brought up.''

The old woman laughed softly, fondly. "Don't you give it a thought," she said. "I myself am prejudiced against women that can't cook a decent meal. I always have been. I'm ashamed of that. Some of those women are in every other respect good fine women, and I ought to be able to remember that and not be so nitpicky.''

"Yes, ma'am," said Jo-Bethany, gratefully, although it wasn't the same thing at all, and she knew it.

"I have a suggestion, child.''

"I'd be very pleased to hear it.''

"Don't you go over to the local hospital a good deal? You do volunteer nursing over there, don't you?''

"Yes. I go once a week, usually.''

"Do they need you over there? What's the government up to? Not putting enough nurses on?''

"No—no, it's not that. It's that nobody here is really very sick, Letha. I go over to the hospital to work with more serious cases, so that I won't get behind, or out of practice. No, they have everything they need. I go for my own benefit, not theirs.''

Letha nodded approvingly, and told her she was a good dutiful conscientious child, and then said, "That means you have free use of the women's chapel at the hospital, then.''

"Does it? I suppose I do have. . . . I hadn't thought of it.''

"I'm *sure* you do. And all you have to do is start your own Thursday Night Devotionals, there at the hospital. Take half an hour, maybe—nobody will mind. Then the husbands could let their wives attend without having to worry about contamination, don't you know. And we'd send one of our women with you to do the Láadan readings a time or two, until you felt comfortable doing it yourself.''

It was an astonishing idea, and Jo-Bethany would never have thought of it on her own. But now that Letha had pointed it out, it was the obvious solution; in a way, it was exciting. There were possibilities . . . every hospital had a chapel for women, where nothing *at all* ever happened. Once in a great while some devout woman might step in there to pray for a loved one gravely ill, but most of the time the room was wasted space. Regular services there once a week would never be noticed. But the nurses at the hospitals would come, and Jo knew that would be a good thing.

She knew how much better she felt, listening to the language, how soothed she was afterward, how it made the tension inside her melt away. She was a better nurse, she was convinced of that, because those services somehow lifted from her the piled-up strain of the preceding week. If nurses in the hospitals could have that, too, it would mean that Jo-Bethany had really done something useful in this world.

She could feel the excitement in her throat; she put it firmly down. A hundred things could happen to stop her. The hospital administrators could forbid it. The husbands could refuse. The women could refuse. It could turn out that she didn't have sense enough to learn to read the Langlish—Láadan?—out loud. She knew the women of the Lines wouldn't have time to do it for her more than once or twice, and then it would be up to her. She must not get her hopes up. But she would try.

"Do you think I could do it?" she asked hesitantly.

"Why in the world not? You're a woman, aren't you? You're literate? Your vocal tract works normally? Of course you could."

"I wonder."

"We'll help you," said the old woman.

"Pardon me?" Jo-Bethany's hands stopped straightening the shelf at the head of the bed; she listened carefully, realizing that this mattered to her. More than she wanted anything to matter. The way Melissa mattered was enough.

"I said, we'll help you. We old doddering ladies, here in this room. We have time. You go to Dorcas Chornyak and you tell her that Letha said to give you copies of some of the readings you like best—short ones, to start with. And you bring them up here and let us help you learn to do them properly."

"You'd do that?"

"We'd do that. We'd be *pleased* to do that."

Jo-Bethany knew she had a silly smirk of delight on her face; she could see it in the eyes of the other women as she looked around her. But she didn't care. They were a tolerant bunch, and it took more than a silly smirk to distract them in any serious way. So confident was she of that tolerance that she clapped her hands for pure pleasure. And they all told her, yet one more time, that she was a good child.

CHAPTER 9

"But why?" asked the child. "Why choose a wild vine wreath? With the whole world full of lovely things to choose from?"

"It was the best choice," said the very old woman. "The very best choice of all."

The child was stubborn; she stood there frowning, and shaking her head, and tapping one foot, and she began listing what she perceived as proper symbols of a faith. "A star," she said firmly. "A lotus. A wooden cross. An elephant. A rose. A coiled serpent, with wings and feathers. A round perfect sun. A crescent moon. A pearl that has no flaw. A—"

The great-grandmother reached out and touched the child's hand, gently. "I do know that list, dearlove," she reminded her.

"Well . . . those things are more suitable!" the child declared. And then she saw the look in the old woman's eyes in their nest of tiny wrinkles, and she added quickly, "In my opinion, that is."

"If I tell you why the wild vine wreath is 'suitable,' as you put it, are you old enough to listen, and not interrupt?"

"Yes, ma'am!" said the child.

The very old woman leaned forward with both her hands clasped tightly on her cane. "First," she said, "the wild vine is always right at hand, even in a wilderness; even in a city, if you look a bit. Unlike elephants. It doesn't cost a penny, the wild vine doesn't; you can be very poor indeed, and still, you can have yourself a wild vine wreath."

"Unlike elephants," said the child.

"I could have sworn I heard you say you would not interrupt."

"Yes, ma'am," the child admitted. "And I forgot. But I won't again."

"Going on," the old woman said, "the wild vine wreath is a

circle moving ever toward perfection, round and round and round and round again. But it is real! *It's a circle with bumps and jogs and rough patches and curlicues and the occasional sharp point—and that is what a human life is like, as* it *moves ever toward perfection, round and round and round and round again. Third, it does not draw attention to itself. A woman can carry a tiny one in her pocket or hang it on a nail or slip it over the strap of her purse; she can toss a bigger one over a fencepost or lean it against a wall or hang it in a tree; and nobody that's not looking for one will see it for weeks or months or years. Or if they do, and they throw it away . . . well, it's always easy to make another one. Or suppose a woman has no out-of-the-way place for it, she can always tie on a ribbon and some trinket and put it up boldly, and the men will remark on what silly things women find pretty and then they'll never think of it again. Are you still listening, child?"*

"Yes, Great-Grandmother."

"Then there's the fact that the wild vine wreath is strong, and forgiving, and it endures. When you wind one, you can feel it take its own sturdy shape in your hands, helping you out, and settling into it for the long haul. Break it somewhere, cut it somewhere, wear it out somewhere, no matter; a woman just tucks in the broken piece among the others, and they keep it whole. It's easy to carry and hard to damage, and it takes no special training to make or to preserve. It can be put to use as well as to ornament; and when it is useful it is still an ornament, and when it is ornamental it stays useful, and there is no separation between ornament and use. Do you begin to understand, child?"

"Yes, Great-Grandmother."

"Going on, every wild vine wreath is known at once for what it is—you couldn't mistake it for anything else—but no two are exactly alike, or ever will be. Suitable, *child, to the human condition! In every way. And that is all the reasons I am inclined to spell out for you. You go observe a wild vine wreath, with your own good mind, and many another reason will come to you. You look at it, and you hold it in your hands, and you smell it all over; press it hard, bend it a little, and listen to the sound it makes. Go make yourself a new one of your very own, dearlove, and pay it close attention as you go along—the wild vine wreath is a fine and patient teacher."*

"Unlike an elephant."

"Oh," said the old woman, *"the elephant is a fine and patient teacher, too! You come upon one, you observe it well, child.*

There's much to be learned from elephants, and stars, and roses,
and every one of those things you were mentioning."
    "But the wild vine is always right at hand," said the child,
and the very old woman laughed, and stood up slowly. "There,"
she said to the child, "you see? There you are, learning already!
Gone full circle and coming around again. . . ."

    (a teaching story, much loved by the women of the Lines)

Heykus Clete was an old-fashioned man; he had old-fashioned
tastes. If there'd been any way he could have done it without
spaceflight, he would have eagerly become a citizen on a frontier
planet where even the wealthiest homes and businesses still had
computers that could only be activated from keyboards, and
where travel by personal flyer rather than ground car was a goal
far down on the list of priorities. He could well imagine himself
being perfectly happy in the primitive bubble huts, robot-packed
at NASA in small cartons, that settlers carried out to the colonies
and called home. He could imagine living without a single
servomechanism; he could imagine being obliged to clean
everything—including his body—with water; he could even imagine living with weather so uncontrolled that you could never
really make plans with any certainty. He could imagine all those
things without a twinge, although the thought of tornadoes and
earthquakes and similar cataclysms happening in populated areas
was a little unsettling.

    But his terror of leaving Earth's atmosphere—very unlike the
abstract uneasiness that comes of knowing there may be
tornadoes—had kept him bound to Earth, and there was nowhere
on Earth that a man could escape technology. For groups like the
Amish, this was a serious matter, a permanent spiritual crisis.
They found it almost impossible to carry out their daily lives
without interacting with the gadgetry their faith called evil; but
that same faith forbade them to use the spacecraft that would
have let them emigrate to colonies where a simple life was still at
least achievable in theory. It made them a denomination in
serious danger of going the way of the Shakers, into extinction;
they held prayer vigils that went on for days at a time, praying
for a revelation that would let them live without violating their
beliefs. Heykus was sorry for them in their trouble, and impatient with them for not simply accepting the obvious rightness of
the mainstream Protestant denominations, but he envied them,
too; because what bound them to this planet was *faith*, not a

shameful womanish cowardice. Heykus was far more afraid of
the daily moonshuttle than he was of any weather, tame or wild,
and that limited his options.

There was no way to do anything in an old-fashioned way on
Terra anymore. It was a sad thing, to Heykus' way of thinking.
You couldn't say, "I won't order my groceries by comset, I'll
go to the grocery store," because there weren't any grocery
stores left. The infrastructure of roads and trucks and docks that
had supported the grocery stores was long gone. You could *play*
at having a grocery store, and find a handful of others to play at it
with you (that was what the Amish did), but you knew it was a
game and you knew it would have to end one of these days.
People who hated modern conveniences were like people who
thrived on violence and danger; they had tremendous value to
society because they were so badly needed on the frontiers. The
government had no intention of providing them with facilities
that would make them less frustrated with the system on Earth. If
they didn't see for themselves that the attitudes which made them
misfits here made them potential leaders in the spaceboonies,
there were plenty of colony scouts always on the stalk ready and
able to point it out to them and move them on out.

But you had to travel through space. There wasn't any other
way to get out there. Heykus was personally convinced that the
Aliens who interacted routinely with Earth did have matter transporters, in the old science fiction sense. Gadgets that would get
you and all the gear you could carry from Point A to Point C,
without having to go through the intervening expanse represented
by B. He was not alone in his suspicions, and one of the
questions that was posed to every Alien at decent intervals had to
do with those matter transporters. But the Aliens weren't telling;
when asked, they would just assume whatever expression signi-
fied mild surprise for their particular Alien face, and suggest that
it was time for the next question. Faster than light travel they had
shared with no hesitation, and for a ridiculously low price. But it
was still travel; you still had to go through B, even if you did it
at speeds previously unimaginable.

Heykus couldn't face it; he would wait for the matter transporters, and if they didn't come along in his lifetime he would
die on this Earth as he had been born on this Earth, innocent of
any other planetary experience. He wasn't sure exactly what it
was that he was afraid of. Not dying, certainly. There was an old
joke about the woman who explained her terror of travel by
saying that she wasn't afraid of dying, she was afraid of *crashing*—
perhaps it was something like that. Perhaps it had to do with

never knowing exactly what would happen if you *did* crash, out in space, showing light you could outrun it. It couldn't be claustrophobia, because the long hours he spent enclosed in his desk never bothered him. Whatever it was, it kept him right here, and he was grateful to the Lord for not having instructed the angel to order him out into space. He was not at all sure he would have been able to obey; no doubt the Lord had known that.

Once in a while, when there was something going on that he would really have enjoyed being part of—the major interplanetary theological conferences, for example—he would hit the database again for the latest statistics on suspended animation. That way, you wouldn't have to *know* you were going through B; the Aliens had been very obliging about helping Earth's scientists get out most of the wrinkles in the process. But it wasn't good enough. Whether you did it with the drugs that moved the metabolism down to just this side of Off, or you used freeze-and-thaw, or you used electrochemical pseudosplice, the failure rate of fourteen percent that the technicians were so proud of was unacceptable to Heykus. He had work to do, and it was important work; he couldn't do it as a vegetable in a medpod, maintained as a ward of the government.

Heykus shuddered, and he wished for the ten thousandth time that Baptists had a good analogue to the Roman Catholic ritual of crossing yourself. Something you could do when that kind of shudder ran down your spine.

He was disgusted with himself. It was womanish enough to be afraid of space travel, something that other men did as casually as he himself took the elevator to his office; it was more womanish still to be standing here staring out the window, spinning fantasies of himself brain-damaged, pod-tended. And this self-indulgence was nothing more than a futile attempt to put off yet one more experience he was afraid of!

Men were not supposed to be afraid of ordinary things; most especially, a man whose trust was in the Lord of Hosts was not supposed to be. He would have been deeply ashamed if his son had ever shown signs of such weakness. And yet here he stood, ten minutes gone by since the courier had brought the chip in, still holding it in his palm as if it would go away if he only ignored it. Doddering over nonsense; trying to put off what he had to do. Next he'd be reminiscing about his childhood, or his wedding night, that had been his first time with a woman. Him with his unshakable standards for other people—what if some of those he'd sent packing knew how he was behaving now?

That was enough, at last, to shake him out of it. He straightened his back, firmed his mouth, went inside his desk and sat down, leaned back and closed his eyes, and inserted the chip into the cognisocket high in his right nostril. Maybe it *would* be a Takeover Chip, sure; it was a hazard you lived with, the way your ancestors had had to live with tornadoes and tetanus. No matter how many and how elaborate the security measures, there was no way to know except to run it, and if it *was* a TC there wouldn't be one thing you or anybody else could do about it; and if you didn't like that risk, you belonged in some other line of work, and that was the way it was. The Takeover Chips had their good side . . . how would you manage mental patients humanely without them, for example? He pressed the chip home with a steady thumb, and he waited.

And this one, this particular chip, was okay. Praise God—his mind was still his own.

He sat and let it play, while the cold sweat dried on his forehead and the pounding of his heart subsided. It was a perfectly ordinary message chip; it would play, and as it played it would erase itself, and an hour from now it would have been absorbed by the mucus membranes inside his nose. It was unquestionably a miracle of technology, by comparison with the memo on fiche that he would stupidly have preferred—there were too many opportunities for security leaks with a fiche.

First there was the formula that identified it as a clean chip, and then the coder introduced himself and the message began.

"EMANYEW BYDORE, PH.D. here, Director Clete. Full professor, Multiversity of California; Colonel, United States Air Force, confidential rank. I am scientific supervisor here in El Centro in that section of the Cetacean project which is making neuron-by-neuron alterations in the brains of decanted tubies according to a computer-generated systematic sequence. As you know, these altered infants are being prepared for Interfacing with nonhumanoid Aliens, and our work is aimed at restructuring their language acquisition processes in such a way that they will be able to undergo Interfacing without the unfortunate consequences experienced in past series. PARAGRAPH. This work has gone very slowly—through no fault of the personnel. As noted in the last report from this site, the supply of captive nonhumanoid Aliens available for Interfacing has been so unreliable and so inadequate in recent years that most of our time has had to be devoted to simply altering the infants and storing them for later use; it

goes without saying that this is a boring way to pass one's time, although the knowledge of the brain's structure that we are acquiring will undoubtedly prove valuable in the future. We have been somewhat restless here. PARAGRAPH. I am therefore delighted to report that two days ago we took delivery of a shipment genuinely promising for our research; I refer to the three specimens brought in from the last GW sweep. I can most quickly describe them as approximately the size and shape of our largest Earth dolphins, with similar brain/body ratio. Amazing that they were unable to escape from the Scoop, frankly, considering their strength and agility— but a stroke of good luck for us. Unlike the dolphins, their bodies are encased in shells; given the pressures to which they were subjected in their native atmospheres, this is to be anticipated. PARAGRAPH. PLEASE NOTE: AT THE END OF THIS MESSAGE YOU WILL BE PROVIDED WITH A VISUAL IMAGE OF ONE OF THE SPECIMENS, OF AP-PROXIMATELY TWENTY-SEVEN SECONDS DURATION. THERE WILL BE MINOR DISCOMFORT ASSOCIATED WITH THE TRANSMISSION OF THE IMAGE DUE TO THE CLUM-SINESS OF STIMULATION OF THE OPTIC CENTERS IN THIS FASHION. MY APOLOGIES. PARAGRAPH. Until now, we have not felt justified in requesting anything more than the minimal budget necessary for maintenance of this facility and for life support of the altered infants. But this new develop-ment changes the situation. These are specimens that can plausibly be assumed to be sentient and to have a system of communication—and we have a group of them. It is plausible to assume that they will interact; we have seen no indications to the contrary in their behavior. Furthermore, their biological needs appear to be such that we can keep them not just alive, but reasonably comfortable. We have an abundant supply of altered tubies ready to be put into service, and we have a superbly equipped Interface ready to be activated. All systems— as the old saying goes, Director Clete—are go. PARAGRAPH. In view of these new circumstances, we request your approval for a stepped-up timetable on this project. We would like to move ahead at the fastest rate compatible with the safety of the specimens. If you have no objection to the expenditure, our budget officer advises me that the deposit of a twenty percent increase in our accounts would be sufficient for im-plementation of the accelerated program. We look forward to notification of the fund transfer, and will of course keep you

informed of progress here. END OF MESSAGE; E.B., PH.D.
[STAND BY FOR VISUAL IMAGE TRANSMISSION!!!]''

Minor discomfort. Heykus smiled to himself. . . . It was like "seeing stars" after being whacked over the head with a club. A substantial club, with a substantial nail in the end of it. It was enough like what Heykus assumed an electric shock to one nostril would be like to qualify in his mind as a good deal more than "minor discomfort." It was also far too delicate a process to make it through either the violent shake he gave his head or the swift rap he gave to his nose directly over the cognisocket. The point of giving you the standby message was so that you'd stay absolutely motionless while the nervebridge was done, instead of leaping three feet into the air when the jolt hit you; Heykus didn't intend to inform Professor Bydore that the warning also gave the knowledgeable individual time to dodge the whole thing. Their "visual image" was superfluous; the statement that the specimens were about the size and shape of dolphins, but with a shell, was graphic enough for his purposes.

Now, while the tingle in his nostril gradually faded, he opened his eyes and began scanning budget displays on the comset screen. Thinking it over. Not because there was any question in his mind about whether or not the request for funds should be granted. But he had to decide which of the slush funds he had access to would be the proper one to stash it in. Once he had made his choice, there was no further delay. It took him exactly four minutes to move the funds to the El Centro account, arrange three interlocking transactions to cover the transfer, and hide the program back inside the larger dummy one.

Members of Heykus' staff with sufficiently high clearance to know about the existence of the program considered its name an excellent joke. Putting a dependent program to launder slush monies inside a sedate file named "All Souls Mission" was, they thought, a stroke of genuine wit; it showed that although Heykus talked the approved Christian line, as was only prudent for any government official, he had a sense of humor. And he was always willing to agree with them that it was a fine joke, on those rare occasions when the subject came up.

For Heykus, however, it was not a joke. One of the things that he knew for certain was that one God, *his* God, had created everything there was, no matter where it might be located. Another thing he knew for certain was that on this planet Earth anything that spoke a language had a soul that could be saved for the greater glory of God. And until he also knew for certain that any given living creature found on any other planet was *without* such a soul, he was taking no chances. First you learned how to talk to them; then you told them the Good News about the Son of God; that was what his life was about. Come the time he was convinced that the primates or the whales had true languages, Heykus was prepared to see that *they* were told the Good News, just in case; this was a situation in which he would always choose to make his errors on the broad side of the line. And "All Souls Mission" was the one and the only and the *perfect* name for that computer program.

II

Jessamin was at her post in the corner, behind the tall five-paneled screen that left her a full view of the girldorm's rows of narrow beds and cribs but kept the small light of her reading lamp from waking the sleeping children. She was staring at a fiche that introduced an entire new set of lexical items . . . the vocabulary she would need, day after tomorrow. The Jeelods were offering to set up an entirely new kind of agricultural station, like a giant clothesline, with protein sheets hung out on it to be— She frowned at the data before her; what *was* it exactly that they were claiming you did? Protein sheets, hung on lines in geosynchronous orbits, that you—rolled up? Rolled up on what? The word was either an entirely new root, or it had an affix she'd never seen before, she couldn't decide which. And she would have to know before she could begin interpreting.

She was staring so fiercely at the baffling words on the fiche that she didn't hear Nizhona come padding across the room to her, barefooted. When the girl grabbed her hand, her own hands like ice, Jessamin jumped; the noise she made was almost a whispered shriek.

"Nizhona Maria Chornyak!" she fussed, as well as she could fuss without disturbing the sleepers. "*Please,* child—don't ever grab like that, out of the air! What have I done to deserve such treatment at your hands—*literally* at your hands? Poor Jessamin, struggling all her life long with the Jeelods, does she deserve such a shockingly abrupt icy greeting from you, eh? And dearlove, how have your hands gotten so *cold?*"

"Jessamin, Jessamin, guess what!" the girl whispered, her voice urgent with excitement. "Oh, Jessamin, *guess!*"

Jessamin put her work aside, drew the youngster inside the shelter of the screen where she could see her a little better, and took the young face between her hands to study it, thinking that the skin was like velvet; she looked closely and carefully, and she thought hard. Nizhona's eyes were bright, almost aglow, certainly dancing; she was terribly *pleased* about something. Her body was trembling with excitement. Twelve years old . . . three o'clock in the morning of an ordinary day, long before dawn . . . and here she was, saying, "Oh, Jessamin, *guess!*"

There was only one single thing it could be.

"*Báa nahosháana ne?*" she whispered, watching. And saw at once that she was right.

"I woke up just now, Jessamin, and I discovered it! It's not just a cut finger, there are little spots of blood on my nightgown!" Nizhona giggled, so very pleased with herself. "And on the floor, too, Jessa . . . I left a trail to you!"

"Oh, Nizhona," Jessamin breathed, "bless you, darling!" And she gathered her into her arms and rocked her, till the joyous trembling quieted and the girl relaxed against her to be stroked and patted, murmuring all the usual words suitable to the occasion.

"I'll bet I'm still leaving a trail," Nizhona whispered, lazily, calm again. "I'll bet I'm making a horrible *mess, Jessa.*"

"Brag, brag, brag," Jessamin teased. "One little quarter teaspoon of blood, and you think you're an instrument of vast and splendid havoc!"

"Yep," said Nizhona, smug and content. "That is exactly right. Splendid scarlet havoc. Jessamin, shall I go sneak through the house like this? Maybe write my name on the floor in the diningroom?"

Jessamin laughed, and gave the outrageous child a swift hug. "Would you accept a compromise?" she asked. "One that wouldn't be quite so exotic?"

"I don't know. I'm not sure I would. This happens only one time, you know, in my whole life. Why should I compromise?"

"All right, then," Jessamin told her. "You go up and see how long it takes you, dearlove, one little drop at a time, to write your whole name in menstrual blood on the diningroom floor. I can't go with you, because I'm on duty; but I'll come by in—oh, three hours, say, you should have it done by then—and I'll put a coat of Permaglass over it so it will be preserved for all of time."

"Would it take that long?"

"I expect so. The very first period you have? What do you think there'll be, child, quarts and buckets and bathtubs full of blood? The very first time?"

Nizhona sighed. "Shoot. . . . Maybe I'll just. . . ." Her voice trailed off before she could outline her next plan, and she smiled. "Maybe I'll just move to *Woman*house," she proposed. "Right now!"

"That," Jessamin agreed, hugging her some more, "you may surely do, with my blessing. Most certainly. I'll call Belle-Anne and tell her to go over to the Womanhouse kitchen and meet you for hot tea and something celebratory; she'll be up, for sure, she always is. Pack quietly, though—the rest of the girls have nearly two hours' sleep coming to them still, if you don't crash and clank and lumber around hooting and thumping."

"I'll only *splash!*" Nizhona declared. "I shall make small soft splashes, as I go."

Jessamin watched her fondly as she headed back across the room, moving as silently as she had come; for all her mischievous talk, she would not have stolen one minute of sleep from the others. And she punched in the call for Belle-Anne on her wrist computer. "Nizhona's coming over," she typed, "and she's headed for the kitchen fit to burst . . . her first period woke her up and she is moving *this very minute*. A good thing she is, too—you should have heard the alternatives she was proposing! Can you go meet her, Belle-Anne?"

"I'm on my way," came the answer, and not a word from Belle-Anne about the project she would have to set aside. "I'll be there before she is, Jessamin, and we'll plan an Osháana Rejoicing to remember, I promise."

"She'll talk you to death—she's wound up like a top."

"Well, of course she is! Weren't *you?*"

Belle-Anne didn't wait for the answer that any woman of the Lines could have supplied. The privilege of moving to the Womanhouse, out of the girldorms to join the women; the festivities of the Osháana Rejoicing party that would be fit into the hours of the coming day no matter *what* extraordinary reschedulings and cancelings and rearrangements had to be accomplished. Those were things you treasured forever. Jessamin remembered her own Rejoicing, and her eyes filled with the tears of memory joyfully welcomed; she knew now that her first period had arrived on as impossible a day for a celebration as could ever have been imagined, with almost every woman in Chornyak Household already scheduled for every last moment the whole day long. But they had held her Rejoicing, and they had never let on for an instant that heaven and earth and all the planets and asteroids had had to be moved about to fit it in.

She saw Nizhona then, holding a bundle in her arms—she must have just wound everything up in her bedsheet, the one with spots of blood, to be washed carefully in icewater and dried in early sunlight and folded away among her treasures. She stood in the dim outline of the door, waving goodbye to her. Jessamin waved back, and the girl disappeared—and then Jessamin remembered, and gasped, and dashed after her, just barely catching her at the foot of the staircase to tuck the pass into her nightgown pocket. "Mercy, girl!" she whispered. "Were you going to go the *whole way* without a *pass?*"

"Nobody will be awake up there yet," Nizhona scoffed. "It's a non-problem, they're all asleep!"

"Maybe," Jessamin said solemnly. "But that's because they haven't heard the splashing yet, as you go through the house. And I don't want some fool man sending you back down here. Or dragging you along with him and waking up everybody in the room demanding an explanation, and me having to spend the rest of the night getting babies back to sleep instead of working . . . no thank you, dearlove. Your pass is in your pocket, if you need it. For my sake."

She set a kiss firmly on Nizhona's mouth, and glanced at the floor; as she had expected, there was no trail of scarlet to be seen. Not this time.

"Off you go now," she said tenderly. "Belle-Anne's waiting for you. And I'll be over, first thing when everyone's up, to get the fandangous festivities started. Hurry, now; and go in lovingkindness, Nizhona Maria!"

The girl went up the stairs at a run, hugging the bundle, not even looking back at this place where she'd lived her whole life; and Jessamin watched her, contented, until she was out of sight and on her way down the corridor at the landing.

CHAPTER 10

"The World They Call Terra"

"Sing me a song!" said the child in the garden.
"Grandmother, sing! I'll sit here by your side . . .
* Sing me a song of the world they call Terra,*
* the world that you came from when you were a bride!"*

"Child, I have journeyed all over the starfields,
* out to the rim of the worlds that we know—*
* child, I can't sing you a song about Terra,*
* for Terra was too many planets ago."*

"Sing me a song!" said the child in the garden.
"Grandmother, sing to me—tell me no lies!
* Sing me a song of the world they call Terra—*
* I know you remember by the tears in your eyes!"*

"Child, I have journeyed all over the starfields!
* Child, I have left all my memories behind—*
* child, I can't sing you a song about Terra,*
* for I have put Terra clear out of my mind . . ."*

"Grandmother, sing!" said the child in the garden.
"I have learned all about stubborn from you—
* sing me a song of the world they call Terra,*
* where the grasses grow green and the oceans are blue!"*

"Child, how you weary me, asking of Terra!
* You are no babe—you should understand why!*
* We who left Terra forever and ever*
* were those who could tell her forever goodbye!"*

* "Child, I have journeyed all over the starfields,*
* out to the rim of the worlds that we know—*

137

child, I can't sing you a song about Terra,
for Terra was too many planets ago .. ."

(folksong, to the traditional tune,
"Come in the Evening")

Benia stood at the round window, stubbornly ignoring the screams
of the furious child on the plastic floor behind her, staring
fixedly out at the landscape past the window as if it had some
attraction to offer. In fact, it had none; it was a vast shelf of dark
blue rock, stretching off to a horizon where she knew that to
stand and look over the abrupt edge would only give you a view
of still another vast shelf of dark blue rock. And so on, for miles
and miles and miles. There were seventeen Indigo Steps, each as
absolutely flat as if a giant laser had sliced them for a colossal
staircase, and her house sat on the fourth one from the top. They
led down, eventually, to a small and boring body of water called
"Harry's Pond"—somebody's idea of a joke. Harry's, maybe?
Benia hadn't bothered to ask. The water was no pond, it was a
sea of sorts, as big as Earth's Mediterranean. But the steps of
rock that led off from it in all directions were so enormous, and
the pitiful little splat of water so lost at the base of the funnel
they made toward the sky, that it *looked* pondlike. Only when
one of the rare boats happened to be on its surface was there
anything to give it scale and perspective, and even then there
was little by which to judge whether it was a liner or a fishingboat.
Benia thought of the fish that swam in Harry's Pond, and
shuddered all over; she would stay with the hydroponics and the
enzyme flats, thank you.

She'd heard that looking out at the Indigo Steps long enough
caused visions. Hallucinations of mountains and caravans and
walled cities, and worse. She didn't know anything about that,
either, because she'd never had the patience to look for very
long. It was boring, like the sea. *Everything* on Polytrix was
boring. The bubble hut was boring, and the landscape was
boring, and the squat plants with their geometric shapes were
boring, and the thologys that came in for the tiny survival comset
were boring, and god knew the baby was boring. He was
supposed to be "company" for her, Daryl said. That had been
the point of having him, that and the usual line about her duty to
increase the colony's population.

Company! She sneered out the window, and her son screamed
even louder behind her, as if he knew what she was thinking.
Perhaps he did. Who knew what being born on Polytrix might do

to the brain of an innocent baby? Polytrix. Daryl thought it was so funny. "It's the name of a magic stone that makes all your hair fall out," he'd told her when they were still just talking about this place. "Isn't that crazy?" What was crazy was having come here. Marrying Daryl, and then coming here.

If she'd been back on Earth right now, if they'd stayed, like her parents had begged them to—but no, Daryl wouldn't even listen!—she could have gone to the Sparkle Club with the rest of the wives. And Bran, instead of screaming himself insane on the floor of this squalid hole that was the very best Polytrix had to offer, would have been in the Tender Room with the rest of the babies, having a wonderful time.

She was going to have to pick Bran up pretty soon; his cries were getting that funny rhythm to them that meant he would be throwing up if she didn't do something. But at least he would be exhausted enough by then to go to sleep and let her be miserable in peace. She had learned, by paying very careful attention, the exact amount of time she could let him scream, that would be enough to wear him out but not enough to make him vomit on the floor. What she would do when he got big enough to walk around in here she did not know; she had no capacity for imagining the stretch of time and tedium that lay between the endless day ahead of her and that day still weeks away, maybe months away, when Bran Daryl O'Fanion would struggle up onto his sturdy legs and begin to add his walking around to her torments.

Daryl loved it here, just as he'd been sure he would. He loved being a forest ranger on Polytrix, where there were no forests. He was out all day six days a week in a two-man flyer with Andrew Felk; the two of them were like kids, laughing and telling jokes and making the flyer do stunts that set the onboard computer whooping alarms and the two men whooping with glee. Chasing the herds of lampa, stupid creatures like big striped goats, away from the agricultural stations. Taking photographs— not even holos, just plain photographs—to send to the so-called capital of this cursed lump in space, for the so-called archives. Watching for the telltale white streaks in the rock that meant deposits of beshokkite crystals, worth far more than gold for all that they were ugly things. "What do they do with them?" she had asked Daryl, the first time he'd brought one back with him, and he'd patted her rump fondly and grinned at her and said, "They use them in biogenetics, baby . . . it's way over your head." Biogenetics. That was boring, too.

Expertly, not one second too late, she stepped backward and

scooped the gulping baby up into her arms, laid him against her chest, and began rubbing him between his shoulderblades, making the soothing noises that the microfiche said she was supposed to make. He was drenched, dripping with a rank mixture of sweat and urine, and she was terribly afraid that she hated him. She had never suspected that a woman could hate her own baby, and if you'd asked her about it before she came here she'd have said without hesitation that such a woman was very very sick. Babies were lovely, and lovable; you put them in their Tender and smiled at them while the Tender cleaned them and oiled and powdered them and dressed them in fresh disposable clothing, blue for boys and pink for girls, and then you took them back out again and played with them. And of *course* you loved them!

But Benia didn't have a Baby Tender. There weren't any on Polytrix. And there wouldn't be any for a long time. Benia had seen the list posted in the window of the station, the sequence of orders for shipments out to the colony set up for years in advance; Baby Tenders weren't even scheduled to be requisitioned yet, and it was a five year list. That was why a Gerber Microfiche was packed for every woman who came out here, so she could find out how babies had been looked after in the Dark Ages.

"Not the Dark Ages, Benia," Daryl had scolded her when she brought the subject up. "You know better than that, sweetie. *All* women took care of their own babies, just like it tells you on the fiche, clear up to the end of the 30's. The Baby Tender wasn't even *invented* until 2037, Benia. Dark Ages, for chrissakes!"

Daryl always knew things like that. When things were invented, and who did it, and where things were located, and how long they'd been there. All those endless boring things that nobody cared about. So far as Benia was concerned, anything before the Baby Tender was the Dark Ages. And it showed how selfish men were, too, because a Tender wasn't anything but a plain old ordinary healthy, like they'd had for sick people forever and ever; it just wasn't as fancy as a healthy. Babies didn't need tubes in their veins and up their noses, and they didn't need something that could sew them up and give them pills. There could already have been Tenders *twenty years* before they came on the market, she'd told Daryl, and he had agreed with her emphatically and said that he only wished to hell he'd thought of it and made the millions of credits that Woo Hee had made. Benia wished so, too, and envied Woo Hee's wife . . . no doubt Woo Hee was the man who *had* thought up the Baby Tender.

She bet Mrs. Woo Hee wasn't stuck off in a bare wasteland of purple rocks all by herself with a baby that stank.

It made Benia's mouth twitch, thinking of it, but not with humor. She had never known that a baby *could* stink . . . her friends had had babies, and her relatives had had babies, but they were always fresh and rosy and fragrant from their Tenders. She wondered what Lu-Sharon Naybers would have said, her with her precious twins, if she'd ever gotten a whiff of what a woman-tended baby could turn into dozens of times a day. Lu-Sharon had had the prettiest dresses in South Philadelphia, and so had the twins, and she'd been Benia's best friend, and she always looked wonderful; but she didn't care much for any kind of *effort*. Probably, if she'd been Benia, she'd have carried the baby down and pitched him into Harry's Pond without giving it a second thought. "I am *not* slave labor!" Lu-Sharon would have said haughtily; Benia'd heard her say it more than once, and about less. And Bran would have sunk like a stone into the deeps of Harry's Pond and that would have been the end of his stink. But Lu-Sharon would never have to deal with any of this, because *her* husband worked for the Department of Education, and Lu-Sharon was never going to find herself on Polytrix.

The baby was limp now, deadweight against her, and the smell wasn't getting any better. At home, she would have said sharply, "*Air* Change!", and the house computers would have removed the odor in seconds; of course at home the odor wouldn't have been there in the first place.

Benia sighed and looked up at the ceiling, less than three feet above her head. The bubble hut had come out with them in a tiny cube that stowed away under their seat; she and Daryl had argued about it. "There *can't* be a house in there!" she had insisted. "Not in that tiny little thing!" And Daryl had chuckled, and reached over to tweak her nipples, and told her that there sure as hell *was* a house in there. But it wasn't really a house. It was a *hut*, which made perfectly good sense when you remembered that its *name* was "bubble hut." You stood out of the way, and pulled the ring on the box with a long string, and it inflated itself majestically, and there it was, ready to be staked down. It had a living room and two bedrooms and a kitchen and a bathroom and a kind of breakfast cubbyhole and a utility room and a tiny greenhouse on one side, and that was *all*. Even if she'd been born poor, Benia thought, even if she'd stayed poor and married poor, she never would have had to live in something like this if she'd stayed in Philadelphia. The government wouldn't have allowed it.

Daryl thought it was cute.

"It suits you, Peaches," he'd said, grinning at her. "It's like a playhouse."

Sure. It was like a *work* house, was what it was like. And now it stank.

Crying, Benia carried the baby into the bathroom to clean him up and throw away the soaking clothes he was wearing. Daryl would fuss at her when he saw how many clothes she'd used up this month, she knew he would, and he'd talk about what kind of mess she was going to be in if she ran out of clothes before the next freighter docked at Polytrix with fresh supplies. But she didn't care. If they were going to have to live like savages, they might as well go naked like savages, that was how she felt about it. Then she could just hose the baby down with the ultrasonics, the way she did the walls. Why not? There wasn't anybody around to care what she did, or even see what she did. There were only five women on all of Polytrix, and not one of the others was like Benia. There were two nurses, and there was a missionary nun, and there was an old woman whose son had brought her with him, nobody knew why; he said she had insisted she wanted to come, and he didn't see any reason why not, which was crazy. But then anybody who would come to Polytrix was crazy. And there was Benia, Woman Number Five. The only one with a baby. There was nobody to be Benia's friend.

"Someday, Benia Sharon," Daryl kept telling her solemnly, "you'll be an important person on Polytrix, you realize that? You'll be *Old* Polytrician, Peaches; you'll be like people in Philadelphia that had family come over on the Mayflower. You'll be able to just *lord* it over all the other women, when they come. I can just see you now!"

Benia couldn't see that bright future, herself. She had this day to get through. Her and Bran. That was as far as her imagination could stretch.

It was funny, how she'd never once thought of herself being a colonial wife. Oh, she knew about the colonies, she'd had to learn all that stuff for Earth History from the mass-ed computers, and she'd been in skits at Homeroom all about the First Colonists, and she'd been as quick as anybody to bring out the champagne whenever a new colony was founded, even if it had started getting a little old after a while. She knew, vaguely, that there was a whole universe of worlds, Out There Somewhere; she even knew that much of her personal comfort and pleasure depended on the products of those worlds, or knowledge exchanged with those worlds. But it had never been *real* to her. Not *really* real. Not like Philadelphia was real.

She knew there were Aliens; she'd watched the docudramas, and once when she was visiting an aunt in Washington she'd even seen one land near the Capitol Building in a big limoflyer. But she'd seen the threedy stars once in a while, too, in *their* limos, and a lot of them looked stranger than the Aliens did. And nobody she knew, nobody her family associated with, went to the colonies. Why would they? Philadelphia was home, and it was wonderful and comfortable and familiar; and her family, and all her family's friends and their families, had lived in Philadelphia for as many generations back as Benia cared to keep track of.

Colonies, in Benia's mind, were for people who were *weird*. People who couldn't get along on Earth. Criminals. Foreigners, from countries where things weren't as nice as they were in the United States. Refugees, maybe; people who had fighting going on in their countries. Or they were for young men, going out just temporarily—not to settle, not to stay, but to make a fortune and then take it home and enjoy it. And for the very *very* rich, of course; people who could afford to buy a whole asteroid all for themselves and bring in a top terraforming company to make it exactly like they wanted it, with a private port and fast offplanet flyers so that they could go back and forth between the asteroid and Earth the way Benia's family would go back and forth between Philadelphia and their vacation homes in Greece and Japan. But not ordinary solid respectable people like Benia, or Benia's parents, or even Daryl's parents.

When she met Daryl, he was working for the Department of the Interior, doing something in management with the National Parks Division, and she'd thought *that* was pretty exotic. Romantic, even. The way he hated being stuck at the office and was always trying to wangle assignments "in the field" and flying off to the Grand Canyon and to Hawaii. *She should have known.* She should have listened to her parents when they tried to warn her. She should have married Victor Harbraccery, who'd gone to Homeroom with her and was going to be a lawyer with the Justice Department till the day he died, if he ever did, and whose wildest dream was to be a Supreme Court Justice someday. But Daryl . . . the sight of him, the smell of him, the sound of his voice, had made Benia's heart pound, made her weak and brainless. It was still that way, in spite of everything; when he called her on their tiny comset, she would be wet and ready for love just listening to him to tell her about the latest amazing thing he and Andy had seen or how late he would be for dinner. Victor Harbraccery had left her as dry and raspy as sandpaper. It had been hard for Benia even to wait till she'd finished her year at the marital academy and earned her wifery diploma before she and Daryl married—she'd thought the waiting would never be over.

And so she had found herself smack in the middle of the Plan. Daryl's Plan. Daryl had signed up for Polytrix before he ever met her, but they'd turned him down; too many bachelors on Polytrix already, the government had decided, time that Polytrix began to have a population of families. Single, Daryl couldn't have gotten the job on Polytrix; he had to go as part of a Founding Family. That's what they were, she and Daryl and poor little Bran . . . a Founding Family. Someday there would be a museum in the capital—where right now there was nothing but bubble huts with signs that said "Capitol Building" and "Courthouse" and "Bureau of Minerals" and "Hospital"—and in that museum there would be an entire holo that was just of her and Daryl and Bran. *First Founding Family Of Polytrix*, it would say. *Bran Daryl O'Fanion, First Human Child Born On Polytrix*. Without her to make him eligible, without her to produce Bran, Daryl couldn't have carried out the Plan.

She wondered: did she mean anything at all to him? Except as part of the Plan? He was kind to her. He made love to her frequently. He was firm about the budget, and about what must be done around the house, and about taking care of Bran, but he spoiled her in a lot of ways. She knew Andrew Felk thought Daryl was a fool for letting her have a servo. He'd said so, the very first time he'd come to dinner at their house, saying that if it had been him he'd have expected her to take care of the yard herself. "You know how many really important supplies you could have brought along," he'd demanded, glaring at her in a way that Daryl never glared at her, "if you hadn't wasted so much of your cargo allowance carting in that servomechanism?" There'd been contempt in his voice, and contempt in his eyes, and Benia hadn't known what to say to him. The servo mattered a lot to her. It was bad enough having to take care of Bran, and not even having a household computer, without having to do the outside work, *too*. And she hated to go outside, anyway; it frightened her to be out there in that looming awfulness of purple rock and sky.

Daryl had laughed, easy and fond, and poured Andrew Felk another glass of the wine he was so proud of, the wine he made himself from some kind of mysterious Polytrix berries. "It's a damn good thing you're not married, Andy," he'd chuckled. "You'd make a lousy husband!"

"Well, what does she need a yard servo for? There's nothing to do out there!" Felk had objected, waving at the yard of bare rock. "It just wanders around, polishing the rock and watering that . . . what is it you've got there, a boll-rose? It wouldn't take her five minutes a day to water the boll-rose, and the rock isn't supposed to be polished. The whole thing is *stupid*."

"Women," Daryl had said, good-humored as ever, "have different needs. They need something . . . something they don't need, if you know what I mean."

"No. I *don't* know what you mean."

"If all a woman has is what she actually needs, she isn't happy. She has to have something she *doesn't* need. It's a symbol. It says: you sweet little thing, you're worth it."

Andy Felk had just snorted, and Daryl had thrown his head back and roared. "You see?" he'd bellowed, and Benia had put her hands over her ears because they were so *loud*, both of them! "You *see?* You don't know the first *thing* about women, Andy! You stay single, my friend, for the women's sake!"

"You can *count* on it," Andy's answered, his voice thick with something Benia recognized only as not very nice. "You can absolutely count on it. I'd rather take a lampa into my house than a woman."

And Daryl had roared with laughter again. He thought Andrew Felk was an unending source of comedy entertainment.

"You could reprogram it, you know," Felk had muttered. "To do something useful."

Daryl had reached over under the table and pinched her bottom, and grinned at them both. "Don't you worry, Peaches," he'd said to Benia. "We aren't going to let Andy the Pirate here take your servo away. I promise."

Benia had heard Felk say "Sentimental fool!" under his breath, and had thought that might make Daryl angry, because in the tiny hut you could hear everything; it wasn't like a proper diningroom. But Daryl had just thought that was funny, too, and had said, "Bigot! Old fart!" back at him, and then they'd started talking about some kind of enzyme strain that tasted like bacon and they'd forgotten all about her.

The servo was out in the yard right now, polishing. Polishing the surface of the Indigo Step, that gleamed even on the duskiest of days, without any polishing. She didn't care. Seeing it out there working away was important to her. It made her feel better about being here. It was something of home.

"Won't they ever run out of colonies?" she'd asked Daryl once when he was holding her, after love, relaxed. He was always relaxed then, and she didn't think he'd ever noticed that she usually wasn't relaxed at all.

"Run *out*, sweetie? Of colonies? What do you mean, run out?"

"Well . . . fill them all up? So there won't be any more of them?" She'd been thinking that if all the colonies were full then there wouldn't be any other women like her, who had to be ripped up out of their real lives to become Founding Mothers.

"Oh, Peaches, for god's sakes . . ." He'd held her close and shaken her gently and told her she was adorable.

"Is it a stupid question?" she'd mumbled through the hair on his chest, knowing it must be, if she was suddenly adorable.

"Benia Sharon O'Fanion," he'd said, grave and fake-pompous, "do you know what *infinite* means?"

"Yes," she'd answered. Of course she did.

"Well, space is infinite, Peaches. And it has within it an infinite number of worlds."

"That means—that means there's never going to be any end?"

"Not so far as we can tell, sweetie. Not ever."

She had thought about that, while he stroked her breasts with a free hand and whispered nonsense into her ear.

"How awful," Benia had said after a while. "That's just awful."

"Awful?" He'd stopped short in his absentminded fondling and propped himself on one elbow and raised his eyebrows and stared at her. "It's wonderful! *Finally*, Benia, there's *plenty of room* for everybody, forevermore, until the end of time! Nobody has to ever go to war again because they don't have room, Benia—nobody has to be stuck in a life that's a dead end. That's not awful, you ninny, that's heaven!"

And then he hadn't let her talk anymore, because he had other things in mind, and she had hushed about it. But she still wondered. If they weren't going to run out of worlds to settle, weren't they going to run out of people to settle them? *People* weren't infinite, were they? And wouldn't people just get *tired* of it and begin to long for something that was *not* new, the way she did? Surely there had to come a day when somebody rubbed his hands together, satisfied, and said, "Well, that's enough colonies. No more; we've got all we need."

It seemed to her that it was as ridiculous to be expanding forever out into space as it had been to be all crowded together and stuck on Earth. Or wherever—if you were an Alien—you happened to be stuck. It seemed to her that there ought to be a middle ground.

"I want to go home," said Benia aloud, to nobody at all. Benia, who was never, never going to go home again. "I want to go home."

CHAPTER
11

Gentlemen: we have now presented to you the first forty semantic units of the interplanetary signal-language PanSig, in three major sensory moralities, together with a brief historical introduction to the system. At this point, it is our experience that someone inevitably rises to make what we at D.A.T. call "the Krawfkelliga Proposal", in honor of the first staff trainee to suggest it. In order to save time for all of us, we are going to run that proposal past you and get it over with; it goes like this:

> *Since the inventory of shapes on which the PanSig vocabulary is based is necessarily limited, each shape should be used more than once, as a mechanism for increasing the vocabulary. For example, take the triangle, which has been assigned the meaning equivalent [LET'S DO BUSINESS TOGETHER]; that's one shape used, and only one semantic unit gained. Suppose we take as vocabulary items one triangle, two triangles, and three triangles, assigning to each of them a meaning-equivalent; then we've still used only one shape from the inventory, but we've tripled our vocabulary for that shape. And so on through the entire set of meaningful shapes.*

Gentlemen, this seems so intuitively obvious, and so right—certainly, if we were using PanSig only with human beings it would be the first step we'd take! But if we were communicating with human beings, we wouldn't need PanSig, remember? Gentlemen, the Krawfkelliga Proposal was tried, and it failed in the most spectacular fashion. It will not work. We will be grateful if you will refrain from bringing it up again in this course.

The reason it won't work is that nothing in the optic system of humanoid Aliens—much less nonhumanoid Aliens—guarantees that the Alien looking at one square or one triangle or one circle

148

(from the Terran point of view, that is) is not already seeing two or more of that shape. Furthermore, we have no way of knowing whether the number of shapes seen remains a stable number over time, the way it does for us. Where the nonhumanoids are concerned, you must remember that we have no way of knowing even if they see the same shape we see; all we know is that, like us, they distinguish among the shapes and see them as differing and unique items. But how many do they see? Gentlemen, for all we know they see hundreds, or thousands! Let us not complicate matters any further than they are complicated already by the simple facts of the situation.

(from Training Lecture #2, for junior staff; Special PanSig Division, United States Department of Analysis & Translation)

"Are you absolutely sure of your facts, Crab?" Heykus was leaning forward with his hands on the seeyum's gleaming surface, half-standing. "Are you positive?"

"Would I have come tearing over here this morning if I *weren't* positive?" the man asked, clearly annoyed at the questions.

His annoyance was justified; Crab Lowbarr had plenty of junior staff he could have sent in his place if he'd thought he was only reporting a rumor. Heykus looked at him a moment longer, thinking hard, and then he made a swift decision. And did something that was so rare for him that Crab Lowbarr was shocked. Heykus sat down and sent for a half-bottle of good wine and two wine glasses.

When Crab had recovered from his astonishment, he mentioned that he hadn't known Heykus drank. Politely. And his chief, who based the decision upon the fact that Jesus Himself had been quite willing to turn water into wine at the wedding in Cana—when He could just as easily have turned it into milk or apple juice or anything else whatsoever—said, "I don't. But sometimes, for a very special and wonderful celebration, I have a glass of wine in joyful fellowship. Weddings . . . births of sons . . . that sort of thing." He did not add that it was also a move that would give him precious time to think, before he had to do any more serious talking, and he sincerely hoped that would not occur to Crab as a possibility.

"And announcements that an ordinary human baby has learned an Alien language," Lowbarr said cheerfully. "I agree. Joyful fellowship! Absolutely."

"Weddings and births come along pretty often, but this has

happened only once, and can never happen again. That makes it especially celebration-worthy."

"Only once, yeah—only one time can be the *first* time. But it's going to happen again plenty of times from now on," Crab said.

"Are you sure of that?"

"Heykus, for god's sake!" protested the other man. "So help me Niobe! What do I have to say to get you to quit with the are you sure and are you positive crap? The Lingoes have been telling us the truth all this time, damn their asses all the way to hell and back, and if I wasn't one hundred and six percent sure of what I'm saying I *would not be here*. Now lay off with the dubious inquiries. *Shit*."

"There really is no genetic difference between the babies of the Lines and other babies?"

Crab shook his head slowly from side to side, one hand laid melodramatically over his heart. "None. *None*. I've called enough of our scientists to run a damn conference, and they all tell me the same thing. They've known for years—'many years' is the way they put it—that any human kid can learn an Alien language in an Interface just the same as a child of the Lines."

"But they didn't feel it was necessary to tell *us* that? During these many years."

"Ah . . ." Crab cleared his throat and looked carefully blank. "They tell me they were instructed to keep their radical opinions to themselves, Heykus, and they didn't feel that it was advisable to argue."

"Pentagon?"

"Yep."

Heykus sighed, and took some more time making a note on his wrist computer; Crab would assume it was a reminder to call in some Pentagon flunkies and kick ass over this. He would have been very surprised to know that what Heykus had entered was the words to the first verse of "The Old Rugged Cross." And then the wine came, and he stopped to pour it and to go through the ceremony of toasting the momentous occasion.

"To the youngster who has broken the monopoly of the Lines," he said solemnly, raising his glass.

Lowbarr repeated that, and added "To the *truth!*" as his contribution. And although Heykus disliked doing so intensely, he had no choice but to join in.

"To the truth!" he echoed, and raised his glass once again, and drank, hoping he wouldn't choke on the wine. It was awkward, drinking to the truth while you did your best to figure out a way to perpetuate what was so far as you knew the most elaborate lie the human race had ever been told. And when the toasts were safely over, he would have to relax and strive for small talk. Small talk that was in preparation for large talk, that he would have to do quickly, as soon as this man could decently be sent on about his business and Heykus could decide how the emergency should be handled.

"Well, now," he began. "Now I've survived the shock, perhaps you could tell me one more time. With a little more detail." He leaned back and gave Crab his most encouraging jovial smile.

"Heykus, there isn't much more detail," Crab answered. "There's a wild-eyed eggdome at Massachusetts Multiversity named Macabee Dow. Powerful man—controls a hell of a lot of money, knows things nobody else understands but a lot of people need, that kind of thing. Shaves his head and stains it blue."

"He does?"

"He does. A militant. You know. 'You wanna hate an eggdome? Hate *me,* here's my eggdome badge!' Anyhow, when his first kid was born, this Dow character just haled himself over to Chornyak Household and talked them into Interfacing his kid along with theirs. He signed a hundred waivers of responsibility, of course, and I suppose it cost him both arms and a leg, but they went along with it. And now, Heykus, little Gabriel Macabee Dow is two years old plus a bit, and a native speaker of REMwhatsis. Same behavior as the linguist kids . . . tiny vocabulary, little baby sentences, you know the kind of thing, but the Chornyaks assure me it's normal language acquisition. And that the Dow baby understands everything the AIRY says, sits around gabbling with the other kids in the Interface— the works. I went over and took a look at the setup for myself, and it's as specified, Heykus."

"How did this professor talk the Chornyaks *into* that?"

Crab rolled his eyes and shrugged his shoulders; Heykus found the man's body language offensively excessive, but at least it wasn't particularly subtle. Massive bewilderment, he was bodyparling, and now he was going to put words to the music. "Apparently it was no problem, and that baffles me. According to Jonathan Chornyak, Muckymuck of Muckymucks, the Lines have never had any objection to Interfacing kids from outside, so long as there was space available. He claims they've made the offer to share the Interface time and time again, direct to this department, and have always been turned down. *Rudely,* he says. He says they got tired of offering."

"He's probably correct," Heykus said. "Relations between this department and the Lines have never been precisely cordial. I can imagine the dialogue. 'Hey, wanna share our Interface?' And one of our prize diplomatic types telling the man where he could take his offer and what ingenious things he could do with it when he got there."

"I know." They both knew, and had been caught in the middle many a time.

"How did Macabee Dow know it was such a simple matter, though?" Heykus asked. "The Lines have certainly not gone around making offers to the general public—they don't have as much contact with the public in a year as you and I do in an ordinary morning."

"Heykus, I don't have any idea how Dow knew, and he isn't telling. He just glares at me like I was the newest fungus and snorts like a horse and mutters stuff about pseudoscience and government claptrap and then claps his mouth shut and smirks at me."

"Smirks at you? Why?" Heykus didn't like the sound of this at all. Somebody was going to have to take a very careful look at Macabee Dow, and at how essential the continuation of his work was; and somebody was going to have to decide whether Macabee Dow wouldn't serve his nation more effectively from a comfortable private room in a federal mental hospital with a Takeover Chip in his nostril and a layer of Thorazine added for insurance. "Why would he feel that it was appropriate to smirk at you?" he said again.

"Well, hell, Heykus, his kid is the very first kid ever, not from the Lines, to learn an Alien language. *Sure* he smirks about it! I'd smirk too, in his place."

Heykus leaned his chin in his hand and closed his eyes, thinking long and hard, while Crab finished the excellent wine. What, precisely, was he going to do now? He hadn't been expecting this, and there weren't any contingency plans for it. He was furious with the Chornyaks for going ahead with it without notifying D.A.T., and he knew that was wasted anger, because there was nothing that would delight the Chornyaks more than knowing that they'd managed to upset Heykus Clete. And Crab Lowbarr was going to expect Heykus really to be feeling the satisfaction he'd been pretending to feel. His security clearance qualified him to know all about the government Interfacing experiments with nonhumanoid Alien languages—the standard classified information about the Government Work projects—but he'd go to his grave as ignorant of the problems of Alien superiority as a servomechanism supervisor. Unless this business with the Dow child had brought on catastrophe, and the whole thing was going to become public knowledge, in which case Crab Lowbarr would have to take his chances like everybody else.

But there was something very strange here, nagging at the back of his mind. Something that did not add up. This had been going on for almost two years, or a little more than two years, and not one hint had come his way? Not one memo? Macabee Dow undoubtedly had the kind of influence that would have kept his child's private life out of the media until such time as he chose to have it there, but it was extraordinary that Heykus had not learned of it long ago. The only possible explanation of that information lag was that the men of the Lines, out of sheer mischief, had taken the kind of elaborate steps that would have been necessary to keep the Director of D.A.T. in the dark and save this little surprise for him. Only the linguists would have the skill, or the motivation, to lay down the kind of smokescreen required and maintain it this long.

"Is something wrong, Heykus?"

Lowbarr's voice seemed to come from very far away, and Heykus heard it through a dull fury that he knew was not helping matters. *Yes, something is wrong.* In a just war, you take a life because it is necessary to do so, and taking Crab Lowbarr's life—and Macabee Dow's, and little Gabriel Dow's—would have been quick and simple. But that wouldn't have been enough. And even if Heykus felt that he was justified in ordering a "natural disaster" that would get rid of a large group, that group would have to include all of the linguists of Chornyak Household, just for starters. Women and children, as well as men. And even then, he would have to start looking for the loose ends. People Dow had mentioned the project to, casually, at parties. Their wives; their children. People *those* people had talked to about it, perhaps because they were disgusted that Dow would even consider doing anything so repulsive. And then there were the staff members here at D.A.T. who'd read whatever kind of disinformational items the linguists had sent along to screw the lid down on the story. And everybody *they* had talked to. . . . It was ridiculous. You'd have to wipe out the population of the Earth to get rid of all the potential loose ends! You might just as well tell the truth and let the population of the Earth do whatever it would do if it knew the facts!

"No, nothing's wrong," he said. "I'm just very surprised. And a little taken aback at the implications."

"It's an unexpected breakthrough, that's for damn sure," said

Crab, comfortably. Just as if he were not sitting there with his survival being considered, pro and con, by Heykus Joshua Clete. Heykus thanked the Lord God Almighty, as he did time and again in the course of any working week, that telepathy was still not among the usual abilities of His children on this planet.

"But do you know what it means?" he asked Lowbarr. "It means that all we have to do in order to double, triple, quadruple, the number of interpreters we have is build Interfaces of our own and stock them with AIRYs and babies. It means we can step up the settlement of space—" He stopped, suddenly.

"What is it, Heykus? What the hell's the matter?"

"It means the Soviets can do the same thing," Heykus spat. "Doesn't it? I don't suppose it crossed anybody's mind that this should be classified information."

"It crossed my mind." Lowbarr wasn't pleased at the implication that he'd been careless. "But Macabee Dow didn't choose to call me on this until *after* he'd held a press conference. I just barely managed to get over here and tell you before you saw it on the newspapes."

"I see."

"I told him what I thought, and he told me how little he cared. He also told me that this hadn't been going on at the bottom of the sea, and if it was such a big deal somebody should have told him so sooner."

Heykus nodded.

"Some kind of hanky-panky's been going on, hasn't it?"

"It doesn't matter now," Heykus told him firmly. "What does matter is for us to move on this. We can build Interfaces bigger and faster and better than the Russians can, and we'll have to. We'll have to do something about the number of AIRYs available to us, and that isn't going to be easy. While the details are being worked out, there are things we have to do *right* now. I want work started on construction of Interfaces here in Washington—the technicians at Government Work will know how to proceed on that. I want liaison men calling at the houses of the Lines, to reserve every space available in *their* Interfaces for infants of our choice—infants chosen by me personally, from the families of our top personnel. I don't want even one more such space to go to an academic with ambitions; they are *all* to go to our people. In fact, Crab, I don't want that put off, I want it done immediately. I want liaison teams on their way by noon today. If this has been gossip around the Multiversity for the past two years, even just within a small circle of Dow's friends, there are undoubtedly other academics who've just been waiting to be sure his child wouldn't die or go mad or turn out not to be able to acquire the language. Now that they know there's no risk, they'll feel the same way we do—they'll want the goodies for themselves. We can't have that."

"Heykus . . ." Crab spoke hesitantly, a puzzled scowl on his face. "Wait a minute."

"What's the problem?"

"Well, isn't that up to the Lingoes? The Interfaces belong to them—it seems to me that who they share them with is not something we can decide."

"They'll cooperate," Heykus said grimly. "You leave that part of it to me."

"And how do you propose to—"

Heykus was suddenly weary, worn out with the sudden crisis and the multiple layers of deceptions, worn out with having to be polite to this man; at such times he understood very well how the good old-fashioned dictator must have enjoyed the privilege of just snapping his fingers and ordering the guards to take whoever it was away to the dungeons and throw away the keys.

"Lowbarr," he said, trying not to let the adrenalin rebound show, "it doesn't really matter whether I'm going to be able to convince them or not. The government still has to proceed *as if* we would be able to do so. Can't you see that?" He didn't wait for the answer; it wasn't relevant. "How fast can you get this organized?"

Crab Lowbarr had begun making notes as soon as he realized that what he was hearing was direct orders and not simply conversation; he looked up from his wrist computer and asked, "With full authority from you, Heykus?"

"Whatever you need. Funds, people, anything."

"Give me two hours—maybe a little less. I'll get it going."

"Good man."

"Is that all?"

"No. It's not. Next, I need a congressman with top security clearance over here. We're going to need a modification of the child labor laws to let children outside the Lines work in the interpreting booths. That's got to be worded extremely carefully; I want somebody good, and somebody effective. Somebody who'll know how to tuck it away in an amendment to a big appropriation bill where nobody will notice it until we *want* it noticed."

"Okay, Heykus. But that's it."

"I beg your pardon."

Crab spread his hands wide and shook them at his superior,

palms up and supplicating. "Look, there aren't many of us around with the necessary clearances for all this, and we're spread damn thin already. There are things we do that can't just be dumped in the ON HOLD file. If you really want teams headed for the Lines in the next two hours, you've given me all I can handle. Let me get on *this* stuff, and then I'll come back this afternoon for the additions to your list."

Heykus nodded; it was annoying, but the man was correct, and it shouldn't have been necessary for him to remind anybody.

"You're right," he said. "You go ahead and get matters underway. I need time to sit down and consider carefully each and every aspect of this development; I need time to set up appropriate strategies. I shouldn't be going off half-cocked like this. Don't come back later today, Crab; get the teams going, send me the congressman, and come back *tomorrow* afternoon. If anything comes up in the meantime that's a genuine emergency, I'll send for you."

"All right." Lowbarr stood up and stretched, groaning aloud. "Too much wine," he said. "This is no time for me to be this relaxed." He reached into his pocket, brought out a strip of Null-Alk capsules, and took two, while Heykus glared at this clear evidence of both dissipation and weakness. "How do you know, Heykus," Crab chuckled, noting the expression on his face, "that I don't carry these for the benefit of other people who lack my sterling character?"

Heykus didn't stoop to answer that. He turned down the volume on the glare slightly, and nodded at Lowbarr as he snapped a mock salute and headed out through the desk exit and toward the office door.

"Crab?" he called after him. "Give me a call in about an hour and let me know how things are going!"

"Right!" the answer came back, and then the door hissed, irising open and then shut. Heykus wanted a good long look at the man on comscreen, to get a chance to study him more closely than was polite when face to face; even more, he wanted a chance to see the fiz-display data. He needed to know if Crab Lowbarr was under any stresses that the effects of the wine had canceled or dulled while he was here; he needed to know if any unusual pattern was going to show up when Heykus asked him a few questions about *exactly* when he had first learned that there was a baby not of the Lines in the Chornyak Interface. And of course, while he was waiting for Lowbarr's call, he would get the man's file from the computer and find out what sort of abrupt exit from this world would be most appropriate and believable, if it turned out to be necessary. It was a duty he found repugnant; it was also a duty he would not have even considered laying on the shoulders of anyone else.

Finally, the moment came when he had done everything that he *could* do right then. He had placed all the necessary calls and was waiting for the replies to come in. He had reviewed all the relevant files, and abstracted the data that had to be remembered. He had made careful notes of the agenda for this day, and, so far as it was possible with the information that he had available, for the next few days as well. He had gone down on his knees and let his God know how troubled he was, and how badly divine help was needed. And now there was nothing he could do except wait for the various wheels to begin turning, for the excellent people who worked for him to do their jobs. There was nothing more that he, personally, could do for a little while, and it was therefore now possible for him to let himself really *feel* what was happening.

The angel had not mentioned this development to him in any specific terms; no doubt it fit tidily into the several broad pronouncements made about anticipating trials and tribulations. It happened from time to time, something major that he had not been told to prepare against, and it always made him feel as if he were flying in heavy traffic with all his instruments broken. He recognized the sensations of his body as panic, and knew that it would be better to distract himself from it. *Review the situation, Heykus,* he told himself sternly. *Get it straight in your head, so that you don't make the stupid mistakes of a frightened man. Lay it out, and take a good long thorough look at it, while you are fortunate enough to have this bit of empty time.*

First point: *the members of the Interstellar Consortiums are fully in agreement with us that Terrans should not be informed of the degree of superiority they appear to have over us.* They *are not going to do anything that will make matters worse, and will do everything they can to make them better. Which means we can rely on them to refuse absolutely all our demands for an increased quota of AIRYs to staff the new government-built Interfaces.*
Second point: *the linguists of the Lines hate us, and with very good reason; furthermore, their livelihood depends on the monopoly of the Alien language interpreting business. Which means that we can rely on* them *to refuse absolutely all demands that they turn over some of their AIRYs to D.A.T. to*

staff our new Interfaces. And we can count on them to take a good long time about it, which will be helpful.

Third point: *the number of lay infants that will acquire native fluency in Alien languages by sharing the Interfaces of the Lines will be very small. Because the linguists—for the same reasons that will guarantee their refusal to give up any of the AIRYs—will refuse to let us put more than one or two infants in each Interface. No matter how much I protest, no matter how much I insist that they show a decent patriotism, no matter what I threaten them with. They'll "discover" reasons why having more than one or two would ruin the whole process, or they'll just flatly refuse to explain. Which means that I am only going to have to put round-the-clock surveillance, complete with electronic ears, on a few dozen children who might somehow know more than they ought to know and spill beans they didn't even realize they were carrying. Nothing that is beyond the resources of this department, or the security groups, is going to be needed.*

Fourth point: *leaking the change in the child labor laws to the media is going to be easy . . . they'll grab it, and they'll take off with it. And we can count on the do-goodys to raise bloody hell long enough and loud enough to force Congress—reluctantly, bowing to the public will—to limit the number of hours the kids outside the Lines are allowed to spend in the interpreting booths. With any luck at all, and enough arrogant kicking and screaming from this department, we'll get a ten-hour-a-week absolute limit.*

Fifth point: *the normal retarding effect of federal regulations will make all of this take three times as long as it ought to take, and we can always get new regulations laid on if the ones we have now aren't molasses enough.*

And there was the extra point, the super-point, the one that was the clincher. *Extra point:* the Lord God Almighty and all the Heavenly Hosts are on *our* side. Which means that we have an advantage. Which means that the Soviets will have a much worse time with this than we are going to have. Which means that we will manage, somehow. We will keep the lid on this, just as we always have, and there is no reason to panic.

His heartbeat was back to normal again; the sinking feeling in his stomach was gone; there was no longer a fine beading of sweat on his palms and on his upper lip. *Good.*

Heykus ordered strong coffee sent in, murmured a prayer of thanks that he was himself again, such as he was, and sat back to wait for the comset call from Crab Lowbarr that ought to be coming in any minute now.

CHAPTER 12

"It is of course utter nonsense to claim that any connection exists between language change and social change, except in the most superficial sense of the word. The fate of the Sapir-Whorf Hypothesis (also known, quaintly, as the 'linguistic relativity hypothesis') is a case in point; it now stands entirely discredited. Its primary advocates were not men, but women, who repeatedly demonstrated the depths of their ignorance even as they made pathetic attempts to teach the concept and to write about it.

"Poor things. . . . They could not grasp the difference between the strong version of the hypothesis—that language controls perception—and the more reasonable (though equally invalid) weak version, which proposed only that language structures perception. They persisted in ignoring the fact that neither Sapir nor Whorf had formulated the hypothesis which bore their names; they never really understood that neither of those great scholars would have supported such foolishness for even a moment. They were incapable of comprehending the massive evidence against both versions of the hypothesis, even when it was meticulously and patiently presented by the most distinguished scholars. They rushed to report, and to elaborate upon, the supporting pronouncements of a few naive males—who, I must pause to add, did not have female gender as an excuse for their disgraceful stupidity—and seemed entirely blind to the manner in which even those men added elaborate disclaimers to their work and in later years withdrew it in its entirety.

"Poor things, I say again! They were like small children, who so desperately want to believe in Santa Claus. They wanted, desperately, to believe in the ABRACADABRA! approach to reality. And what could be more natural? After all, it was the words *of misguided and overindulgent men that had 'turned them*

into' doctors and professors and scientists and corporate executives and even—horrifying as it seems to us today—religious officials. Naturally, like those same small children, they believed that when someone put 'Ph.D.' or 'M.D.' or 'CEO' after a woman's name she was thereby magically endowed with the abilities necessary to carrying out those functions. The fate of those women was not pretty. Their panic and disarray, their suicides, their nervous breakdowns, their endless personal tragedies, inspired compassion even in those who had tried hardest to convince them of their folly beforehand. And I am not ashamed to admit that I feel that same compassion now, even at this historical distance. One does not expect a legless person to become a figure skater, and it would be disgustingly cruel to do so; the situations are painfully similar.

"Today, the Sapir-Whorf Hypothesis lies buried beside the Flat Earth Hypothesis, where it most assuredly belongs, and the dear ladies have been restored to their proper place in the world, allowing us all to both work and rest in peace. It therefore becomes possible at last to turn to the systematic examination of the linguistic phenomena associated with the so-called 'Women's Liberation Movement' purely as linguistic phenomena, and to subject them to historical analysis, free of the unfortunate emotionalism with which they were heretofore associated. For the sake of historical accuracy, I will begin with the rather silly topic usually referred to as 'the pronoun question' and dispose of it promptly; we will then move on to less trivial aspects of the subject."

> *(from a paper presented at the annual Exotica Colloquium of the Department of Language Sciences, California Multiversity - La Jolla Campus, by Associate Professor John "Norm" Smith of Stanford University)*

If you were a linguist, you lived at a pace unknown to the rest of Earth's population. You were up every morning at five; you were at some negotiation or meeting by eight; you were lucky to be home by dinner time; and there was still a schedule to deal with after dinner was over. If you were a child, there was homework to be done for the mass-ed computer courses, followed by private lessons in as many foreign languages as the family could manage to squeeze into your head. If you were older, there was always preparation for an upcoming job, or there was practice in the language for which you served as the backup interpreter. Or there were Household business meetings.

The daily work schedules were now so crowded that almost everything to do with internal business had to be postponed for meetings that began after dinner and lasted until midnight or later.

If you were a man, there was occasionally time to send for your wife to come from the Womanhouse and join you in a rendezvous room for at least part of an evening, if you had energy enough left for such things.

And it went on six days a week. There were so many different religions on Earth and on the planets with which Earth interacted—there was no day that wasn't a sacred holy day for *some*body. The intricate interweaving of the schedules (done by the computers, thank all the various gods involved) demanded six of the seven days of the Terran week. Which made Sunday—*their* holy day—precious to the linguists of the Lines, even encumbered as it was by the obligatory morning trek to church.

That religion was necessary for women was something the men had no doubts about; it was the single most reliable way to maintain in women not just a decent awareness of their proper role but a serene satisfaction in that role. It was *doubly* necessary for linguist women, whose work as government interpreters and translators might otherwise have bred in them a dangerous tendency toward unwomanly independence and arrogance. The children had to go to church because church was one of the very few areas of their life in which they could function within their culture in the same way that other children did. And if the women and children must go, the men had no plausible excuse not to; you couldn't insist that your sons pay attention to what they heard from the preachers, including the necessity for being there every Sunday, and not put in an appearance yourself.

But *before* church, there was a luxurious chunk of real leisure time that every linguist male treasured. Church didn't start until eleven, breakfast wasn't served in the diningroom until eight-thirty—you could legitimately sleep past seven, and that was bliss. If you were sufficiently enterprising to get yourself decked out for church before you went to breakfast, you could spend as much as two full hours lounging around. Doing things that had no connection with languages or politics or business. Talking to your buddies—plain oldfashioned mantalk, that could recharge you for the whole blazing week ahead. The women insisted on rushing through Sunday breakfast and being gone before nine, to do god only knew what mysterious female things between nine and eleven, and the children always seized that time to watch trash on the comsets that they weren't allowed to look at any other time. Eight-thirty to nine in the diningrooms was like eating in the middle of a six-way groundcar intersection with three lanes of flyer traffic overhead. But at nine, like magic, the women and the children were gone, vanished, and the men had the place to themselves. They could lean back and relax and enjoy one another . . . you looked forward to it all week long.

This Sunday morning's stampede was over, leaving behind it the usual extraordinary silence. That silence, to Jonathan's way of thinking, contained more genuine reverence than any silence he'd ever experienced in any church. A genuine, heartfelt, soul-nourishing, "Thank God, they're gone at last!" reverence, that could be recognized as a valid religious emotion by every man in the room. He had once told Nazareth that if he could find a church that would give him the kind of peace and satisfaction he experienced every Sunday morning in the diningroom during those two hours, he would volunteer for its priesthood—or whatever it had of the kind—instantly. It was the sort of thing you could safely say to Nazareth; she never gossiped, and she never asked stupid questions. She had smiled at him, her eyes dancing with a pleasure he didn't understand but that he knew was no threat to him, and had said, "Ah, yes, my dear. Brotherhood with a capital B! Fellowship with a capital F! Than which there are few things more seductive . . . with a capital S!" He remembered that there had also been a look of approval on her face, which was rare; she'd gotten to be a crochety old thing.

He realized then that he must have a foolish expression on *his* face, from the way the three other men were looking at him and exchanging significant glances with one another. They had the best spot in the room. The corner table against the wall, from which you could see everybody else and watch their comings and goings, but where nobody could get behind you. And they were grinning at him, waiting for him to snap out of it, nobody having the decency to say something that might hurry him along. Bastards, he thought fondly; while he was at it, he said it aloud.

"Bastards! All three of you."

"Are we? You've got balls, Jonathan, sitting there smirking to yourself like a baby at the tit, and calling *us* foul names."

Jonathan chuckled. "A baby at the tit, as you so elegantly put it, does not smirk. It cannot smirk, Leo, because if it did there would be no suction produced, and all the nice milk would *stay* in the tit. If you'd get married and fulfill your responsibilities by producing some offspring for us, you'd know these basic facts."

"I'd rather be shot," Leo declared flatly. "Much rather."

"Makes no difference." Conary Lopez, who had married one of Jonathan's most spectacular younger sisters and had no regrets, was always willing to put in a good word for the married condition. "You'll have to do it eventually, and you won't be allowed to choose shooting instead. Duty is duty, Leo."

"I don't want to talk about duty this morning," Jonathan announced.

"How about talking about whatever it was you were thinking about before you regained consciousness?"

"No—you wouldn't find that interesting, I give you my word." He reached into the inside pocket of his jacket and pulled out a hard copy, folded three ways, and slapped it down on the table in front of him. "*This* is what I want to talk about! You've got to hear this, my friends . . . I'm going to read it aloud to you. For free. Gratis."

Because he was Head, they didn't get up and move to another table; but because all but Conary had lived their whole lives in this house with him, they didn't bother hiding their disapproval. His cousin Tom provided a skilled raspberry, Conary and Leo jointly seconded the motion, and Leo stated firmly that they had not come to his table to be read to, unless it was something dirty, in which case he had no business making a hard copy and carrying it in his Sunday suit jacket.

"It's worth your time," Jonathan insisted. "Would I be bringing it up if it weren't? Would I spoil Sunday morning? Where's your faith, for christ's sakes? This is going to brighten your day."

"And the corner where we are."

"I solemnly swear it. You wait till you hear this. I almost missed it, myself." Jonathan paused and looked at each of them, and then he tied it off. "I don't spend a lot of time reading the *Journal of American Religious Ethnomethodology*."

That brought the protests he was expecting, and hadn't been able to resist provoking, and he wigwagged at them with both hands and went on talking, drowning out their objections. "It was one of the automatic datasweeps that flagged it!" he shouted over their racket. "I never would have seen it otherwise. Shut up and listen, will you? This thing is called . . . get ready . . . 'Liturgical Language in an American Religious Cult: A Unique Development.' By . . . let me see here . . . by Searcy Waythard, Ph.D."

Leo Chornyak was not going to let this be easy. He leaned toward the others, elbows solidly on the table, and asked them if they knew that professors used to be called doctors.

"What?"

"Shit!" Tom laughed, and punched Leo's shoulder. "You'd know that kind of thing wouldn't you? That's why you're always screwing up your honorifics, your mind is full of junk like that."

"It's true. You had doctors of medicine, you had doctors of zoology, you had doctors of literature—"

"How the effing BEMdung could there be a doctor of literature? What's to doctor? That's ridiculous. That's the—"

Leo cut him off in mid-sentence. "Exactly," he said. "Exactly! And that is why, instead of a semantic mess, doctors are now doctors and professors are now professors."

"And assholes," Jonathan noted, "are still assholes."

"What?" asked Conary again.

Jonathan laid the hard copy down in front of him, patted it smooth with elaborate ceremony, poured himself a fresh cup of coffee from the gravytrain, and folded his arms across his chest.

"You've got a choice," he said calmly. "You can listen to me read this, without any more interruptions, or any more attempts to change the subject—as if anybody gives a slim pallid odiferous shit for the historical tidbits Leo is expounding for us—or you can go sit someplace else. Because I *am* going to read this out loud."

"To an audience of nobody but your elbow?"

Jonathan's voice was soft, and his eyes were locked with Leo's. "The microphones in this room are programmed to respond to just two signal inputs," he crooned. "Anybody's pronunciation of the words *emergency alert*. And the sound of my voice. If you'd like me to share this with the entire room, I can manage that."

"Leo," Tom added, "this man here is not just the Head of the Chornyaks. This man is the Head of Heads. If he wants to read us the latest editorial on how many rows of lace the ladies prefer on their panties this spring, that's his privilege."

It was partly a joke, and partly a game, and partly a serious warning. Jonathan *was* the Head of Heads, and if he cared to pull that rank he could make their morning very unpleasant. On the other hand, they all happened to know from many a solemn contest over the years that any one of them could pee a bigger circle in the snow than Jonathan could; if they cared to pull *that* kind of rank, they could ruin *his* morning. The silence got thicker, and they watched one another with narrowed eyes, while everybody considered the various possible moves and their probable consequences. And then, because it was the only Sunday morning they'd get for a whole week, Leo grinned in a swift flash of gleaming white teeth and raised his coffeemug in a good-natured hail to the chief, and the others immediately moved in to make it unanimous.

"*Go,* Jonathan!" Conary said. "It's not much of a floor, but you've got it."

"Okay," he said, relaxed now that the moves were over and the points were his. "Your spirit of enthusiastic cooperation is duly et cetera et cetera. Now, this starts off with some stuff that's not so bad, considering the source. What's normal language; what's not normal. Next step, the special nature of religious language—no need to read you any of that. Then Waythard makes a distinction that's not quite as typical, between what is normal *religious* language and what's not. Noting that whether it makes any sense isn't one of the criteria, right? Stuff like 'in the name of the Father, and of the Son, and of the Holy Ghost' is normal religious language; if there were a religion of the Pig In The Poke, he says, it would be normal religious language to say 'in the name of the Pig, and of the Piglet, and of the Holy Poke.' Et cetera, et cetera. He tries to explain what is *not* normal religious language . . . puts glossolalia in there, and some other stuff. None of it very well argued, but what the hell. And then we get to the good part. Listen, please, to this:

'Recently, however, a unique case has arisen in this country which is not so easily classified as normal or abnormal, as religious language or as secular language. I refer to the phenomenon of Langlish (also know as Láadan) which had its origins with the women of the linguist families known as "the Lines" and is used for at least some portions of the liturgy in the religious cult called "Thursday Night Devotionals."

'The cult is itself interesting, as a cult sheltered within the framework of an accepted religion—usually one of the Protestant denominations of Christianity. And the language in question forms an interesting parallel, inasmuch as it is an artificial language sheltered within the framework of a real language. The sample of Langlish/Láadan which the Chornyak family was kind enough to supply to this researcher for examination is—however much the ladies may have convinced themselves that they have done something creative—quite transparently nothing more than a computer deformation of ordinary Panglish, with a few frills added to make it seem exotic. Now, the question is—' '

"Hey! Hang on a minute!" Tom slammed his coffeemug

down, skillfully spilling almost none on the table. "Just hold
on!"

"Problem?" Jonathan hadn't expected to get this far before
they ran out of patience and interrupted him. "Something wrong?"

"Yeah, there's a problem!" Tom said. "Our women have
been doing that Thursday night piddling ever since the Womanhouses were built and somebody decided it would be good public
relations to include a chapel in the floor plan. How in the name
of Patrick the Perpetrator did that get transformed into a *cult*?
Furthermore, how does anybody outside the Lines even *know* our
women like to get together every Thursday night and play church?"

"Well," Jonathan explained, "as always, we are the last to
know. Listen to this—

> *'We cannot state precisely when it was that the Thursday
> Night Devotionals—which had until then been confined exclu-
> sively to linguist women—began spreading outside the Lines.
> The first recorded example we are able to verify took place in
> the women's chapel of Mercy Hospital in Belleglade, Vir-
> ginia, near Chornyak Household. Since that time, services
> have sprung up in hospital chapels and private homes all
> across the country, and have come to constitute a distinct
> religious movement.' "*

"Jesus H. galloping Christ," breathed Leo, grabbing for more
coffee as the gravytrain paused over their table. "It was started
here? At Chornyak Household? Johnny, did you know about
this?"

"I knew about the services at the hospital. Of course. The
women came and asked me for permission, and I saw no reason
not to give it. It was a worship service in a hospital chapel,
remember; they weren't asking to go to a witches' coven in a
bosky dell! As I remember, it was the nurse—that Schrafft
woman, you've seen her around the place—who was the reason
for the request. She'd gotten interested in the Thursday night
meetings at Womanhouse, and some other women she knew . . .
her sister, I think, and some nurses, maybe some friends . . .
had gotten interested from hearing her talk about it, and they all
wanted to go to a service. But there was some problem about the
other women's husbands not being willing to let them travel over
here at night. I saw no harm in it . . . I told them sure, they could
go, as long as it wasn't more than once or twice a year."

"It must have been more than that, to have turned into a cult,
god damn it!"

"I looked into it," Jonathan answered steadily, "as soon as I read this. And our women have got nothing to do with it. I made absolutely sure. I'd told them twice a year, and twice a year is all it's been. They went that first time, and they went again for a Christmas service. They've gone twice a year since. But our *nurse*, now—that's another matter. She's been holding a service on her own every Thursday night, apparently, and that's what has turned into a cult. Our women aren't involved any more deeply anywhere than they are here; I put in a conference call to every one of the Heads, and they have the same report I have. Their women go to nearby hospitals for the services that the nurses sponsor, once, twice, maybe three times a year—always with permission—and that's it."

"But we get the blame, by christ!" Leo made another rude noise.

"Well, what do you expect?" Jonathan asked him. "Some innocent nurses go to a pissant Thursday prayer meeting in a Lingoe den, and suddenly they're 'sweeping the country' with an effing *cult!* Naturally we get the blame. Especially since Langlish got dragged into it. Let's not forget the crucial fact that it's Langlish—not the cult itself—that is the subject of this article."

"Oh lord . . . Langlish," moaned Conary. "That pathetic monstrous pile of tangled offal. . . ."

"Accurate," Jonathan agreed. "Precise."

"Can you imagine a—what is it, this liturgy? Prayers? Hymns?"

"It's their eternal translations of the King James Bible, according to the article. Recited aloud, mind you. *In chorus.*"

"Ah, shit," said Leo. "How could you for chrissake make anything usable out of that mess?"

The linguist men monitored Langlish routinely, as they monitored every activity their women were involved in. It had seventeen distinct verb tenses, each of which had to be assigned one of seventeen distinct verb aspects every time it was used. It had eleven separate noun declensions, without a single shared affix. It had enough stuff in it for a dozen ordinary languages, and a couple of dialects left over. It was a baroque travesty of what languages were really like, and it was exactly what you would expect a group of women to construct when left to fool around on their own without guidance. It was a disgrace, and if it hadn't always seemed like a harmless diversion it would have been squelched long ago. The idea of it spreading outside the Lines was not something that had ever crossed their minds.

Jonathan knew what they were thinking; it had been his first reaction, too. It had taken him a while to get past the kneejerk distaste he felt for the women's foolishness and see what really *mattered* here. He wanted them to see it, too, but he didn't want to have to spell it out for them; he wanted them to see it themselves. It was so damn funny, once you saw it. It was more than just funny; it was a wonderful, magnificent, splendid *hoax* being perpetrated on the public, and the fact that it was an accident took away very little of its charm.

"It *is* a mess," he agreed, carefully keeping his face bland and unaware. "That's the point. That's what this Waythard is talking about. Here's something that is ostensibly a real language—artificial, sure, but put together by honest to god linguists—and when you take a close look at it, it's a godawful mess. Okay, Waythard wants to know: since it doesn't mean a cursed thing, really, to the women who are saying it—I mean, they *think* they are saying a translation of the Twenty-third Psalm, but in reality you can't translate the Twenty-third Psalm or the Twenty-third Telephone Book or anything else into Langlish, so what they're really saying is equivalent to 'Sasparilla please and thank you ring a lady, O!' So, does this constitute normal religious language, he wants to know, or *ab*normal religious language? Or something else entirely?"

They were frowning at him, but they still weren't getting it; but then, they hadn't read the article.

"It's an interesting question," he went on, watching them. "It's not like glossolalia, speaking in tongues, because the nice nursies and their lady friends from the wide-eyed public *think* they know what they're saying. On the other hand, it doesn't really mean that, so it's like . . . Waythard suggests that it's a little like a cargo cult. You know. The great gods fall out of the sky and they say 'Have you people got a comset?' and you think that 'have you people got a comset' has religious significance because the great gods said it."

"But holy shit, Jonathan, this isn't the same thing at all. Our women didn't fall out of the sky, and the other women aren't savages—it's not the same."

"He doesn't claim it is; he's just hunting for something in the same ball park. But it doesn't matter how far off base he is. Perceive . . . you've got a ladies' Thursday night religious meeting. With guest speakers. Everything that goes on is mostly plain old ordinary Protestantism. *But it's in a ritual Langlish frame.* Now what *is* that, he asks? This is a very serious problem. This is maybe a dissertation topic. This is maybe a *symposium* topic. This is maybe the basis for a major *grant* proposal."

He felt the change, felt the loosening of the tension as it began to dawn on them, too, how funny it was.

"Oh, god," Leo said, almost whispering, "do you suppose the women did it on purpose?"

"I wish I could think so," Jonathan told him. "But I checked, remember? They genuinely have not been involved in this—they're as innocent as babes. And come on—they aren't capable of thinking up anything this elaborate, Leo. They've got no political savvy at all, and almost no sense of humor—it couldn't be deliberate. But think about it, will you? So it's an accident, a glorious miracle of an accident. So what? Does that make it any less beautiful?"

He could feel them, pondering the question. All over this country, lay women had fallen for this. There were actually women, coast to coast, prattling memorized chunks of Langlish, that unspeakable—literally—monstrosity that the women of the Lines had been fooling with for more than a century. And it had assumed enough significance within the public reality consensus to inspire an article by a real professor, in a real scholarly journal. . . .

The effect, when they finally got it, was everything he had hoped for. If there'd been any way a man could roll on the floor laughing without spoiling his Sunday suit, they'd have been polishing the tiles; as it was, they were roaring and wiping their eyes, and that drew more of the men over, demanding to be let in on the joke. Before it was over Jonathan had a good crowd, and an enthusiastic one.

They were all in agreement; this was much too good to waste. It was a good thing, they decided, that the women had done it by accident, because this way you didn't have to take it away from them—they didn't know there was anything to *be* taken away, and that simplified matters. There wasn't much time left before church, but they managed to map out a rough strategy, all talking at once, shouting one another down.

The first step would be a letter of comment to the *Journal of American Religious Ethnomethodology*, responding to Waythard's article. Something truly incomprehensible, but so full of linguistics jargon that the editors wouldn't dare not print it. And then some responses to that from other linguists at other Households, working it up back and forth, until they suckered in a few professors. Papers on the subject at some annual conferences—parodies from the men of the Lines, naturally, and serious efforts from the real academics, who would never catch on to the parodies—that would come next. Leaks to the media . . . Leo knew somebody at Shawnessey Household in Switzerland who was tops at media-leak techniques.

It was going to be one hell of a lot of fun, and Jonathan saw no reason why they couldn't get two or three years out of it before they withdrew and left the scholars to discover that they'd been sandbagged. Maybe they'd get a little comset newspape going, pull in a few distinguished whatsits to serve on its editorial board . . . leave them sitting there with their asses waving in the wind when All Was Made Clear. God, it was beautiful. And it was only a matter of constructing perfect questions, that the academics would be unable to resist answering. Child's play.

"One day," Jonathan proposed as they were trying to get out the door fast enough not to be late for church, "we are going to have to do something nice for the women, to pay them back for this."

"A fountain," Conary suggested. "They're always wanting a fountain, for the racket. We could put a brass plaque on it: 'In Honor of Langlish.' " That set them off again, till they had to lean on the walls of the atrium for support while they laughed, and then they *really* had to hurry. The slidewalk was almost empty, a sure sign that the church was already full and the service about to start. The last thing they needed was for the men of the Lines, in a group, to come marching into church in the middle of the opening prayer or some such shit. Dignity didn't allow them to actually run, not in their Sunday suits and with no obvious fire or flood or maiden-in-peril as an excuse, but they moved it up to the briskest walk that was plausible, and thought grim thoughts to restore some semblance of order to their faces before they had to meet the public view.

"What about if we—" somebody began, ten yards from the church door.

"Shut up," Jonathan ordered. "Don't even think about it. Think *reverence*. Think *damnation*. Think *original sin*. The mode, gentlemen, is *grim*—keep that thought firmly in your mind, and follow me."

II

The Annual Caucus of the Encoding Project, which the women referred to among themselves as the Annual Circus, had been superfluous for at least fifty years. The task of the Encoding Project—to secretly construct the woman-language Láadan, using the ridiculous Langlish as a dummy inside which Láadan could be hidden—had been finished generations ago. But the women of the Lines could not have been made even to hint at that, not if you'd used thumbscrews. The only way they were able to obtain this one weekend in each year when women from all the linguist Households were allowed to travel to a single hotel, with no men other than the legally required escorts during the actual travel period, and to then be left in peace for the entire weekend without male supervision or constant interruption, was by the firm pretense that the Encoding Project still existed. There was a century of tradition behind the Caucus; permission for it had been granted at a time when the linguists were less busy than they were today, and at a time before the construction of the Womanhouses, when the men welcomed an excuse to get rid of all the women for a weekend. To forbid it now would be like canceling Christmas, or the Fourth of July—a shocking break with the established customs. But if the women were to give it up voluntarily, it would be the end of their precious respite from the normal routine—there was not the slimmest prayer of a chance that the men would let them substitute a similar meeting for some different purpose. They couldn't spare the women now, not even for forty-eight hours, and nothing but tradition was protecting the disgraceful waste of time that the Caucus represented in the male eyes. They grumbled, letting it go on but fighting it from all directions, managing in the weekend hours involved to create vast messes that obliged all the women to go on double and triple untangling shifts on their return. The women ignored this guerrilla tactic, it being normal male behavior and entirely to be expected; it was a small price to pay for the two blissful days of conference time.

However, keeping the men convinced that nothing had changed meant that a large bustling decoy conference had to be set up every year and run by the conference committee. With programming tracks. With panels and lectures and discussion groups and a banquet. With keynote speakers and workshops and plenary sessions and opening and closing ceremonies. All the trappings of a genuine old-fashioned conference, done well enough to fool even the expert male eye.

It had not been easy. And it had been Nazareth who saved their skins, once again, when things had become not just difficult but desperate. They had revised Langlish and reformed it and reworked it until they'd run out of ideas. Human languages only offer a set of about seventy meaningful sounds to choose from; there are a multitude of possible noises, but only a finite number actually usable for linguistic purposes. And they were *linguist*

women; their men would not have been fooled by a proposal that
Langlish be revised to consist only of consonants, or any one of
a number of other theoretically possible but pragmatically ridiculous alternatives. There are only six possible word orders that the
elements subject/verb/object can take in a human language, and
only a small number of mechanisms for indicating which is
which; when you've exhausted all of those, what do you do
next? For the women to be absurd was allowed, because it was
expected; but if they had tried behaving like women ignorant of
the characteristics of real languages, the men would instantly
have been suspicious. It was a fine and perilous line to have to
walk, and the necessity for continual changes within a web of
absurdities made it very hard to keep track of what they were
doing, much less what had already been done.

The year the women had tried proposing that subject be indicated in Langlish by simply *repeating* it had been the year they
almost lost the Caucus. That had caught some man's eye as he
was looking over the conference transcripts or watching the
tapes, and suddenly he had paid attention instead of just skim-
ming. Two hours later there'd been a woodshedder at Hashihawa
Household, with three senior males calling in a half dozen of
their women to discuss the matter.

"Let's see now . . . if we compare this to Panglish, and we
consider a simple sentence such as 'the men canceled the annual
Caucus' and we use this new rule, all of the following will be
grammatical, right?" they'd begun. " 'The men the men canceled the Caucus.' 'Canceled the Caucus the men the men.' 'The
Caucus canceled the men the men.' 'Canceled the men the men
the Caucus.' 'The Caucus the men the men canceled.' Have we
got that straight?"

And there had been menace in their eyes. *Are you trying to be
funny?* their eyes had demanded.

"So, we could have a sentence like this one: 'The women who
had abundantly demonstrated that they hadn't the faintest idea
what they were doing and were only behaving like idiots the
women who had abundantly demonstrated that they hadn't the faintest idea what they were doing and were only behaving like idiots
regretted it.' Is that right, ladies? We are expected to seriously
believe that this proposal took two hours' time? For women of the
Lines? *Trained linguists?* And that it was *passed?*"

The Hashihawa women, badly scared, had introduced on the
spot two subrules limiting the length of the duplicated subject
noun phrase and specifying that any subject longer than three
words would require the repetition of only its final three words.

And had explained courteously that the subrules had—with inexcusable sloppiness—simply been taken for granted by the women, which accounted for their absence from the tapes and transcripts. And had maintained staunch innocence while the men, obviously suspicious and justifiably so, set up one trick question after another. Requiring mental gymnastics that would have been a challenge even if the proposal had been *real,* so that a background of data and discussion would have existed for them to use as a basis for those gymnastics.

It had been awful, and a very near thing. They had managed to leave the men convinced that this was no more than typical female nonsense and excess, not worth worrying about no matter how deplorable in terms of wasted time. But they would be watching more carefully from then on; the women had slipped badly, and had drawn attention to themselves. Something new had to be done, or they would lose it all.

Nazareth's solution had provided the men with material for months of jokes at the women's expense, but it had solved the problem. Certainly, if you were developing a language to express the perceptions of women, and had brought it along to a point where it was at last roughly stable, you would want to find those last weak spots in its structure and vocabulary that needed shoring up and adjusting. And what better diagnostic probe could there be for finding areas where the perceptions of women were difficult to express than the monumentally male King James Bible, in the old unrevised version? With its kings and masters and battles and rods and staffs and foreskins and so on? The men had agreed with that judgment, struggling to appear at least minimally serious; they had choked their laughter back long enough to agree that if there were areas of Langlish not yet adequate for expressing women's perceptions, translating the King James Bible into the language would unquestionably locate those areas.

"The *whole* King James? *All of it?*" the men had demanded, half strangling. "You're proposing to translate the whole goddamn *thing* into Langlish?" And the women had assured them that only the whole thing would suffice, and that it was expected that it would take quite some time.

"Oh my god, I should think *so!*" the men had moaned, giving up the attempt at courteous consideration, pounding one another on the back and roaring with laughter, and the Caucus had been safe for another century. Nazareth had dutifully submitted to the men a conference resolution in which it was unanimously agreed that the Langlish word for *Langlish* should be *Láadan;* for the women, this would mean an end at last to always having to guard their speech against an accidental saying of that word. The men had been unsurprised, and had declared themselves ready to be presented any day now with the Láadan name for Langlish, agreed upon unanimously by the women at the Caucus in plenary session. By acclamation, perhaps.

"I think if we were to do that," Nazareth had said, frowning a little, "there would be a demand for a roll call vote." And then she had sat smiling vaguely through the usual incantations about the impossibility of ever understanding women, quite content.

When Nazareth had first suggested the plan, a horrified woman from Verdi Household, already worn out with the lengthy discussion that had come before, had cried, "But Nazareth! The King James! You could spend hours on a single verse, Nazareth—it will take *forever!*"

"I do hope so," Nazareth answered, her hands folded quietly in her lap and her eyes downcast to hide their expression. "I certainly do hope so."

And hours *had* been spent on single verses, ever since. It had been impressed upon the men that the women could not possibly be comfortable with a translated verse, be it ever so flawless in its grammar and ever so magnificent in its style, if they had to worry that the translation had somehow caused a theological wrinkle; this required endless multiple sessions. *Women,* groaned the men, *and their pathological religiosity!* And the women admitted it, and expressed their regret, and were told that no one held it against women if they behaved in a way characteristic of women. The women had been properly grateful for the understanding the men showed of the matter, and for their forebearance; and they had been properly grateful to Nazareth Chornyak Adiness for preserving their Caucus, perhaps unto the very end of time. All those begats. . . .

CHAPTER 13

"The human brain has a hard time handling sentences when they're embedded inside one another. We can manage 'The man the woman spoke to left the room' without much trouble; that's just one embedding. But make that 'The man the woman the child kissed spoke to left the room' and our minds begin to gasp for clarification. And with each additional sentence embedded inside a sentence embedded inside a sentence it gets more impossible to understand. Now that's a handy thing to know, because it has applications well beyond the construction of sentences.

"I knew that a single plan, standing all alone, was sure to be noticed and interfered with eventually by those who had the power to interfere, no matter how carefully it was camouflaged. But suppose you took the plan that really mattered, and you embedded it inside a plan that was embedded inside a plan that was itself embedded inside a plan? And suppose you made each of the other plans as you worked your way out toward the edges less and less worth interfering with?

"It was obvious to me that there could be no better way of protecting the real plan from all harm; and that the more useless layers of planning there were to be stripped away before you got to the real plan, the better. Furthermore, the more frivolous the plans on the outside seemed to be, the more the whole structure would look like something that was more trouble to interfere with than it was worth. It took a certain amount of ingenuity to keep it all going, and a tremendous amount of help from other women. Sometimes I wish I had not had to burden them so heavily; other times, I am sure they welcomed the burden because it represented doing *something, taking action instead of just sitting around and letting things happen. But I have never yet had any reason to regret making this my method of choice. . . ."*

(from the diaries of Nazareth Chornyak Adiness)

176

*   *   *

Father Dorien Pelure sat at the head of the long table; he was
well aware of the dramatic note provided by the rays of late
afternoon sunlight falling through the narrow window behind his
head, and he was taking full advantage of it. It was the sort of
thing that appealed to the uncomplicated minds of women, and
Dorien never overlooked any such detail. During his first year as
Abbot here he had kept a scrupulous calendar, noting precisely
where that ray of light fell throughout each and every day for the
entire year, so that he could schedule his appointments accord-
ingly. He had moved the table, and moved the chair, checking
and rechecking in a large mirror set before him, until he knew
the one perfect spot for them in terms of putting the light to use,
and he had put tiny dots of permanent black on the floor to mark
where each leg should go. So that there could be no mistake. He
did nothing carelessly.

The meeting with Fathers Claude and Agar had been set for
three o'clock, while the light was golden and hearty and clear;
then he had scheduled Sister Miriam to join them at four sharp,
when the slant of light would make it seem that he had first the
finger of the Holy Spirit at his shoulder and then, as the minutes
went by, an unmistakable halo round his head. It would impress
the sister, and amuse the other priests.

They had been severe with him. As they properly should have
been. Forty-five minutes of interrogation. Was he absolutely
positive that *this* nun was the right one? She was still young—
could he be sure she had the necessary firmness of purpose? The
ability to deal uncompromisingly with women older and more
experienced than herself, and to keep them properly in submission? Was he certain of her dedication? Of her devotion? Of her
virtuousness? And even if he was, was he certain of her intelligence, due allowance being made for her gender? Had she the
proper skill of voice? Was she pleasant looking, but not beautiful, since beauty would make her task more difficult, causing the
women she supervised to be jealous of her? Was she sufficiently
learned? And so on, and so on. He had answered all the questions patiently, knowing they were wholly appropriate, and had
let them wear themselves out and fall silent for lack of anything
else to ask.

"You will be satisfied with her, I promise you," he told
them then. "I've chosen her very carefully—she is exactly
right."

"I still wish," fretted Father Agar, him of the cavernous

cheeks and temples and the incongruous little pot belly straining against his robes, "that the task could have been given to a *priest*. I would feel so much more secure, so much more confident, if a man's strong hands were at the helm of this project!"

Father Dorien nodded, and shrugged his elegant shoulders, but he said nothing; they had been over this again and again, and there was no point in doing it yet one more time. A man could not do what must be done; it had to be a woman. He reassured them again: "You will be satisfied with her." And then he lifted the heavy silver bell and rang it three times—once for the Father, once for the Son, once for the Holy Spirit—to call Sister Miriam Rose, of the convent of Saint Gertrude of the Lambs, into the room.

The door opened soundlessly and closed the same way, and the nun stood in front of it, her hands properly hidden away in the sleeves of her habit, her eyes cast down, her face serene, waiting. The priests stared at her, noting that she was tall for a woman, and too thin; unlike Father Agar, she had no round belly spoiling her Gothic lines. Her hair was hidden entirely by the wimple and coif, but the black of her lashes and the clear ivory of her skin hinted that the hair was also black; the perfect oval of her face was the classic oval of the traditional Madonna. Father Dorien knew what the others were thinking—that he had misled them, that this woman was too beautiful to work successfully in the supervision of other women, that he had made a mistake.

"Good afternoon, Sister Miriam," he greeted her, tilting his head just the slightest fraction so that the halo would backlight him but not blur her sight. "You may speak to us now."

She raised her eyes first—they were a brilliant dark blue, almost a violet—and then her chin, so that she stood absolutely straight before them. None of the hunching into herself that was so often a problem with these religious.

"Good afternoon, Fathers," she answered. "I am here as you instructed me; please tell me how I may serve you."

Father Dorien kept his face expressionless, but he risked a swift side glance at his colleagues. Ah yes . . . they were both leaning toward the nun with their lips parted and their eyes alert, and they had forgotten all their reservations. It was the woman's magnificent voice. A voice that Father Dorien was confident had been given to her by God, specifically to enable her to serve his purposes in this project. As he had anticipated, she had only had to speak one sentence to put an end to their objections. He had heard that voice many hundreds of times, because he was her confessor, but it never ceased to be something he marveled over.

It was not just a voice, it was a musical instrument, and she was a virtuoso in its use.

"Be seated, please, Sister," said Dorien. "We will need you here quite some time; we do not wish you to stand." No doubt both Claude and Agar would have a good deal to say to him about that later; it was not customary to allow a nun to sit in the presence of priests, no matter how long the time, unless she was ill, or aged, or an Abbess. Sister Miriam was none of those, and caution about setting precedents is forever necessary with female religious. Anything a priest does risks being dubbed a tradition; let him do it twice, and the term will be "hallowed tradition." It required constant vigilance.

But Dorien knew this woman, and he knew what he was about. If they'd sat there and talked to her, and listened to her answers, the combination of her voice and her height would have emasculated Claude and Agar, and he was by no means sure he was himself immune; before it was over, they would have been hanging on *her* every word, looking up at *her* with respectful attention . . . it wouldn't have done at all. And so he had made provisons in advance. The seat he directed her to with a gracious flicker of his hand was a low wooden stool. She would not be particularly comfortable, she would lose the advantage of her height, and she would be obliged either to tilt her head up to look at the priests or to keep her eyes modestly lowered. It was just the thing, and Fathers Agar and Claude could be glad they'd had his prior knowledge to safeguard them.

"You may speak, Sister," he added.

"It is my privilege to obey," she murmured, correct in every way, and she took her place on the low stool and waited for them to tell her what they wanted of her, her eyes safely on her feet.

"Sister Miriam," said Father Dorien gravely, "we call you here today to give you a holy charge—a mission for the Church and for the glory of God. We charge you to keep secret, even unto death, every word that we say to you here this day, and we ask your pledge in the name of the Blessed Virgin. You may speak."

"I swear," answered Sister Miriam, without raising her eyes, "in the name of the Blessed Virgin, Holy Mother of God, that I will guard the secret of this meeting and the words spoken here today, even unto death. It is my privilege to obey."

Dorien looked at his two brother priests, with raised eyebrows, posing the question. *Well? Will she do?* It was a silent question, but clear, and they nodded. So far, so good; a dutiful religious, seemingly well suited for a difficult job. Despite her irritating attractiveness, about which perhaps something could be done.

"Sister Miriam," Father Dorien went on, "we are about to speak to you of a perversion of faith—it may be, although we cannot yet be sure, an actual heresy. Let your mind be pure, whatever your ears must hear, Sister; guard your soul. You may speak."

"It is my privilege to obey," she said.

"You will have heard, even within the convent, the gossip about the religious fad that has been spreading across the country— the so-called 'Thursday Night Devotionals' movement originating in the houses of the linguists. Specifically, in the dwellings of their women. It's like any fad—its hold on the female masses is fierce right now, but it will not last long. We applaud the wisdom of our Protestant colleagues in making no move to interfere; they are right that the more freely the flame is allowed to burn, the more swiftly it burns itself out. However, with the usual naiveté of Protestants, they are missing a number of important points. We do not propose to miss those points." He paused, and made a gesture of permission; then he realized that with her eyes downcast she couldn't have seen it, and he added, "You may speak."

"I am listening, Father. It is my privilege."

"Sister Miriam, look at me," he directed, and admired the grace with which she obeyed. "I will tell you what our Protestant brothers, in their carelessness, have overlooked. Listen most carefully; again, guard your soul! You may speak."

"It is my privilege to obey," she murmured.

"First," he stated, "only shameful theological ignorance would let this fervor be *wasted*; one does not let such opportunities pass. Since the Protestants have no interest in gathering in these souls in the service of their churches while the women are still in the grip of the fashion, we will be only too happy to do that for Holy Mother Church. You will begin that task for us, Sister Miriam. These women are meeting all over the country, always in the chapels of hospitals or in private homes; they have chosen Thursday nights for their effusions, and that's very convenient. It is a proper fad, Sister. Uniform to a fault. Always in chapels; always on Thursday nights. Very easily managed. You will attend some of these meetings locally, Sister, to become familiar with their form. You may speak."

"It is my privilege to obey."

Do they ever find it monotonous, saying that, he wondered?

He supposed they did it so automatically they weren't even aware of it, after a while. Unfortunate that it wasn't a *single* word.

"Then in about two weeks," he went on, "you will be sent to a retreat house in the Ozark hills, where nuns from all over the world will join you at the direction of the Church. You will shape these nuns—who have been carefully selected, Sister, for this role—as a holy task force; you will of course have a priest in residence nearby to assist you. The sisters are to go back to their convents at the end of their session with you and attend all the Thursday Night Devotionals held in their areas—as many as possible. Your function and theirs is to seize this sudden religious fervor, passing fad though it may be, and win it for Holy Mother Church. We can make good use of that fervor, and we are confident that you and the other nuns will be able to devise ways to keep it *from* burning itself out. It's a matter of timing; it is a force without direction or control, that must be caught and turned while it is at its most powerful. You will simply use its momentum for the purposes of the Church."

He saw the frown, and knew he had been meant to see it; he gave her permission to speak.

"How are we to reach these women, Father Dorien?" she asked. "What role do we have in their gatherings? I don't understand how it is to be done."

"No problem at all," he reassured her. "You, and the other nuns as well, will be sent to these meetings as guest speakers. The ladies positively dote on guest speakers, the more exotic the better. You'll tell them what it's like to be a nun, which is what they are curious about, and that will give you an opening. Remember that to Protestant females a nun is as mysterious and exotic as an Oriental harem dancer, inappropriate though it may be; answer their questions, spin them some tales, charm them. And then you will be able to ask them to tell *you* about their liturgy."

Her eyes widened in courteous inquiry, and Father Agar, whose specialty was religious language, interrupted the dialogue to add his part.

"My dear Sister," he said, chirping at her, "it appears that these linguist women have, over the course of the past hundred years or so . . . astonishing! . . . constructed a language. As a *hobby! Isn't* that astonishing, Sister? They call it 'Langlish,' also 'Láadan,' and of course I've no idea why two names are needed for one language . . . it seems like a great deal of bother . . . and they have been translating portions of the old King James

Bible into the stuff and reciting them aloud at their Thursday
night chapel services. The men of the Lines—you do know,
Sister, that the families of linguists are called *the Lines?* Yes, I
see you do. Well, the men of the Lines have allowed them to do
this, which I am not at all sure was a good idea; on the other
hand, I can see that for women who are themselves linguists the
construction of an artificial language is perhaps an appropriate
pastime. Still . . . still, this is where you and the other dear
sisters will be able to gain a foothold, win hearts. If you show an
interest in their precious Langlish, they'll take you to their
bosoms at once. Figuratively speaking. At *once.*''

"And it is in this 'Langlish,' Sister,'' said Father Claude,
raising a cautioning index finger, ''that we suspect there may be
heresy. Despite the way it fascinates Father Agar.''

"We are in fact almost sure,'' put in Father Dorien quickly,
"that there is heresy there. This language, whatever its name, is
said to be—'' He looked down at the notes he had prepared, and
read aloud exactly what had been said to him by the pleasant
woman he had queried on the matter. ''—is said to be 'a language
constructed by women in order to express the perceptions of
women.' ''

"We don't have any samples,'' said Father Agar, unable to
resist interrupting again. ''We've asked for them, of course, and
have been told with the most *charming* courtesy that nothing is
available that would be interesting to us, that the ladies would be
embarrassed to have us see their poor amateurish efforts, and so
on. All just so much persiflage, of course, and don't think we
can't spot it, but they were . . . well, perhaps clever is the word.
It's clear that they have no intention of letting us examine the
material. And since not a single one of the Lines is Catholic, we
could compel them to show it to us only by going to the *men* of
the Lines and asking that they have it sent. We could do that
easily enough . . . it's no problem to pretend an anthropological
interest of some kind and send a seminarian along, and I must
tell you that some of the correspondence the linguists have been
sending to the theological journals on the subject is *extremely*
interesting, if a bit hard to follow. But we prefer not to call the
men's attention to the fact that we are interested. You will not
understand that, Sister—I will explain. If they should suspect
that the Church has an interest in their females, they not only
will not allow you nuns to attend the meetings, they will send in
a regiment of Protestant Bible-thumpers in your place to make
certain that their women toe the line! And those Bible-thumpers
will wonder why we are interested, and they will begin to see

what we had in mind, and we will lose all those souls, with their delightful fervor. We do not wish to do that, you see; we wish to win those women—and through them, their men—and in the fullness of time, the Lines and all their power. You may speak, Sister."

Father Dorien had long since fixed his eyes on the ceiling, praying for patience, and Father Claude was glowering at Agar as if he were about to hit him, but Sister Miriam showed no trace of irritation at the rambling monologue. "Thank you, Father Agar," she said placidly. "I believe I understand; thank you for the explanation."

They were talking around and around the delicate issue, because all of the men found it distasteful even to think about it, much less speak of it. Worst of all was the need to talk about it to a woman. Father Dorien could see that they might go on in this way for hours . . . Agar was given to the impromptu speech form, particularly when he was handed a topic that he found so alluring; Claude was less so, but would inevitably feel compelled to pontificate in competition with Agar. Father Dorien, on the other hand, wanted his dinner. Much better, he decided, just to speak up about it himself and get it over with, forestalling the orations. It was natural that the other priests, who did not know Miriam, would feel inhibited with her.

He broke in abruptly, without any preamble to spare her feelings or those of the priests. "What we suspect, Sister Miriam," he said, while Claude and Agar assumed expressions of elaborate indifference, "is that somewhere in these Langlish/Láadan materials you will find mention of a goddess rather than of God. I apologize for being so blunt, but that *is* what we suspect. A score of little things . . . a simple consideration of where 'a language to express the perceptions of women' might be expected to lead, if nothing more. We may be quite wrong, Sister. It may be that in suspecting the substitution of a goddess we are only expressing the perceptions of *men*—it may be something we don't suspect at all. But we suspect the seeds of an attempt at a 'feminist' religion once again, goddess or no goddess. If we are right, that is heresy; if they are practicing it openly, in these rituals, it is blasphemy and unspeakable perversion. A great danger, Sister—a great danger, and something that must be stamped out. We want you to find out for us, and to have the nuns helping you find out for us. You will come back here and tell us what you have found, and if the women are innocent we will praise God for that and ask forgiveness for our over-active imaginations. You may speak, Sister."

"What if you are right, Father?" she asked. "Then what?"

"Then you will stamp out the heresy," he declared, repeating the words with deliberate vehemence. "With our help. With all of the resources of the Church that you may find needful to do so. And we will gently turn that heresy around, and change it ever so carefully—we will cause it to become devotion to the Virgin Mary. That is always the best way to deal with these female flareups, whenever they occur. We will shelter these imperiled souls beneath the skirts of the Blessed Mother, where they will be safe from harm. Do you understand, Sister?" It occurred to him, too late, that his metaphor had been badly chosen; it had occurred to Claude and Agar, too. They looked shocked. "You may speak," he said hurriedly. And then, to their surprise, he added, "I apologize for my clumsy figure of speech, Sister Miriam—it's a traditional figure, but grossly out of place in this situation. As I said, you may speak."

She was nodding, the smallest hint of a nod; and because he knew her innermost thoughts as only a confessor can know them, he was reasonably sure he knew what she was thinking. She was thinking that they were hoping she *would* find the suspected heresy. And she was right, in a very limited way; a perverted leaning toward goddess worship was always a fertile source of souls, first through the innocent devotion to Mary and then on past that into true and wholesome worship of the Lord and of His Son. It was one of the most reliable of all conversion mechanisms, reaching back into the most ancient times. It presented a challenge, and the Fathers were too human not to welcome a challenge. But Miriam said nothing of her thoughts, and the expression on her face would not have betrayed her to anyone except him.

"I understand, Father," she said calmly. "It is my privilege to obey."

He looked straight at her, and she dropped her eyes immediately; in that privacy, he looked inquiringly at the other two priests. As he had expected, they signaled their full approval. She was exactly what was needed. And that was very good; he could save a great deal of time now, not having the nuisance of interviewing other nuns for the post, and he could work quickly with Miriam; she was intelligent and cooperative, and he understood her completely.

"Sister Miriam," he said, pulling a small case from the pocket of his robe, "unless you have questions you wish to discuss with us, we don't need to keep you any longer. You will find full instructions on the microfiche in this case, as well as all

the relevant background information. Instructions have been given
to your Abbess; she is to cooperate with you in every way. She
will be informed that as of this date you are released from all
other duties except those of worship. You'll find all the details
on the fiche. *Do* you have questions, Miriam? You may speak."

"No, Father. Not at this time. It's all quite clear."

"You do understand the importance of your mission? You
may speak."

She did not look up, and she said only, "I do understand,
Father. And it is my privilege, as ever, to obey."

She remained where she was, her eyes still down, until she
was directed to stand. And then she stood motionless while the
priests filed from the room, without a word.

CHAPTER
14

"Had a dog and her name was Quark,
had a dog and her name was Quark!
Had a dog and her name was Quark—
she ran faster than light, had a four-part bark!
Hey, Quark . . . lemme hear you bark!"

"Spacewarp travel on an average day (three times),
meet ol' Quark goin' back the other way!
Hey, Quark . . . lemme hear you bark!"

"Quark knew e equals mc squared (three times),
mighta made a difference if Quark had cared!
Hey, Quark . . . lemme hear you bark!"

"Quark chased every relativity spike (three times),
never met a constant she didn't like!
Hey, Quark . . . lemme hear you bark!"

"When Quark died it was somethin' to see (three times),
she went nova in four-part harmony . . .
Hey, Quark . . . lemme hear you bark!"

(folksong, set to traditional tune, "Had
a Dog and His Name Was Blue")

He was a career man. His navy-blue denim jumpsuit, with the
full legs correctly cinched tight at the ankles, demonstrated that.
So did the eyeglasses with their black horn-rims, which he
needed not at all, nearsightedness being one of that small set of
things that the med-Sammys could actually cure, but which he
wore as dutifully as he wore his discreetly stylish AT&T wrist
computer; he would have felt naked without either, and in fact

186

removed them only when making love. His wig was of the best quality, and had a fine pepper-and-salt coloring that he knew gave him a look of distinction he might otherwise have had trouble achieving; the wig had cost more than all the rest of his outfit put together, but had been worth every last credit. It had been hard enough getting to his present post when his wife's uncle was an eggdome, without being condemned in advance by his own prematurely bald scalp . . . it seemed to him sometimes, although he would not have admitted it because he knew he could not defend it logically, that it was his wife's fault that he'd lost every last hair on his head before his thirtieth birthday. As if she'd brought a taint with her that had destroyed the very roots of his hair; to balance the obvious *benefits* she'd brought with her. He was looking forward to the money that Uncle George was leaving to Brenda, and when he lost his hair he'd been able to stop feeling guilty about having married her only for that reason. His hair had been surrendered in exchange for that money, that was how he felt; and it had been worth more than that to him.

He didn't like the assignment he was carrying out today. It made him nervous just to look out through the transparent walls of the building that housed the Cetacean Project, and he appreciated the docking tube that had allowed him to step straight from his flyer into its air-conditioned comfort. That people had once actually lived out there in that wasteland inferno was a matter of historical record; there had been a town there, called El Centro, with houses and schools and churches . . . there had even, so said the history books, been a college. But Paul couldn't imagine it. He couldn't even begin to imagine that human beings no different from himself could have voluntarily condemned themselves to live in such conditions and survived it. There was nothing *out* there . . . nothing but some kind of pale brown bushes that looked completely fried, and the shimmering heatwaves, and a collection of cacti and boulders that had been carefully arranged by the landscapers—who had had to *work* out there, he realized with a shudder—to lead the eye past the desolation toward the line of mountains on the horizon. Paul didn't find *them* a comfort either; they were just piles of bare desolate rock. No doubt they provided a spectacular effect at sunset, but he didn't plan to still be here at sunset.

He hurried past the tourists (all three of them) who were gawking at the whales swimming round and round in their tank of sparkling blue water and the solemn baby watching them swim; he took the elevator down one level, transferred to the

service elevator marked "No Admittance—Employees Only,"
and went down one level more. Hating it all the way.

Nothing could have brought home to him more forcefully how
different eggdomes were from normal people than his knowledge
that the Cetacean Project scientists not only worked down here in
the bowels of nowhere but actually *lived* down here as well,
because of the highly classified nature of their work; he'd been
told that some of them had not been topside even for earned leave
in as long as three years.

"How can they *do* that?" he'd demanded, horrified. "There's
not enough money in the effing universe to pay a man to do
that!" And the guy who'd told him had shrugged and said
something about eggdomes being almost as weird as Lingoes.
Which was probably true. But there was a difference. He hated
the eggdomes, but they didn't make him queasy the way the
Lingoes did. He could have put up with his sister marrying an
eggdome— hell, didn't he have an eggdome for an uncle by
marriage, and a pretty nice guy he was, too?—but if he'd
thought she was going to marry a Lingoe he'd have had her
institutionalized without a second thought. If he'd had a sister.
According to Brenda, the day was coming when his prejudice
was going to cause him trouble; she claimed that since they'd
begun putting normal human babies into the Interfaces along
with the Lingoe cubs, the Lingoes were beginning to be looked
at differently.

"You're going to have to give up being so bigoted about
them," she'd said, licking trankdust off her fingers and grinning
at him the way she always did when she thought she was hitting
a nerve. "You're going to find them right beside you everywhere you go, and you're going to have to just forget that they
turn your stomach, and socialize with them. You'll see. I may
not get out of this house much, but I keep up with what's
happening. And that's what's happening."

Paul had given her his coldest stare, and told her to please
remember that he'd *always* had Lingoes all around him. Any
federal employee had to get used to that. The Lingoes were part
of the working environment, and you had to be polite to them.
But everybody knew it was an act, including the Lingoes. And
that wasn't going to change any, even if some people's kids had
to spend a little time with Lingoe cubs as a way of gradually
taking over the linguistics business.

"I admire those people," he'd told Brenda. "I admire their
guts. I couldn't do it."

"What people? Do what?" Brenda, and her tiny brain.

"Well, it's one thing to do something like that your own self—that's different. But to send one of your kids? That takes a kind of moral fiber I haven't got, I can tell you. You know what it makes me think of? You remember the history tapes where the little black kids walked into the schools between rows of policemen with dogs, and white people spitting and screaming and throwing stuff at them . . . rotten eggs, rocks . . . you remember that?"

"No, I don't. And I don't believe it ever happened."

"It happened, Brenda. More than once, it happened."

"I don't believe it, Paul." Stubborn. "Not in *this* country."

Paul had given up immediately, because any other decision was a waste of time. His wife's ignorance was impenetrable, and that suited him just fine. She was a hell of a lot easier to keep in line than the wives of some of his friends, who'd had more education than was good for them. He hadn't pressed the point; but it was a very real point to him. He'd always thought that maybe he could have walked up those school steps through all that hatred himself, but that he never could have found the guts to send a child of his own. He would have said: send somebody else's kid, not mine. Somebody's kids had to be the ones, in a time so barbaric that people based their estimate and treatment of others on skin color. . . . Jesus! It was like hearing that your ancestors were cannibals; no wonder Brenda had blanked it out. But he felt that way about the babies going into the Lingoe Interfaces—somebody else's kid, not mine, that was how he felt about it.

He'd heard a rumor around D.A.T. that Carl Crewvel's wife Nedralyn had actually been going to private religious club meetings that were connected in some way with bitch Lingoes; he hoped it wasn't true, because Carl was a good man, and he liked him. That kind of thing could ruin a man. Sure, you had to let them into the public churches, this was a free country, but that was a long way from what sounded like joining a Lingoe *cult*. Jesus.

He'd been watching the numbers on the doors he passed, absently; they were coded, but he'd dealt with coded numbers so long that he wasn't conscious of them any longer. This one said "Radiated Legume Storage—Caution" and under that "Do Not Enter Without Permission From the Officer of the Day." That'd be it. Room 09-A, where the meeting was scheduled. He was supposed to go right in, and that made him jittery . . . you walk right through a door inside a top secret project like this, you could get your brain fried like those bushes outside in the desert. But he'd been assured that all alarms were turned off and that all servomechanisms except the ordinary cleanup ones had been deactivated for this occasion.

"Yeah," he thought aloud. "And my Aunt Tildy flies a Greyhound Rocket. Sure."

Still, Paul was accustomed to following orders, and he followed them now. He put his hand on the door, palm flat on the lock, and pressed gingerly, and when it slid smoothly aside for him he walked straight on into the room with the hair on his neck prickling and his heart pounding out "The Stars and Stripes Forever" in his chest. The guard that stopped him two feet inside the door was a human being, and that helped a little; he laid his fingertips on the portable ID-platter the soldier held and saw the blue light flash just like it was supposed to, and that was even better. "Take your seat at the table, please, sir," said the guard, respectfully.

Paul straightened his tie—a double one, and a little daring, but he felt like he needed *something* to serve as a personal fashion statement, and the tie was just enough, and wouldn't offend anybody—and went to take his seat with the rest of the men. He was the last one to arrive, apparently; but then he was the only one who'd had to come all the way from the opposite coast. And they couldn't start without him.

There were the usual introductory moves. The man in charge was a general . . . Paul wondered what he had done to get stuck out here. There were three eggdomes, whose names he paid no attention to; you just called them all Professor, the way you called all med-Sammys Doctor, and that saved a lot of effort and energy. There was an underling named Tatum Jorgen Pugh, some kind of computer specialist; according to Paul's briefing fiche, Pugh's father had also worked here. A family tradition? You'd think the father would have seen to it that his kid had it a little better than he'd had it, but there was no accounting for computer people. Paul had a wary respect for them, but he didn't pretend to understand them. He respected the money they made, and when he needed one to do something for him he respected the incredible speed with which it always got done. He gave this Pugh a polite nod to let him know that he recognized another team player when he saw one, and then he bowed his head politely for the invocation and the national anthem. Both supplied on tape, which was another good sign. Paul was always uneasy when a live chaplain was on deck for government meetings. It meant you had to spend half your time tiptoeing around the edges of everything, trying to avoid the Ethics Bog, and it meant you had to talk like a Wimpoe. Nothing stronger than

"Golly" in front of a federal chaplain. The tape was much more efficient.

"*Okay!*" he said briskly, once the formalities were over. "I know you've got a lot of work to do, and I know I have—I've got another meeting back at D.A.T. at exactly sixteen hundred hours. I'd like to simply lay out the department's position for you, without any interruption, if you don't mind, and then I'll welcome your comments." He looked at the general to see if any objections were headed his way, and saw none. Good. No chaplain. No objections. Batting nine-ninety-nine so far.

"Now as I understand it," he continued, "you're doing a hell of a lot of fine work at this installation, but you're not getting much of a return. No criticism implied, gentlemen—we know what you're up against—but we're getting to the end of our string here where funding is concerned, if you know what I mean. According to the reports I've seen, you have just about done everything there is to do in the way of altering the brains of the tubie infants you've got here—" He noticed the frowns gathering on the eggdomes' faces, and he held up one hand to remind them about no interruptions. "I don't mean," he said carefully, "that there aren't umpty-squared other neurons in their brains that you haven't fooled with yet. I just mean that according to the computers you have carried out a sufficient number of such alterations to complete the projected set that you were budgeted for. And unfortunately, gentlemen, nothing much has come of this. You've been Interfacing these babies with the new nonhumanoid AIRYs—which was supposed to be something with real potential—and you've been getting the usual crap. They're going to run out of funds at the Arlington orphanage, too, if you keep on like this."

The eggdomes looked sullen, and the general looked distressed, and the computer whiz looked bored; everything was going just as planned, and he could move along to the important part.

"Now . . ." He slowed way down, and he swept the group with his eyes to signal that something was coming that even the computer whiz should listen to. "Now, the department would like for you to move on to a new phase of this project. *Now,* General, Professors . . . Mr. Pugh . . . it is Director Clete's opinion that we've got to produce some return to justify the expenditure here at El Centro. And what he wants you to do—"

They were all looking at him, and he liked that; he paused, and let them wait, six full counts.

"What he wants you to do—and he has full backing on this,

all the way to the top—what he wants you to do is stop putting infant humans of any kind into the Interface on this floor. There'll be a baby in the display Interface upstairs, as always, of course; but down here you are to Interface infant *whales*, gentlemen. And I am authorized to tell you that a consignment of two . . . uh, let me see here . . . oh yes, two infant humpbacks and their mothers, is already on its way here by special transport. Also a team to make whatever adjustments are required for the Interface on this level. We realize it won't hold all four animals, but we decided it would be cheaper and more practical to send spares just in case—considering the past history of the project—and you can of course put the extra mother and baby in the upstairs exhibit on hold. The public would be delighted, and the whales won't care. My job here is to let you know what the new plans *are*, to warn you to expect the shipment of animals, and to find out if there's anything you need that we haven't anticipated. I'll take the information back to Washington with me when I leave, and any oversights will be rectified immediately. You have my word, and Director Clete's word, on that. Now! Are there any questions?''

He looked around with that cheery but businesslike expression—as if he knew a great deal more than he'd felt obliged to tell—that always served him so well in dealings like this, and raised his eyebrows to indicate how willing he was to listen.

"Well?" You had to encourage people. "Please don't hesitate. We know we're not experts on . . . uh . . . cetaceans. That's *your* field, we just push the paper around. Just tell me what you think we might have overlooked, and I'll see to it.''

The eggdomes had the strangest expressions on their faces; he wasn't sure exactly what to make of it. He'd been expecting resistance, because eggdomes always resisted—they weren't good at handling change, and that was normal for the role. But these men didn't look resistant, they just looked baffled. The computer guy was looking mildly interested, but that was probably because he'd thought of something fun to do with his machines. He turned his attention to the general, since nobody else seemed to be quite ready for any give-and-take.

"General?" he asked. "Would you like to begin?"

"Well . . . Paul, is it?"

"Yes, sir. Paul White."

"Paul, this isn't really *my* field, either. I'm an administrator, not a scientist. It sounds damn exciting to me, but I have to rely on the judgment of my men here."

Ball neatly fielded. Now they were all staring at the eggdomes, who were moving around in their chairs as if they itched. And finally one of them did manage to put a few words together.

"Why are we doing this?" he asked.

Why are we doing this? What was that supposed to mean?

Patiently, Paul began again. "Professor, there is just a limit to available funds. Especially with all the new colonies opening up—the taxpayers out there on the frontiers have a right to expect that we'll put as much money as we possibly can into making their lives a little more bearable. Not that—" He paused to chuckle, as does a man who knows the facts but is willing to indulge those who would romanticize them a little. "—their lives are a lot worse than yours, I must say, in many cases. But we're under a great deal of pressure at D.A.T. to prove that there will eventually be some return on the investment here, and—"

"That's not what I meant." The eggdome looked both sullen and belligerent.

"I'm sorry. What *did* you mean?"

"We understand about funding problems. Every scientist understands about funding problems. But why *this* particular shape to our new 'phase,' Mr. White? *Why* are you sending us baby whales, for the love of christ?"

For an eggdome he was downright agitated, and D.A.T. didn't like its eggdomes agitated; Paul moved right in with professional soothing noises.

"Professor," he said, smiling his most competent friendly smile, "it seemed to us that since the new AIRYs are whales it was the obvious thing to do. I realize you've put years of time and effort into the tubies, but—"

"The new AIRYs are *what?*"

This was a different eggdome; the other one was looking at Paul as if he'd farted.

"The new AIRYs are whales . . . oh, I get it. Sorry. The new AIRYs are *cetaceans.* I'm afraid we laymen have trouble with that word. Since that's true—"

"But it's *not* true."

Nobody, nobody in the solar system, did more interrupting than eggdomes. Paul knew that, but it was beginning to get under his skin.

"I beg your pardon?"

"Where did you get the idea that the current AIRYs are cetaceans, young man?"

Young man. They were going to start *that* now.

"Professor," he stated flatly, giving the wig just one brief touch to draw attention to the pepper and salt effect, "everybody is aware that the AIRYs we got in the Scoop last time were whales. That's a matter of common knowledge—that is, it's common knowledge to everybody with a clearance high enough to be familiar with this project. I don't understand your question.''

The eggdomes were looking at each other, and their faces had that US WISE MEN, HIM NINCOMPOOP expression that Paul hated most in dealing with them. He didn't intend to let it get to him; he concentrated on looking resolute, and waited for their move.

At last one of them said, "Mr. White, do you have with you any kind of description of the Aliens? That is, when they are discussed at D.A.T., how are they described?"

Paul blew a slow small stream of air between pursed lips, and scanned the hard copy he was carrying on pliofilm. It was there somewhere . . . oh, yeah.

"It says here," he answered courteously, "that they are like the dolphins of Earth except that they have a shell. Because of, it says here, the extreme pressures they were subject to in their own planet's atmosphere. Dolphins . . . dolphins are whales, right?"

"Naw," said the computer whiz.

"Yes, they are," said the eggdomes. "Small toothed whales." Of the order mumbledy, something else mumbledy—Paul didn't follow the rest of it. And then, like some kind of comedy team, they all laid their heads in their hands and sighed, and Paul finally ran out of courtesy.

"Gentlemen," he snapped, "I'm sorry if my lack of scientific expertise offends you. But I am genuinely doing my best here, and I've got to get this meeting finished and head on back to the port. That rental flyer they gave me in Los Angeles Diego doesn't strike me as overpoweringly reliable, and I'd like to allow myself a little extra time to make the shuttle. If you would just explain to me what the problem is, I'd be extremely grateful—and so would the Department of Analysis & Translation."

To his surprise, one of the eggdomes turned out to be a pretty decent guy after all. He apologized, for starters, and said they hadn't meant to act as if Paul were lacking in scientific knowledge.

"The problem," the eggdome went on, "and what made us collapse like that, is that we all saw immediately how this got started. And it hit us all the same way. We try so hard to avoid this kind of mess, and we so rarely succeed, you see. It was that description you read to us that set us off."

"It's the official one." No one disagreed with him, and he shrugged. "It's the one we were given at D.A.T. when the Scoop brought the Aliens in and you people reported to us."

"I'm sure that's true. My name is Bydore, Mr. White—I did the report myself. It was my own description."

"Well? Is it wrong?"

The eggdome looked sad, and frustrated, and burdened with the weight of the centuries, and before he started talking again he chewed first on his upper lip and then on the bottom one, while the other eggdomes glowered.

"Mr. White," he said slowly, "there's not the slightest reason to believe that these AIRYs are cetaceans. It's true that their bodies, except for the shells, rather resemble the bodies of dolphins, and I used that fact—God forgive me—as a way of saving time and avoiding a lengthy technical anatomical description. But it's nothing more than a chance physical resemblance. A golfball resembles a bird's egg, Mr. White, but it's a meaningless resemblance. It's an accident, you see. And it makes this new idea of D.A.T.'s pretty ridiculous."

The general moved in swiftly with the necessary question, and Paul was grateful; it was always best to move the target of annoyance around from one member of the team to another in a situation like this one. "You say there's no reason to believe that these Aliens are whales," he said roughly. "All right, Bydore, we'll accept that—you're the experts. Now I want to know: is there any reason to believe that they *aren't* whales? Alien whales, that is?"

"The question is almost meaningless," protested Professor Bydore. "Like the resemblance."

"The question is perfectly straightforward," the general answered coldly. "Do you or do you not have reason to believe that these Aliens—which you admit bear a close physical resemblance to whales—are *not* whales? Do you or do you not have evidence that would *support* the contention that they're not whales? There's nothing wrong with that question."

There was a muggy silence, with the eggdomes scowling and fidgeting and looking disgusted, but the other men present were used to that, and not bothered by it. One characteristic found in ninety-nine of one hundred eggdomes was an absolute inability to stay silent for more than about sixty seconds if their scientific field was the subject of discussion. The three in Room 09-A did not fall into the exceptional one percent; they all erupted into confused protest simultaneously.

"*Please*, gentlemen!"

The general's voice was the standard military voice of high rank, and it shut the eggdomes up again. In the hush, he said, "One at a *time*, if you don't mind! I want your answers, one at a time, and I want them right now!"

He got them; in sequence, tight-lipped.

"There is no logical reason to believe that the Aliens either are or are not whales."

"There is no way to determine at this time whether they are or are not whales."

"We have no evidence, nor have we any basis for conjecture, as to whether they are or are not whales."

The general snorted and admonished them not to try that crap with him. "It walks like a duck, it quacks like a duck, that's reason to believe that it *is* a duck!" he said emphatically.

"An *Earth* duck!" pleaded Bydore. "Only an Earth duck, General. If two creatures of a single planet strongly resemble each other physically, then *maybe* there is a relationship. But stop and think, General. Just for a moment. Think about the Emperor penguin—it resembles, *very* strongly, a small portly human male in evening clothes."

The General suspected that he was being made fun of; his brows locked over the jut of his nose, and his next question came snapping out, ratatat. "And how, precisely, would you proceed to find out if the penguin was in fact a new variety of human male, of small size? If you didn't already know, that is?"

"You'd do tests," said the eggdome reluctantly, seeing where they were headed.

"You couldn't just conclude, because the penguin has webbed feet and is three feet tall, and the human being has unwebbed feet and is much bigger, that they are different species?"

"No."

"Then," the general summed up, "you cannot just conclude—because the Aliens have shells and the Terran whales don't have shells—that they are different species. Using the term *species* loosely, of course."

"General—"

"No further discussion is required," the general announced. He stood up, put both hands behind his back, and shifted to parade rest. "The department has decided to test this physical resemblance and is sending the necessary animals. We *will* proceed with the tests. When and if we have evidence that the AIRYs are not whales, we'll stop the tests. You *will* direct your attention, as Paul White has requested, to the simple question of whether we have all the necessary equipment, supplies, and personnel."

"*But, General—*"

If the general had given Paul any opening at all, he would have found a way to let the eggdomes talk; he could tell that something else was wrong. If it had been only the scientific question of whales-or-not-whales, they would have stated their objections, heard them called garbage by the nonscientists, and retired into dignified contemptuous silence. They wouldn't be going "But, General," the way they were doing now. They wouldn't have stooped to bicker with nonscientists. But General Charing had been annoyed, he'd felt that his authority was being challenged and his competency ridiculed, and he wasn't going to stand for it; he'd made his speech and he intended to entertain no rebuttals. Paul noted the strategic error, and would include it in his report when he got back to D.A.T., but he stayed out of it now. He was the messenger here, no more; it was not his place to get involved in inhouse politics at the project.

"Well?" demanded the general. "Has anything been over-looked, or not?"

"Probably not," Professor Bydore answered icily. "We won't be able to determine that until we've put this absurd project into operation. And I want it a matter of record that we're opposed to it."

"Noted." The general's intonation carried the same weight of ice. "I will then direct Mr. White to report that all appears adequate, and to indicate that if there turn out to be missing items the department will be promptly so advised." He looked at Paul, then, and asked, "When should we expect the animals to arrive?"

"Failing a specific order to the contrary," Paul told him, "within the next two hours. Perhaps you might want to get started making preparations."

The general abandoned parade rest and assumed some version of alert for action. "Certainly," he agreed. "At once. Gentlemen?" And then he was gone, presumably off to find the Cetacean Head Keeper, or whatever it was he had on tap of that kind. He did not bother trying to disguise the eagerness with which he was leaving.

When they were alone, Paul White leaned forward with his elbows on the table, and spoke very gravely and carefully. "All right, Professors. What's the real problem here?"

"I should think it would be obvious," said Bydore.

"No, Professor, it's not a bit obvious. But I'm willing to be told."

"At least you could see that there *was* a problem—unlike our military friend."

"The general is trained to command soldiers, chimps, and

military robots; the commanding of scientists was not part of his curriculum at the Academy. Be reasonable. How good do you think you three would be at coordinating a laser attack?''

"Then what the bloody hell is he *doing* here?''

"All operations at this level having military implications or national security implications *must* be administered by individuals with high military rank and the necessary security clearances,'' Paul recited, straight from the manual with very few modifications.

"It makes no sense.''

"Not scientifically, perhaps. Administratively, it makes excellent sense. Now please, instead of attempting to reform the Department of Analysis & Translation, tell me what it is that is so obvious and let me get on back to Washington. I may even be able to do something useful.''

The eggdome nodded slowly. "All right,'' he said. "*This* is what is obvious. The human beings of Earth, as of this date, are not capable of communicating with the cetaceans of Earth. Suppose the Aliens that the military is pleased to assume are whales—no matter what they really are—do interact with the animals you're sending, in such a fashion that the end result is a Terran whale that has acquired an Alien language. So what?''

"So,'' said Paul, "then we have to Interface some human babies with that whale, so that we can get access to the new language. An extra step, that's all.''

"Mr. White—that's what we've been trying to do here for decades.''

"What?''

"What do you think is going *on* up on the first floor of this installation, damn it?''

The eggdome was actually bellowing at him. Paul felt a vague alarm; eggdomes bellow at one another, but they do not bellow at the ignorant layman. It seemed improper, and undignified, to Paul.

"First floor?'' he echoed, playing for time. What had he missed on the first floor?

"That's an *Interface* up there, man, with a couple of whales on one side and a human infant on the other. For god's sake!''

"But that's just for show, Professor,'' Paul stammered. "I mean, it's just a cover for the real work done here. It's not—''

"*Listen*, White!'' Professor Bydore slammed both hands on the table, and Paul stopped talking, astonished. "That is a *real* Interface! It contains *real* whales, and *real* babies! And that is all there is in *any* Interfacing!''

"Now, Professor—" Paul began, but the man only threw up his hands, shouted that he gave up, and implored heaven to be his witness that the level of stupidity he faced was more than any human being should be expected to tolerate in one lifetime. Paul was astounded; he'd heard plenty of jokes about eggdome tantrums, he even had a few in his own repertoire, but this was the first time in his life that he'd actually *seen* such a display. In his personal experience the academics and scientists were slow-moving lethargic creatures given to grunts and mumbling; he'd had no idea that one could behave with so much passion.

The computer whiz put in an oar, then; whether out of sympathy for Paul, or some personal motive, nobody would ever know. He had all the dates and names and places right on the tip of his tongue. It was an impressive performance, making Paul wonder obscenely about Interfacing humans and computers. The end result was not ambiguous—many experiments had been tried with human/whale Interfacing, and every last one had failed.

"Why?" Paul asked. "Do they know why? Some of those were done a long time ago—don't we know a lot more about it now?"

"Mr. White," said another of the professors, "we don't know one thing more about Interfacing than we knew by the end of the first year that it was done. That's how long it took to find out everything we know. Oh, we know more about the engineering—it doesn't take us as long to get the right mix for the atmosphere the Alien breathes, we have better barriers between the Alien's quarters and the area where the human infants are placed, that kind of thing. But the basic process is exactly what it always was. You put a human infant on one side of the barrier, you put a cooperative Alien or two on the other side, and you let them spend a few hours a day together interacting for four or five years; the result is a human infant that is a native speaker of the Alien language. But the important word here, the crucial word, is *cooperative. The Terran whales won't cooperate.*"

Paul was intent now—this was important. "Are you serious?" he asked. "Can you say something like that and not be . . . what's the word . . . anthropomorphizing?"

"I can," the man answered. "In every experiment that has been tried, the whales have simply done a Ghandi. They don't object, they don't charge the barrier, they don't turn belly up and die, they don't refuse to eat . . . they give us no trouble. But so long as a human infant is on the other side of the Interface partition, the whales do not make a single sound. Nor, so far as we can tell, do they make any movements—any body language—

other than what is necessary to their survival. They just wait until somebody removes the infant and then they resume normal behavior. This has been true for all types and varieties of whales studied. Why else do you think that after all these years we are still without any results to report from upstairs?''

''Well, I'll be damned,'' breathed Paul, leaning back in his chair. He ought to have known about this; he ought to have been briefed on it. Even if it was only a cover operation, it had clear—and as the eggdomes said, obvious—bearing on the current project. They'd had no business sending him here to collect egg on his face, half-briefed, and somebody was going to be sorry, once he got back to D.A.T. and found out where the information gap was originating.

Bydore spoke up, calm now after his outburst. ''There's no possible way to misunderstand the message, Mr. White,'' he said. ''A long time ago, we called in a linguist to observe and comment, a man from the Lines. And he gave us a solemn translation, which I now quote: 'The whales say, "We won't play your silly game."' '' And that was that.''

''I see; thank you.'' Paul sat there, thinking, and then he decided to cut his losses, because pretending wasn't going to work with these men. ''Gentlemen,'' he said, ''I think I finally understand what you're telling me. I apologize for having arrived here so badly prepared, and for having been so goddam slow after you began helping me out. I understand the problem you face now—I *do understand*. But I am going to ask you to do me, and the department, a favor. I am going to ask you to go ahead with this project, in spite of the difficulties you have been kind enough to make clear to me, while I explore ways of dealing with the whales' determination not to help.''

''We can't communicate with the whales,'' the professor objected. ''How are you going to 'explore' anything, as you put it, when they won't have anything to do with us?''

Paul smiled, and began gathering his files together. ''We *have* communicated with them,'' he pointed out. ''The message was completely unambiguous, and—as you of course were demonstrating—we didn't need a linguist to tell us what it was.''

''A refusal to cooperate does not constitute language,'' said the scientist. ''An earthworm digging desperately to escape the light you shine on it is not communicating.''

''Tropism,'' Paul said, guessing. It was close enough. ''The whales' behavior is not like that. And I've seen human beings do precisely what you describe the whales doing. *That*, gentlemen, we know how to deal with.''

Bydore closed his eyes. "Vee half vayss," he murmured, "uff making zem talk."

Paul laughed, and stood up quickly, tucking the files under his arm. "I'll ignore that," he said. "And I want you to know that *your* cooperation—without benefit of cattle prod or Takeover Chip—is greatly appreciated. But trust me, please. I am a government troubleshooter. My function is to find out what's wrong and find out who can fix it and order it done. *Your* function is to start Interfacing these Aliens with infant Earth whales. You leave it to me to put together whatever it will take to deal with the subsequent stage of this project, which is years in the future. And I'll be in touch with you—or someone else from D.A.T. will be—as soon as we have something useful to tell you."

"You really think something can be done? In spite of all the evidence? After all these years?"

"Something can always be done," Paul told him. "The only question, ever, is whether it's worth doing. There's plenty of time. Set your minds at rest, and let me get started on this. Let me see what I can find out . . . let me get in touch with some people. Don't worry about it—you fulfilled *your* obligations when you took the time to get the facts into my thick head. Now it's up to D.A.T., and I have got to get going."

Hands were shaken all around, even if reluctantly, and he backed out of the room, Mister Joe Cordial all the way, smiling and nodding, and praise be to god he was again in the elevators and on his way back to civilization. With a lot more to do than when he'd arrived, but that was all right; keeping busy was Paul White's middle name. He ate and drank and lived and breathed and *thrived* on keeping busy. Some men cared about sex; Paul didn't mind it. But work, now—that was what really mattered to him. And if he could find a way to break this particular logjam, which had obviously been sitting around forgotten in the files, a plum just ripe and red and waiting for the plucking of some enterprising individual, why then, by god, you'd see some *action!*

He was looking forward to it.

CHAPTER 15

"I am Selena Opal Hame, and this is what I want to say to you."

I do know what they are doing. I have known for a long time. Yes, I do know. I can see what it is. Here is what I do know.

I know that when their mouths move and noises come it is because they are sharing what is inside their heads. They can show each other, or they can do it when no other person is there. (I do not understand that part, no. Why would they want to show their own selves what is in their own heads? But when there is more than one person there, then I understand what they are doing.)

I know that sometimes when their bodies move that is a way to show what is inside the head, too. Not always. It is very hard for me to know which moving is about the real things in the head and which moving is only *doing*. Cutting is doing. Sewing is doing. Digging is doing. Eating is doing. But I cannot always tell.

And I have seen another thing. I have seen persons that shape their hands and arms and move them in a way that is a *special* doing. Those persons move their hands and arms and faces the way others move their mouths, to show what is inside their heads.

All this is magic, and I do not have any magic, you see. I never have had it. Only wonderings. How do they do it? I think I know what must be the *what* of it. I think there is first the real chair, inside their head . . . that chair is what is real inside their head. And then, some magic how, there is a noise that they hook together and make with their mouth and it tells another person

202

that what is real in the first one's head is CHAIR. Then, you see, they both know! And that must be a joy. Sharing what is in your head. That is what I cannot do.

It took me a long time to learn even this much. I did not always understand the what of it. When I was a small person, I saw their mouths move and their hands move and it was a great wondering and nothing more than that. For a very long time, while cold times and hot times came and went away and came again.

I remember well when I was one of the small ones, but that was very long ago. Now I am a large person, that has gray lines in the hair. No small ones ever have gray lines in the hair. And now that I am a large person, too, I understand that much— but I do not understand the *how*. I do not understand how a person decides which noise will be for which real thing, or which shape of the fingers and hands will be for which real thing. Who decides? How does one of them know which noise the other one has chosen to be the real thing? How can they remember which noise it was, when all the noises are so different, and none of them go together in the air? No, I do not understand that, except that it is magic.

I am not the only broken one there is. Where I lived before, there were other small ones almost like me, that could not do the magic either. Almost like me, but not exactly like me. Because now I am a person with gray in the hair, you see, and every single one of those other small ones was there only as many hot times and cold times as I have fingers, or maybe a few more, and then they grew very white and thin. And then they were gone, in the sleep that does not have a waking. So that I was all alone at that place among the ones that know how to make the noises and shapes and hook them to real things. Alone. I was so alone.

Those other small ones that were broken like I am broken— they tried to show me what was inside *their* heads. They did try. Their mouths did not move, their bodies did not move, but they caused a noise to happen in my ears. But I could not understand their noises. I was so sorry, but I could not understand. They made a noise like the dog makes. A noise like the noise when glass breaks and falls. A noise like when persons walk over many small rocks. A noise like the noise when much water is coming from the wall. Or just noise-noise, that nothing else makes. . . . They did not have the magic, either, and their own magic did not work with me. I do not know if it ever worked between some two of them, but I think probably it did not. If it had, why would they have gone away so quickly?

Many times large persons came and looked in our ears, looked in our mouths, put little wires on our heads. Always I thought they were bringing the magic to me, and to the other small ones, and when it was over I would turn and look at the mouths or the fingers, and think MAYBE NOW I WILL UNDERSTAND. But it never happened.

I don't know what in me is the broken part. My ears work; my eyes work; my head works. My fingers are not broken; I can cut and sew and dig and stir and cook. All the doings. I can go where other persons go, I know it is not my legs. My mouth opens like their mouths, but it does not make any noise . . . perhaps it is my mouth that is the broken part.

And when I was all alone in that other place, where all the small ones are together with only a few large persons to look after them, a person came and brought me to this new place. Where at first it was the same; I understood the what, but I did not understand the how.

But now, there is a new thing! This is what I want to tell you. There was a day, in a cold time. I was rubbing the long table in the eating room with a soft cloth and a kind of stuff like butter, that smells of lemons. To make the table shine in the light, you see. I know how to do this. One of the persons here taught me, the first day I came. This person stood behind me and held my hands and moved them. This person helped me pick up the cloth and put the lemon stuff on the wood. Moved my arms making circles on the wood, making it shine, until I knew what the doing should be and did it myself. Every day I do some of the wood in this house, so that all of it shines in the light. I am very strong; I do this very well.

And that day it was the long table for eating that I was making bright, when suddenly one of them came up to me holding a small box in the hand. So small it could be hidden away in the hand. This one touched me, so that I would look. Took my hand and put it on the small box, to feel that there were buttons on it. Took one of my fingers and touched three of the buttons on it. And the box made noises! Noises! But it was the *other* kind of noises, the kind that stay the same and make a real thing in the air! Like a very little piece of what comes from a much bigger box that is in one of the other rooms—it makes long strings of noises that are real. Whenever that box is making the noises, I always stop and I wait until *it* stops, if they will let me. They have seen me do that, and almost always they let me, unless it goes on for too long. It's wonderful, it makes noises that hold together and don't just leak away like the noises the persons make, like water running into the ground leaks away.

When the person showed me that the small box made noises like the large one, I stopped rubbing the table and I held my breath, wanting. That person, that has gray in the hair like I do, took my finger and touched it to three buttons on the small box. And again there was a noise that was real, and had all its parts together! And while the noise was there, that person raised a hand of its own and hit the table.

I stepped back, very fast, in case I would be the next thing that was hit. But the person stood there looking at me, and over and over again did the same two things. Touched the three buttons on the small box, to make the real noise in the air. Hit the table, while the noise was doing. Over and over again.

I knew it was important. I could feel that. I am not stupid. I knew I must *look* and *wait* and *think*. Was it a new kind of work that I was being taught to do?

The large person stood still a little time, and moved the face in places, and then took my hand and led me to a chair. Went down on the knees on the bare floor beside the chair. Set the small box on the chair. Touched three buttons—but not the *same* three buttons. It made a different real and whole noise in the air. And while that new noise was there, hit the chair gently with the hand.

Oh, my head hurt, I could not breathe! What *was* it? I could not just stand there, I had to try, I had to *do*. I reached out my hands, I dropped the cloth that I use to make all the wood shine in the light, and I rubbed that person's hands with my hands to make *them* bright, so that I would be able to see!

We looked at each other. And then that person began to do a certain thing. Sat me down in the chair and put the hands one on each side of my face and looked at me hard. Touched the forehead to my forehead, so gently. Caused the small box to make the noise with its three parts, and tapped the chair with its finger, *hard*. Went to the table, carrying the box, and caused it to make the other noise with *its* three parts, and tapped the table hard. Went back and forth, making me stay where I was. The noise; the chair. The other noise; the table. Over and over and over.

When the magic came, it was like what the lightning does to the sky in the hot time! It was a great crashing and a tearing inside my head, and a great light flashing through me! I understood, oh I understood, I could not be still, I ran! I went to the table, I took the small box, I pushed the three buttons that make TABLE, I ran to the chair, I caused the box to make CHAIR! I did it twice, I did it again! And then I turned to that person, and it was clapping the hands together and its mouth was moving and noises were coming and others came running into the room all together in a great hurry!

That person took my shoulders and held them, then, and looked hard at me again and took a long breath—we were at the table—and did not move the mouth, but made CHAIR somehow with the mouth all closed, just like the small box. And looked at me, so hard.

I knew what to do. I knew the magic! I ran to the chair, I took the small box. I made CHAIR with the buttons on the small box. And every single person in the room, every single one, was clapping the hands together!

Oh, it is true magic, and I understand it. This is what I understand.

On the small box that I can hold in my hand, there are buttons to push. One for each of the fingers I have and then enough for one of my hand's fingers more. When you touch the buttons, a real noise comes. And if you press three buttons, or four buttons, one after the other, it is a string of noises that holds together and is a real thing in the air. And then, you see, you have one string of noise like that for each one thing in your head that you want to show to a person. This is what I want to tell you.

I learned, so fast. There is a string of three that is TABLE. A string of three that is CHAIR. That is APPLE. That is FLOWER. That is HEAD. That is EYE. That is HAND. There is a string of three parts that is LARGE-PERSON, and then if you push one more button to make it a string of four parts it is for showing a SMALL-PERSON!

Do you see? Do you hear, do you understand? Or are you broken?

I can know in my head that it is WINDOW, I can push the buttons to make WINDOW, and the person with me will know what was in my head, will go to the window and touch it to show me that we are sharing it.

It is hard for them, though. I don't know why. Perhaps it is a way that they are broken. When I cause the box to make a WORD (that means, a string of noises that is a real thing and holds together), often the person will look at a paper in the hand, that has marks on it. Does the paper tell them what the word is? I don't see how that could be, but if it is not so why do they look?

And very often they make mistakes. But I am so patient. I will wait and I will make my word as many times as it takes, until they understand. Because we are sharing it. Oh magic, oh magic, and more and more magic!

But I am crying now. Because I am wondering . . . the other small broken ones, at the place where I used to be, all the small ones that lasted only a handful of cold times and hot times, that were trying to make words and could only make empty noises. . . . What if they had come here? What if they had had one of the small boxes, as I have? Could they have shared words with other persons, as I share them now? Perhaps they were only broken in the same way that I am broken. Perhaps then they would not have gone to sleep forever, while they were still so small?

They are sorry that I am crying. They want me to share the why. But I can't. There are no words on the small box for what they want me to tell them. They are so sorry.

And I am so sorry. I am so sorry because all the poor small ones are gone, before I can show them how the magic works. It is a sad thing, to go with the new happy things. This is what I want to say to you.

CHAPTER 16

"It's all very well to talk of faith transcending language, and of the pettiness of quibbling over the little touch of sexual gender a language may drag into a sacred text here and there. I do understand, and of course it is only primitive superstition to visualize the Lord God Almighty as either male or female, in the sense that a human being is either male or female. But have you ever considered what very odd images come to one's mind if one says "The Lady is my shepherdess, I shall not want?" One can just see the dear little creature, with her petticoats flying in the spring breeze, and the big pink satin bow on her crook . . . don't you think?"

(Langtree Moulineux, Professor of Religious Studies, Midwestern Multiversity, speaking on the newsthology talk show, "Meet the Clergy" . . .)

"Fathers, I am sorry—it is just as you suspected it might be," said Sister Miriam; her voice was grave, and measured, as was suitable for speaking of things of this kind. "Of course I am not qualified to say if it is either blasphemy or heresy. But I am very sure that it is not something that you, or Holy Mother Church, would approve of. And if you will allow me an opinion . . ."

She paused and waited until Father Dorien said that yes, she might express her opinion, and then she went on.

"It is my opinion that it contains at least the *seeds* of goddess worship," she told them, not hesitating at all over the words of condemnation. Her face had the expression appropriate for removing a small dead animal from the hotbox of a flyer, but she did not stammer over the word; she spoke straight out.

Father Agar's breath hissed through his clenched teeth, betraying his fascinated interest in what he should not have found interesting, and Father Claude glared at him fiercely. Father Dorien ignored them both, and spoke to the nun.

"Please continue, Sister," he urged. "You may dispense, for the duration of this meeting, with the requirement to wait for our permission to speak."

"It is my privilege to obey," answered Sister Miriam, "and I thank you for the courtesy—it will certainly save a great deal of your time. But there's little more to report, Fathers. The other nuns and I have followed your orders; as you anticipated, we were welcome as guest speakers at the women's chapel meetings. We had no difficulty obtaining materials for examination, and I have brought you some samples."

She laid three microfiches on the table, each in its own sheath, within their easy reach; and she stood quietly waiting while they inserted them in the readers that hung on black cords round their necks, her hands clasped properly behind her back. They made the sort of noises fussy spinsters make when faced with the private reading collections of healthy adolescent males, and Father Dorien suspected that Sister Miriam was perhaps amused at the variety of clucks and sniffs and snorts that she was witnessing from the end of the table; if so, no trace of that, or of any emotion other than courteous respect, appeared upon her face.

Dorien was the first to move; he pulled the fiche from the reader with the tips of two fingers as if it were something slimy and decomposing, set it into the comset recess on the tabletop, and pushed the stud that would display a selected page on the overhead screen.

"I direct your attention," he said sternly, "to the tenth line and to its translation. Sister Miriam Rose, do you vouch for the accuracy of that translation?"

"I do, Father," she assured him. "It has been done morpheme by morpheme. However, some details have perhaps not been made entirely clear. Do you wish me to comment on it, Father Dorien?"

"Please."

"*Boóbin Na delith lethath oma Nathanan,*" she said easily, reading off the line. "You see that it is easily pronounced, Fathers."

"Indeed. As one would expect."

"Yes, Father Claude; just as you say."

"Please continue, Sister," Father Dorien directed. "And I will be grateful if my colleagues will refrain from interruption—

this is quite difficult enough for the sister without our intermittent comments."

"A word at a time, Fathers," she said, nodding her agreement to the command. "*Boóbin*: that is the verb, to *braid*. It has no other meaning, although it has a transparent relationship to the numeral three, which is *boó*."

"Charming!" warbled Agar, drawing the glares of both the other priests at once. "Well, it *is*," he insisted defiantly; he knew he was safe from Dorien's tongue as long as the nun was present.

"Go on, Sister Miriam," said Father Dorien harshly. "Please."

"*Na*: that is the subject pronoun, second person singular, with the suffix from the grammatical class designated as 'beloved.' Perhaps 'Beloved Thou' is the closest I can come to it . . . and it should be noted that it begins with a capital letter to denote reverence as well. *Delith*: that is the noun meaning 'hair.' Human hair. *Lethath*, next: that is the first person singular pronoun, marked with the possessive and objective case endings. The choice of '-tha-' for the possessive indicates that the reference is to something possessed by reason of birth. '*Delith lethath*'; it means 'my hair, that I was born with,' and is the direct object of *braid*. *Oma*: that is *hand* or *hands*; in this context, it is plural. And finally we have *Nathanan*: possessive-by-birth, in the pattern meaning beloved and revered, second person singular, and marked for the instrumental case. Referring to 'Thy (Beloved) hands,' plus the instrumental 'with.' "

The priests listened to this torrent of grammatical terminology without difficulty; they knew all about such things from the painful learning of both Latin and Greek, and Fathers Dorien and Agar both had a smattering of Hebrew as well. They sat nodding their heads as she went along, watching the screen, punctuating each chunk of information with a small movement of acknowledgment.

"And the whole line," said Father Dorien slowly, "is to be translated 'Thou braidest my hair with Thine own hands.' 'Thou' and 'Thine' being understood as containing in addition the morpheme 'Beloved.' Is that correct, Sister?"

"Yes, Father. Quite correct."

"And that is supposed to be the Langlish translation of 'Thou anointest my head with oil'?"

"Yes, Father."

Father Dorien glowered at the line, and glowered at her, and then realized that his display of emotion contrasted badly with her serenity; after all, if anyone here should have been shocked, it was the good sister. Hastily, he composed his face.

"Very different from the King James," he observed. "They've taken extraordinary liberties."

"Yes, Father. It's not even a close approximation."

Dorien steepled his slender white hands before him, the heavy ring with its single square stone catching the light, and looked at his colleagues. In a voice of grim determination he said, "Father Agar, Father Claude—I have had the benefit of a brief prior discussion of this material with Sister Miriam. And I would like you to hear what she has to say about the *interpretation* of this particular line, which might seem at first to be no more than a glaring example of feminine inability to translate accurately. Sister, please tell them just what you told me."

Miriam allowed herself a expression of faint reluctance, and was not surprised when Father Dorien interrupted her opening words to tell her please to sit down, obliging her to begin again. She did as she was told, and then said, "This is an excessively feminine recasting of the line, Fathers, in my humble opinion. First, it was necessary to render the sense of Our Lord performing some act that would be an honor to a human being. And a woman, Fathers—" She cleared her throat, very quietly, and let her eyes fall modestly for a moment. "A woman would *not* wish to be anointed with oil. That would be a messy procedure, you see; afterward, she would have to wash her hair, and probably her clothing as well, since drops of oil would inevitably trickle slowly down. . . . If God were anointing you with oil, even a very small quantity of oil, you could hardly avoid that. It would not be respectful, or worshipful, to avoid it. That is the first point."

Father Claude broke in, his voice almost petulant. "So they replaced it with having their hair braided? Sister, I don't see it. What is there about braiding hair that could be viewed as an *honor*? It's such an everyday, trivial . . . No, I don't see it at all."

Sister Miriam looked down at the gleaming boards of the floor; they were real wood, very old, and they pleased her. And she spoke in such a way that it was as if she were only agreeing to something that Father Claude had been thinking of himself. "When the Son of God washed the feet of His disciples, one wonders if they were not perhaps honored. . . ." She let the words trail off, and added, "Of course, Fathers, the translators are women. One must remember that. And they are theologically without any training at all."

Father Dorien picked up the dropped ball on the first bounce, secretly amused, but too well-bred to let it show. "I believe you had finished with your first point, Sister," he said. "Please go on."

"Yes, Father," she said. "It is my privilege to obey. Well, then! There is the substitution of the act of braiding the hair, which does not carry with it the physical consequences—that is, oil in one's hair and on one's person—that anointing does. If I may speak *as* a woman, Fathers . . . I would consider it an inexpressible honor if divine hands were to braid my hair. It is an intimate service, and one that demands closeness."

She saw something on their faces—the beginning of a hint of comprehension, perhaps? Agar had begun to fidget and would be breaking in on her with a speech if she didn't take the floor quickly.

"Secondly," she continued, "and I believe most significant, is the fact that—if you will forgive me for pointing out what you have of course already realized—the braiding of hair is not something that men *do* in our world. Or know how to do."

She let that hang in the air, just under the seventeen-second limit, and then observed politely that of course God knew everything, and how to do everything, but that the point undoubtedly remained clear to the Fathers . . . who must remember the theological ignorance of the women who had written the translation of the line.

There was that hissing noise again—Father Agar sucking his breath in through his teeth. And Father Claude, to everyone's astonishment, pounded on the table with his fist and very nearly shouted at her.

"For *these* women, then," he demanded angrily, "the act would have to be performed by a . . . a female god? That's what you're saying, *isn't* it? You're saying that the reference is *perforce* to a goddess, aren't you, Sister Miriam?"

"Well, Father," answered Miriam, still looking steadily downward, "they could of course defend themselves against any such charge by pointing out that (a) it is a sin to anthropomorphize God, so that to say that He is male or female is idolatry; and that (b) God has been here since before the Beginning and has seen many a period of human history come and go during which men braided their hair; and that (c) even to suggest that there is some human act of which God is ignorant is heresy."

The summary had come so swiftly, and had been so unlike her usual submissive murmurs, that all three men stared at her, startled.

"Of course," Miriam added, "none of that is, to my mind, what they *were* thinking. I believe that the image intended is, unfortunately, the image of a—" She stopped short, and put the fingertips of both hands over her lips, moving her head from side to side, helpless in her distress.

"The image intended is the image of a *goddess*," announced Father Agar gallantly, seeing that she was unable to bring herself to use the word. "A *goddess!* Sister, you are quite right; the theological subtleties that would constitute a defense would be far beyond their capacities. They would have had to be spelled out by a man, as they were for you. And, dear child—"

Father Dorien cut in, right across Agar's bow, leaving the other man sputtering with outrage, but silent. "Let us remember," he snapped, "that we are not dealing with ordinary women here. These are women who have spent all their lives taking part in *interplanetary negotiations,* and who are able to provide simultaneous interpreting between Alien languages and the tongues of Earth. It would be foolish to assume that they are incapable of subtleties."

"May I remind *you,* however, Father Dorien—"

"Father Agar—"

"Allow me to remind *you* that the 'negotiating' you attribute to these females is nothing but a mindless following of instructions. They do not act *alone,* Father Dorien; they simply function, much as a servomechanism would function, for the linguistic convenience of the skilled men present who *provide* them with their instructions. I don't approve of it. I never have, and I don't mind saying so. A way should be found to restrain the greed of the government so that only males of the Lines would be involved, to avoid *precisely* this kind of needless—and, I might add, unscientific—confusion in the minds of the ignorant. Not that I am referring to *you* as ignorant, Father Dorien, I hasten to add, but, really Father! I must object to your mode of expression in front of Sister Miriam Rose! You risk introducing serious confusion into the sister's *thoughts,* Father!"

Had Miriam not been present, Father Dorien would certainly have told Father Agar what a tiresome and insubordinate old fart he was; hampered by her presence, he could only nod and look wise and hope the tiresome and insubordinate old fart would shut up shortly. It added nothing to his peace of mind when Father Claude leaped in to remind everyone how many times the linguists had made the point that there is no significant correlation between intelligence and the acquisition of language in infants and small children—a fact which Agar immediately challenged, parading his ignorance for the delectation of one and all and providing Father Claude with an opportunity to present a full-scale introductory lecture on the subject. He carefully did not look at Sister Miriam.

Being surrounded by nincompoops was a situation that Dorien had deliberately brought upon himself. Keep the nincompoops at home where he could deal with them, that was his policy, and send the brilliant priests out into the world where they could be of use without having to be saddled with the nincompoops. By and large, it worked well, and was no doubt good for his character; occasionally, it could be embarrassing. And he realized that no matter how absurd it might be, he was embarrassed at the way his stupid colleagues were flaunting their stupidity before Sister Miriam. The idea that she might be more intelligent than either one of them—or both of them put together—was both improper and inescapable.

"Sister Miriam," he said abruptly, grabbing a small gap in the dialogue when Agar and Claude had paused simultaneously for breath, "we Fathers are agreed, I am certain, that this example does represent heresy; it does indeed manifest the taint of goddess worship. If not in full flower, at least in the bud. And the example is by no means unique."

"*Tell* me, Sister," Agar piped up, and Dorien smothered a curse that *would* have been the end of dignity before the nun by turning his head away and pretending to cough, "do these frightful females address Our Lord with the feminine pronoun? That would settle the case, you know."

Sister Miriam smiled the modest and soothing smile of the nun whose purpose is always to be a comfort. "Father," she replied, "one cannot know. The pronouns of the language are not marked for sexual gender."

"Barbarous!" Agar exclaimed, taken aback. "Just barbarous! Why, how could a language call itself a language without masculine pronouns, and feminine pronouns, and—"

Father Dorien moved instantly into the breach. He was certain that Sister Miriam was too well-bred to humiliate poor old Agar by listing for him the multitude of living languages on this Earth in which a single pronoun form is used for masculine, feminine, and neuter; but he did not trust Father Claude not to do so. He cut Father Agar off in mid-babble, and spoke directly to the woman.

"My dear Sister," he said tersely, "if I might have your attention, I think what we must do is consider the question of our next move. That it's necessary to stifle this heresy before it condemns the immortal souls of these foolish women to perdition, and before it spreads beyond the present groups, is overwhelmingly obvious." *That you speak in clichés and platitudes, Father, is overwhelmingly obvious.* "That our goal should be to transfer the present fervor to a seemly devotion for the Blessed Virgin is not in dispute. The materials you have brought us—and we thank you for your industry in that regard, Sister—demonstrate that the heresy is real and that we were not just imagining the problem. *All these things are clear.* In that context, then, what should we do next?"

"Why, we tell their *clergy!*" puffed Father Agar. "We *tell* them, at once, that the women of their flocks are being led into the foulest temptation and the most seductive evil, and that unless they make an immediate effort to counter this phenomenon it will be the Almighty they have to answer to one day!"

Sweet suffering saints, thought Father Dorien; Father Claude gave the ceiling his total attention, and Sister Miriam favored the floor with *her* glance. Neither would meet Dorien's eyes, and he did not blame them."

"Father Agar," he purred, "will you be so kind as to explain to Claude, and to me, how we are to accomplish the goal of converting these women to Holy Mother Church if we call in their ministers and alert them to our opportunity? Haven't you been listening at all? Where is your *mind?*"

When the head of your monastery speaks to you in that fashion, and in that tone, you know yourself rebuked; Father Agar was grateful that no one except Claude was present to witness his humiliation.

"In my concern for their, uh, immortal souls," he stammered, his lips stiff and his eyes averted, "I perhaps lost track of . . . of less vital issues, Father Dorien. I beg your pardon."

"Less vital issues? *Less vital?*" The rays of light radiating from Father Dorien's head, although you knew very well that they were only coming from the sunlight through the window, seemed to Agar to gain in brilliance with the outrage in the abbot's eyes. "What, may I ask, is more vital than the winning of these souls to the True Faith?"

Father Agar *was* a nincompoop, but he was not stupid; he simply lacked foresight and resolve. He knew that Father Dorien was deliberately shaming him, and it seemed to him especially cruel of Dorien to do so when a nun was watching, though of course her opinion was unimportant and if she did gossip about this no one would pay any attention to her nonsense. He knew Dorien was perfectly well aware that Agar had only lost track for a minute of the drift of the discussion. Now the question was whether he should be defiant—as he certainly had every right to be, because Dorien's behavior was inexcusable—or humble, which was safer, because Dorien was capable of doing a good deal worse if you made him really angry, and he did seem to be angry. Agar was sufficiently worried about this that instead of being offended when Sister Miriam spoke, he was pleased. Now *she* would be rebuked, and that would distract Dorien. What had she said? Something about an urgent appointment with her Mother Superior?

"Sister Miriam Rose!" Father Dorien thundered. "I was addressing a question to Father Agar—I had *not* given you permission to interrupt!"

He had forgotten, for the moment, that he had opened the meeting by excusing her from the obligation of waiting for permission to speak; he remembered the instant the reprimand was given. But it didn't matter; there was no way that she could have contradicted him, or protested the injustice. And she did not try. Before he had even come to the end of the angry speech, Miriam was on her knees on the floor beside the wooden stool, her head bowed in contrition. It earned her no points with Father Dorien, who ordered her to get up at once and take her seat again, but it did cause him to drop his interrogation of Father Agar.

"You are finished with your melodramatics, Sister?" he asked her coldly, when she was decently seated again. "We can proceed?"

"Yes, Father," murmured the nun. "It is my privilege to obey."

"Try to do it with less fuss, then. We are not a frontier parish frolic!"

"Yes, Father. I am deeply sorry, Father."

"The question was: what are we to do next? *Not* alert the Protestant clergy—let that be stated at once and not mentioned again. But what? Sister Miriam, the next step in the plan, once it had been determined that our suspicions were justified, once the nuns in your group had established themselves within these devotional meetings, was for you to begin a systematic modification of the language of the heretical texts. Are you prepared to get that task underway? You have permission to speak."

"That is the plan you proposed, Father. And you will recall that you thought it would be an excellent idea for us to set the resulting texts to music, so that we could perform them for the women present—women, you will remember remarking, are so susceptible to music, and especially to religious music. And I of course agreed with your suggestions, Father.''

What Father Dorien actually recalled was that the idea of setting the modified texts to music and performing them, to take advantage of the power of the melodic line to reinforce mere words, had been Sister Miriam's. And unlike many men, he did not immediately decide that it was an idea he had been just on the point of presenting when the woman rudely appropriated it for herself. He understood—unlike many men—that "less intelligent" was not synonymous with "stupid." But he appreciated Miriam's fine sense of decorum, and he allowed her to proceed as she thought was proper; it would do him no harm, and she would be spared the distress of yet another verbal confrontation.

"Are you ready to move ahead with the plan, Sister?" He spoke warmly now, to let her know that he understood the strategy she was following and approved.

"There is a significant problem, Father," she answered, surprising him. He had given her the best nuns he could find, and ample funds, and she had had no difficulty finding the damning materials; he had not expected to hear that there was a problem.

"What problem, Sister? Why should there be a problem?"

"I am not a linguist, Father," she answered. Quite superfluously. He knew she wasn't a linguist.

"I am aware of that. Please continue."

"A linguist might well be able to work out the grammar of the language from the texts that we have collected, and then make the necessary changes. I can't do that, Father; I would not even know how to begin.

Dorien leaned toward her, frowning. "I'm not sure I understand you, Sister. Are you saying that the grammar of this language—made up out of whole cloth by a pack of women—is beyond your abilities?"

"I would not be at all surprised, Father," she said quietly. "I am not a learned woman, and I know little of grammar, for *any* language. But that is not yet the point. The point is that no such grammar exists."

"That's impossible!" he snapped. "Don't be absurd!"

"I beg your pardon, Father, you are quite right—it *is* impossible. I should have said: no grammar is *available*, neither on microfiche nor on chiplet. There is no course in the subject that one may take by comset, or anything of that kind. The *only* grammar, Father, is in the computer databanks of Chornyak Barren House. To which I have no access."

"The only one?" Dorien was very dubious; it was so unlikely.

"Yes, Father. And I must tell you that it was not easy for me to determine that even *that* one existed."

"Why not?"

"Because the women were extremely reluctant to tell me, Father. Only when I made it clear to them that I was not to be put off with nonsense about there being no written grammar at all—as if they could have done those translations without one— would they tell me that a single grammar does exist. In the databank, as I said. There are no hard copies."

"But it can be called up at any time by any *other* computer, at any of the other Households of the Lines, and printed out on the spot," put in Father Claude dryly. "Instant grammars, in any quantity desired."

"I am not familiar with computer systems, Father Claude," said Sister Miriam, "except as we use them in the convent for simple accounts and letters. I regret my ignorance—and I assure you, and the other Fathers, that I am taking steps to correct it, since I must do the programming for the revision of the texts. But I have only just begun my studies."

"Your ignorance is expected and appropriate," Claude responded testily, "and I personally wish that it could continue. You do not need to apologize, my child. But you may be sure, anything that is in any databank owned by the linguists is also available to every single one of their computers, and hard copies are a simple matter of pushing a button or speaking a command."

"Indeed," Miriam said. "How very clever, and how useful . . . and of course frugal, since but one copy is needed to serve for all. Thank you, Father; I am pleased to learn something new."

"Not at all, my child," said Father Claude, feeling somehow soothed. "We are here to *help* you in this project, in every way we can."

"That is my good fortune, Father Claude," she answered.

Father Dorien broke in, feeling that Claude had had all the sugar and cream that was good for him in a single serving.

"You need this grammar, then, in order to proceed," he said, and she agreed that she certainly did.

"Did you ask for it? That is, did you ask that a copy be made for you?"

She didn't answer, just stood there biting her lip and looking at her hands, and he grew impatient. "Sister Miriam Rose?" he asked sharply. "Did you hear my question?"

"Father Dorien . . . may I speak frankly? Expressing my own opinion, which may be quite wrong?"

"For heaven's sakes . . . of course. Please proceed."

"Father . . ." She said the word, and then looked directly at him, so that he was suddenly aware of those disconcerting eyes. "Father, it is true that most of the women attending the Thursday services are exactly as you have described them. Silly ignorant women playing at religion, taking part in a fad because it *is* a fad. They think it fashionable to flaunt their liberal ideas. . . ."

"Linguists are becoming *chic*, eh?"

"Yes, Father. Now that infants from outside the Lines are sharing the Interfaces. . . . You do *see*, Father."

"I do. And it's as ugly as the prejudice was."

"As you say, Father."

"Your *point*, Sister!"

"My point is that the women of the Lines are something else entirely. They are a good deal more than silly ignorant women leading a fad and glorying in their chance to do something fashionable for once in their poor dreary lives. Father Dorien, the women of the Lines are dangerous."

"Dangerous. Indeed."

"Yes, Father. I refer to spiritual dangers only, of course—for other women. And among the dangers they represent is this one: they are *not* going to let me have a copy of that grammar."

"Ah!" Dorien rubbed his chin, considering that. "Do you know why that should be, Sister? A polite request from a harmless nun, refused in that rude way? Did they offer you an explanation?"

"Oh, yes."

"May we hear it?"

"They would be humiliated to have me see it in its present state," she told him. Grimly, looking down again, and he was glad of that; her eyes distracted him. "It's no more than a rough *draft*. Much too unformed, much too embryonic, to be examined by anyone outside the family. The men of the Lines would be *extremely* angry if anything so clumsy were to be seen by a stranger. They are *working* on it—when they have a spare moment or two, which is not often—and when it is fit to be seen they will just be *delighted* to give me a copy. And so on, Father."

"This . . . rhapsodizing. It does not represent genuine womanly modesty?"

There were those eyes again, and he very nearly looked downward *himself* to avoid them.

"I am *absolutely* certain that they are lying," she stated. "Deliberately and willfully lying. No question about it."

"Hmmm. You're most emphatic about it, Sister."

"It sounds very unwholesome," put in Father Agar. "Disgraceful. I don't like it at all."

"Do they," Dorien wondered aloud, "like so many Protestants, look upon you as a sort of distant relative of Satan? Lechery in the convent basements, and you its representative? Is that the reason for the lies?"

Sister Miriam looked uncomfortable, but she said only, "Perhaps that is the explanation, Father."

"But you don't think so."

"No."

"What *do* you think it is, then?"

"I think they are up to something," she said flatly. "And I say again—I think they are dangerous. I think they need curbing."

"They are only women, Sister."

She made no reply, but the weight of her doubts hung heavy in the room, and the four of them sat a while in silence, thinking. Until finally Father Dorien spoke, disapprovingly.

"Sister Miriam," he said, "I will make no comment at this time on your assessment of the situation. Frankly, if it were any woman but yourself speaking, I would tell you that I considered your remarks to be symptomatic of hysteria. Since it *is* you speaking, I will reserve my judgment, but I ask that you guard your tongue in future. And of course, if you have convinced yourself that the women are a threat, it will be an additional motivation for you to carry out your assigned tasks; perhaps a touch of hysteria is not misplaced in these circumstances. But as for the grammar in that databank . . ."

"Yes, Father?"

"Don't concern yourself about it, Sister. A copy will be made available to you. What format would you prefer?"

"Could it be a paper copy?"

"Isn't that an unnecessary extravagance?"

"Forgive me, Father, but I would find it easier to plan the changes in the text if I could sit down somewhere alone with a paper copy and a pencil. I would be uneasy displaying those texts on a comscreen in the convent."

"She has a point, Dorien," said Father Agar. "Some of the nuns are so brainless—the chance of contamination, if they saw this stuff, or at least of unseemly gossip, would be considerable. Sister Miriam, I commend you for your scrupulous concern for your weaker sisters."

"Thank you, Father," she said.

"Get her her paper copy, Dorien, for goodness' sakes," Father Claude said crossly. "We can certainly afford one."

Father Dorien nodded. They certainly could. "All right," he agreed. "As you wish."

Can you really do that? her eyes were asking him. *Can you really get into the computer databanks of the Lines?*

Even from this woman, whose soul he had guided since her fourteenth year, and for whom he felt a respect he accorded few men, he would not tolerate impudence. An impudent woman, especially with this woman's gifts, was the first day of a plague. Encouraged, she would be the second and the third and the fourth. That had happened on this Earth before—it was not going to happen again. He locked glances with her, and felt something he could not have named, a kind of giving way, a joint snapping somewhere, as she looked down. He would show her who needed curbing!

"The material will be in your hands within forty-eight hours, Sister." He kept his voice as impersonal as any robot's. "I will then expect you to move quickly, and to keep me informed at every step. Do not take it upon yourself to decide that this is too trivial to tell me and that is too obvious to tell me, and so on—*do not presume*. You will report every detail to me, and *I* will decide what is to be ignored. You will remember your station, or you will be removed from this task and replaced by someone more suitable."

"Yes, Father," said the nun softly. "It is my privilege to obey."

"You will keep your absurd opinions to yourself," he continued, angry now, and not sure why. "You will not express them in front of the impressionable sisters participating in this project with you, nor will you express them anywhere *else*. I am disappointed in you, Sister Miriam Rose. *Deeply* disappointed!"

He could feel the eyes of the other two priests upon him; as they had thought him too indulgent when he ordered Miriam to sit in their presence, they now thought him far too rough, he knew that. And what they knew about controlling women would not have constrained a girl of three; he only hoped they would have sense enough to keep their unsolicited opinions to themselves, because he was in no mood to be gentle with *them*, either.

"This meeting is adjourned," he announced brusquely, jabbing the stud for the comscreen to banish the offensive text. He stood up swiftly, gathering his belongings as he did so, forcing the other men to follow his example or join the standing-versus-seated split in the rank of Sister Miriam. This brought them to their feet with astonishing speed, as he had intended that it should, and he led them out of the room as rapidly as was consistent with any semblance of propriety.

Sister Miriam brought up the rear, well behind the men, too far back to hear Agar's sputtering or Claude's complaining or Dorien's fierce order to them both to shut up for the sake of Christ, which he meant literally.

CHAPTER 17

"Dearest Allegra Anne,

"My poor little girl! you were absolutely right *to contact me* at once *when you found those disgusting holograms hidden in Beverly's study-chaise! Of* course *you should have written! Of* course *you did the right thing! And of* course—*of* course, *Allegra Anne—you can trust me not to say one single word about this to anybody else! Haven't I always told you that you could come to me with anything, no matter* how dreadful? *Heavens, what an* awful *experience for you! You are Mother's brave good girl. (And no, I certainly will* not *say anything to your father!)*

"I know, darling, that I can rely on you to spend as little time as possible with that awful Beverly until I can arrange to have you moved to another room. And you do remember, don't you, sweetheart, that Mother always *told you it would be best for you to have a private room instead of sharing one? And Mother was right,* wasn't *she?*

"Now, you must just put this whole nasty episode right out of your mind, darling, and concentrate on learning to be the very best wife any man could possibly want. We will never mention this again, and you are not to think *of it ever again. Mother will take care of the whole thing, don't you worry!*

"Many, many tender kisses, from . . .

Your proud and loving Mother"*

"Dear Mrs. Qwydda:

"I regret to inform you that my daughter Allegra Anne—who has the misfortune to share a room at Briary Marital Academy with your daughter Beverly—has written to me in great distress to tell me that your *child has a sizable collection of pornographic holograms hidden in their rooms. Including, my dear Mrs. Qwydda,*

sets of holos depicting Terran males engaged in sexual acts with both humanoid and nonhumanoid alien females!

"You will of course understand the nausea I feel, as well as my concern for my daughter's welfare. I have taken immediate steps to move my daughter to a private room, and have notified the Dean of Students at Briary of the reason for that action. I have also notified the Membership Boards of the major national women's clubs and their junior auxiliaries to be alert for any membership application from your daughter. I think I can safely say that my influence is sufficient to guarantee that Beverly will have no opportunity to become a member of any club worth joining.

"I respectfully suggest, my dear Mrs. Qwydda, that you seek immediate psychiatric treatment for your unfortunate child; you have my profound sympathy.

"Very truly yours,
Evvalinda Eustace (Mrs. B. B. Eustace)"

When Jo-Bethany was paged and told that she had a visitor, she was surprised, because she had been nearly three years at Chornyak Household and had never had a visitor before, nor had she ever expected to have one. When the visitor turned out to be Ham Klander, the surprise became astonishment—and cold suspicion. If Ham had wanted to see her, he would have sent a message summoning her to appear; he would never have made the effort of traveling to Chornyak Household for that purpose. And the idea that he would do so on one of the three days of the weekend, when he was ordinarily free from the brain-curdling tedium of his job, was too implausible even to consider. That he was here, nevertheless, meant that he wanted something from her; that he wanted something from her meant trouble.

She faced him, her hands clasped behind her back, and waited. In this place, in her uniform, he did not outrank her in quite the same way that he did in his own home, where he was undisputed potentate. She saw puzzlement on his face, while his mind—slow, but full always of an animal cunning—gradually sensed that there was a difference, and then even more gradually figured out what the difference was. That face of his had always been her most dependable source of information about him; it was as easy to read as foot-high block letters in black ink. She watched the realization of his disadvantage appear on it, and the petulant displeasure, and she braced for the inevitable bluster.

He didn't let her down. "Think you're smart, don't you?"

was his opening remark, with a matching sneer. "Think you're really *some*body, don't you, Jo-baby?"

"Good morning, Ham," said Jo, ignoring it. "What can I do for you?"

"Maybe I'm here to take you home for *good,* Scrawny . . . looks to me like you could do with a little reminding of your proper *place!*" He had his thumbs in his belt loops, and he was rocking on the balls of his feet; no doubt he was thinking of himself as the Big Bull of the Pampas. According to Melissa, that was what he fancied himself in bed; he would, she had told Jo-Bethany, stand in the doorway of their room naked, waggling his bulky erection at her, and shout, "Get ready, you lucky little bitch, here comes the Big Bull of the Pampas!" What happened after that, Jo-Bethany had carefully managed never to find out; what a pampas was she did not know, and she was very much doubted that Ham did.

"Ham," she said calmly, "that's just fine with me. Shall I go pack, while you tell Jonathan Asher Chornyak we're leaving?"

"God damn you to hell," said Ham, his speech slurred by the whiskey he'd obviously added to the strange brew that served him for consciousness before he arrived here.

"Thank you, Ham," Jo replied. "I'm sure I'm very fond of you, too."

He wanted very much to hit her; she could see the lust for it in his eyes. But he was not on his home turf, and he couldn't be sure what would happen if he tried that here; it was against the law in the United States to hit a woman. He was *afraid* he would hit her, as he was afraid of so many things, and she too felt a kind of lust—to step closer and provoke him further, here where he would not dare even the kind of clumsy shoves that he'd had to make do with when she was under his roof. Her hatred for him was at the root of that lust, and she was ashamed of it; she put it under firm control, and reminded herself that tonight she must pray she would not feel it again.

She stepped back from him, then, and kept her face blank; if she annoyed him further he would take out his frustrations on Melissa, and Jo hated the idea of that. Damage done to a woman in the marriage bed, unless it was very unusual and extensive damage, was acceptable, since it was only "normal male passion" and an expected part of married life for any woman paired with a sufficiently lusty husband. Any old bull. Like this one, or any of his brothers. How did women bear it, she wondered?

For Melissa's sake, and mindful of the gratitude she should be feeling because she was not Melissa or any of those other

women, she made an effort to be polite to him. She asked him
into the atrium around the Interface, where there were comfortable chairs and benches to sit on, and—for a linguist dwelling—
reasonable privacy. He followed her sullenly, but without protest,
and the way he stared at what was going on in the Interface
convinced her that she had made a wise choice. It was possible
that the exotic atmosphere there would make him forget his foul
humor. It was one thing to watch the brief docuclips of Interfacing that the linguists now and then allowed on the newspapers; it
was quite another to be there in person and see it happening right
before your eyes. She was sure that the two Aliens-in-Residence
now at Chornyak Household were humanoid, because the Lines
accepted no AIRY who wasn't; but they were sufficiently bizarre
in appearance, especially with the tufted tails whipping along in
synchrony with their speech, and the four separate triple-jointed
arms, to distract Ham Klander.

He stumbled over the edge of a bench, because he was looking
at the Interface instead of watching where he was going, and he
muttered at her. "They can't get out, can they, Sis?"

"Get out? Sit down, Ham, won't you, and make yourself
comfortable. . . . Can what get out?"

Klander made a large vague gesture toward the Interface.
"The whatsit—the AIRYs. What's it . . . I mean, what are *they*
doing?"

Jo-Bethany turned her head to look. The AIRYs were sitting
in what appeared to be some extraterrestrial variant of a lotus
position, side by side on the floor in their half of the Interface;
on the human side beyond the transparent barrier there was a row
of four solemn infants. One was still fastened into a babypod; the
others, old enough not to need such trappings, lay stretched out
on their stomachs facing the AIRYs.

"I don't know exactly, Ham," she said. "Maybe the AIRYs
are telling the kids a story; maybe they're just talking to each
other or to the kids. Whatever it is, they all seem happy enough.
And no, Ham—the AIRYs can't get out. Not without special
equipment being brought in. They'd die in Earth's atmosphere."

Klander looked relieved, and turned unsteadily sideways so
that he could stretch out his legs and put his feet up on the
bench.

"Well, I wasn't worried about it," he said.

"I'm sure you weren't, Ham," said Jo-Bethany. He had been,
of course, and he still was. In spite of the fact that every single
day there were humanoid Aliens from all over known space
carrying on business in the government buildings, with nothing

more unusual about the situation than the necessity for special environments and interpreters, and he knew that. Still, he was alarmed by the AIRYs. As much time as the Aliens spent on Earth, they were familiar to Terrans only as threedys or holos, because with few exceptions their problems with Earth's atmosphere restricted them to specially-equipped buildings and vehicles. You didn't run into them at your friendly neighborhood bar, or strolling down the city streets. And although the holos were faithful in every detail—you could look at a hologram of an Alien and be able to see it, hear it, and smell it—there was still a vast amount of information missing. Not only the entire sensory system of touch, but also the information from the less elementary senses; no amount of technological skill had been able to endow a hologram with "presence," for example. So that even if you had money enough to buy the fanciest projectors and were looking at lifesize holo Aliens, there was no possibility that you could ever fail to distinguish them from the genuine article. Ham was looking at the genuine article—*two* of the genuine articles— and it was different. He didn't like it. An Alien in a holo was exotic; an Alien in the flesh was *alien*. Jo hoped he would have nightmares; she *knew* he would not only make up a story about his total indifference to the AIRYs, and about their horrid appearance that would have struck terror into the heart of an ordinary man but caused him not so much as a quiver, he would also manage to *believe* the tale he concocted. It was an astonishing skill.

Because AIRYs ordinarily stayed for a period of four to five years, the present pair were the only ones Jo-Bethany had seen, and she had gotten used to them. They were not *that* horrible.

"Ham?" she hazarded; perhaps he'd watched the Interfacing long enough for the novelty to wear off. "Do you want to tell me why you're here?"

He looked at her as if he didn't know who she was, and then his face cleared and he rewarded her with a lopsided bleary grin. Looking at him, she was surprised he'd been allowed in; he must have put on a pretty good performance for whoever was on the door this week.

"My mind," he said. "It was wandering. You know. They're ugly." He waved at the Interface again, and Jo-Bethany wondered how he would have reacted if he'd been with her the night she had accepted the family's invitation and gone down to the computer room to watch the display of what they called "the Album"—a series of holos of each and every AIRY that had occupied the Interfaces of the Lines since the beginning of the process. Including the two nonhumanoid pairs that they'd accepted before they understood how dangerous that was for human infants. It had made her a little sick, and their Alienness didn't seem to get any less striking no matter how many you looked at or how often.

She tried again. "Ham, is everything all right at home? With Melissa and the children?"

"Oh, yeah. Melissa's fine, and the kids are okay. You oughta come home some Sunday and get to know your new nephew, Jo-baby. He's quite a boy."

I'll bet he is, she thought, and said, "Thank you, Ham, I'd like that. They keep me awfully busy here, but I'll certainly come home one of these days when I get a chance. Now maybe you'd like to tell me why you came to see *me?*"

He leaned forward a little, and studied her closely, as if he'd finally realized who she was, and she went on waiting, trying to avoid his breath. Finally he spoke to her, but without the usual bull-bluster; he was almost whispering.

"You're really in tight here, Jo-Bethany, aren't you?"

"I'm very satisfied, Ham, thank you."

"That's not what I mean. I mean you're in *tight.* You're like part of the family. You've got some *clout* here, right?"

She looked at him, uneasy, and he grinned again and jabbed at her knee with the toe of one shoe.

"Come *on!*" he said. "Never mind the innocent act, Sis. You're not like Lissy, I *know* you. You'll have the effing Lingoes eating out of your hand by this time. Don't try fooling me, Jo; it won't work."

"Ham—*what* do you want?"

He chuckled, and stretched his powerful arms, and folded his hands behind his head to lean on.

"I've got a plan," he told her. "And I'm here to explain to you what you're going to do to help."

"I see."

"And I don't want a lot of shit out of you, Jo, you got that? You give me a hard time, I'll give you a hard time. *And* your precious baby sister." He snickered. "It's just that simple. One, two, three, baby, down the track. Even *you* can follow my dust."

"Ham, you haven't told me what I'm supposed to do. How do you know I won't be glad to cooperate?"

"Because you think you hate my guts," he said comfortably. "You've got your little legs crossed so tight that you've cut off all the blood supply to your twat, you know? I'm *exactly* the kind of man you need, Jo, but you haven't got enough guts to admit it, so you think you hate me.''

''Ham—''

''I'm talking to you! You'd never cooperate with me if you could get out of it, and it's just too effing bad for you that you're such a pussy where your baby sister is concerned. That gives me lots of leverage with Miss High-and-Mighty-Hard-Ass-Uppity Jo-Bethany Schrafft!'' He slapped his thigh, delighted with himself and his wit. ''You don't like hearing that, do you, Sis? No, you don't like hearing that one bit. Well, that's tough, Jo! My heart aches for you.''

Jo-Bethany knew what he was after right now. She'd seen him do this with Melissa so many hundreds of times—she knew what he wanted from her. He wanted her to do what Melissa would have done. She was supposed to plead with him, beg him to tell her what he'd come here for, while he teased, and pretended he wouldn't tell, and started to tell and then said, ''Oh, never mind,'' and so on, for however long it took until he got bored with it. She wasn't going to play that game with him unless he began to seem angry enough again to be a danger to Melissa. She sat quietly and smiled at him, fully attentive, waiting, but she said nothing at all.

''You're no fun, Jo-Bethany, you know that?'' he said after a little while, his lower lip jutting in a sloppy pout.

''I do know that, Ham. I'm sorry.'' It must be awkward, wanting to order a woman to do something that your manly image wouldn't allow you to admit you wanted.

''Well, I don't have all day. So I'm just going to tell you.''

''Good enough,'' she said. ''What is it?''

''You know this new deal they've got set up, Jo, where they put just ordinary babies from anyplace, just plain ordinary ones, into the Interfaces? Just like they do the Lingoe pups? The new government program?''

''Sure. The youngest child in that Interface there right now isn't a Chornyak, it's one of the outside kids.''

''Well, I want you to get my boy into that program. I want you to do that *fast.* I called the people at D.A.T. that are in charge of it and told them I wanted Danny in, and they gave me a whole planeload of shit about a waiting list, and special qualifications . . . all that stupid shit. So I came straight to you. I'm not about to miss out on this, and it's only for babies, right? Danny's the right age now, and god knows I don't want any more kids. I want you to get Danny in the Interfacing program *right now,* Sis. *Here,* with the effing *Chorn*yaks, so I don't have to commute someplace with him all the time. And so I don't have to listen to Melissa having hysterics about her baby being too far away and all that crap. That's what I want, Jo-Bethany, *and what I want, I get.* You just look at my track record, any time. I mean to have it, and I *will* have it.''

Jo-Bethany leaned back in the chair, glad of the sunlight that gave her an excuse to close her eyes, praying for patience to deal with him without irritating him, and inspiration to say no to him in a way that he could not quarrel about. She realized that she ought to have expected this. Ham was dead set against work for himself, but he had no objection to others working on his behalf. The kind of money an interpreter of an Alien language could earn would draw Ham the way naked women drew him, and the fact that the boy could start earning that money while he was still only a child would look to Ham like Christmas In Perpetuum. She should have been expecting this, from the very first day that the news of the Interfacing breakthrough had been leaked to the media by the Multiversity professor.

"Well, Jo? Come on, say something." His voice was truculent; he hated being here where he wasn't top dog; he hated being so near the AIRYs; he hated the constant flow of people through the atrium; she could hear the unease in his voice, and she knew it wasn't a good sign. She could not risk his making a scene, not here.

"Ham, I don't think I can help you," she said slowly. "I'd be glad to, of course—I'd love to see Danny here, it would be a wonderful opportunity for him, and it would be nice to have someone from the family around even just a few hours at a time. But I don't think you understand the situation."

"*No?* Listen, Jo-Baby, I *always* understand the situation! *The situation is:* you work here, and you've got all kind of stuff you can hold over the Lingoes. Somebody's got a little touch of something nasty, you'd know about it. Somebody's a little warped, maybe shows up in your office with a foreign object in a place it shouldn't be, you know? You'd be the one that knows about it, in a case like that." He snickered, and winked at her to signal the conspiracy of nice powerful *filth* they could wallow in together.

Jo-Bethany fought her own bad temper—she spoke as evenly as she could. If she let him provoke her, he'd start a fight right here in the middle of Chornyak House. She didn't want that— she wanted him to *leave*. And that meant not upsetting him.

"No, Ham, I wouldn't be the one. In a case like that, the person would go to an emergency room, not to me."

"So, maybe that's not a perfect example; you know what I mean, all the same. There's bound to be plenty of dirt that gets into a clever little ugly head like yours, Sis, because that goes with nursing. People tell you stuff. And I expect you to show a decent loyalty to your family and put that dirt to good use. Like I said—don't give me a hard time. Just do your thing. Get your butt in gear and do your thing for the sake of your sister's kid, and her peace of mind. You understand me, Jo?"

"I understand," she answered.

"Well? How long will it take?"

She was thinking. She would have to stall him as long as possible. And she could hope that before it came right down to the wire something else would happen and he'd lose interest in this. She would have to be convincing. She wondered . . . what *were* the special qualifications for the babies sharing the Interface? She had no information that would help her, and no recollection of having heard anything about it from the Chornyaks. *Fake it, Jo-Bethany,* she told herself, but *go slow.*

"Ham, it's a great idea," she said. "You're right—it *should* be in the family! And it's just an indication of how stupid I am that you had to come all the way over here, and miss work besides, to point out to me something that I would have thought of myself if I'd had one brain in my head!"

She was watching him as she spoke, watching for that subtle change in his expression that would mean she was going too far and he was about to realize that she was putting him on. But he seemed genuinely pleased—unless he was putting *her* on . . . did he have that much imagination? She saw no signs of suspicion. It was astonishing how easily a man could be made to believe you when you were saying exactly what he wanted you to say, no matter how improbable it was. And she realized suddenly that before she had come here and lived among the Chornyak women she had not suspected that for an instant. She had learned that here, without even realizing that she was learning. Strange—and very welcome; perhaps this was part of the curriculum at the marital academies.

"Well, that's more like it!" announced the head of the Klander family, swinging his legs around and sitting up, so that he could slap his thighs with his hands and gather himself together to leave this creepy place. "Maybe I was wrong, Jo," he said. "Maybe having to live here with the Lingoes has given you some sense of what *normal* family feelings are like." He looked around him, and grimaced. "I'd go crazy in this place! No wonder they call them Lingoe dens—*hive* would be more like it, the way you're all crammed in here together."

"I've gotten used to it."

"Well. Nurses can get used to anything, right?" He reached over and patted her knee, willing to be pleasant now that he thought she was going to oblige him. "I appreciate your help, Jo-Bethany. And Melissa will be grateful, too. This is a great chance for Danny!"

A great chance for Danny. Jo-Bethany thought of how the children of the Lines lived, racing from one work site to another, always studying in every spare minute, trying to keep up, forced to fill adult roles when other children were still sucking their thumbs. Poor little Danny, if that happened to him.

"I'll do my very best, Ham," she said, putting into her voice all the warmth she felt for Melissa and Danny and Flowerette. "I'm glad you took the time to come point this out to me." She resisted the temptation to warble "Silly little me!" and wave her hands around and twitch . . . surely that would have been too much? Although she'd seen Melissa do *precisely* that, many a time, and Ham had not appeared to find it too much. It might help to have long red hair and a pretty face.

"I've got to go, Sis," he mumbled, looming over her, much too close. She wished he were only a hologram. "I've got a lot of work piled up."

A lot of work. One button to push, every thirty minutes.

"I know you do, Ham," she said sympathetically. "You go ahead—I'll get right on this. And I'll keep you posted; I'll let you know exactly how it goes." She lowered her lashes, trying to remember how Melissa did that, trying to *feel* like Melissa for just the necessary tiny bit of time. "It's the men here who decide things, of course," she said, all modest reluctance and timid flutters. "And I'm *afraid* of them." She smothered her distaste, drew a timid little gasp of a breath, and said, "Ham—you don't know what they're *like!*"

It was the right flourish, apparently; he gave a grunt of sympathy, and reached down to give her a hug that made her skin crawl.

"I understand, Sis," he said roughly. "You bet I do. And listen—if they give you any trouble . . . you know, if they try to push you around? Try to take advantage, just because you don't have a husband to look after you? You just let me know, and I'll punch their effing faces through the back of their heads. You get that, Jo-Bethany? You don't have to take *anything* off the sons of bitches."

"Thank you, Ham," she said, extracting herself from his grip. "You're—you're very kind. It's good to know that I have someone I can count on."

She watched him from the window, going out to the flyer with the swagger that she knew he practiced in front of a mirror. She was crying, she noticed; her cheeks were wet with her tears. Why was she crying? She had pulled it off; she had gained herself time. She'd be able to get weeks, months perhaps, out of her Scared Maiden skit. It had been absurdly easy to do. Why was she crying?

And then she knew, and she put her hands up to scrub away the tears that were betraying her. It was because she would far rather have taken her chances in a bed with one of the AIRYs . . . she had no idea which one was male, but she assumed one must be . . . than with Ham Klander. Who was supposed to be her species. Blood of her blood, flesh of her flesh, in some dim recess of pre-pre-history. A human man, as she was a human woman. Both of them, she and Ham, the descendants of Adam and of Eve.

Still. It was Ham Klander that Jo-Bethany found alien. Four arms, she could understand. They might even be useful. Ham Klander, on the other hand, was an absolute mystery. How could there *be* something like Ham Klander? And it survive, and flourish?

She hurried out the door and ran for Barren House, ran for her room, desperate to get out of her clothes and into a shower. To try to scrub from her skin the taint that came of just being *near* this man, of her own species. He would punch their faces through the back of their heads, he said. And he would, too. If somebody would hold them for him while he did it. He would name his daughter Flowerette, and he would punch their faces through the back of their heads with his meaty fists, and he was her own kind.

Barren House was not close enough; Jo-Bethany vomited, ignominiously, in the daylily beds beside the walkway.

II

Father Agar stood in front of the abbot's worktable, bouncing cheerfully on his heels, and asked, "Does it seem to you that our nuns are more than usually enterprising lately, Dorien?"

Father Dorien frowned at him; he certainly *hoped* not. The last thing Mother Church needed was "enterprising" nuns.

"Explain, please," he said. "In that way, enterprising?"

"Well, you know, it's not just here." Bounce, bounce.

"It's not just here? What is that supposed to mean? What's not? Not just here what? Lord, you're irritating, Agar! You look like a child that needs to pee, you know that? The behavior of the nuns is not your responsibility—you're perfectly safe reporting their outrages."

"Oh, not outrages, I assure you." The bouncing stopped. "In fact, I find it rather admirable, to be perfectly frank. I'm not sure I would have their courage."

Dorien let his head drop into his hands, and closed his eyes. "Father," he pleaded, "either tell me what you're referring to, or go on about your business and let me get this program cleaned up. One or the other. *Please.*"

"Sorry," Father Agar said. "It may be only a coincidence, of course." When that provoked nothing from Dorien but a groan, he went on hastily, "I just meant that they tell me nuns all over the country are requesting transfer to the colonies, and I think that shows real *pluck*. To go from a cloister, out into space, to primitive conditions, all that hustle and bustle—or all that desolation and wilderness, depending—that takes a little something extra, Father, to my mind. Just imagine it!"

Dorien stared at him. "How *many* nuns, all over the country?"

"Oh . . . ." Father Agar waved a vague arm. "Half a dozen or more, I'm told."

Dorien's eyebrows shot up, and he made an irreverent reference to several of the Apostles. "Good *lord*, Agar! I thought there were hundreds of them, all clamoring to desert us for the hinterlands, the way you were carrying on! *Half a dozen!*"

"I don't remember *any* such requests in previous years," Father Agar objecting, looking injured. "That's a large jump, from zero to six!"

"Certainly! Six hundred percent. I can see the headlines now. Father Agar, six is only six. There are thousands of nuns in the United States alone—six of them hardly constitute a groundswell. What sort of nuns are these, according to the gossip that I assume is your source? Senior sisters? Major losses to their communities?"

"Oh, no," Agar reassured him. "All quite young, and not in any way crucial to their houses. As I understand it, several of them happen to be illegitimates turned over to the Daughters Of Genesis and raised in the convents."

"Well, that makes perfectly good sense. They're probably finding the normal pathways for moving upward in the convents blocked, Agar."

"Sister Miriam Rose was one of the illegitimates," Agar noted, looking carefully at the wall behind Dorien's right shoulder, "and it hasn't held *her* back."

"She's hardly typical," said Dorien, striving for patience. "She had exceptional qualifications, and I went out of my way to create an opportunity for her. That doesn't usually happen." He picked up the printouts he'd been poring over when Agar interrupted him, and held them in an ostentatious manner that the other man could not possibly fail to see, and added, "Let's be frank, Agar—a sister who not only brings no dowry but is the product of fornication or adultery, a child of disgrace, is going to have a difficult time. There's no way to keep a thing like that secret within a community. No one's going to be openly unjust to the poor things, but they're scarcely on the ladder of progress."

"Uhuh. Uhuh." He was bouncing again. "Naturally, it would occur to them that they might do better if they went out to the colonies, where their origins wouldn't matter much. I hadn't thought of that."

"Obviously," sighed Father Dorien. And then he asked, struck by a sudden thought, "They aren't asking for places like Arya, or Baron, or—god forbid—Gehenna, are they? It's not some kind of mad idea of civilizing the barbarians with the gentle touch of the virgin?"

"No, no. Nothing like that, although that would be very interesting, wouldn't it? I think . . . let me see . . . oh, yes, I remember. They've been asking for Horsewhispering, I believe, and for Strawberry Fields. And Harmony—two of them wanted to go to Harmony. Places with enough population and settlement to make the services of a nun desirable and useful, but far enough from Earth—and new enough—to give them a pretty open territory. I mean, now that you've pointed out what's going on, I see the pattern."

"Plenty of women at those locations," Dorien commented, "and that's the main thing. Perhaps some of our good sisters can manage to set an example for those ridiculous people on Strawberry Fields; I'd certainly approve of *that*."

Agar looked blank. "There are so many colonies now," he said mournfully. "It must have been so much simpler when there were only a dozen. What's so ridiculous about the Strawberry Fielders, or Fieldites, or whatever they are?"

"They're hippies, Agar, that's what's ridiculous. They could *use* a nun. If anybody asks for my vote, I'll say by all means send them *several* nuns."

"What's a hippie?" Agar looked even blanker than before, and Father Dorien gave up trying to keep a Christian calm and smacked the worktable with his free hand.

"Damnation, Agar!" he roared. "Go read a history book! Try the infamous 1960's! Don't you know anything at *all?*"

"I resent—"

"And as for it being easier when the only colonies we had were the ones on Luna and Mars, that's ridiculous! Before we even *thought* of colonies in space, people in this country couldn't tell you where Denmark was, or if New Zealand was part of Africa! People—including you, Agar, know damn little, and nothing that doesn't affect them personally! Now go on about your business and let me get on with mine, before I lose my temper!"

"It appears to me, Father Dorien, that you have already lost it," remarked Agar with great dignity, and he folded his hands before him and strode stiffly from the office as if he were trying to balance a realbook on his head.

Dorien stared resignedly after him, regretting his irritation; it wasn't fair for him to deliberately choose nincompoops for colleagues and then torment them for being nincompoops. But the computer program he was trying to sort out was one of those projects that requires a man's full attention, where every interruption means starting over from the beginning, and he was already late setting it to rights. Agar had caught him at a bad moment; he would apologize to him later, and explain.

He made a brief note on his wrist computer, reminding him to check in six months and be sure that the number of nuns wanting transfer into space remained as trivial as it was now. And then he put the matter out of his mind and settled down to work, praying for just one hour without interruptions. "Please, God," muttered Father Dorien, "Occupy my beloved nincompoops with some sort of nonsense, just for sixty of your blessed minutes. Amen."

CHAPTER
18

"Anything whatsoever that can be said in one human language can be said in every other human language; that is true. But a thing that can be said quickly and with ease in one tongue may require a great deal of time and many many words in another. As the centuries go by, and a language grows and changes, there may be a skewing of its development in one direction or another; certain parts of experience may become inconvenient and cumbersome to talk about. Not that they can't be talked about, but just that it becomes so complicated to do so that it's hard to find anyone willing to listen.

"There was English, for example, and then its development as Panglish. Suppose you were a speaker of Panglish and you wanted to talk about war, or killing or violence. There was no weapon, and no smallest variation on a weapon, that did not immediately receive its own convenient Panglish name, easy to pronounce and easy to remember. If there were fifty different subtle variations on the use of one's hands to take a human life, you could be sure that Panglish would provide you with fifty different subtle manners of expressing those variations with speed and ease in conversation. But not all of life was so well provided for as were those parts most closely associated with violence. There was the word 'love'; it was almost impossible in Panglish to say which of the many subtle and different kinds of love was the one you felt toward someone in less than ten minutes; if it was a man you were talking to, he would leave or fall asleep before you could finish what you were trying to say. (As for the act *of love, there was not one single word for a woman's part in that!) Panglish society found itself obliged to create a separate class of special persons who were paid by the hour,* just to listen; *and their work was considered so unpleasant that the standard*

fee for a therapist's time as early as the year 2000 was one hundred twenty-five dollars an hour, a very large sum at that time.

"It is an interesting fact, linguistically, that the most common complaint of Panglish-speaking men toward women in conversation was this sharp question: 'For god's sake, will you get to the point?'"

(from the diaries of Nazareth Chornyak Adiness)

There were eleven nuns in the narrow room with Sister Miriam, lined up in two rows that faced the cubicle where Miriam herself worked; she could sit at her own computer and watch them through the arched door. Each one was bent over the primitive terminal that had been assigned to her, and each one was aware that it could have been much worse. There had been a time when they would have had to make do with typewriters, and not so very long ago, either. A vow of poverty was a vow of poverty after all.

It didn't occur to Sister Marisol, the youngest nun present, that before typewriters there had been a time when the sort of work they were doing had been done by hand, with paper and ink, and that before that there had been parchment, and papyrus scrolls, and tablets of clay. . . . She was a devoted and industrious nun, and good at what she did, but her total education in the history of this world had been a series of fourteen mass-ed computer lectures titled "Great Events Through the Ages." It had been strong on wars and kings and explorations and conquests; it had not taken up the matter of how people had managed to write things down in the ancient past.

If you had sat Marisol down and ordered her to think about it, she would have been reasonably prompt in saying that of course the Old Testament Prophets and the Early Christian Fathers had not typed the Bible; she was not stupid. But it wasn't something she gave any thought to, any more than she thought, of her own initiative, about what life in the Bronze Age might have been like. Nudged a little, she would have remembered seeing monks portrayed in religious paintings, scrawling away on unknown surfaces with pens and inks, and she might have thought of that as romantic. She most emphatically did *not* consider the Apple 79R's with which she and the other sisters had to make do romantic. Not in any way. She wished they could have had modern equipment to work with, and had twice been obliged to do penance for saying so.

Now she was keeping her eyes on her work, squinting at the screen, but all the rest of her senses were tuned to Sister Miriam. Marisol could see why Sister Miriam had been put in charge of this project—she was just the sort of person you would *need*, if you wanted a woman to be in charge of it. And as the good Father had said, it made no sense to put a man in charge of revising texts in a language constructed specifically for women. That was clear enough, and although no one had asked for her opinion she had been in full agreement. Nevertheless, she regretted it. Because it would have been so much easier to work under the supervision of a priest, who would always have been making allowances for the fact that you were only a woman. Sister Miriam made no allowances, not for gender or for anything else, not for herself or for any of the women whose work she was responsible for. She was made of stone and steel and plastics, and Marisol had twice been obliged to do penance for saying *that*.

She hated it when Miriam managed to sneak up behind her. There Marisol would be, craning her aching neck at the cursed old screen where the text was displayed, trying to make out what it was supposed to mean without having to call up the dictionary—because that would mean reducing the size of the letters even more to make room for it—and suddenly there'd be Sister Miriam at her left shoulder. Marisol would have heard not one sound . . . she wondered if Miriam went barefoot . . . and suddenly there would be that iron grip on her shoulders, bringing her bolt upright at her station and gasping with the surprise of it. And then the voice. *More* iron, and ice-cold iron at that, like the convent gates in February. How could any woman, allegedly filed with the love of God and of His Son and of the Blessed Mother, be *so cold?* Sister Miriam—Sister Miriam *Rose,* actually, though nobody could possibly look at her and think of roses, and Marisol had never heard her called anything but Sister Miriam—was a mystery. An enigma. Everyone agreed on that. Perhaps it was because she was a bastardess, born of wicked dissipation and scandalous lust; Marisol knew that she was not supposed to consider that Sister Miriam's fault, except in the sense that original sin was Sister Miriam's fault as it was everybody's, but she couldn't help it. And now she'd thought of it again, and she would have to confess it, and there'd be a penance again for her lack of charity; there was no end to the burdens Sister Miriam imposed on you, just by her skinny presence. It wasn't fair.

Miriam was coming down the row now, and Marisol tensed,

but she didn't get that far, praise be. It was Sister Tamarah that had the rotten luck this time, and Marisol was sure she heard Tamarah's shoulderbones crack under the other nun's powerful hands. Give her a priest any time, thought Marisol, especially if he could be well into his sixties and a bit addled. She would not have enjoyed one of the young firebrand Fathers; but then nobody would have put a priest of that kind in charge of eleven nuns revising Bible translations.

"Display, Sister Tamarah!"

Sister Miriam's voice cut the air right down the middle, if you could imagine air having a middle; listening to her, Marisol could.

The text went up on the big screen at the front corner of the room, left of the door, keyed from Tamarah's terminal, and Miriam began at once to lecture them on its various inadequacies. That was all right. "Inadequacies" were easily handled. What made the nuns anxious, and sometimes more than anxious—because most of them were genuinely afraid of Sister Miriam—was when she began speaking of "excesses." "Inadequacies" meant there was something you ought to have put in (or something the creaking old computer ought to have put in) that had not appeared. "Excesses," on the other hand, meant you had put something in that neither you nor the computer had been authorized to insert.

When that happened, it usually happened for reasons of style. "Felicity of expression," it was called. The style every one of the nuns was striving for would have been *characterized* by felicity of expression, and sometimes that led to difficulties you never would have foreseen. You would look at a passage from the materials that the linguist women had prepared, translated from the English—not even Panglish, but English!—into their "Láadan." And the computer program would already have done all the automatic things to it. The series of masculine pronouns that Sister Miriam had added to the language would have replaced the sloppy genderless ones the women of the Lines had used, unless of course the reference was actually to a female, and then the computer would have put in *that* set. Everywhere that one of the multitude of words for "love," each referring to a special kind of love, had been, the program would have substituted the neutral Láadan term Miriam had selected for that purpose. Places where "child of the Holy One" had replaced "Son of God" would have been corrected and restored to their earlier form; places where metaphors of battle had been tampered with would have been automatically restored. The program that did all this was named "Patriarch," and Sister Miriam was said to have written it herself, apparently not the least bit disconcerted by having to do it in a computer language that had the same relation to contemporary ones that Middle English had to contemporary Panglish, or worse—and it worked very well, thank you. When it got through, you still had a Láadan text, but it was free of every single one of the routine blemishes of feminism.

But the result was not always *felicitous*. All those rules interacting, in the mindless way that was the best these old machines could manage, sometimes produced results that were free of feminist slant but were offensive for other reasons. And then the nuns were expected to fix the problem, which was where "excesses" originated. None of them knew Láadan; they had to make their alterations with the help of the dictionary and grammar in the computer's memory. Their intentions were good, but their results all too often set Miriam off, as if they had done it on purpose to annoy her.

Marisol remembered a time when the offending "excess" had come from Sister Ann Martha . . . a Láadan word she had selected to replace a name of a female animal had turned out to include in it somewhere a mystifying reference to "sexual congress with someone you dislike but have respect for." And Sister Miriam had turned on them all, furious as they'd ever seen her, and had almost screamed at them: "Don't any of you know *anything* about morphology?" They had stared at her, shocked into stillness the way rabbits are shocked by the sound of an eagle shrieking, and indeed Sister Miriam had reminded them of an eagle, standing the way she was with her arms spread wide in the long black sleeves and her eyes flaming in her face. And then she had shaken her head slowly and let the black sleeves fall and folded her hands over her heart, and said, "No . . . of course you don't. I beg your pardon, sisters. You don't even know what morphology *is*, do you?"

They didn't know. And they had no reason to be ashamed of that. If it had been something a nun needed to know, they would have been taught about it. Marisol would have let it pass; but Ann Martha was still bruised at Miriam's vehemence, and she had insisted that the senior nun *explain* morphology, if it was so important.

"It isn't that important," Miriam had said, with a gentleness that was unusual for her. "Please forgive me—I think perhaps I am a little overtired."

Ann Martha was stubborn; she would not let it go. "Nevertheless," she said, and stuck her chin out for emphasis. "We would prefer not to be . . . not to be ignorant, Sister. We would prefer not to be in a position where others can *call* us ignorant.''

She had looked at them, thinking it over, and then nodded very slowly.

"A morpheme," she had said, in the cold voice that was her accustomed voice, "is the smallest piece of a language that has an independent meaning. The combination of morphemes into words is called morphology. It is morphology, sisters, that tells you the words 'sign' and 'signature' and 'insignia' have related meanings. The morphology of Láadan is so new that it is transparent. Think of 'mid,' which means 'creature', and 'balin', which means 'old'. When you see that the Láadan word for a tortoise is 'balinemid' you have no trouble understanding the morphology. And if 'woth' means 'wisdom', finding the mule named 'wothemid' in Láadan tells us—through morphology—something about the way the women of the linguist families view the world.''

There had been a soft murmur among the nuns, moving round the terminals, because this was an interesting idea, and each one could see examples they had not seen before.

"I should have spoken to you about this when we began our work," Sister Miriam had added. "It would have been helpful to you. But sisters—truly, I did not realize that you were unaware of these things.''

She let them hear that, and understand it, and then she was through being helpful. No doubt it had been a strain on her, being pleasant through four consecutive sentences.

"But now I *have* told you," she snapped, "and the concept is clear, and if you see a Láadan morpheme that has a feminist taint lurking inside a word in future I shall expect you to recognize that and remove it! For example, sisters, I shall expect you to be alert to any words that may hide within them the morphemes for 'water' or 'wet' or 'rain'—anything of that sort. They are all too often suspect, and frequently blasphemous. Is that clear?''

Up went Ann Martha's hand, to ask if they might spend time studying the Láadan dictionary, so that relationships among the words and parts of words would come more readily to their minds.

"Absolutely not!''

"But, Sister—''

"It's bad enough that you must be exposed to these foul writings! I am concerned for the welfare of your souls; I wish we could leave the entire task to computers, which have no souls to lose. You are *absolutely* not to add an additional source of contamination to what already endangers you! You are forbidden to study the dictionary *or* the grammar—the computer knows what they contain, and will provide you with what you absolutely must have to do your work. And *that will suffice,* sisters."

"Sister, may I speak?" Young as she was, and frightened of Miriam as she was, Marisol still had wanted to point out that they were really not so feeble of faith that just looking at feminism could corrupt them. But Miriam had said only, "You may *not!*" and had left the room with a "God be praised" that sounded like a curse.

Her harsh manner surprised no one. She was known to be a hard taskmaster and a pitiless supervisor; it was expected of her. If she hadn't been that way, the other nuns would have been disappointed in her. And it was not surprising that the program called Patriarch, written as it was in the outdated language, often provided results that were unsuitable for any church service. But there was something else, something that genuinely *was* surprising, something that perhaps went with Miriam's prickly, unyielding personality but seemed inappropriate and inexplicable nevertheless—who would have suspected that Father Dorien's precious Sister Miriam Rose would have a terrible tin ear? It was shocking, the way she would take a properly defeminized section, with a lovely ring to it when you read it aloud, and fool around with it until it went clanking and stumbling over the tongue, completely ruined.

She knew both Latin and Greek; she knew English of several periods, and could have read Shakespeare in twentieth-century texts; she knew French well; it was rumored that she knew Aramaic, and a little Japanese; a sister whose tongue was not as tightly attached as it ought to have been claimed to be certain that Sister Miriam knew and used Sign. Most curious of all, she sang like an angel. Trite; but true—like an angel! When she took the solos before the choir, and her voice soared with a magnificence and power that seemed entirely effortless, even the women who disliked her most held their breaths to listen. Given all that, how *could* she take something theologically correct, and lovely to say, and turn it into the sort of unreadable rackety clatter that she did? It was more than any of the nuns she supervised could comprehend.

"Perhaps she does it on purpose," Sister Gloria John had muttered to the others, after one especially unpleasant sequence produced by Miriam's tinkering had been entered into storage as a final version.

"Why? Why on earth?"

"Because," Gloria said, "the longer she can keep us at this, the longer she can avoid doing any real work herself. And when the Fathers read the garbage she has produced, they'll make her throw it all out and start over again from the beginning."

"That's a terrible thing to suggest!" Ann Martha protested, even though she secretly suspected that what she felt for Sister Miriam was not simply dislike but fullblown hatred. "Have you no charity at all?"

"So it is, and perhaps I don't," Gloria admitted. "But I tell you, uncharitable or not, I think I prefer it to the idea that she doesn't even *know* when what she writes hurts everybody's ears!"

Maybe. They hadn't been able to decide which was worse, ignorance or sabotage. Neither alternative was acceptable. Because as much as they disliked and feared Sister Miriam, every single one of them respected her completely and without reservation.

"Maybe we should speak to one of the Fathers about it?"

"Gloria John!"

"Well? Isn't it our duty?"

Sister Fiona, a sturdy woman of forthright habits and expression, had set both her arms akimbo in a gesture having not one feature of humility and demanded, "Are you out of your mind? Do you realize what Sister Miriam would do if one of us went to the priests and complained that her literary and liturgical style doesn't meet our standards?"

It was a sobering thought, and one that kept them silent while Fiona embroidered on it.

"And do you have any idea what the priests would say *back* to a complaint such as that, if one of us was fool enough to make it?"

"We could all go together, in a group," suggested Sister Gloria slowly. "We could tell them what we all agreed, so that they'd see it couldn't just be spite, or one of *us* with a tin ear. Sisters—the things she does to these texts are . . . repulsive!"

"You will go without me, if you go," declared Marisol instantly. "I do not wish to spend the rest of *my* days scrubbing plastic floors on a frontier planet, Sister!"

There had been a little additional muttering and fretting, making Marisol think of a poultry yard that had been a hobby of her mother's. But eventually they had all hushed and gone back to their work, keeping to themselves the certainty that if they did it well they could rely on Sister Miriam to spoil it. It was the only safe thing they could do.

There was no lack of women to fill convents. A convent was

one of the very few alternatives that a woman on today's Earth had to a life of unrelenting silliness. If you thrived on silliness, that was all very well—you'd be treated to it in heaping portions. But if you were an intelligent and ambitious female, you suffered. If you'd been lucky enough either to be born Roman Catholic or to belong to a family that would allow you to become Roman Catholic, the convent was a compromise of sorts. Life there was not all excitement and danger—if that was what you wanted, you did your best to marry a man who would take you out to the colonies—but it was not totally absurd, either. And you didn't have to spend every moment of your time catering to the whims of some human male. Catering to the whim of God had more appeal; if He made messes, they had grander scope.

But you could be expelled from the convent, your place given to some other eager woman, for nothing at all. At the whim of any priest who chose to denounce you, for whatever infraction, however trivial, or even imaginary. There was no real appeal, if a priest decided that he didn't wish to tolerate your presence in a convent for which he was advisor, although of course there was a paper appeal that you could waste your time going through if you were so inclined. And then what did you do? If you had spent all your life in a convent, what did you do, out in the world of men?

Sister Miriam's revisions bruised the ears of the other nuns, who were accustomed to magnificent ritual language, and they winced as they entered them in the files; but they would keep their esthetic judgments to themselves.

CHAPTER 19

TO: All Homeroom Teachers, Grades 1–12
FROM: United States Department of Education, Curriculum Division, Subsection Four

Please be advised that no further requests for deviations from the established schedule of official Holiday Observances will be tolerated by this department. The current calendar of one Holiday Observance per week constitutes maximum efficiency coupled with maximal educational opportunity, and the recent agitation regarding the Fourth of July Observance must be the *last* such episode. No competent Homeroom Teacher should have any difficulty explaining to his students the appropriateness of celebrating the Fourth of July in January, since:

1. Homeroom is not in session during July;
2. January, like July, begins with the letter "J";
3. No other month of the school year begins with "J".

Student proposals in this regard are to be *firmly* ignored; students who persist in efforts to have established HO's removed from the calendar, or their official dates changed—or who attempt to add unauthorized observances to the list!—are to be assigned Penalty Essays in one-thousand word increasing increments until they understand the futility of their efforts. (NOTE: Any Homeroom Teacher who allows a student to wangle an expulsion from Homeroom by such transparent tactics will receive a single warning; a second such incident shall be grounds for immediate dismissal without appeal. Such naiveté in teachers is *not* acceptable.)

Homeroom Teachers are reminded that the vigorous and enthusiastic observance of our national holidays during Homeroom is crucial to the social development of the American child. Neglect of this principle has repeatedly been proved (see Hynderson & Whiplash 2026, Volume III, pp. 1349–1477) to represent a major barrier to normal cultural functioning. The list of the thirty-six official holidays for in-class observance during the school year is attached to this memorandum, together with the latest chart of suggested holiday-coordinated classroom activities.

G.R.E.

TEACHERS! DO YOU HAVE A NEW AND ZAPIPPY IDEA FOR HOLIDAY CLASSROOM ACTIVITIES? A SPECIAL WAY TO TIE IN GEOGRAPHY WITH EASTER? A UNIQUE CRAFT IDEA LINKING SOCIAL STUDIES WITH REA- GAN'S BIRTHDAY? A NEW HISTORICAL SKIT FOR THANKSGIVING? SEND IT TO SUBSECTION FOUR TO BE SHARED WITH OTHER TEACHERS, FOR PUBLICA- TION IN THE MONTHLY ACTIVITIES BULLETIN! YOU WILL BE CREDITED WITH ONE DAY'S BONUS PAY FOR EACH SUGGESTION ACCEPTED AND PUBLISHED! (THE DEPARTMENT RESERVES THE RIGHT TO EDIT YOUR SUGGESTIONS, FOR LENGTH AND FOR STYLE.)

The room would not be appearing in the Terran Homes section of *Planet & Asteroid*. It did not have warmth, it did not have charm, and it was difficult to believe that it was intended for human occupation. It looked like the inside of a giant egg, emptied and scrubbed. High on the rear wall (in the sense that it was the surface farthest from you as you came in through the door) was a desk; like the room, it was absolutely white, and shaped like an egg. The curving walls were punctuated seem- ingly at random by niches, in which were stowed realbooks, microfiches, electronic gadgets, and a few personal items. The niche locations were in fact not random, but computer-generated according to an optimum equation for the purpose; Macabee Dow did not do anything randomly if he had control of the situation, and he had had total control of the construction and arrangement of this room. It was his study, and he cared nothing at all for the fact that it was spine-chillingly unwelcoming. So was he. The colleague foolish enough to suggest to him that what he was after in both study and desk was a womb had been informed that that was imbecilic, that wombs were dark red inside and their walls lined much of the time with blood, that it was pitch dark inside a womb, that the interior surface of a womb was soft rather than hard, and that the inspiration for the room was the number nine. As Macabee *Dow* visualized the number nine.

Macabee was not bothered by the fact the floor was not flat; he never used it, and the ultrasonics that kept the study spotless cared nothing for the shape of what they cleaned. There was no "decoration" of any kind, not so much as a print or a flower or a holo; there were no lights or lamps, because the walls were translucent glow-sandwiches and the light came from everywhere. The indispensable blackboard (which was of course not black), the comset screen, anything that might have interrupted the smooth flow of glowing white, all were safely inside the desk where they could not offend the eye. As was Macabee, most of the time.

Gabriel Dow was only eleven, but he had sense enough to realize the strangeness of the study. He strongly suspected that when his father looked at the small garden his mother insisted on maintaining at the center of the apartment he saw it the way he saw the study. Maybe as the inside of a green egg instead of a white one; maybe as the representation in the natural world of the number eleven or the number seven-and-a-half. Gabe was nearly certain that when his father granted the world the privilege of his glance he imposed this kind of order upon it . . . he bet his father shit geometrically perfect ovoids.

Gabe was nervous; he was pretty sure what this morning's conference topic was going to be. He'd been expecting it for weeks, and was surprised that it had taken this long; probably they'd been trying to make special allowances for him because he was the very first ordinary kid to have native fluency in an Alien language, the very first one that didn't come from the thirteen linguist families. Probably they'd kind of hated to spoil his image. And more importantly, they were scared of his father; for *sure*, they were scared of his father.

Almost everybody was. Gabe wasn't. He hated him, but he wasn't scared of him. He knew what his own place was in the world of Macabee Dow; he came after mathematics, and before every other human being dead or alive. It wasn't the worst of places.

He crossed the room, liking the cool of the floor against his bare feet, and used one toe to touch the spot exactly beneath the center of the door to the desk; soundlessly, the desk extruded the elegant set of eleven steps that Gabriel's mother refused to climb because they made her dizzy. It was their narrowness, and their steep angle, and the fact that they were so transparent as to be just this side of invisible, that made her dizzy, of course. Gabe had fallen off them dozens of times when he was little, before he got the hang of it—the important thing was not to *look* at them, just let your feet do it all for you.

"Macabee?" he said, uneasily. "Okay if I come up?"

"Would I have sent for you if I didn't want you to come up?"

Gabe shrugged, and took the steps swiftly; as he lifted his foot from the top one, the whole staircase folded itself back into the base of the desk, and he saw his father's fingers touch the spot that would put the stairs on LOCK. So that nobody else could join them.

There was no point in putting it off, and a certain number of points to be acquired by taking a confident stance. Gabe looked his father right in the eye, pitched his voice as low as it would go, and demanded, "Well? What have I done to disgrace us all now, sir?"

"Sir" was all right; it was a title of respect, untainted by emotion. It was words like "Father" and "Papa" and "Dad" that were forbidden, all of them being what his father called "terms of slop."

"Sit," said Macabee. "I'm not pleased."

"No," said Gabe, sitting as directed. "I guess you're not."

"You do know what this is about, Gabriel. *Don't* you?"

"I guess so."

"How long?"

"How long, sir?"

"How *long*, my son who is named for an angel, have you know that you were getting unsatisfactory evaluations as an interpreter?"

"Six weeks, maybe. Maybe a little longer." Lots longer, really; six months, a year . . . he wasn't sure. He wasn't telling, either.

"Six weeks! They said nothing to me, not one single word, until yesterday afternoon!"

Gabriel shrugged again; everybody, he had noticed, shrugged a lot around his father. Or twitched. "They were afraid to tell you, I expect," he said.

"You think so?"

"I know so. Everybody's scared of you, Macabee. You know that."

"Except you."

"And Raphael. And Michael." His younger brothers, also named for angels. Who, his father had explained to them, were not to be confused with the feathered lady harpists in billowy skirts that you saw on Christmas cards. An angel, Macabee had told them, was an abstraction of splendor suitable for the focus of spiritual energy; they had not argued with him.

"And your mother?"

Don't shrug, Gabriel—he forced his shoulders to stillness.

"She's a woman," he answered. "Women are scared of *everything*."

"I see. Well, since you know what it's all about, and you're not afraid of me, that saves us time. You can begin by explaining it to me. I do not expect to hear the words 'I don't know' used in this explanation."

Gabriel stared hard at the bare white floor, trying to think. He'd known this was going to happen *some*time, and he'd known he would be ordered to explain; he'd intended to work out a really clear concise logical speech of explanation and have it ready, have it memorized. But he hadn't gotten around to it. He'd considered being a smartass and constructing the speech in his Alien language, of which Macabee understood not one word, but he hadn't gotten around to that either. He hadn't really wanted to *think* about any of this, that was why.

"Gabriel—*explain*. Why must I be told that you are, and I quote, 'inattentive, slovenly, careless, and entirely inadequate' in the performance of your duties? Why *is* that, Gabe?"

"You're not going to understand," the boy said miserably. "I don't know any way to make you understand."

"Try me."

"You're just going to say 'you had an opportunity, and you had an obligation, and none of your remarks are relevant.' What's the point of trying to talk about it?"

"The point," said Macabee Dow, "is that I need to know. If I don't understand at first, you can tell me again. As many times as it takes, until I have sufficient data *to* understand."

"Jesus, I'll be here all morning."

"If necessary."

Gabe glanced at his father, and back at the floor again, and apologized; just because he hated him, that was no excuse for being rude. Macabee was never rude to *him*. "Sorry I cursed, Macabee," he said. "I was showing off."

"You were. It's understandable. Now begin."

The boy sighed heavily, and he let his arms hang aimlessly beside his knees. "I don't know any way to *do* this, sir," he said again, hopelessly. "I don't know how to start, even. And I know you said I wasn't supposed to say I don't know, but I *don't*."

"Try linear mode. One word after another; full stop, every now and then. Until it's all said."

Gabriel put his face in his hands, and he moaned. He knew how much that would irritate Macabee, who would not have moaned if you'd dipped his face in a vat of boiling oil, but moans were Gabriel's style. He was hoping for irritation sufficient to draw something in the way of a lecture on manliness and fortitude and assorted other good qualities from the professor, as a postponing strategy, but when he peeked through the cracks between his fingers he could see that it wasn't going to work.

The expression on Macabee's face came from the set titled "Grim & Patient," at the extreme end of the set, and it would be there all morning. All day. *Just say it, Gabriel,* he told himself fiercely, *just go on and say it! What's the worst thing that can happen? He can't do anything about it, even if he'd like to kill you. And he wouldn't like to kill you. Because you and Raphael and Michael, abstractions of splendor in the making, represent Macabee Dow, Continued.*

"Okay!" he blurted. "Okay! Macabee. . . . Macabee, I don't *want* to be a *linguist!*"

His father frowned through the grim and the patient. "You're *not* a linguist," he observed. "What does that have to do with it? What's that got to do with you going to sleep during negotiations? What's that got to do with you elaborating an Alien delegate's speech—during a labor negotiation, Gabriel, of considerable importance—by adding a dozen unprintable Panglish obscenities? You're not a linguist, and nobody ever said you had to be; you're a simultaneous interpreter of a significant Alien language, who was given a spectacular opportunity guaranteeing you a spectacular future. All you have to do is interpret. You don't have to live in a herd underneath the ground, you don't have to do group gymnastics at six o'clock in the morning in the middle of winter, you're not required to spend all your spare time hacking away at *more* languages—you don't have to do any of that stuff. Just interpret. And your command of the language is flawless." He stopped and tapped the scrap of pliofilm he was holding . . . the hard copy of the comset message complaining about him, Gabriel supposed. "Even these men at D.A.T. agree on that. They all say you're very good indeed at what you do, if you choose to be."

"It's a *joint complaint?*"

"Five of them are signing, Gabe. *Five.* All disgusted. They have, they say, given you every possible chance, and I believe them. From the look on your face, I assume they've gone beyond that. What's the matter with you, exactly, to make them say these things?"

"Macabee, listen to me," the boy said urgently. "Try to just listen for a minute. I'm not going to be able to say this nice and neat, it's gonna be sloppy and all messed up. But I mean every word of it, and I'd like to get it over with. Without you doing a kind of running review as I go *along,* Macabee."

"Agreed. You tell me when you're through." And Macabee leaned back against the curving wall of the desk and folded his arms across his chest, staring at his son from under half-closed eyelids.

"Macabee," Gabriel began, "you say I don't have to be a linguist, I only have to be an interpreter. But it's not that simple. The Lingoe kids are crazy—" He stopped suddenly, and backed up. "I'm sorry I said 'Lingoe'; I didn't mean to. The *linguist* kids are crazy. They don't *mind* sitting in the damn interpreting booths from eight o'clock in the morning until noon, and then all afternoon long, listening to people go on and on and fucking *on*—sorry, sir—about should we put two hooks on the top of the box to hang stuff from or *three* hooks on the top of the box to hang stuff from. You know what they do, Macabee? When lunch finally comes around, you know what they do? They sit there and argue about verb endings, so help me god. . . . And they really care about them—I mean, they *really* care. When they're hassling a verb ending they're in heaven, they think case markers are more fun than baseball, they eat prepositions for breakfast . . . they're all crazy. They do that six days a week, and they don't do anything else, Macabee. When they go home at night I guess they sit around like old people, discussing the 'implications' of verb endings—I know they go home and study half the fucking night after they're through with their regular homework. Hey, Macabee, come *on*—that's not a way to *live!* It's not *human! Shit,* who *cares* about all that stuff? No, don't say anything, Macabee, you promised me you wouldn't interrupt! Look, I want to spend time with my friends, and I want to watch the holos, and I want to go *do* stuff! The linguist kids *don't,* or at least if they do, they sure do a damn good job of hiding it from everybody. And that's the *point,* Macabee!" He gulped air and swallowed hard; he was already shaking, god damn it.

"Listen," he said, desperate to make the man understand, "you put me in that Interface with the Chornyak kids when I was too little even to turn over by myself. And you proved—*proved,* just like you meant to do—that the linguists are telling the truth when they say any human kid can acquire an Alien language just the same as their kids. You proved there wasn't any genetic difference, and you were right, and I'm sure that's good. Because it's hard to be prejudiced against the linguists if you know for absolutely sure and certain that they really *are* just like everybody else. They were telling the truth about not having any special language genes other people haven't got. And that means they're probably telling the truth about refusing to try for non-humanoid languages because you can't do it without hurting the kids, too. That's good to know, Macabee, and I'm glad you were in on that. It makes it a lot harder to go around saying the Lines are traitors to Earth, and all that crap. But Macabee—Macabee, listen to me, because *I* am going to tell *you* something that is the truth. Okay—it's not genetic. A linguist is a human being is a linguist is a human being. They weren't lying. You proved it—*I* proved it. But nevertheless—get ready, Macabee, here it comes, Gabriel's First Law Of Linguadynamics, are you ready? It goes like this: TO BE AN INTERPRETER FOR THE GOVERNMENT YOU HAVE TO BE A LINGUIST, BECAUSE YOU HAVE TO BE *CRAZY* LIKE A LINGUIST. Have you got that, Macabee? Ordinary normal, sane human beings can't *do* it, Macabee! You have to be an effing *fanatic!* You have to grow up thinking there's nothing else in the world worth caring about except languages—the way *you* grew up thinking there was nothing else but numbers! *Jesus,* Macabee!''

He stopped, and leaned back against the wall, almost sobbing, closing his eyes, and this time he didn't apologize for all the swearing. He moaned, too, and he didn't apologize for that either.

The silence went on and on; it went on so long that it started to be scary. Had his father fainted from the shock? Had a heart attack? He was bracing himself to open his eyes and look when Macabee Dow, in a voice his son had never heard before, and using words his son had never heard from his mouth before, said, "Why, those filthy clever effing sons of lust-crazed *whores!*'' Gabriel's eyes flew open, and he forgot all about his own distress. It was like a mountain breaking into song, or something. Breaking into an *obscene* song! *Macabee Dow did not curse.* Curses were the expression of excessive and uncontrolled emotion. Curses were for lesser mortals who were unable to perceive the universe as a confluence of numbers or whatever.

"Macabee?'' Gabriel whispered, tentatively, ready to throw himself out through the door of the desk to safety if he had to, even if the staircase was locked, if his dad had finally fulfilled all the predictions and gone clear over the edge into insanity.

"Gabriel!" The words came fast and steady and thumping into the acoustic space of the desk like bursts from a rapid fire automatic weapon. "When I went to propose that you should be Interfaced with the Chornyak infants, I was prepared to have to fight for it. I was prepared to pay an enormous sum of credits. I thought it might take a lawsuit to force them to let you do it. I was prepared to take them to court and charge them with denying you your economic civil rights—I thought it was going to be *hard*. And when I told them what I wanted, and they just said, 'Oh, fine, we'll start Monday,' I couldn't believe what I was hearing. The bureaucrats over at D.A.T. came around, after they'd sewed up all the Interface places for D.A.T. employees' kids, and asked me how that figured—they couldn't believe it either—and I told them I didn't know. I think we all just decided—like you, Gabriel—that linguists are crazy. Crazy enough to give up what had been, up to that point, a total monopoly on a profession that brings in enormous wealth, without a quibble. Without even a discussion. For *free!* They had to be crazy, we thought . . . but we were wrong, Gabriel. They weren't crazy at all. They knew *exactly* what they were doing, from the first minute. Sweet shit, how they must have been laughing at us, all these years!"

Macabee let out a long breath in the silence, *loud* in the silence, and his mouth twisted as if he had been hurt. "Gabriel," he asked abruptly, "do the other kids feel the same way you do? The other kids that aren't from the Lines?"

"Yes."

"All of them?"

"I don't *know* all of them, Macabee. But those I know, they hate it. Just like I do. I mean it was fun at first, when we were little, getting to travel and go all those places and do grownup work, and having people treat you like you *were* a grownup—and earning all that money. But it wears off fast, let me tell you. They hate it, just like I hate it. And they all goof off. Just like I goof off."

"Gabriel, we can't have that." Macabee Dow's voice was urgent, tense. "These matters are too important for anyone to be 'goofing off' with them."

"Then let the *Lingoe* kids do it, damn it, the way they used to! They don't know *how* to goof off! They beat it out of them at home, or something!"

The mathematician wasn't looking at the boy, he was looking

at something he remembered, but he kept talking in that lasergun way, and Gabriel was fascinated. Usually Macabee only talked that way when he was talking about math.

"*They knew,*" he was saying. "And they slipped it over on us like a bib on a baby. When they said sure, we could put you kids in their Interfaces, and build Interfaces of our own if we could get AIRYs to staff them and put more kids in those—but that was *it,* as soon as the Interfacing session was over we had to pick you up and remove you from their premises—*they knew.* They knew perfectly well that without the rest of the life, the activities that the children of the Lines spend all their time in from infancy, they weren't risking one thing. Not one thing! They knew it wasn't going to work . . . could not possibly work. Damn their souls to the innermost crypts of hell!"

Gabriel waited a minute, to be sure it was over, and then he added some more data. "Macabee," he said, "there's so many other things to do, don't you know that? Nobody wants to stay here, on Earth, fooling around with a lot of stupid federals and ET's! You know? There's a whole *universe* of stuff to do out there—" He waved one arm, showing the universe, and slammed his elbow painfully into the wall of the desk. "There's planets to see, and planets to explore, and planets to conquer, there's the whole effing *universe,* Macabee! And you really expect me to sit all day long, six days a week, in an interpreting booth in Washington or Chicago or some such place? Bored out of my mind? Macabee . . . if that's how you see it, just because of the money, you're as crazy as the linguists are."

"It wasn't the money," his father said gently. "I don't care about money, Gabe, not the way you mean. It was the *power.* I wanted the power for you. I still do."

"Well, I don't. I want to have some fun. I want to live like a normal person. Power! Macabee, there are ten thousand million ways to get power, and every last one of them is more interesting than being a linguist."

"You don't understand. You don't understand, Gabriel, that the Lines literally control the fate of entire planets, and of whole alliances of planets."

"Who cares?" Gabriel shrugged. "What good is it? If I want power, you know what I can do? I can buy myself a whole asteroid—I've got enough money, the way you've invested it, the way it'll earn more money while I'm getting old enough to have control of it—and I can be *king!* I can run the place, a whole asteroid of my own, just exactly any way I please! *That's* power, Macabee!"

"It's not the same thing at all." His father's voice was as cold as Gabriel's drenched armpits. "It's little puny power."

"It's enough for me, sir."

"You really don't understand the difference, do you, Gabriel?"

Gabriel could hear the sadness in his father's voice, and he was sorry. It was the same sadness that Rafe was going to hear when he had to give up and admit that he hated mathematics. And Michael would hear it when he got a little older, too, unless Macabee just happened by a fluke to choose for his youngest son some passion that the child would have chosen even if left to himself. Gabriel didn't care. He'd always known this was coming. And no, he didn't understand. Why *wouldn't* a whole asteroid of your own be power enough, for anybody?

He sat there stubbornly, and waited, not saying anything more. Whatever was going to happen, it would happen. And finally Macabee Dow released the lock on the staircase and let down the steps.

"You want to quit right away, Gabe?" he asked quietly.

"If I can." That was a little scary, because he hadn't ever done much else, but it wasn't a chance he dared pass up. His father might change his mind if he said he wanted to think about it or something. "Yeah. Right away."

"When you are a grown man, Gabe, I want you to remember this morning. And I want you to promise me now that you will forgive me. Because when you are a grown man, you *will* understand about the difference between real power and the illusion of power. I want you to engrave this morning in your mind, and I want you to remember that this was your own choice, freely made. Do you understand me, Gabriel?"

"Sure. I understand."

"You don't, Gabe. But it doesn't matter. It's eleven years too late to set this right, and making you go on doing something you hate won't accomplish one single useful thing except to amuse the men of the Lines. You go on, Gabriel—I'll see to this."

"Really, Macabee? You really mean that?"

"I really mean that."

"*Jesus!*"

"Please, Gabriel."

"I'm *sorry*. It's just . . . it's not what I expected. I thought you were going to try to argue about it."

"You go on now," said his father. "And you think about what you might like to do. Not with your whole life, Gabriel, I don't mean that. I mean, what you'd like to do with the empty hours you're going to have now."

"You're really going to get me out of D.A.T.? I don't have to go back?"

"I really am. I will be just delighted to do so," said Macabee. Thickly, as if he'd been drinking; but he never drank anything except a very good wine, with a very good dinner. "It's not your fault that I've been had, Gabe—me and the whole United States government. There's no reason why you should have to pay for our stupidity."

"Who's going to do my language?" Gabriel hadn't thought about that before. "'We were right in the middle of that new clause . . . sir, who's going to take care of that?"

Now it was Macabee Dow who shrugged.

"That's their problem," he said flatly. "Let 'em call a linguist."

CHAPTER 20

"It wasn't that we didn't think it would be wonderful, and valuable, to have a Womansign—a sign language that would express the perceptions of women, as Láadan expresses them through oral language. At the beginning, deafness was still a common problem on Earth, and we spent many anguished hours trying to decide how a Womansign project could be managed. One of the very first things we did, just as soon as our alphabet was firmly established, was to work out a manual alphabet that allowed the fingerspelling of Láadan. Not because fingerspelling was even a small step toward a Womansign, but because we wanted to demonstrate our respect for the tactile mode of language—and because it was something we had enough time to do. And because, unlike a complete sign, it was something that could legitimately be done by hearing persons.

"But things were so difficult for us then. . . . All information about Láadan had to be exchanged in our recipe codes. We worked in constant fear that the men would discover what we were doing and put an end to the Encoding Project. We had to work in scraps of time, five minutes here, ten minutes there, stolen from other work or from badly-needed sleep . . . sometimes we considered ourself lucky to find thirty uninterrupted minutes for the language in a whole month. If there was any way that we could have constructed a Womansign at the same time, we were unable to perceive it.

"Later, when we no longer had to maintain such secrecy, when Láadan had begun to be spoken by women throughout the Lines, we had to face the enormous, awe-inspiring, almost paralyzingly difficult task of trying to move the language out into the world of other women. And by that time deafness had ceased to be a problem; by then, deafness was as much medical history as

smallpox was, so that there was serious concern for the preserva-
tion of existing sign languages.

"The dream of a Womansign remains, because the love for
communication by sign remains. But I think it is a dream that
will have to wait for the work of women who have great genius
and great love and great skill, and—most difficult of all for the
women of the Lines—who have abundant leisure. It will not
happen in my lifetime, not this time round."

(from the diaries of Nazareth Chornyak Adiness)

Cassie St. Merill is not just failing to enjoy herself. It's much
worse than that. She is furious; her narrow strange face is
distorted and ugly with her petulance, like the face of an Egyptian cat slightly crushed by some accident. She is furious with
her hostess, who has played a cheap trick and managed to take
Cassie in completely—not for the first time. Cassie is thinking
that she ought to have known; that she ought to have asked her
husband for permission to turn down the invitation; that she
should have found some way to avoid this humiliation. O.J. is
going to make her pay for this for a long time; she can hear him
already, every morning at breakfast for weeks and weeks, finding a way to bring up this night at the Coloridons' and Cassie's
incomprehensible stupidity and the way that she is forever dis-
gracing him and making it impossible for him to advance in his
career in the way he would advance without her as baggage. He
will say, "Can't you *ever* find a way to outsmart Burgundy
Coloridon? For the sake of your own self-respect, if not for my
sake?" She will plead, "O.J., how could I have known? She
swore it was an informal dinner party, a little simple dinner for
four couples! How was I supposed to know she was setting me
up?" And he will say, "Isn't that why you spent two years at the
marital academy, Cassandra? Isn't that what your father's money
was supposed to be paying for? Learning how to deal with
people like Burgundy Coloridon? Who *always* whips your ass, I
might add!" And Cassie will have nothing to say back. She
never has anything to say back. She does not know how to talk
to him without getting caught in the traps he sets; it would be
bad enough if he were only a man, but O.J. is a psychotherapist.
She cannot say that the academy she attended wasn't even in the
same league as the one where Burgundy went, not without facing
O.J.'s icy stare and a severe, "Do I hear you criticizing your
father again, Cassandra?"

It hadn't been Daddy's decision to send her to Briary Marital

Academy, it had been her own. They had had plenty of money, she could have gone anywhere; he had told her she could choose and she had picked one that she thought she would like, from looking at the catalogs she'd dialed up on the comset. It had looked so pretty . . . she had chosen it for its pretty name, and for the pretty rooms in its dormitories, with their canopy beds, and for the way the rosebushes trailed over the stone arches of its handsome old buildings. Burgundy now, she had gone to Mary Margaret Plymouth, one of the very best—perhaps *the* very best— and she apparently majored there in Dirty Tricks & Deceptions. Cassie hates Burgundy fiercely, and envies her; she knows not a single woman in the circle of friends selected for her by O.J. who doesn't feel the same way about Burgundy that she does.

There are to be four couples at the dinner party. There are their hosts, Krol and Burgundy Coloridon; there are Doby Phalk and his wife Brune; there are herself and O.J.; like him, Krol and Doby are successful young psychotherapists. And like Cassie, Brune is wearing a simple spraysheath. Brune's is a silver and gold stripe; Cassie's is scarlet with a narrow band of white fur around the hem. Just right, both of them, for a small informal dinner party for four couples.

But Burgundy Coloridon isn't dressed like that. To the uninformed eye, Burgundy Coloridon is clothed only in miniature roses, palest yellow through delectable peach to deep rose-gold; Cassie wishes bitterly that the roses were real instead of holograms, so that they might attract real bees with real stingers. The dress is magnificent, and it is set off by a ruff of golden lace that rises high behind Burgundy's head and out of which she herself seems to rise, like a final perfect rose. She is wearing contacts that exactly match the tint of the most dramatic of the holo flowers, and the rose-gold eyes are glorious in her tanned face. She is exquisite, and Cassie wants her dead.

Brune and Cassie know that Burgundy has only rented the dress; Krol Coloridon is doing a little better than their husbands, but not so much better that he could afford to let her buy that dress. But that makes no difference, it's not the kind of dress that you could wear more than once a year anyway, and *tonight* it is Burgundy's, and that is all that matters.

It could have gone differently, if they'd been lucky, Cassie thinks. It could have happened that Brune's and Cassie's husbands would have decided that Burgundy's dress was overdone and exhibitionist and that they would have been sorry for Krol and proud of their own wives' good taste. But Burgundy has been very careful; not one other detail is anything but the most classic conservative style, making her the single item of display and thus an acceptable ornament. The dinner table floating in its nook beside the tier of three reflecting pools is bare of any cloth—just the crystal acrylic, almost invisible with the lights from the pools glowing through it. Square acrylic plates with a single silver stripe around the border; glassware to match, and serving pieces to match, and flatware of massive sterling without any decoration but its flawless *shape*. No centerpiece . . . Burgundy is daring, she is not afraid to do things like omit the centerpiece at a dinner party, and she is right, of course, because through the bare central space of the table you can see the water lilies in the pools, and an occasional flash of color from the giant carp. A centerpiece would have ruined that. Burgundy has carefully spraycovered every room of the house to coordinate with the dining area; everything is silver and white, with just a touch here and there in rich genuine wood to set it off. And in the midst of all this understatement and elegance, there is Burgundy, wearing the full spectrum of shades of gold. It is *absolutely* perfect! Cassie knows that O.J. will expect her to top it sometime in the next month or two when they return the social obligation and ask the Coloridons to *their* place, and she is frantic just thinking about it—how do you do better than absolute perfection?

Brune is ashen, a color that does not go well with her dress, and her eyes are wide with a fear she is not able to conceal. Cassie knows that Doby makes Brune's life miserable, using a twisted vicious teasing that is much more ingenious than anything O.J. would ever consider doing with Cassie; she also knows that Doby treats Brune that way because what he would *really* like to do is hit her. Brune could report Doby to Family Court, and Cassie knows that she sometimes secretly records the interminable verbal battering she endures from him, just in case. But then what would she do, even if the court took her seriously? It would only make Doby worse, and the chances are ninety-nine to one that what the court would do is send *Brune* for counseling, not Doby. Already Brune's father blames many of his own problems in the House of Representatives on Brune's social failures—and that is ridiculous, but what can Brune do about it? If she turned in her own husband, who supports her in luxury and has never laid one harsh finger on her, even in the marriage bed, her family would consider themselves disgraced. And they would probably be right. The word would get around. Brune would find herself divorced and living in a Federal Women's Hostel before she could say, "But I just could not stand it any longer!'' If she were lucky. If she did not find herself in a tasteful mental hospital instead. Poor Brune. . . .

The fourth couple is not here yet, and Burgundy has refused to tell them who is coming. It's a surprise, she says charmingly, raising one luscious shoulder high and turning her lovely head to shelter in it. Burgundy is the only woman Cassie knows who is able to carry off that particular piece of bodyparl, although every woman who attends a marital academy is required to learn it. Most women who chance it only look like they're trying to check their armpits. But not Burgundy. When she does it, it works, it is alluring, delightful, exchanting; even hating her as they do, Cassie and Brune can admire her skill.

The men are on their best behavior until they find out who they are sharing this evening with. If it turns out to be someone they know well, the Coloridons will bring out the innocent-looking fruit drinks laced with forbidden chemicals for which they are famous in their social circle and soon Doby and O.J. will abandon all pretense of good manners. But not yet. Not while for all they know the fourth husband invited is an important client, or the head of a famous clinic, or a celebrity with enough public clout to do their reputations harm. Krol and Doby and O.J. have not gotten where they are, young as they are, by risking their reputations.

The men are standing by the oval window, talking shop talk, and Cassie thinks how unfair it is. When they go to their offices, they wear their white labcoats and the antique stethoscopes and they are impeccably attired; when they go out in the evening all they have to do is switch to black labcoats and pin miniature stethoscopes to their neckties, and they are impeccably attired; even the most formal occasion requires of them nothing more than a silk shirt beneath the black labcoat, perhaps with vertical tucks, perhaps with a narrow black cummerbund. They have no decisions to make, they have no conception of what a woman goes through. She wonders how they would like it if they could never set a foot outside their homes, or invite guests into their homes, without the obligation of earning points for their spouse by being the best-dressed person present.

"There can only be *one* best-dressed woman in any group of women, O.J.," she had pointed out to him once when he was complaining about her own performance of this obligation, "and *all* the rest of the women have to be the losers and go home and be tormented about it."

"Please," he had said, turning his back to indicate that he

couldn't bear the sight of her. "Do not make yourself even more ridiculous by attempting to express mathematical concepts."

She is aware of Brune beside her now, and she turns her head to smile thinly at the other woman. At least they are failures together. At least Brune has not worn anything enough better than what Cassie is wearing to let her try any sort of alliance with Burgundy.

Brune says, "I could kill her, you know."

"I could help you," Cassie agrees. "How will we do it?"

"Slowly! Very slowly, with lots of little tiny pins, so she is completely spoiled a long time before she is dead—so she has time to know it and think about it a long time before she is dead."

"Brrrr. . . . Brune, don't!" Cassie knows Brune is not serious; she has seen Brune carefully carry a spider outside her atrium area and set it down gently in her yard in a safe place. Brune is gentle; still, Cassie does not want to hear the vicious talk with the ugly pictures that it makes in her mind.

"I'm sorry. Maybe. But you know she did this on purpose. She knew what it would mean for you and for me, and she did it on purpose all the same, curse her!"

Cassie shrugs, trying to seem indifferent; sometimes Brune is a little melodramatic. "Oh, well," she says. "That's what women *do,* Brune."

She is conscious that she might not be so calm if she had Brune's problems to deal with. O.J. has told her about Doby Phalk being recruited for colony placement by the Department of Health, and about the game he is playing—pretending he prefers to remain here on Earth, so they'll offer him better terms; O.J. tells her that Doby is sure to get what he wants, because they want *him* badly. "Ideally suited for colony placement," is what they say about Doby. Cassie will be sorry to lose Brune, but maybe Doby will be kinder to her when they get out to the colonies; she hopes so. She doesn't like always having to feel sorry for Brune; it distracts her, and it makes her feel uneasy and insecure.

"Who do you suppose the other couple will be, Brune?" she asks softly, to change the subject. "Maybe the woman will be even more spectacular than Burgundy is. Could we get that lucky?"

"We could pray," Brune says sullenly. "Dear Heavenly Father, may whoever comes through that door be an even worse bitch than Burgundy is."

The door speaks immediately as she pronounces the last word, making Brune jump, and Cassie giggles and pats Brune's hand a couple of times, reassuringly.

"Leonard Joseph Verdi," says the door in the precise Irish accent that is so fashionable this year. "And Mrs. Leonard Joseph Verdi, born Elizabeth Caroline Chornyak."

There is a stunned and total silence, which is what the Coloridons had intended, and Krol is grinning the satisfied grin of a triumphant man with a triumphant wife at his side as he tells the door to open and it slides silently into its case to let the new couple in.

Verdi! And Elizabeth Chornyak Verdi! If it had been only the man, it could have been a coincidence—after all, there are tens of thousands of people with names like Verdi and Jefferson and Noumarque and Hashihawa who aren't linguists of the Lines. But no Verdi who was not one of *the* Verdis would have a wife born a Chornyak; that is farther than coincidences can be made to stretch.

Brune has prayed for a bitch, and her prayer is answered. There in the doorway, handing her plain brown cape to the servomechanism, stands what is without any question a bitch of the Lines. A Lingoe bitch! Her straight pale hair is cut short like a child's and it is obvious that nothing has been done to it except to brush it. It just *hangs* there; it is shocking and ugly. She is wearing a garment of a good quality beige fabric, but it is only a straight tunic with square ample sleeves and a square neck; it reminds Cassie of the garments that are issued to women prison inmates. There are beige clingsoles on the creature's feet, she is wearing a wrist computer and narrow plain gold wedding ring, and that is absolutely *all*. Neither Cassie nor Brune would have gone alone into a dark closet dressed the way that this woman has seen fit to come to the dinner party at the Coloridons. (The man is not as interesting; he is dressed like any man, in a pair of dark trousers and a shirt and a jacket and a tie. His hair is in a moderate reagan cut. Nothing there to remark upon. But the *woman!*)

Behind her, O.J. grabs her elbow with his fist (she has not heard him coming up behind her) and hisses. "Close your *mouth*, Cassie, for god's sake!", and she realizes that she is standing there gaping at the new arrivals with her mouth hanging open, and that Brune is doing the same thing, and that Burgundy is smiling the rapturous smile of a woman who has just tasted something delicious and knows that there is much more of it to be tasted. Burgundy moves forward as Cassie's mouth snaps shut; she welcomes the linguists into her home, taking the woman's arm and leading her into the room. And now the slots in the walls are all glowing and the servomechanisms are moving swiftly, silently, to take the trays of appetizers and drinks from them. There aren't going to be any unusual chemicals in these drinks, Cassie realizes, and she is grateful for that; she hates the way O.J. behaves when he uses them and is—as he puts it—"nicely relaxed." And it means that O.J. won't insist on putting the flyer on illegal manual control when they go home; Cassie is terrified without the automatics, especially after dark, and terrified that they'll be caught; it makes her furious that O.J. complains about the potential for disgrace when she doesn't come out first in some trivial social competition like being best-dressed, and then risks the *total* disgrace of being arrested for endangerment of traffic and flying under the influence of controlled substances.

Cassie's mind is racing . . . what does she say now? She knows Brune is thinking the same thing, and that for once their husbands are not precisely comfortable either. Lingoes! How could the fourth couple at this "informal dinner party" be a pair of *Lingoes?* Cassie knows very little about them, but she knows this: *they do not mingle socially with people outside their own families and business circles. It does not happen. Ever.* How has Burgundy pulled this off? And what should Cassie do? She sees herself assuming an expression of *very* wellbred distaste, inventing some sort of gracious excuse, floating elegantly from the Coloridon house with a quick smile back over her shoulder, showing them all that *she* knows what constitutes decent behavior, even if Burgundy doesn't . . . should she do that? Would that be the right move? What if that's not what O.J. wants? What if it would be a serious mistake? And what is Brune going to do?

Cassie is almost grateful when Brune grabs her wrist, mumbling an excuse, and flees for Burgundy's powder room, dragging Cassie with her; at least that way the exit is Brune's fault, not her own, and it will give her time to think. She knows that it is *important* for her to think, before she has to go back out there.

Alone in the little room with her, Brune stands pale and shaking, leaning against the lady-vanity. It is playing something romantic that Cassie does not recognize, and the mirror behind it clears for service, showing Cassie that she does not look one bit better than Brune does. "Revert!" Cassie spits at it, and the mirror clouds again obediently.

"Cassie," Brune is asking, "how did she do this?"

"I don't *know*. How would I know?"

"Does this mean we're going to have to sit at the table with them? And *eat with them?*"

Aha! Cassie hears the bell ring—her first chance this evening, this terrible evening, to score even one point. She can't let it pass, sorry though she is for Brune; she has her obligations to O.J. She looks casually past Brune, as if to spare her the embarrassment of a direct glance, and she says sweetly, "Why, *Brune*, dear . . . I had no *idea* you were prejudiced!"

It will be something she can tell O.J. later, if she needs it. How Brune looked, caught flat out like that. Cassie feels a little strange at the idea of eating with Lingoes, too—that's normal. That's reasonable. That's forgivable. But Cassie knows better than to ever *admit* that she feels that way! Only a very ignorant woman could be unaware that although prejudice is a perfectly normal human failing, only someone from the lower classes would ever admit to it aloud.

She is still standing there, smiling, waiting for Brune to stop breathing fast and shivering and say something back, feeling the warm satisfaction of the earned point, when the door speaks to them. It says, "Ladies, your husbands require your presence." Of course they do. Cassie can just imagine. The door waits thirty seconds, and when there is no response it says it again. It will keep that up until something happens to stop it. But it isn't a sophisticated model, it will be easy to fool; Cassie reaches over and opens it wide, then lets it close again. The door is convinced that she has gone out; it stops delivering its message. This won't gain them very much time—the men will only punch it up again—but even a minute or two will help. And Cassie, from the vantage point of victory, feels inclined to be protective toward Brune right now.

"Cassie," Brune is saying, "I can't go back in there. I can't."

"You can. You have to."

"I can't do it, Cassie."

"Brune, stop talking nonsense and help me think what to do. We have to do the right thing, and we have to figure out what that is, *fast!* Stop being an idiot, and help me *think*."

"Why? So that you can tell O.J. and he can tell Doby? About what I said, about eating with them?"

"You say something useful, and I won't tell," Cassie offers promptly. "I promise."

"I've remembered something," Brune says slowly. "I know how Burgundy did this. Is that useful enough?"

"Tell! Hurry!"

"Burgundy belongs to the Hospital Auxiliary, Cassie, right?

And what they did this year for their annual project was to redecorate the women's Chapel at the hospital.''

"So?"

"So, remember the Thursday night whatever-they-ares, those religious kind of club meetings, where the nurses go, and sometimes the linguist women? Remember, Cassie, it was on the popnews? Thursday Night Devotionals! Remember? They said women all over the country had been going to those.''

"Krol would *never* have let Burgundy go to something like that, Brune! You're crazy!''

"For a psychotherapist's wife, you use the term a bit loosely, dear,'' Brune coos, and Cassie swears under her breath. O.J. will be livid if he hears about that, and he *will* hear about it if Brune tells Doby.

"All right, Brune, we're even,'' she admits, furious with herself for being caught in such a baby mistake. "But I don't have time to let you gloat about it right now. Just tell me what you mean so we can decide what to do.''

"It's obvious,'' Brune tells her. "Burgundy must have met one of the linguist women when she was over at the hospital doing something on that decorating project! They would get to talking, about how things looked—''

"You *saw* how that woman was dressed! She doesn't *care* how anything looks!''

"But Burgundy wouldn't have known that, Cassie. It would have been perfectly natural for her to start up a conversation, and then one thing would lead to another, and pretty soon. . . . You know how she is, when she wants something, Cassandra Joan—she always manages. And that would have been the perfect opportunity.''

It makes sense. It is the only likely explanation. Krol couldn't have been the one responsible, because the Lines never went near psychotherapists or any other kind of therapist. Brune is undoubtedly right. Burgundy must have wandered in on a Thursday night when she was at the hospital with Krol, with a plastispray sample or a holo for the chapel wall or some such thing, and met a lady Lingoe and struck up a conversation. Leading to this. Cassie doesn't like accepting it so fast, but it makes sense, and nothing else makes sense. There is no Rent-A-Linguist service; it has to be Burgundy's doing, and where else could she have met a woman of the Lines?

"All right!'' she snaps. "It sounds right. So what do we do?''

The door is haranguing them again, at thirty second intervals. The men will be angry by this time.

"Brune, we've got to get out there," she whispers urgently, feeling certain the men have turned the door's ear on now. "And we have just one decision to make." She runs the plan by Brune . . . inventing an excuse to go home, sailing fastidiously away, demonstrating their good breeding, leaving Burgundy stuck with the collapse of her dinner party and the unspoken trashword "Lingoe-lover" hovering over her exquisite perfect dinner table. But Brune shakes her head, firmly, angrily, and hisses at Cassie, "No! Absolutely not! Things have been changing. I know several very high-placed families whose children have been in the Interfaces with the linguist babies! You can't talk against the linguists the way our mothers do any more . . . Cassie, I heard on the popnews that at Georgetown University the Department of Language Science is changing its name back to Department of Linguistics!"

Cassie feels dizzy. Thank god Brune knew! What if she hadn't known? God, what a near thing! And now she knows she is in Brune's debt, and she hopes Doby will take her out to the colonies *soon*.

"Well, all right—what are we going to *do*, Brune?" Cassie demands. "Tell me what we're going to *do!*"

The two women stare at each other, both contemplating the same horrors, and Cassie thinks with sudden dismay that Brune is going to vomit, and then there will *really* be trouble, because with the room's ear turned on everyone will hear her. But Brune shudders once, all over, and she pulls herself together. A remarkable performance! Straightening; smoothing; gathering up. Blood does tell, and training, too. Brune comes of a good family, her mother belongs to the very best clubs, and Brune went to Midwest Oak. Not as classy as Mary Margaret Plymouth, but several cuts above the place Cassie had been fool enough to settle for.

"Silly Cassie," Brune says, managing the cool smile from some reserve for which Cassie cannot help admiring her. "Of course I'm not prejudiced, any more than you are. Of course we won't leave, and make ourselves look ridiculous. But quick— what are we going to *talk* about?"

It's a good question, Cassie thinks. The right question. Obviously they can't talk about fashion. Or about managing the home or decorating it—the Lingoes live communally, like animals. It can't be clubs—the Lingoe women have to work all day every day, they wouldn't have time to be in social clubs even if you invited them. Only men talked either politics or business. . . .

"Oh!" Cassie has a sudden inspiration, and she is the one

now who grabs Brune and pulls her along. Under her breath, very fast, as Brune stumbles to keep up, she says, "We'll talk about the colonies! She'll know all about them, the Verdi woman I mean, because she's a linguist. And that's always a safe topic!"

Back in the recreation area, Cassie sees that the linguist woman is standing, just like a child would stand, in front of the antique color-fountain that Burgundy Coloridon picked up once at an auction. The woman claps her hands, and the fountain rewards her with a shower of rainbows, and then she laughs. She whistles, a long liquid trill, and gets a different rainbow pattern, and she laughs again. Just like a child! How can she dare do that? Cassie would have been so ashamed. . . .

What happens next brings all the other women to stunned attention. Even Burgundy. To their complete bewilderment, the four husbands begin to laugh, too, and go straight over to join the Lingoe bitch at the color fountain. While Cassie and Brune and Burgundy stare, they begin a syncopated pattering of clapping hands and snapping fingers and whistling, and the fountain's display becomes a glory of color, a tumult of rainbows, all around them.

Cassie and Brune have both come back with the same thought, that Burgundy cannot have this new plum all for herself, that they must find a way to invite the couple from the Lines to parties at *their* houses, that the only question is which one of them will accomplish that first. They have both been planning their campaigns, anxious to begin. Now they have forgotten all about it. Watching their husbands, their husbands and the woman, having a wonderful time—they have forgotten what it was they wanted to do. Cassie dares to sneak a look at Burgundy, and it delights her to see that even the holodress is not enough to make her hostess invulnerable. She feels left out, too, just like Cassie and Brune are feeling left out; like them, she is frozen in place and doesn't know what to do.

Elizabeth Verdi turns around then and sees the three of them standing there watching, and she does something with her hands—Cassie doesn't know what, some gesture—and although the men go on playing with the color fountain they do it more quietly.

"It's so beautiful," Elizabeth Verdi says to them, smiling at them, *not* embarrassed, how can she not be embarrassed? "I've never seen one before—I didn't know such a thing existed! Imagine, playing with a rainbow, and bossing one around!"

Behind the woman, her husband's arm moves to touch her,

and Cassie winces a little; he will move her smoothly away from the group now, before she can disgrace him further, and when they come back she will have a properly chastened look; she will look white and strained, and she will have a hard time not crying.

But the Verdi man does nothing of the kind. He touches his wife's hand and leans toward her, whispering, and she listens, but she doesn't turn to him, she just listens and nods her head. And then she speaks to the silent women staring at her.

"My husband says to ask you to join us," she tells Cassie and Burgundy and Brune. "And he is quite right—you're missing all the fun. My dears, won't you come play, too?"

CHAPTER 21

"The Seas of Space"

"Oh come and sail the seas of space,
that have no shores . . . and their waves are light!
Come sail with me; be my constant friend
on the journey out that has no end.

"I'll show you wonders on every hand
you'll never see on any land;
and Terra wrapped in endless light
and wound around in blue and white.

"And if you mourn what you've left behind,
I'll hold you close—I'll ease your mind—
and we both shall weep for those who roam
the seas of space, and can ne'er go home.

"For they are strange, the seas of space;
no dolphin leap there, no seaweeds sway;
and the solar wind, though it fills our sail,
is a foreign wind, in a foreign gale."

> *(Twentieth-century folksong, set to the tune*
> *of the much earlier "The Water Is Wide")*

There had been no reason at all for the agent to worry about discovery. Terran perceptions were so limited that she could move about with complete freedom and never do anything more in the way of trying to conceal herself than being quite sure she didn't actually *touch* anyone; humans were sensitive enough to tactile sensations to notice (and be mystified) if she did that. But they couldn't see her, or hear her, or smell her; and she had no reason to go into the few places where there were sufficiently sophisticated scientific instruments to betray her presence.

It was a boring assignment. Something you took your turn at because it had to be done and it was only fair to share the boredom. Or, as in her case, it was an assignment you took because you were being punished for fouling up some other assignment. She didn't want to think about how badly she had failed on the archipelago, had been absolutely determined not to think about it—there was nothing she could do now to change it, and no reason to torment herself with it, and there was good reason to believe that the new team in place would be able to repair the damage or at least lessen its effects. But Earth duty was so stupefyingly boring that her mind kept going back to what she had done, the scene playing over and over inside her head . . . it was maddening. If she'd been anywhere where caution was necessary, her state of distraction would have worried her; on the other hand, if she'd been anywhere where caution was necessary, her mind would not have fallen constantly into useless rehashings of the past.

To be "sent to Earth". . . . It was an expression of her people. Faced with something unpleasant, you said "I'd rather be sent to Earth." But she *had* been sent to Earth, and the expression now had a dreary reality for her. How did Terrans stand it? She shuddered, and forced herself to pay attention; not that there was anything to pay attention *to*.

The agent understood, intellectually, why things had to be this way, why so little could be done to help these pitiful people, why even the slightest changes had to be introduced with glacial slowness. She knew the theory. But her *heart* did not understand, and her most constant impulse was to round up the entire population and take it somewhere where it could live decently, at once. If not sooner. There was a Panglish word for that; it was called "paternalism," and it was not allowed. And of course she would not do anything of the kind; she would obey her orders down to the last comma. She had done too much damage the last time, when she took it upon herself to make what had seemed to her no more than a minute alteration in her instructions, to ever do such a thing again. It was that previous folly that had gotten her sent to this pesthole; and she deserved it. She had *agreed* with them that she deserved it, and had been grateful that this was all, because she had been afraid they would tell her it was time to take up some other sort of work. What would she do, if that happened? What would she have done? She didn't know. She loved what she did, loved it passionately; she could not imagine doing anything else.

"Just gather data," they had ordered her sternly, though with less contempt than she had been expecting. *"Don't do anything . . .* just observe. Gather the data that the sensors aren't capable of interpreting properly, and be sure you miss nothing important."

She had been almost through with the assignment when the trouble occurred; she had spent one unit of time in each of the other twelve Households of the Lines, without incident, without a ripple in the smooth fabric of her scrupulous observation and reporting. She had saved Chornyak Household for last, because it was likely that if she found anything important she would find it there—almost anything new in the Lines began with the Chornyaks and then moved to the other families.

She'd been on duty at Chornyak Household in recording mode through three Earth days before it happened, and she had not been especially careful. Her only precaution had been to stay well away from the Interface, since the current Aliens-in-Residence *would* have been able to see her. They would never have betrayed her deliberately, but the linguists were capable of astonishingly acute observations, and she could not take the chance that some slight unintentional change in the AIRYs' behavior would catch the Terrans' attention and disturb their state of placid ignorance. Placid ignorance was the Consortium prescription for Earth, for the very best of reasons. But other than that one small concession, she had been completely relaxed, completely invulnerable, completely unaware. And that was how it had happened.

There had been a disturbance in the spectra around her, and she had tensed immediately, startled, searching for its source. And then she had seen the Terran woman staring at her.

She looked like any ordinary woman of the species. She was standing in the doorway of the room; she held some cleaning implements in her hands and was clutching them as if for protection. Her knuckles were white with the effort she was making. She had graying hair—an older woman, then—and was a little thicker of body than the other women of Chornyak Barren House that the agent had seen. She wore the same clothing that any of them wore, was groomed the same way that any of them were groomed. . . . The agent could find no difference at all; she looked like an ordinary woman of the United States of America, Planet Earth.

But the woman could not have been ordinary, because she had perceived the agent. The nature of that perception was not something the agent could be sure of. It was possible that she

saw nothing, but smelled a smell entirely new to her experience
or heard a sound that could not be identified as anything of her
world. It was a defining characteristic of these people that only a
few of their senses were sufficiently developed for use, and even
those had a pitifully narrow range.

There was no help for it now, and the sensory modality was
irrelevant; the agent had been spotted. Her mind raced franti-
cally. How could it have happened? It wasn't possible, how
could it have happened? And what would the consequences be
when the agent removed the woman from this spacetime? How
could it be done without causing a *disruption* in this spacetime? A
simulacrum . . . could she substitute one without creating multiple problems?

The agent knew what despair was now. Next to this, her
previous error had been a matter of no significance. She would
go down in history now, but not for her distinguished achieve-
ments. She would be remembered as the agent who had somehow managed to fail in her assignment on the planet Earth,
despite the fact that such a thing was as nearly impossible as any
event in the known universe could be. *Congratulate yourself,* she
thought bitterly, *now you have* really *done it! Now you will
spend your life sorting cajederai-lipoba into neat small stacks,
like an infant; perhaps the Consortium will allow you to do this
in the company of others in disgrace, who will look at you with
awe, your disgrace being so much greater than theirs.*

The Terran woman was obviously in great distress; any minute
now she would scream and bring others running. And what
would she say? She was of the Lines—she would scream, "Perceive! *Perceive!*" And point at the agent, and explain. And then
what? The end of the world? The agent could not even begin to
imagine what that might lead to.

I am standing here, she thought then, *doing nothing at all,
watching the world collapse. How very admirable! How professional!* She shook herself, snapped herself back to awareness,
and did the thing she should have already done, wondering how
much precious time she had wasted; she queried her datary. *Who
is that woman?* She specified full information, although she
would only scan it; somewhere in the data there might be the
single item that would help her understand what had happened
. . . there might even be something that would help her decide
what to do next.

Making the query was a very simple act, but apparently it
caused a perception that was more than the human woman could
tolerate; some defense mechanism in her nervous system took

over and she fell to the floor in the pattern Terrans called a "faint" as the agent began extracting items from the cascade of information.

THE WOMAN IS SELENA OPAL HAME . . . IN SIXTH DECADE OF LIFE . . . IN GOOD HEALTH . . . MOTHER KILLED IN ACCIDENT WHEN HAME WAS ONLY A FEW DAYS OLD . . . FATHER TURNED INFANT OVER TO AGENCY CALLED GOVERNMENT WORK . . . FROM THIRD WEEK OF LIFE, GIVEN DAILY DOSES OF DRUGS TERRANS CALL HALLUCINOGENS . . . NOT A SINGLE SUCH DRUG, BUT A VARIETY Of THEM . . . AT FOUR WEEKS, PUT INTO A STANDARD INTERFACE . . . RESULT, ALMOST INSTANTANEOUS DEATH OF QTEQN CITIZEN SHARING INTERFACE AND TRANSFER OF INFANT TO FEDERAL ORPHANAGE . . . MOST OF LIFE SPENT AT ORPHANAGE, NO SIGNIFICANT EVENTS UNTIL TRANSFER TO CURRENT RESIDENCE AT REQUEST OF CHORNYAK HOUSEHOLD . . . NOTE SERIOUS DISABILITY CONFINED ONLY TO THIS CLASS OF INFANTS—SUBJECT HAS NO LANGUAGE, CAN NEITHER SPEAK NOR WRITE NOR SIGN, REPEAT SUBJECT HAS NO LANGUAGE . . . FURTHER DETAIL??? WAITING. . . .

The agent made the necessary hasty queries and scanned the answers as rapidly as possible, keeping one wary eye on the woman lying on the floor, demanding repeats when what the datary displayed seemed too good to be true.

The woman was stirring now, but the agent was no longer concerned about the consequences, other than for the poor creature herself. The agent was weak with relief; if "fainting" had been a process available to her physiologically she would no doubt have done that in her turn.

Talk of miracles! Of all the hundreds of thousands of people she might have encountered on this planet, she had managed to run straight into the one and only unique individual capable of perceiving her. The one and only individual whose nervous system had been altered early enough and drastically enough, at the time of greatest plasticity, to make that perception possible. And then, in that bizarre situation of improbable catastrophe, it turned out that the same neurological alteration had still another consequence—it left the woman without language. How awful for her . . . how wonderful for all other persons on this planet!

The woman could not tell what she had seen. Ever.

And now she was getting up, weeping, brushing the tears away with clumsy swipes of her hands across her cheeks. It was over.

Dataries do not present erroneous data. This woman, this woman now leaning against the wall, huddled into herself, her face distorted by her distress, lacked the mechanism of human communication, for all that she was truly and wholly human. This woman had eaten and slept, had done household tasks, had cared for infant and young humans, had walked about, had seen to her personal grooming and her bodily functions; she was capable of many things. But she was not capable of communicating to any other human being the message: THERE IS SOMETHING ALIEN HIDING IN THIS HOUSE!

Because the agent wasn't human, she was not subject to the human temptation to conceal this event. It might be exceedingly important at some future time, in some other place. Its consequences, for all she knew, might be significant; she did not know how they could be, but that was not her field, and she had been wrong in that way before. She had been positive that what she had done on the archipelago could not possibly have any consequences that mattered, and she had been terribly wrong. When she returned to her locus, she would report this occurrence, and that would be the end of her service as an agent of the Consortium. She would not be trusted with any other assignment, because there *were* no assignments less important than the one she just failed in, and there was nowhere worse to send her even if they had been willing to permit it. None of this was open to question or discussion.

But *catastrophe* was not going to happen. The agent would never know anything more than that she had been perceived. It had taken her only seconds to make certain that Selena Opal Hame was not capable of communicating with *her,* either, except in the form of an attempt to escape from her presence. The agent would never know whether she had been seen or heard or smelled by the human woman, or if the alteration of Selena's nervous system had activated in her one of the normally nonfunctioning sensory systems. But no one else would ever know, either, because Selena Opal Hame had no way to communicate what had happened. And that was what mattered.

The woman gone, the danger past, there was time to spare; the agent entered into the state of prayer, for she had much to be thankful for. And when the prayer was complete, she advised her datary that the time had come for her to return; she could be of no further use here. Nor could any other agent, for so long as Selena Opal Hame lived at Chornyak Household.

It was categorically forbidden for any agent to cause distress to any Terran, and there was no question about Selena Opal Hame's distress. The three buildings of Chornyak Household—the main house, Chornyak Barren House, and Chornyak Womanhouse—would be added to the list of forbidden sites for so long as Selena lived. The harm done to her could not be undone, but no *further* chance of harm would be permitted. It would not be necessary to remove her from this site, or to disturb her life in any other way whatsoever. Her file would be flagged in the master dataries as a routine measure, to provide an alert if ever she *did* begin to communicate, but that was only a formality. A human being of her age who had never acquired language would not do so—the Terran brain did not work that way. No one but the agent's superior would ever know what had happened; Selena Opal Hame could be left in peace. And in time, in the way of humans who have endured shocking experiences, the memory would be buried in her mind, walled off and harmless, explained away as a dream or a hallucination, and then forgotten.

It was all right, then. Everything was going to be all right.

Except that the agent's career was over, and her life effectively at an end unless she could learn to enjoy her exile from everything that she valued. Except for that.

CHAPTER
22

The White House has just announced that the President will not veto the tax reform bill passed last night by both houses of Congress. According to White House Spokesman Chad "Bull" Whipple, the President continues to disapprove strongly of the provision canceling the requirement for all American Earth colonies to remit one percent of their annual income taxes to the Internal Revenue Service in Washington DC. However, he will not—repeat, will not—veto the package, since he finds it otherwise acceptable. Spokesman Whipple added that the President sincerely hopes the colonies will voluntarily continue to return the monies in question.

"Well, Senator, how do you feel about the President's position on this bill?"

"Brodo, do you have any idea how degrading it is for our colonies to have to apply every goddam year for exemption from that stupid one percent levy?"

"No, Senator, I can't say that—"

"And do you know that not one of those requests has ever been turned down? Do you know how long it's been since any taxes were actually paid by a colonial government? Would you believe sixty-three years? And do you—"

"Wait a minute, Senator! Are you telling our viewers that the Soviet Union allows—"

"Oh, the Soviet Union! What the hell does that have to do with this? I don't pretend to know what the tax arrangements are for the Soviet colonies, Brodo, I am talking about the great and glorious United States of America! And I am saying that although of course the President had to make some ritual noises of protest—"

"Are you saying that the one percent tax levy is only a symbol, sir?"

"Well of course *it's just a symbol! If anybody should be paying taxes, we should be paying them, to the colonies . . . do you know how many billions of credits—trillions of credits— our colonies save us every single year? That levy has never done one damn thing but cause bad feeling and rotten public relations!"*

"Then you're on the record that the President made the right decision, Senator?"

"Brodo, do you have *to ask stupid questions? Is it part of your job description? Or is it some kind of personal fetish?"*

(excerpt from an interview in SPACETIME HOLOMAGAZINE)

It was such a small meeting that it could actually have been held inside Heykus Clete's desk; the desk had been built a little larger than was usual, to accommodate Clete's unusual bulk and to make room for his specialized gadgetry. It would have provided space enough for three men who had no active dislike for one another. But Heykus didn't want to do it that way, despite the fact that his desk offered some of the best security to be had in any federal building in Washington. He didn't like the *scope* that kind of crowding seemed to give to a discussion; it was too much like three criminals huddling together in a back room somewhere. It would have hung a seedy psychological miasma over their heads, and he vetoed the idea at once when the General suggested it.

"We'll do it out at the farm, Stu," he'd said. "I'd prefer that."

"That's damned inconvenient, Heykus!"

"It is?" Heykus let the surprise show in his voice; you could not be subtle with a prototype Good Soldier like Stuart Charing, or he'd miss half the conversation. "What difference does it make to you and your computer expert whether you land in downtown Washington or a farm in Maryland? There couldn't be thirty seconds travel time difference!"

"Hell, I didn't mean inconvenient for me and Tatum Pugh, Heykus. I meant inconvenient for *you.* As compared with just having us meet you at your office—which, as you so correctly point out, wouldn't take us any longer." The general knew he was appearing on Clete's big screen; he was sitting tall, and his shoulders were thrown back, and all his brass was polished to a fare-thee-well. "The farm's nice, Heykus, but hell, you don't need to go way out there on *our* behalf. We're used to El Centro, remember? Washington's not going to faze us."

"All the more reason," said Heykus courteously, "why you should have something pleasant in the way of an environment for a change. Let's do it at the farm." He paused, and raised his eyebrows long enough to be sure the general was following him, and added, "If you are absolutely determined that it has to be person to person."

"I am."

"You do know how many scramblers and safeties and cob-webbers we've got between your installation and my office, Stu?"

Charing muttered that he did know, but *still*, and looked vaguely uncomfortable, confirming Heykus' original estimation of the situation. The point of coming to Washington, obviously, was that Stu Charing had cabin fever there in El Centro, three levels down below the surface of the desert, and presumably had already used up all the leave he was entitled to for the year. It was a shame about Stu Charing. He was in many ways a very good man. If Heykus had had to trust his life to Stu Charing, he would not have had an instant's worry about the man's loyalty or his integrity; *nothing* short of the most advanced and illegal techniques of interrogation could have made Charing betray Government Work, and anyone using those would have discovered that as a side effect they had turned their victim into a *dead* victim. Death was hard-wired into Stuart Charing so many different ways that only a truly ignorant interrogator would have bothered even to ask him his name, rank, and serial number. In addition to all that, the general was hardworking, and conscientious, and pleasant; he was the sort of person that subordinates could tolerate easily. He wasn't charismatic, but he was a good officer. Unfortunately, he had a flaw. He was the master of the *tiny*, but devastating, forgotten detail. If you trusted your life to Stu Charing he would remember ninety-nine out of one hundred items, but the single item he forgot would be the toilet paper. It was an uncanny anti-talent, and it had landed him at the Cetacean Project, where it was felt that he was too far underground and too far out of town to do any serious damage. And he got tired of being there.

Heykus didn't blame him for that. What was amazing was that none of the scientists sharing El Centro with Charing, or the computer expert who would be flying in with him, ever seemed to feel that way.

"All right, Stu," Heykus said, "I'll defer to your judgment. You think face-to-face is necessary, I'm sure you have your reasons. But we'll do it at the farm." *And you, dear Stuart whose middle name I happen to know to be Vivian, and there's damn few of us that know that, will not have the fleshpots of Washington to console yourself with after all. Just the government's spread of pretty posies.* The Maryland farm (unlike some other federal "farms" of less savory reputation) was an agricultural experiment station, covered with plots of plants brought in from all over the galaxy, all being tested to see what sort of conditions they could survive in, and what kinds of practical uses they might have, and what hazards they represented. But the small conference room where Heykus would meet with the other two men didn't look out over the experimental gardens. It was at the very center of the acreage, in a grove of tall pines and cedars. At least it would be a nice change from the desert.

"You want to give me a small hint, Stu?" Heykus asked as they exchanged parting remarks. "So that I can prepare?"

The general shook his head. "There's no way to get ready for *this* shit, Heykus," he said sadly. "Trust me."

"You're sure?" Heykus spoke emphatically, closing in on the source of the general's famous weakness. "You're absolutely sure we won't get over there in Maryland and you'll suddenly remember that the one essential item for the meeting is only to be had somewhere else entirely? I am *safe* trusting you, without so much as a clue?"

The general's face went blank; he did the Military Blank Face, Just Doing My Job, extremely well. "I'm sure," he answered. "Nothing to worry about."

Heykus waited, maintaining eye contact, but the general was as good at maintaining the expression as he was at assuming it, and no flicker of expression marred the military visage.

"In that case, I'll see you tomorrow." Heykus blanked the screen without waiting for any more amenities. General Charing would forget something, as sure as the coming of spring, but there was no point in worrying him about it. And it was probable that Tatum Pugh, after working with the man all these years, would be carrying the forgotten item in his pocket or in his head, depending on what sort of item it was.

"Dear Lord," muttered Heykus testily as he watched the fiz-status display tell him the familiar facts about the general's low blood pressure and rapid heartbeat, "I'm a little tired of failures and catastrophes and disgraces and cataclysms over at Government Work. It would be nice if this were something minor, Lord, if You've no serious objections."

But it wasn't minor. If it had been, even Charing's desire to be sprung briefly from El Centro wouldn't have driven him to interrupt Clete's busy schedule for an emergency meeting. It had been an empty hope all along, and an empty prayer. Just a word with the Lord in passing, not any *real* prayer. Heykus was careful about prayer, as he would have been careful with explosives. There were a lot of problems associated with it. You take its power—what, exactly, was supposed to happen when two men of equal faith prayed on opposite sides of a question? It made Heykus think of two lightning bolts tangled in midair, and it made him uneasy. He was sure the Lord had ways of handling it, because that went with omnipotence, but he couldn't imagine what they were. As for that bit about being able to order mountains to cast themselves into the sea if you had as much faith as a grain of mustard seed . . . Heykus was not going to test that one. Suppose you *did* have faith enough—and Heykus knew beyond all question that he did—and it didn't work? Suppose the mountain didn't move? The blind didn't see? The lame didn't get up and walk? Then what? How were you going to handle that? Or suppose the mountain *did* move—what did you do about the resulting mess? You move a mountain, there'd be sizable disarrangements of such things as the geotectonic plates, not to mention the real estate; and the animal life would definitely not be prepared for a marine existence. No, Heykus didn't care to test that one, and he didn't want to see anybody test it, either.

Although at the moment, he might have been tempted to throw the *general* into the sea, along with the cetaceans. He knew *they* could swim, and he didn't give a hoot for the fate of Stuart Vivian Charing.

"Let me see if I've got this straight," he said through clenched teeth. "Let me just see if I understand it fully."

"All right," said the general. He was trying to look both concerned and serene, and doing very badly. It wasn't one of the standard GI expressions, or GW either.

"You haven't left anything out?"

"No, Heykus, I haven't. Have I, Pugh?"

The computer whiz drew his shoulders up beside his ears and rubbed his arms with his hands, delicately. "General," he stated, "this is your party. I am not a guest. I am here in case you want something out of the databanks and aren't sure how to get it without disturbing security. Do not ask me silly questions."

The general glared at Pugh, who was unimpressed, and then turned to Heykus and declared that he had not left anything out, so help him god. "And thank you very much, Tatum, for your unfailing dedication to the cause," he added.

"Any time," said Pugh. "Any time at all."

"*So,* Stuart!"

"So?"

"So you have known about this particular—difficulty—for at least a year. You were warned about it, by unanimous joint memo, by all three of the senior scientists at El Centro. Before it even began? Is that possible?"

"At that stage of the operation I thought they were simply in error, Heykus."

"All of them?"

"Certainly, all of them. They've been wrong—all of them—many times. I felt that this was one of the times. And I saw no reason to trouble you with what I was certain would turn out to be yet one more mistake."

"Why, Stuart? *Why?*"

"I *told* you why. You have more than enough work to do without having to review the imbecilities of my scientific staff."

Heykus sat there and stared at this man who was a good friend and a man of his own generation and wondered if he could be speaking the truth. It was *possible,* maybe. Just barely possible. If he was, the implications were not pleasant.

He leaned back in his chair, fixed the general with his eyes like a moth on a very short pin, and ticked off the points on his fingers.

"ONE!" he said. "The physical resemblance between the AIRYs now at El Centro and the Earth whales is *not* just a coincidence. They are in fact . . . what would you call them? Cetaceanoids? Whatever you call them, their brains appear to be related to the brains of Terran cetaceans in the same way that humanoid Alien brains are related to the brains of Terran humans. That's point one.

"TWO! Interfaced with the AIRYs, our Earth whale infant did in fact, so far as we can tell, acquire the Alien language. Scientists observing the Interface agree that the young whale is actually communicating with the AIRYs.

"THREE! This constitutes the first—*the first*—example of a Terran organism acquiring a nonhumanoid extraterrestrial language. Which is something you put in the history books, right? *Don't answer that, Charing!* Don't even think about answering it. So: we now have cracked a nonhumanoid Alien language."

"Maybe!" put in the general, desperately.

"Maybe? Why maybe?"

"According to the eggdomes, maybe the linguists are wrong in thinking Earth whales aren't human. Or something like that. I don't understand it completely, except that they do not find the idea that these whales have a language something to be happy about. Maybe the Terran whales, *and* the Alien ones, are really some kind of humanoid.''

"And we've just drawn our lines in the wrong places,'' summarized Tatum Pugh disgustedly. ''That's stupid. That's just whatever-you-call-it. That ism. The one about man being superior to everything else. Species-ism or whatever it is.''

"You think that can safely be ignored, do you, Pugh?'' asked Heykus.

"Damn right. Our eggdomes have been underground too long.''

"Then I'll ignore it. That leave us back at point three—we have now acquired the first nonhumanoid Alien language. *Except*— and this is point four—except that we don't have any access to that language because we don't happen to speak *Whale!* Is that right, General? Have I phrased that right?''

"Yes, and—''

"FIVE!'' Heykus thundered. ''And this is the most outrageous item on the list, General! Five: you were warned about this a year ago. *A year ago.* And in all that time, you never saw fit to pass the warning along to me.''

Blank Military Face. Stiff upper lip, rigid jaw.

"That's essentially correct,'' the general replied, ''but it's not exactly the way I see it.''

"I'll bet it's not! How *do* you see it, Stuart?''

"In the first place, I thought they were wrong. I told you that. That was my own judgment, based on the data I had. And I saw no point in passing on erroneous information to you.''

"That's in the first place. What else?''

"In the second place, I assumed you already knew about it.''

"*What?*'' Even for Stu Charing, this was a little much. ''You assumed what?''

"Paul White knew about it,'' said the general, getting stiffer and stiffer with every word. ''He's your own liaison man. You sent him out to tell us about the project at the very beginning, Heykus. I assumed he'd told you.''

"And I just mysteriously had never mentioned it.''

"I assumed that you agreed with me in my opinion that the eggdomes were mistaken, Heykus. I assumed you had noted the report from White, had decided it was ridiculous for the eggdomes to come to the conclusions they'd come to, and had put it out of your mind. As I would have done, in your place.''

Heykus got up from the chair, turned his back to the General and walked over to look out the window. It was pretty out there. Groves of evergreens. Slabs of wood for steppingstones . . .

steppingslabs. Whatever. Carpet of needles, piled thick, but not a one out of place. Babbling brook, with *real* steppingstones. Little clumps of columbines, here and there. It was absolutely the splendid handiwork of the Almighty, and it was a consolation to have it to contrast with the pitiful example presented by Stu Charing.

If the poor slow sonofabee was telling the truth about all his assumptions—and he probably was—he'd gone wrong in what was for him the classic fashion. Among all the other things that he had assumed, he had assumed that Paul White had gone on back to Washington and reported in the usual way, and *he had not checked that out*. It being a small detail. In fact, White had never made it back to Washington. An intercept courier had caught up with him over Little Rock, Arkansas and handed him emergency orders for an entirely separate trouble-shooting mission way to hell and gone out past the commercial routes, on the planet aptly named Sorry Prospect. Where White still was. Still patiently slogging away at a mess that was just his kind of thing, and no doubt doing a fine job of it.

"You know where Paul White is right now, General?" he asked casually, not turning around, keeping his eyes on the wonders of the carefully-assembled woodland glade beyond the window.

"Of course not. Why should I?"

Heykus told him.

"He never got back to you? Not at all? Well. . . . Heykus, his report should have reached you all the same."

"It reached me. White is reliable. Always. But he wouldn't have put your scientists' speculations about this matter in a routine report, Stu, even if it was coded. It was the kind of thing he would have told me only in person, under strictest security."

"Well, hell*fire*, man!" the general blustered. "*That's* no excuse. Why didn't he *make sure* somebody had told you?"

Pugh's voice sounded as old and weary as Heykus felt. "Because," he drawled, "in view of the fact that at least three senior scientists at El Centro knew about it, and had protested to White in the strongest terms, and would *absolutely* have gone straight to their chief—that's you, General—and told him, probably three or four times a week, it never crossed White's mind that Director Clete would have to rely on his report to get the information."

Heykus turned around, then, and leaned against the window, with both hands splayed and braced on the broad wooden sill. "And I've seen you twice during this past year, Stu," he said softly. "Once at a Christmas party. Once for lowgrav tennis.

And neither time, *neither time,* did you see fit to mention this. Or ask me what I'd thought of White's report. Or anything of that kind.''

"There were people around," protested the general. "It wasn't safe."

"It wasn't safe to ask me what I'd thought of Paul White's last routine report."

"No, it wasn't. Not in my judgment. Somebody might have made something out of it."

Tatum Pugh snickered, and the general glared at him, and he snickered again.

"Ah, sweet suffering saints, Stuart," mourned Heykus. *"What am I supposed to do with this mess?"*

"I don't know," said Charing. "I really don't know."

"What made you decide to tell me now?"

"This was different."

"In what way?"

"I had new information. I had the actual report, from the eggdomes, stating the conclusions they had reached. And I had not seen Paul White or anybody else, in the interim, who might have passed it on to you. It therefore became my duty to report to you myself. In person."

"You'd just gone on hoping, all this time, that your staff— your scientific staff, Stuart, who you persist in calling 'eggdomes' as if you were a recruit fresh off the boonies rocket—you'd just gone on hoping they would be wrong."

"Yes. I don't think that was unreasonable. They were wrong when they informed me that the physical resemblance between the Earth whales and the Aliens was only a coincidence. They talked about it being like the resemblance between a penguin and a short man in evening clothes. They talked about golfballs looking like eggs, for chrissakes. They were wrong, and we were right. Why shouldn't they have been wrong about the rest of it?''

There were a number of things that Heykus might have said to him if Pugh hadn't been there. *I always knew you had a blind spot that made you overlook small things that turn out to be important, Stuart, but until this moment I never thought you were actually stupid. Now you have changed my mind.* He did not choose to say that, or any of the other remarks along that same line that occurred to him, in front of Tatum Pugh. Not so much because Pugh might have wondered why he'd left a stupid man in charge of the Cetacean Project; often the very best place for a stupid man was the "in charge" position, leaving people who knew what they were doing free to do it, while he spun his wheels. But he could not afford to encourage the sort of disrespect for authority that he already saw in Tatum Pugh's face.

"Dear Lord," said Heykus fervently, and he meant no disrespect for *his* superior. He went back over to the table, dialed for coffee, and watched the gravytrain float over. Meticulously, tenderly, as he would have cared for a badly flawed child, he poured coffee for General Stuart Charing, and handed it to him. He took his own cup, black and strong, as he preferred it, and he let Tatum Pugh fend for himself. The silence thickened round the table; and in that silence, Heykus stirred his coffee with a spoon. There was nothing in it to stir, but he stirred it nonetheless. It filled the silence, while he thought about what he would say next.

"Stuart," he began, finally, "I'm afraid there's a piece of the problem that you didn't look at from precisely the right angle. You see, this was always a no-win situation. Right from the beginning. Paul White wouldn't have realized that—he hasn't had that much experience, and he doesn't believe in making that kind of judgment in any case—but you ought to have known."

A line of beads of sweat stood out across the general's upper lip, and he sputtered at Heykus; what the sputter meant was impossible to determine.

"If the scientists were right, and the little whale did *not* acquire the Alien language," Heykus said, keeping his voice casual, "we lost. We'd wasted time and resources and a lot of money. If, on the other hand, the little whale *did* acquire the Alien language, we still lost—because we can't communicate with whales, right? They told you this, at the very beginning. They came to you, in a group, and they explained that all attempts to Interface whales with humans had been failures. Without exception. And they told you that they, and the men of the Lines, were quite certain that this was deliberate on the whales' part—and would not change."

The general cleared his throat and raised his hand in the gesture that means wait-a-minute-there's-something-I-want-to-add-right-here, and Heykus stopped for him.

"Well, you see, Heykus, that's just the point. Now, it seemed to me—I mean, I have been there, all these years, while those whales up on the first floor were in the Interface with tubies, and I have *seen* that nothing whatsoever was happening. I *knew* about that. It was just a cover, anyway, and nobody cared. But it seemed to me that this was a whole new ball game, Heykus. It seemed to me that the whales of Earth might well feel that now there was a *reason* to communicate with us. They might want to *share* with us this entirely new set of circumstances."

Heykus and the computer whiz exchanged glances, and Tatum Pugh shook his head sadly; and Heykus shouldered the burden and went on speaking in the same compassionate tender mode he had been using before the general pranced through the linguistic environment stark naked in that awful fashion, with his thoughts hanging out.

"This one little whale," Heykus mused, "this infant whale, alone of all its kind, and with no other whale for company but its mother. It might know all the past history of human/cetacean Interfacing. And it might decide, on the basis of its ample knowledge, that the time had come to . . . to what, Stuart? What did you think it was going to do, demand to be put in the first floor Interface so it could teach the current tubie? Or was it going to rely on its mother to make that demand? Or what?"

"When you put it that way," said the general slowly, "it does sound a little unlikely."

"*Does* it?"

"But I wasn't thinking of it that way."

Heykus wasn't angry with Stu Charing any longer. Anger was an emotion that he reserved for his peers, for equals, for those who were equipped to defend themselves as rational adult males. This man wasn't stupid. This man was mentally defective. He had been under stress too long, had suffered the humiliation of too many failures for which it was clear that he had been the cause; he had broken under the weight of it. He should not have been in charge of *any*thing—he should have been in a sheltered environment where he could have been looked after. And he wasn't angry with Tatum Pugh, because he knew about really good computer people; they reported trouble with computers. Period. Human being trouble was not their province. "I don't do humans," they'd tell you if you asked. The better the computer man, the more that was going to be true. But the anger Heykus felt toward his subordinates in D.A.T. was a mighty anger. They should have spotted General Charing as a man who—however capable he had been before—was now as useless as a chocolate computer chip. They were there so that he, Heykus, would not have to worry about pathetic creatures like Stuart Charing. He recognized in his anger a core of passion that would not do; if it was still there by the time he got back to Washington he would spend an hour on his knees in prayer before he called in any of the upper level men who ought to have alerted him to Charing's breakdown. Anger was permitted to him, but vengeance was the Lord's; he would pray for the breadth of spirit to remember that.

"Heykus?" Charing's voice was trembling now.

"Yes, Stuart?"

"What's the next step? Do we negotiate with the whales now, or what?"

"How would you suggest we do that, General?"

"I don't know." Charing swallowed hard. "But there has to be a way. Heykus, it's intolerable that there's a nonhumanoid language that's been cracked by a Terran, and we can't get at it. It won't be easy to live with that, Heykus."

"Astute observation."

"Nobody could argue with that," Pugh said, adding his contribution.

"What are we going to do, Heykus?"

"*I* don't know."

"I thought you *would* know," the General said. "I was counting on you."

"You thought I'd have a magic solution? Stuart, I'm an administrator, not an animal trainer. How would I know what to do about an ocean full of whales that won't stoop to talk to human beings?"

The general sat there blinking at him, and Heykus couldn't bear to look at the man any longer; he turned his attention to Tatum Pugh. "Mr. Pugh," he said. "Do you have anything to contribute? You've had very little to say."

"He never talks," the general said. "Never."

"I have a suggestion."

"Make it, Mr. Pugh."

"I suggest that you ask the Lingoes what to do."

Heykus saw the general open his mouth to say what he thought of that, and he told him to shut it. He was kind, but he was firm. "You think they'd help?" he asked Pugh, well aware that the man was making a vast concession in even taking part in this discussion.

"No," answer Pugh. "I don't think they'd *help*. But I think they'd be just purely fascinated, and that might sucker them in. A nonhumanoid language . . . god almighty, can't you just imagine how the Lingoes would want to get at that? After all this time? I don't think they would help, because—once again—you've ignored everything they said and gone right on fouling it all up just like they told you you would. But I don't think they could *resist*, Mr. Clete. If you just told them what had happened, and then you got out of the way, I think they'd come in. And while they were around, they just might do whatever there is that could be done."

"You think they could get the whales to cooperate?"

"I don't know. But I don't think anybody else could, and I think they *might*."

"And if they did . . . then what would we do?"

Tatum laughed. "Then," he said, "we *would* have to negotiate. With the Lingoes."

"Could you handle setting that up?"

"Absolutely not," said Pugh. "I don't do humans."

"You must have somebody on your staff that could do it," said Heykus.

"Nope." Pugh's voice was flat. "The General here can't do it. The eggdomes won't—they hate the Lingoes. And there's nobody else at our installation that I—or you—would trust with the arrangements."

"All right," Heykus sighed. "I'll see to it. I'll contact the linguists myself."

He kept confidence in his voice, still working on subduing the unwholesome rebelliousness he sensed in Tatum Pugh; but if he had been forced to state his expectations they would not have matched his tone. The linguists functioned by a code of ethics so bizarre that Heykus could not ever be certain what they would do or how they would react in a given set of circumstances. He was *grateful* for it—without it, he was sure they could never have been forced to lead the lives of constant sacrifice, cradle to grave, that were essential to D.A.T.'s plans and to the Lord's. Still, sometimes it was awkward.

He could just hear the linguists now. Explaining. That the whales had made it more than amply clear that they did not choose to communicate with humans. That they had every right to make that decision. That if the whales had found a creature they *did* choose to communicate with, the linguists were happy for them. That come the day the whales wanted to communicate with humans, they would no doubt make that desire known. And until that day—Heykus could just hear the linguists. Saying:

"We don't do whales."

CHAPTER 23

"I was so very slow to grow up; I don't suppose I began to approach anything like *adult womanhood before I was thirty years old. And it was terrible, then, when it did come, to awaken into life no longer young and with children of my own, and to discover that almost everything that made up the reality in which we lived was simply lies. I didn't know what to do. Fortunately, I was the sort of awkward and cumbersome personality who makes no impassioned speeches and wouldn't be listened to if she did; I managed not to make a complete fool of myself. I looked at all those lies, and I saw at once that not one stood alone. Every lie was intertwined with every other lie; every lie was wound into a dense fabric of lies that seemed impenetrable; there were so many lies that existed only to protect people from the consequences of other lies. And that structure went on, layer after layer; I had lived within it for thirty years and never guessed that it was there.*

"When I recovered from my astonishment all I could think of was that something must be done, and that whether I was the only one who felt that way or one of countless millions who felt that way, it was my place to do *what had to be done, to the limits of my strength. I thought then:* no matter how deep the dung, no matter how long the task, if you just go at it one shovel at a time the day will come when you can see clean earth at the bottom of the pile.

"It is possible—barely possible—that I was right. I'm not sure, though I have now lived three times thirty years and more. But right or wrong, there was one way in which my error was large, was vast . . . Never, you perceive, did I so much as begin to guess at the scale of time with which I was dealing. "No matter how deep the dung," *I thought.* "No matter how long the

task.'' *I believe I was thinking of decades, of tens of years; and I do believe that I was considering myself a remarkably patient woman! My arrogance, like my ignorance, was almost as abundant as that pile of dung . . . that pile of preprocessed lies, excreted all tidy and steaming by our culture . . . that I fancied I might be able to at least make smaller.*

"I know better now. The unit of time that must be taken into account here is not decades but centuries, and tens of centuries. It has meaning only in the context of eternal time. Imagine eternity, where a million centuries might still be ahead of you before some event that you were anxious for, and the Holy One would say to you gently and honestly, 'Wait . . . it will only be a minute.' That is the sort of time we are speaking of."

"Well . . . I was a human being, a woman of Earth, a Terran female; I was ill-prepared to set my mind to plans that must be based upon thousands and thousands of years. Nothing about me was large enough to stretch itself to such a scale. And so, because there was quite literally nothing else to do, I set Time aside. I pretended that there was no such entity as Time; I abandoned it utterly. And then I set my shovel to the pile. I began to do whatever I humanly could. Outside the context of Time.

"It would have frightened me, I think, if I had allowed myself to think about it."

(from the diaries of Nazareth Chornyak Adiness)

Belle-Sharon lay in the broad firm bed in the rendezvous room, as carefully arranged for Jared's pleasure as an earth-wise plant arranged for sunlight or for rain. Like the plants, Belle-Sharon was earth-wise, but she had the additional benefit of conscious intention. She had washed her long hair that afternoon, and had dried it in the sun while she took her turn at watching the little ones in the Interface, and when she came to her appointment with her husband she loosed her hair and let its ends sweep the pillows and sheets, to loose also the lilac scent that Jared preferred. At first he had wanted that perfume so strong and so pervasive that she had found it hard to breathe; over the months she had decreased it in almost imperceptible steps until it was no longer overpowering. She had been scrupulously careful, and Jared was not aware that there had been any change.

He was calling her "sweetheart," over and over again, and setting rows of kisses along the side of her throat and down over her breasts; he had come upon the spot between her breasts where she had touched the lilac oil directly to her skin and he was nuzzling there now like a blissful infant. As he moved, she felt his penis touch her hip and noted that it had begun to harden; soon he would be ready to enter her for the act itself. She shifted her body carefully beneath him, so that although he could still reach the nuzzling-spot his penis would lie cradled against the inner surface of her thigh, to make the erection swifter and easier for him; with both strong hands she stroked the long muscles of his back and buttocks.

Jared's murmuring had stopped being recognizable words and become a blurred babble of passion and pleasure; she fit her own murmuring to his so that it would form a constant background. Not that he really heard her; she could have lain there under him saying "Hail Columbia, let the good times roll" or "when in the course of human events" or "six times six is thirty-six" or anything else whatsoever; it was the intonation of her voice, the melody to which she set the syllables, that he heard, and not their lexical form.

He gasped, and his hands were busy at the fork of her body; she arched her throat to give him a place for his mouth while he fumbled, because she knew he didn't like her to see his face at this particular moment, and as soon as she felt the tip of the penis within her she moved her hips to grasp him and settle herself around him so that he would have maximum contact with her vagina. An ugly word, *vagina*; like that ugly word, *penis*. Their ugliness would serve her purpose, however, as Jared began to move, moaning with each thrust, the carefully prepared surfaces that sheathed him offering no resistance except the skilled grip of her inner muscles tightening around him to increase his ecstasy.

"Vagina," Belle-Sharon repeated to herself, aloud. If he did understand her he would think only that in her passion she was talking a bit scandalously, and he would be delighted by that; at the same time, her careful consideration of the word's ugliness was a helpful distraction. She had had difficulty early in her marriage with Jared, because despite her best efforts she would become aroused. But she had gone immediately to the more experienced women for advice and they had described to her a dozen ways to manage. Ugly words always helped, they told her, and there are plenty of those ."Menstruation," she said— now there was a *truly* ugly word! The n-s-t-r sequence before the vowel was so un-English, so un-Panglish, that it fought your mouth when you tried to pronounce it; she had heard many a med-Sammy slip and say "menestration" instead. She said it again, softly, correctly; Jared was moving more quickly now, well into his best rhythm; it would soon be over. And if things became truly serious she could always switch to Nazareth's favorite technique. "Oh, the times tables are useful," Nazareth had said to her, and "verb conjugations have their place, but the very best way I know to avoid going so far into arousal that you suffer is to say the alphabet backward. It takes an extraordinary amount of concentration!" The old woman had chuckled, and added that if the time came when the alphabet in reverse had been so well learned that it lost its efficiency as a distractor, you simply turned to the alphabet of the Alien language you were interpreter for, and so on down the list. "But don't get *too* distracted, now," she had warned. "There is a moment when your attention must be on your husband."

Yes. Jared had almost arrived at that moment, and Belle-Sharon was aware of it. She began to pant, tiny gasps like a woman in labor; when the spasm took him, her own body was arched tight against him, and she screamed sharply—just once—and allowed a series of shudders to race through all her muscles as he climaxed. She was as good at those shudders as any woman in Chornyak Womanhouse, and she prided herself on their perfection. Her mother had begun her instruction as soon as her breasts had shown curve enough to draw the attention of the unmarried men, and before pronouncing herself satisfied with Belle-Sharon's performance she had brought in her *own* mother to observe the demonstration. Only then, when Noura Hashihawa Adiness had said, "Yes, my dear—that is exactly right," had the instruction come to an end. And if Noura said it was exactly right, you could be certain that it was; she was well into her sixties, but her husband still called her to the rendezvous rooms weekly, and sometimes oftener. Belle-Sharon had known herself complimented, and she had said, "Thank you, Grandmother," and been kissed in reply. "You are a good child," Noura had said, "and you will be a superb wife."

Like any woman of the Lines, Belle-Sharon thought. It was a matter of courtesy, that one should be a superb wife. "My darling," she said to Jared, "you give me such joy!" He had lifted his head and was looking down at her; she let her pupils dilate, as she had let her vagina dilate, and she drew a long sighing breath—the sigh of a woman replete. That, too, was courtesy.

"And you, my sweet lady," he said to her softly, taking a long strand of her hair and curling it round one hand so that he could smell it more easily. "No man ever had a better woman in his bed than you, Belle-Sharon Adiness Chornyak."

She smiled and thanked him, and touched his cheek with her fingertips, and when the tug of his hand on the lock of hair hurt her scalp she did not let that show on her face. It was a tiny inconvenience, not a real pain. The real pain—the pain that she had known too many times before she brought her body under control—was the pain of letting yourself truly take part in this act that Panglish called "sexual intercourse." Or "fucking." (More ugly words!) It had taken Belle-Sharon nearly six months to achieve fully the control that would spare her that pain, and there had been many nights when she had gone desperate and frantic back to Chornyak Womanhouse to be soothed and comforted by the other women, who had been through it themselves before her and knew what she was enduring.

She wondered how on earth she would have survived that period if Jared had been one of those overly romantic young men who insisted on taking a bedroom for the two of them adjoining the rendezvous rooms, where she would have had to sleep with him all night, every night. There *were* such men; and often they clung to the arrangement for a year or more before the pressure of the other husbands' teasing finally put an end to it and the wife was released to Womanhouse. Belle-Sharon was absolutely certain that she could not have lived through that without a distortion of her mind and spirit; it had been horrible for her even as it was.

"It can't be helped, sweet Belle-Sharon," the women had told her, soothing, stroking her hair. "It takes a little while to get the knack of fulfilling the demands of courtesy to your husband adequately and at the same time never letting yourself become too much aroused. It takes *every* woman a while to get it right, and some far longer than others."

Sometimes she had screamed at them that she could not bear it, could not possibly bear it, and then they had sent for Dorcas to brew the bitter tea that would bring sleep within minutes, giving her peace and letting the swelling of her body, so ready for what Jared could not be expected to provide, go away during the long drugged night. And while she waited for the tea one of them would hold her, saying, "Hush, hush now," and rock her in gentle arms.

There were some women, Belle-Sharon knew, who drank the tea and slept deep and long, but woke the next morning still tumescent, to linger that way for days at a time, not eased even by the orgasms any woman could of course provide easily enough for herself. Poor loves, thought Belle-Sharon. Poor tormented loves. She was grateful that she was not one of those, also.

Jared lay now with his hand still tangled in her hair, still pulling at her scalp, sound asleep, softly snoring. She moved just a little, to ease the tug at her hair and to get one cramped leg out from beneath the weight of his knee, but she was cautious; he woke rather easily and if he woke and wanted her again it was important that enough time should have passed so that any stray touch of passion that might have gotten through the barriers she raised would have subsided. It would not do for him to take her again until she was entirely calm.

Jared had no complaints about her, she knew that. He would not have been so rude as to speak them to her openly, even if there had been things he disliked; courtesy bred courtesy. And he was a man of the Lines—he did not betray himself by posture or expression or tone of voice unless he did so by deliberate choice and for a reason of his own. But he was like any other man, linguist or no linguist, when passion took him; he had no skill left at dissembling then. As *she* also would have had no skill, she reminded herself, noting her unbecoming vanity, if *she* had been overtaken by passion. A woman was fortunate; the passion need not be real, and still she could be all that her husband wanted. For a man matters were very different, and unless he truly meant the passion he would be as helpless as a dead stick. Rather more helpless, in fact; a dead stick might still be of some use.

She lay resting, quiet, waiting until he either woke or was so deeply asleep that she could leave without his knowing, listening to the soft sound of the rain. It was not real *rain* either; no downpour, however torrential, could be heard through the earth piled over the roof of a linguist household. It was a recording of rain falling on a roof open to the sky; like the lilac perfume, it was Jared's favorite. Belle-Sharon's ear, that could distinguish easily more than thirty different varieties of the unit of sound symbolized by the letter "t", caught a hint of a hiss behind the rain, and she made a mental note to get a new copy. This one was worn, from too many men of the Lines fancying rain on the roof while they took their pleasure.

Sometimes, in the early months when she had still been so miserable, she had thrown wild oaths around the table in the kitchen at Womanhouse, swearing that if she bore a daughter she'd see to it that every last *scrap* of desire was stamped out of her before ever she married, to spare her that same misery.

"Tsk, child," they'd said to her. "For shame . . . that's only your pain talking."

She had been fierce, and stubborn. "I mean it! I swear I won't let any child of mine go through this hell!"

"Belle-Sharon, please do think," they'd said, after more clucking of tongues. "If true passion is driven out of our women . . . and certainly that's easy enough to accomplish, if we were such fools . . . then what hope is there? How are the men ever to *learn,* if we do that? Do you want your granddaughters, and their granddaughters, still to be spending half their lives, or all their lives—horrible thought!—wedded to men who have no more idea what to do with a woman in bed than a blue-balled baboon would? Is that what you would choose?"

And when she had insisted that there was no possibility, ever in all this world, that a man *would* learn, they had all laughed at her. The Young Wife's Complaint, it was called. So predictable that they were able to finish it for her, almost word for word, while she fretted at them to take her seriously.

"Belle-Sharon, there are many men who learn."

"*I don't believe it.*"

"Nothing in your experience so far would lead you to believe it. But then nothing in your experience so far would lead you to think we would lie to you, either."

"You might. To make me more patient."

"Did we lie when we warned you it would be like this?"

"No," she admitted. "But you didn't make it *clear* to me!"

That had set them off again, of course, and deservedly so; how were they supposed to make it clear to her when they had no way of knowing what sort of man Jared would turn out to be? Or how she would react to the sort of man he turned out to be?

"Belle-Sharon," they had chided her, when they could stop the loving laughter, "if it weren't that quite often men do in fact—over the course of time—manage to learn what a woman wants, and if it weren't that quite often such men are willing and able to give her ecstasy instead of what you are bearing now, we women of the Lines would long ago have done just what you are threatening. We would have found an efficient way to simply put an end to desire, for all of us."

"That is *exactly* what you should have done!"

"That is a very *male* solution," Dorcas had observed. "If it can't be made right instantaneously, throw it out. Downright manly thinking, Belle-Sharon . . . set it to music, we'll call it the Testosterone Rag."

"It's a stupid, stupid system!" she had cried, and had—if she remembered correctly—smacked the table so hard with her fist that it had made her cup rattle in its saucer. *Not* courteous, to be sure, but everyone had pretended not to notice.

"It certainly is stupid," Nazareth had agreed, and had spelled it out for her, her lips thinner with indignation than they were with age. "Raise the boys 'decently' so they have no experience at all before they marry—unless it's stolen experience, and done in such a terror of getting caught that the only goal the poor youngster has is to get it *finished* as quickly as possible. Which, for a male human, is very quickly indeed. Then give them wives with no experience of any other kind either, and no training except the marital academies' lessons in the choosing of nightgowns. And then leave the couple to batter away at each other in total ignorance, while the wife grows ever more bitter and vicious and the man wonders what happened to the nice girl he married. Perhaps, if she is *very* lucky, he will be so decently raised that he'll never read any of those books that bring up the concept of preparing a woman for his sixty seconds of attention. On his own that will never occur to him, it not being 'natural,' and in a year or two the wife will be sufficiently dead to all passion to get by."

"How can they *possibly* let that go on, century after century?" Belle-Sharon had demanded when the old woman paused for breath, her mind finally off her own selfish frustration and contemplating the awfulness of what women outside the Lines had to endure. It did change your perspective about your own problems, remembering how much worse it was for most women. Each one of them all alone, in her own house with her children, with no other woman to comfort her or help her or advise her. And the women of her family as ignorant as she was, even if they happened to be close by when she was miserable, by some accident.

Dorcas had shrugged her shoulders. "Dearlove," she said, "it comes of so many things, all working together. The idea of a decent Christian upbringing—that's so powerful. The idea of not wallowing in filth, which I must say is one we also support, if we could only get rid of the confusion about what is and what is not filth. And then American men are extremely attached to the myth that a spectacular act of love is one that lasts three whole minutes. . . . I don't know about men elsewhere, my dear, not from direct experience, but I suspect that it's much the same wherever you go. The idea of a decent Moslem upbringing. The idea of a decent *religious* upbringing, period. After all, men would tell you that during the twentieth century of Earth an attempt was made to dispense with that—the decent upbringing—and the result was movies about hacking up young women with power saws and group sexual acts with whips and chains. Not to mention drug addiction, poverty, juvenile delinquency, the decline of Western Civilization. . . ."

Belle-Sharon had made a rude noise. "It makes a good excuse," she scoffed, "all that nonsense. But do you know what it *really* is?"

"What?"

"What it *really* is is that men are just *lazy!*"

"Mmmm . . . There's that. Some men are lazy, just as some women are lazy. But what it *really* is, sweet Belle-Sharon, is that the men are perfectly contented with what they're doing. Why should they change it, when it suits them so well?"

"Exactly! And so they never will learn!"

"They do. Not always. Not even most of the time—we will not lie to you. But it does happen. It *has* happened. We know, therefore, that it is possible. And so long as it is possible, we must try to help."

Belle-Sharon had said a word that made even Nazareth jump, and Dorcas had thrown up her hands and gone for the bitter tea, because it was clear that she was not going to be reasonable that night. But she had known *they* were reasonable, even though she was unwilling through the aching of her breasts and loins to speak up and admit to what she knew. It was a principle as basic as breathing; the teacher does not give up while there is still the possibility that the student may learn.

Furthermore, she was a woman of the Lines; she was *not* all alone and locked into "decent" ignorance! Thanks be to the Holy One, into Whose hands she wished she could give the responsibility for helping all those other women out in the world. And she had mocked herself, disgusted even in her disarray—*Now who is lazy, Belle-Sharon Adiness Chornyak? You are the one who is lazy!* Those women were her responsibility as long as she lived and had her wits about her; it was something she must keep firmly in mind, even when she was in a foul temper because the whole process was so abysmally slow. She was most emphatically her sister's keeper.

Beside her, as she was admonishing herself to patience and yet more patience, Jared opened his eyes and reached one hand casually for her breast. "Hello there, sweetheart," he said, and his voice was not the voice of a man preparing to "make love" again. It was the voice of a man contented and happy, finished with all this folderol as a man properly ought to be, and ready to go on about his business or get a good night's sleep, whichever happened to be his preference. Very good! Belle-Sharon could relax and spend as much time in pleasant conversation as he wished, until he suggested that they leave. After which the bed, skilled servomechanism that it was, would strip itself of the used linens and drop them through the slot in the floor beneath it, and remake itself all fresh and new and inviting for the next couple, and the folderol would begin all over again. Belle-Sharon would go back to Womanhouse and tackle a problem in sentential complements that had been set aside when Jared sent for her; Jared would go join his buddies in the big diningroom and brag a little about what a marvel she was. Meaning what a marvel *he* was, of course.

She smiled at him, and told him hello in return, and waited for the ritual that would open his aftersex conversation. It was always the same line—and there it came.

"All right, woman," he said briskly, leaning up on one elbow and peering at her. "Tell me the truth. Would you rather just cuddle than fuck?"

It had been a "scientific poll," long long ago, that started that line. Thousands of women, allowed to answer that question anonymously, had startled the men of America by declaring that they would *much* rather cuddle. That was not surprising to Belle-Sharon; a woman would have to be out of her mind to prefer the systematic teasing her husband considered to be valid sexual experience to the consolations of mere affectionate touch. But the men, who must have been very like the men of today, had been so flabbergasted by the nearly unanimous indictment that it had become part of their folklore. Apparently they were never going to forget it; Belle-Sharon knew three other women at Chornyak Womanhouse whose husbands had the same post-sex verbal lucky charm dangling about.

"Jared, my darling," said Belle-Sharon with complete honesty, "that is such a foolish question."

"I don't want any semantic wiggling," he insisted. "Speak up, woman—cast your vote."

"You want a declaration? A proclamation? A manifesto?"

"Any one of those will do," he told her, grinning happily, sure of her answer.

"Jared Joel Chornyak, my dear husband," she said solemnly, leaning forward to softly kiss his handsome bare chest, "of *course* I would not rather 'just cuddle' than have you make love to me!"

It was what he wanted. Satisfied, he grinned at her again and

began to discuss the negotiation he had scheduled for the following day, while she listened, and spoke if she had anything to say
that might be useful to him.

It seemed to her at times that he was in some ways improving;
she had told Nazareth so, and Nazareth had agreed that it was
certainly possible and had kindly refrained from reminding her
that people had told her so. "Continue to set him a good
example," Nazareth had advised her, "and perhaps he will
improve even more rapidly. It is often that way, dearlove."

"Perhaps he will turn out to be one of those miracles, the man
for whom it is not totally stupid to feel a little hope?"

"Perhaps."

It was a matter of common knowledge that Nazareth's husband
had *not* been such a man, and Belle-Sharon felt suddenly
ashamed—she had taken Nazareth's hands in hers and laid her
cheek against them to show that she had not meant to cause pain
with her thoughtless talk.

Nazareth had looked at her fondly, and let Belle-Sharon sit
there with her without speaking for a little while. And then she
had said, "*Bíi dóhúuya ul beyeth hath nedebe wa.*"

*In my experience, and according to my perceptions, I say to
you: hope rarely does anyone harm.*

II

"Sister Miriam, I don't understand your request. I'm sorry—it
makes no sense."

He knew he sounded cross; he *was* cross. Just looking at her
irritated Father Dorien. He knew what the years had done to *him*.
The elegance he had always relied on, the fair slender manly
beauty that had made it acceptable for him to sit haloed in light
from the window at his back, had failed him. Instead of becoming more and more impressive with the passing years, instead of
taking on the distinction of an ascetic, he had softened and
blurred and spread. His clerical collar was too tight, even in the
larger size, and his cassock did not disguise the ample belly that
afflicted him in spite of many a good resolution. He was a priest,
an abbot, soon to be a bishop; he was obliged to spend much of
his time wheeling and dealing over banquet tables, or in intimate
opulent lunches. And he had not been blessed with the sort of
genes or bone structure that allowed that to go on year after year
without a penalty of the flesh.

But Sister Miriam, now! She, who had once been merely an

attractive young woman with an imposing voice and manner, useful for his purposes, now had *exactly* the look he longed for and could not achieve—in its female version, of course. She seemed even taller; certainly she was thinner. The thinness might have been upleasant under ordinary clothing, because it was unfashionable for women to be thin, but the black folds of the nun's habit concealed any distressing angles. The headdress hid the raddled neck (if it *was* raddled . . . he had no way of knowing), and the only visible effect of the gauntness was a wonderful bony face exquisitely sculptured. Sister Miriam Rose looked like an El Greco saint. Father Dorien knew that he himself looked like one of those dumpy little country priests who got painted with mug or glass in hand, drowsing over a table where the debris of a generous meal testified to his recent excesses.

Dorien felt himself disliking Sister Miriam, and he despised himself for it. Here was a devout good nun who had devoted herself without stint or reservation for years to a project of his own choosing. And the best he could manage as a man of God was a shameful envy because the years were treating her less badly than they were treating him. Disgusting! He could imagine how tiresome his confessor must find him, always having to admit that he was still just as vain as he'd been the time before.

But it was *not* fair! She had no right to still look like that, to command the room she entered and the attention of everyone in it that way. That sort of effect was the natural right of men; it had no place in the life of a woman. He, Father Dorien, needed that effortless dignity, that power—he might just as well admit it, because that was what it was—she had *power*. She didn't need it at all; it was no use to a woman. The Lord's finger had slipped somewhere along the way, and Dorien resented it. And now here she was, asking to be relieved of the pleasant assignment she'd had for so long and sent into the public wards of the city hospitals. Bad enough that she should *appear* saintly; Dorien felt that he as not going to be able to bear it if she really *was* saintly.

"Sit down, Sister, for heaven's sake," he said, to put an end to her looming over him; and then when she had murmured the usual nunly tripe about the pleasure of obedience and done as he ordered, he regretted it. He'd forgotten to have the low wooden stool set at the end of the table for her, and she'd had no choice, in her obedience, but to take one of the elaborate high-backed chairs. In which she did not look like a humble nun being obedient, but rather like a medieval queen affecting a simple throne, meeting perhaps with one of her slightly dissipated advisors. *I am getting old*, Dorien thought, *and I am going to get older; I make foolish little mistakes. I hope I do not start making foolish big ones.*

She sat waiting patiently, her eyes cast down and her hands folded decently inside her sleeves; as always, the perfect nun. She could not initiate a conversation without his permission and he hadn't given it; he let her wait, while he glared at her and thought about what he might want to do about her request.

It had come through proper channels, a discreet note hard-copied from his secretary's comset, saying only that she considered her usefulness in her present post at an end and humbly requested transfer to a nursing position in one of the large public hospitals in Washington. Signed, "In obedience, Sister Miriam Rose."

Why? Why would she want to do that? Now she had nothing to do but supervise a dozen well-trained nuns at their terminals, correct their work when it wasn't precisely right, push papers around now and then, report to him once in a while. Why would she want to trade that sweet sinecure for a hospital nursing post? It made no sense. No sense at all. He regretted that he had allowed another priest to become her confessor, just because he had been so busy; if he had seen her regularly he would have been prepared for this instead of being taken by surprise. *Why* would she want to go into—of all things—nursing?

True, nursing today was not what it had been in former times. There were healthies beside every bed in the public wards, even in the poorest areas. (Not that Earth had anything that could accurately be called poverty any more, but such judgments are always relative; citizens who had nothing but ample food and clothing and housing and education and medical care *considered* themselves poor.) And with healthies there, a nurse no longer had to do the grubby things. If the patient was in a medpod, she didn't have to do anything except be available if something in the pod malfunctioned or the patient developed a sudden craving for the flesh-and-blood presence of a human being. The healthies kept the patients clean and dry and at a proper temperature and properly oxygenated; they kept them fed and hydrated and medicated; they turned them and exercised them and entertained them; they dressed and tended wounds. And every smallest item of relevant information about the patient's condition and care was monitored by the healthies and transferred constantly—all nicely summarized and charted—to the central terminals at the nursing stations.

Nevertheless, a nursing post meant spending all your time

with sick people, and if you were not doing grubby work yourself you were still responsible for making sure that it had *been* done, and there was nothing attractive about it. Why would Sister Miriam trade her quiet small office in the convent, opening on the soft hum of the computer room, her windows overlooking the gardens and the brook, the peace and quiet and order of the religious life, for the pandemonium of a big city hospital's public wards?

Be careful, Dorien! he told himself. *Be extremely careful. This is only a woman, but this is not an ordinary woman.* And when an extraordinary woman makes a request that is itself extraordinary, she is probably up to something.

"Sister!" he said, not kindly. She looked up without expression, as if she had not had to spend a full ten minutes waiting to be addressed. She was still beautiful, he thought, if you weren't enthralled by dimples and curls and curves. "Sister, your request is absurd. I am inclined to refuse it for that reason alone, without further discussion. Except that your dedication over the years has been exemplary, and I have no reason to believe that your mind is weakening. I will therefore permit you to tell me why I should allow you to do something so stupid. You may explain yourself, Sister—*briefly*. You have my permission to speak."

"I dislike being useless, Father," she said, her voice quite flat and unexpressive. "I am quite useless at this time."

"*How* are you useless?" he asked her sharply. "You may speak."

"I have supervised the revision of all the materials that the women of the Lines are likely to use as devotional items, Father; you will realize that although they insist on translating every last begat into Ládan they will never *use* most of it. There are parts of the Bible that are suitable for reading aloud as devotions, and then there is all the rest of it—suitable only for including in sermons or for reading to oneself. Since women do not preach, Father, none of that is likely to be widely circulated."

"But it will be *read*, Sister. You may speak."

"Within the Lines—not beyond. I beg your pardon, Father; I do not mean to sound disrespectful."

Still that flat dull voice . . . what had happened to her magnificent voice? Without the voice he realized that she wasn't half so imposing, and he felt a bit more charitable toward her; perhaps she looked better than he did, but she certainly didn't sound any better. He spoke to her more gently, from this new perspective. "Sister Miriam," he said, "I'm either missing a point or I don't have the information necessary to follow you. Please—speak freely. What, precisely, is the situation?''

"All those materials," she answered, "the Psalms, the Beatitudes, the Nativity Story from Luke, the Easter sections and the Creation Story—all that sort of thing, suitable for reading aloud—has been carefully revised. You have my word, Father, to the extent that I am competent to give it: there is now no hint of feminist taint in any of those materials. Where references to the Blessed Virgin could be made more prominent . . . foregrounded . . . that has been done. You have seen all these items yourself and have approved them. The computer program for automatic revision has been refined to such an extent that the nuns rarely need to change anything—and Father, when they do, always remembering that they are presently working with the less essential materials, they have had years of experience. They don't make errors as they did in the early stages. They do not *need* my supervision any more. As more materials are completed, they will simply be forwarded to you for reading; if there is any problem, you will send them back. I have prepared a detailed manual for use when the computer does not seem adequate, or when the wording provided by the program is for some reason not entirely suitable. If a new nun were added to the revising staff tomorrow, Father, she would not need me; she would have the program in the computer to do most of the work, the manual available in case of difficulty, the other nuns with their years of experience to advise her if the manual is not enough, and *you* as final arbiter. What possible need could there be for me, in these circumstances?''

"In sum," he observed slowly, "you have successfully completed your task. You may speak, Sister."

"I am very sorry, Father," she said, surprising him, "but that is too complimentary; I could not accept it in good conscience."

"My dear Sister, your description certainly *sounded* like an account of a successfully completed project! Please explain—you may speak."

"Father," she said, "there were two tasks assigned to us. One—the revision for the Láadan materials—is well in hand, yes. Everything has either already been finished or its completion is assured without further assistance from me. But the other task— that of transferring the women's fervor to the Blessed Virgin and thus leading them to Mother Church—in that, we have not done so well. We regret that, Father—we are indeed sorry."

Father Dorien shrugged his shoulders and made a careless gesture with one hand. "Sister Miriam," he said indulgently, "it's true that you and the other sisters failed to bring about a *mass* conversion . . . you did not gather in tens of thousands. But you did well enough, and you need not reproach yourself. Have I ever complained? You may speak."

"You haven't complained, Father—no. You have been most generous. I am afraid the task was just beyond us. Perhaps, if we could have had priests at the devotionals, to truly fire the women, things would have gone differently. But Father, the fad is almost over now. Except within the houses of the Lines, where things are as they always were, women no longer hold Thursday Night Devotionals. Not even in the largest cities. And so you do see, Father; I am not needed. Not any longer."

Dorien thought of the last set of revisions she had sent to him. It wasn't surprising that they kindled no religious fire in women; women were theologically illiterate, and they had to be attracted to the Lord by the rhythm and power of words and music well assembled. He had tried reading some of those recent bits aloud, and it had been like reading a comphone directory. *Less* effective than that, in fact, because alphabetized names in lists have a certain hypnotic quality. He didn't understand why the revisions necessary to clean up the heretical tendencies should have resulted in such dull and plodding and unmelodious stuff, but he did understand why the results could not hold the frail attention of women.

"All right, Sister," he said suddenly, making up his mind to be done with it. "I understand. I agree that the other sisters can go on without you, and no doubt they, too, will be free of this before long; the King James is large, but it isn't *in*finite! I even agree that you should be released from what must have become no more to you than a running in place. However—" Here he stopped, and raised his right index finger beside his face. "—that does not explain why you have requested transfer to, of all places, the public wards of a huge urban hospital! You've done your duty, Sister, and done it well and faithfully. If you want something new, why not something a bit more tasteful? You may speak."

"I enjoy nursing," she answered. "I have always enjoyed it."

"Then why not private nursing, Sister? Or nursing in a small hospital in some pleasant place? In the mountains? At the seashore? In a lovely little New England town? Why, in the name of all the saints, *Washington General?* That terrible place! Why there? Or anywhere else of that kind?" He shook the finger at her. "It smacks of excessive religiosity, Sister! One thinks of the ancient nuns and their barbarous habits—kissing the sores of lepers and so on—and much, much worse. Is that what's going on with you, Sister? If it is, I won't allow it. You may answer."

She raised her eyes and looked directly at him, for the first time since the interview began. But there was nothing compelling in her glance. They were bland, dutiful eyes; a pretty color, nothing more.

"Father," she answered, "I tell you from my heart; I am *bored* with peace and quiet. A fault of character, I know. But I have had peace and quiet and tranquility until I am sick of them all. I would like some excitement . . . some bustle. A *change*, Father."

"Oh. Yes, I see." It was reasonable enough. He should have seen it for himself. "Do you want even more excitement, perhaps?" he asked her, teasing. "Shall I send you out to a frontier colony? You may speak, Sister."

"If you wish, Father." Her eyelids dropped. "It would be my privilege to obey."

Dorien drummed his fingers on the table edge, considering the idea. Should he do that? No . . . no, he didn't think so. "No," he told her, "I don't want you where—if those bizarre females took it into their heads to translate . . . oh, Confucius, for example . . . it would be hard for me to get you back. If I send you out to the colonies you'll be indispensable in a month, and they'll insist on keeping you. No—I won't do that. But I'll make you an offer, Sister Miriam Rose the Bored. I'll transfer you to Washington General, as you wished. *On the condition* that if I need you back again you will come without protest or delay— and that if you find Washington General more than you bargained for and would like to be bored again, you'll send me a message and I'll find you something more pleasant. Will that do, Sister? You may speak."

"I would be grateful, Father," she said. He could see that she was pleased. "You are very kind."

He was, thought Dorien. He was *damned* kind. But he could afford to be. She might have stayed elegant, but she'd gotten dull. Insipid. All that boredom she'd been talking about—it had leaked through her pores and made *her* boring, too. She didn't even seem beautiful, now that he thought about it, especially sitting there slumped the way she was. He resisted the urge to order her to sit up straight and throw her shoulders back; you couldn't say that to a woman. Why, she was only passable to look at. All bones. Poor old thing, of course she was bored. And she needed other women to gossip with, and so on.

It gave Father Dorien great satisfaction to let her have exactly what she had asked him for; he was embarrassed now, to think that he'd been suspicious of her. Granting her request would be a kind of recompense for the insults she'd suffered from his overactive imagination. She thought him very kind, and so did he; but he would deny it.

"Not at all, Sister Miriam," he said cordially. "Not at all."

CHAPTER 24

"This year's Pulitzer Prize for Colonial Literature is sure to be a matter of intense controversy everywhere except on Terra's Eastern Seaboard. We can now look forward to renewed—and wholly justified—demands, especially from Luna and New Evergreen, for the Colonial Pulitzers to be chosen and awarded by colonial juries. The ossified pedants who made this year's award (only one of them under seventy-five years of age!) have again ignored reality and remained with their distinguished bald heads firmly encased in the literary sand.

"The obvious winner, not only this year but for the preceding three years, is the brilliant young symphonovelist Kalaberra Courtney. It is a disgrace to the planet Earth that the award went instead to the tiresome semi-autobiographical warblings of Hassan P. E. Pritchard, the only frog in the tiny pond of Settlement Thirteen. Never mind that Pritchard's life is boring, his style unreadable, and his personality insufferable! He is the product of a Terran Multiversity, and his tedious works can be recognized as novels even by small children—that is apparently all that the Pulitzer Committee demands.

"'Meanwhile, the work of the true literary giants of the colonies continues to be almost impossible to obtain here on Earth even in cheap chiplet versions. Under the circumstances, the simple fact that Pritchard accepted the tainted award is proof enough that he is nothing but a hack."

(from "Bookbits," by literary critic Lincoln-Jefferson Stratargee, SPACETIME HOLOMAGAZINE)

"This room has a genuinely awe-inspiring ugliness," Heykus said solemnly. "It must have cost . . . oh, as much as the setup-pack for a new colony of one hundred settlers. On an Earth-type planet, of course. A man wouldn't want to overstate the situation.''

The other men, already seated and waiting for him, looked at one another and then at their surroundings, while Heykus stalked to the head of the table—if something shaped like your average amoeba on the move could be said to have a "head." The tallest and most cadaverous of the group was an old-line bureaucrat named John Charles Sundbystyner, who'd known Heykus for fifty years; he closed his eyes, sighed as if he were in mild distress, and answered with his usual dynamic intonation . . . absolutely flat. It's not easy to achieve a controlled monotone in Panglish, but Sundbystyner was famous for his. "Heykus," he droned, "you say that every damn year. It's tiresome, and I've told you so before. In fact, last year you gave me your word that you'd get somebody on your enormous staff—for which there is *no* conceivable excuse—to write you a new opening line.''

"Get off him, Sundy," snapped the man at his right; to his left, the last member present added, "Second the effing motion, John Charles. We're not here for a seminar in stylistics.''

Sundbystyner's eyes opened, his eyebrows climbed his forehead, and he snorted. Heykus noted appreciatively that even the snort did not deviate from the monotone, and considered congratulating the old fart for his consistency and his prosodic skill, but he discarded the idea as inappropriate. Aldrovandus Barton was absolutely right; stylistics was *not* the point. And if Sundy were given the least encouragement he'd go on for half an hour. Heykus settled for a comment as predictable as his opening complaint had been.

"The reason I say that every year," he noted, sitting down, "is that this cursed room is *redone* every year. Aren't they ever going to quit?''

"No," Aldrovandus answered. "Not as long as this room is used for greeting Soviet cultural exchange delegations. You know that.''

"Can't have Moscow thinking we aren't up to the very latest thing in ugly, eh?''

"It's not that ugly, Heykus.''

"It *is* that ugly, Lo Chen. The Capitol Architect has surpassed himself this year. Pale lavender? With a narrow silver stripe? Live fish swimming in the windows? And a *transparent floor?*''

The other three glanced down and looked at the crowds of tourists aimlessly wandering in small groups on the museum floor far below them. Phong Lo Chen snickered, and remarked that if they only had transparent chairs as well as transparent floors the tourists would be able to add a quartet of famous bureaucratic crotches to their travel recollections. "Perhaps it would become fashionable," he mused. "Snapping holos of famous crotches, above your head."

"What's sad, Lo Chen," Heykus observed, "is that you meant that to be funny, but it's very probably a statement of solemn fact. Gentlemen—let's pretend we are not on public view; let's pretend that we are not bathed in an ethereal glow of lavender and silver; and let's begin. The sooner we get through this, the sooner we can go back to the ordinary ugliness of Washington's classic disrepair." He frowned for a moment, and glanced at reliable Sundbystyner. "I have completely forgotten why it is that we always have to meet here," he said slowly.

"Regulations," Sundbystyner told him.

"You're joking."

"I am not joking. The Feder—"

Heykus raised one hand beside his head, signaling silence. *"Do not explain!"* he ordered. "I have recalled the idiot regulation in question. We are now in session, and I apologize for the delay incurred as the direct result of my superfluous speeches about the decor. Somebody send me a memo of reproof. *Now*. This meeting is a routine meeting, in the sense that we have to do it whether anything has happened or not. But it appears that something *has* happened, this time, and I'm not pleased about it."

"You got our memo chiplet."

"I did."

"It's an accurate statement of the situation," Sundbystyner stated; there was a murmur of agreement.

"You all agree?" Heykus asked, making certain. "No dissenters? No reservations? No qualifications?"

"None. No dissenters present, and no dissenters elsewhere," Aldrovandus told him. "You talk about a consensus—we have one of those."

"I see." Heykus remembered the memo, verbatim; it had been terse and unequivocal. It had used the word "failure" twice. He had a strong dislike for that word. Temporary setback, perhaps. Unanticipated delay. But failure? Heykus didn't believe in failure. Not at *his* level of government.

"All right," he said. "Let's just run through it, one at a time. John Charles, you start us off."

Sundbystyner pulled a fiche from his case, inserted it in his viewer for a ten-second perusal, and put it away again. The expression on his face was not pleasant.

"There has been absolutely no progress," he said, "and I wish to emphasize the word 'absolutely,' in getting an agreement from the Consortium to increase the quotas for AIRYs. On the contrary. They will not even discuss an increase, much less agree to one. They are inflexible, gentlemen—the quotas, we are informed, will remain just as they are, and that is not open to negotiation."

"Do they understand the situation, Sundy?" demanded Heykus.

"I'm sure they do. We have repeatedly sent in crack teams from the Lines, with completely native fluency in the major languages, to guarantee that there could be no problems due to a barrier of language. They understand that things have changed; now that we can Interface children from outside the linguist households we *need* more AIRYs. They understand that we are willing to build new Interfaces, with much more space and more creature comforts. They've heard all our arguments about the resulting improvement in interplanetary commerce and diplomacy. They know all this. They've been told. We've tried every conceivable angle of persuasion. They will not budge."

"*Damn,* but that's frustrating!" Heykus declared.

"Yes, it is. But they've always been inflexible on the quotas. I don't know why anyone should have expected them to make changes just because we ourselves had made some, however drastic."

"I keep thinking we might wear them down," Heykus sighed.

"You've thought that for decades, and you've been wrong the whole time. Nevertheless, we will—if you so direct—try it again at the next contact we have with them, just as we have on each preceding occasion. I must say that by now the speeches are well memorized; it's no work to run through the performance twice annually and on miscellaneous occasions."

"All right, Sundy; I agree that yours is probably a lost cause," Heykus said. "'But do it again anyway. Since we don't know why they always refuse, we can't anticipate factors that might cause them to agree. Go on as you've been doing."

"Certainly. Glad to oblige. It won't do any good whatsoever, but we'll go on doing it."

"Thank you. Your optimism is always appreciated. Lo Chen?"

Phong smiled; his role was a less burdensome one than poor Sundbystyner's and he could afford the better humor. "No progress," he said. "The linguists will *not* surrender any of their AIRYs to the Department. Not for any price; not under any circumstances. *Still.* Their arguments vary from session to session, Heykus, which means we don't have to do set pieces at them the way John Charles does, but that's just because they're playing games with us and *they* prefer the variety. They don't have any intention of ever sharing the quota with us and letting us use their AIRYs to stock government Interfaces.''

''And they can make that stick.''

''Damn right they can.'' The man laughed, showing beautiful white teeth. ''We try to do anything clever, Jonathan effing Asher will just pull every last member of the Lines out of whatever negotiations are ongoing until we stop being cute. Total strike, in other words. And there we'd be—I assume you can imagine the chaos that would create. We're short-handed now, even with every available linguist working full forty-hour weeks—'' He paused, and the smile left his face. ''Let me take this opportunity,'' he said gravely, ''to point out to you again that this means every available linguist now earns twenty hours a week overtime wages. As long as we are discussing extravagances, Heykus. The taxpayers don't like that, Heykus.''

''Noted. The damn fools that put them on hourly wages in the first place, instead of flat rate contracts, are all dead. Do not inflict upon me the abuse that is rightfully theirs.''

''Noted right back at you,'' said Phong. ''And continuing . . . even with all the linguists serving double, we don't have enough staff to get everything done efficiently. If they went on strike I don't know exactly what would happen, but I do know it wouldn't be nice.''

''I might add,'' Sundbystyner put in, ''that we can be ninety-nine percent certain that even if the linguists would agree to loaning out, or renting out, their Aliens-in-Residence, there's very little chance the Consortium would go along with it. We risk having the quota *reduced,* for example. Or cut off entirely.''

''Which might be a good thing,'' said Aldrovandus Barton. ''Then we could drop the whole goddamn farce and settle down to work with the status quo. I do *not* see what is so wonderful about acquiring ever more Alien languages, and I will *never* see it—my god, if we'd stopped with the first one we'd learned and never learned another, we wouldn't be anywhere near the end of what could be gained from that.''

The point of ever more languages was not that it was wonderful to acquire them, like collecting ever more varieties of butterflies, but that without them you could not spread the Word of God to all the peoples of the universe. But Heykus assuredly could not say that, and so he said nothing and allowed Barton to glare at him. He was accustomed to the reaction, and understood it.

"On the other hand," Lo Chen went on, aware that there was no hope of a productive discussion on the preceding point, "the linguists have been extremely cooperative about letting us Interface infants, selected by Government Work, with *their* infants. All they've ever required is that the government should provide the additional Tenders needed for convenient care of the smaller babies, plus a standard fee per child to cover insurance and administrative costs. We've run nearly two hundred infants through their system to date, without having even minor hassles. Oh, the usual drivel from the infants' mothers, sure, but no problems associated with the Lines."

"So it's good news and it's bad news," Heykus proposed. "That doesn't sound to me like 'total failure,' which was the unfortunate phrase used in your memorandum."

"Barton will be happy to explain to you why my good news is not good news," Lo Chen told him. "That's his department. But I have one more item."

"Go on, then—sorry I interrupted."

"Last item from Phong Lo Chen, liaison man with the Lines, coming up. There has been *no* progress in getting the linguists to go to the alternate plan you suggested three years ago, Heykus. They think it's a hilarious idea—at least that's the public pose, and I have no way of knowing what the private one is, if there *is* a private one. They will not—repeat, not—agree to Interface linguists who are native speakers of Alien languages with infants, as if *they* were AIRYs. Not at any price. Yes, it has been explained to them that since no physical 'Interface' is required for Terrans plus Terrans, a single native speaker of one of the major tongues could serve as language acquisition datasource for perhaps fifty or more infants at a time. We've offered money, we've offered ample staff to look after the infants physically, we've appealed to their sense of patriotism, we've tried everything. They just tell us the idea is stupid."

"Stupid!"

"Their very phrase. They seem to feel that they're doing more than enough already, and arguing against *that* claim isn't easy— see above, right? They will—as I notified you almost a year ago—teach classes in the languages for us, provided all students allegedly aiming at native fluency are no older than ten years and preferably younger. They have agreed, without any hesitation that I can see, to let adults sit in on these classes up to the capacity of the rooms, provided two conditions are met—and I will again give you their own words: (a) the adults promise to keep their mouths shut unless specifically asked to talk, and (b) it is fully understood that the adults should not expect to achieve native fluency.''

"So?"

"What do you mean, 'so'?"

"So that's *good*, isn't it? So we're grateful for their cooperation. So why have no such classes been initiated?''

Phong sagged in his chair and thrust both hands deep into his pockets. "Shit, Heykus" he said disgustedly.

"Well? What's holding them up?"

"*Shit*. You know perfectly *well*. Whole thing has to go through department channels, right? Okay. First decision: which languages will be taught. There are hundreds of them. There are at least thirty that involve extremely critical interactions with Alien populations. The linguists' schedules are already impossible; they've told us that they can manage classes in three languages, maximum, and have directed us to choose them. And that, Heykus, is where we are stuck.''

"That is. . . ." Heykus' voice trailed off; he found himself with no word to complete the sentence. And Phong was nodding agreement.

"It is," he said. "It sure is. *But*, you have this very important top dog official who insists that it's got to be REM-X because that's the minilaser people. And you have the very important top dog official who insists that it's got to be REM-Y and REM-Z because that's the medical drugs people. And you've got—''

"Never mind, Phong," Heykus interrupted. "I surrender. I understand. Is that the only hitch?''

"*Oh*, no. We've also got the entire teaching staff of the Foreign Service threatening that *they* will strike, quit, riot, you name it, if we allow so much as one filthy Lingoe to put his little toe in a federal language classroom. If Alien languages are to be taught, by god, *they* will teach them!''

"But they don't *speak* them!''

"Heykus, that is the great American tradition. Don't be ridiculous. They can *pronounce* them, after a fashion, and they can write tests over them, and they have *text*books of them, and they have graded *readers* for them. Oh, and let's not forget folksongs. The Foreign Service language teachers know Alien folksongs.''

"Sweet suffering saints.''

"It's our own fault," said Barton. "We should have listened to the linguists a hundred years ago when they told us to let them do the language teaching.''

"And had our buildings burned down?" Heykus allowed shock to tint his voice, just a touch. "Now who's being ridiculous?''

The silence in the room went on and on, as the men contemplated the set of interlocking absurdities with which they were struggling, until finally Barton asked Heykus if he might be allowed to make his report or leave, whichever Heykus preferred.

"Judas, Aldrovandus, please do," said Heykus. "Sorry. This business is so infuriating that I lose all track of what I'm doing. You say total failure, too, don't you?"

"One hundred percent. No—make that ninety-six percent, Heykus. Let's not overdramatize. It's not really *total* at my end of the string. But it's very close."

"All right, Aldro. spell it out."

"May I? Just spell it out, without bullshit? Yes? All right, here you are: NO CHILD NOT OF THE LINES IS GOING TO BECOME A LINGUIST EXCEPT THOSE EXCEEDINGLY RARE CHILDREN WHO HAVE AN *AVOCATION* TO BECOME A LINGUIST. In the same sense that the word 'avocation' is used in religious orders, gentlemen. There *will* be a few lay linguists, yes. But we're talking extremely small numbers."

"Like what?"

"Oh . . . let's see. The original charter group was one hundred infants, which is handy for the math. Maybe six of that hundred are like the children of the Lines . . . their desire is unto nouns and verbs. But the other ninety-four, gentlemen, are going to be doctors and lawyers and pilots and artists and technicians and explorers and military men and politicians and colonists and so on, *just like everybody else.* They are not going to spend their lives the way linguists spend their lives. And I do not blame them one damn little bit."

Heykus leaned forward, his hands holding the edge of the table, and spoke harshly, protesting. "Barton, hold on—that was supposed to be a major point, something made exquisitely clear to every one of the youngsters. They are supposed to have been made to understand that if they will just stay *with* it, and the next group and the next, then pretty soon a linguist will be able to put in a four-day week, and a four-hour day, just like the rest of the working population."

"Sure! Fifty years from now! Look, Heykus, that's not going to apply to these kids—they'd be retired before there was any real change in their working conditions. They're not willing to sacrifice their lives for The Plight Of Linguists, or some such sanctimonious thing. They want their *own* lives—and they want *normal* lives. If they've got to work like slaves, they want to do it out in the colonies where it means carving out something substantial for themselves and their families, not in some effing interpreting booth in Washington, DC!''

He looked at Heykus' stricken expression, and moderated his tone a little, leaning toward the other man in turn and speaking with equal intensity but less venom. "Clete," he said gently, "come on. Don't look like you've lost your last friend. This is something that we *ought* to have known. That we ought to have been prepared for, if we'd stopped to think. *You* think about it, will you?"

"I'm thinking."

"Heykus, my youngest son was one of the charter group. And I'm ashamed of myself, as his father, for ever thinking it would work and allowing him to be involved."

"Tell me."

"Well . . . the linguists have an accurate analogy that they always use."

Heykus nodded. "The circus families."

"Yeah. The old circus families—hell, I don't know why I put it that way, they're still going strong. After hundreds of years. Just as the linguists, Heykus, will still be going strong hundreds of years from now. Look, a linguist kid is born into an enviroment where all that anybody does is work with languages. He stays in that environment, is educated there, has all his social life there; he doesn't even know anybody who isn't part of that environment except in the most superficial way. The indoctrination is total, from day one, every day of those kids' lives, and there's a whole peer group all in the same bucket to shore it up. Traditions. A long family history. But when my boy comes home from the interpreting booth all excited about the interpositional classifiers or whatever the hell it is, who's he supposed to *talk* to? Sure, there's some glamour to it for a while, but it wears off in a hurry. And any normal kid sees, real quick, that it's not as much glamour as he could find if he went out to the colonies, or went into the Space Corps, or did any one of a hundred other things that are readily available to him."

Lo Chen spoke up to add support. "He's *right*, my friends. And he's right to say that we ought to have known. You know what it's like? It's like we had volunteered all those boys for the priesthood . . . celibacy, poverty, obedience, the whole bag . . . and had expected them nevertheless to go on living out in the world where everybody else has full access to all the goodies. And we were counting on the *glamour* to carry them through, don't you see? The linguist children are in communities, where the constant sacrifices they make are sacrifices everybody else is making. Our kids are not in that situation. They have to spend their time off duty in the company of their siblings and their friends; they're all alone. Heykus—this whole thing was a really dumb idea."

Heykus was being very quiet. He was being careful not to talk, or move. This was difficult for him; because he was a man who *did* have an avocation, and he had to continue to perform in this discussion as would a man who had none. He could not sit here and continue to feel that those little boys should have been thankful to the bottom of their hearts for the opportunity to carry out the Lord's holy work. It wasn't like that for them. They had a different view of things. No angel had dropped by to speak to any of them. And this was not the only aspect of deliberate deceit that he was obligated to maintain.

"Heykus, are you still with us?"

Heykus made an effort to pull his attention back to them, and to exclude firmly the attitudes and prejudices of the man that he must not, really must not, appear to be. Fortunately, at his age the others expected a certain amount of doddering and absentmindedness; he could always fall back on that.

"I suppose it *was* stupid," he managed. "It didn't seem stupid at the time . . . but perhaps it was."

"Like I said, there are a few exceptions."

"*Six.* Of one hundred."

"Maximum. Maybe less than six."

Heykus drew a long weary breath. "You think this whole project ought to be shut down for good, don't you? All of you?"

"Heykus," Sundbystyner put in, "we think the opportunity should be left open. We think that the rare child who comes to his parents at the age of three or four and swears with shining eyes and a passionate little voice that he wants to be a linguist when he grows up should be encouraged to go into the Interfaces. But our current program is so ludicrously irrational that it's an embarrassment to every one of us."

Heykus nodded slowly. "It makes good sense," he said. "It makes excellent sense. And it is . . . as you say . . . embarrassing. Because it is just beginning to dawn on me that the linguists of the Lines have been having a great deal of fun at our expense. If I appear to be slightly stunned, gentlemen, it is because I'm having a very bad time with what I am starting to see far too clearly. I assume that all of you are getting the same impression I am. That we have been providing extensive entertainment, god help us, to the linguist households, for quite some time."

"You are putting your finger right on it, Heykus." There was almost a hint of emotion in Sundbystyner's voice. "They must sit around at night telling layman stories. Slapping their thighs. Rolling on the floor."

"Shit, Sundbystyner," pleaded Androvarus Barton, "cut it out, will you? I think we all realize the extent to which we have been suckered."

"They wouldn't see it that way," Heykus noted.

"No. They'd say we came and asked them—begged them, they'd say—and that they courteously allowed us to indulge our whims. And they would be right. But we should have known that *they* were not that stupid . . . you realize that. The idea that they didn't even feel that they needed to make a *pretense* of arguing—that they were so sure we were that deluded, and were right—dear god, that's hard to live with." Barton's voice trembled, and he added, "I can understand why there's been so little difficulty in persuading people to hate them. I'm having a hell of a time not hating them, for this. It's not their fault—it's our fault—but I hate them anyway."

"There's never been even a hint from them."

"No. They've just let us toddle down the road, swinging our little pails and singing our little songs, and they've never said one word to stop us."

"How could they be like that?" demanded Lo Chen bitterly. "It's not *human*, damn it. How can they hold off like that . . . not one dig, not one hint. . . . I couldn't do that. I would *not* be able to hold out like that. Jesus . . . it's been *years*. And they've just been waiting all this time. Knowing that eventually—*eventually*—we'd find out and feel like very tiny flat little shits. Heykus, that *isn't* human. Not really human."

"Perhaps," said Sundbystyner, "they felt that we had it coming. And the longer it went on, the worse it would be. They wouldn't have wanted to spoil it."

"It must have given them great pleasure," said Heykus huskily.

"I'm sure it did. Enormous pleasure."

Heykus sat there looking at these men, his colleagues, his good friends, thinking how they had been writhing under the humiliation of this since the pieces started falling into place, and he felt a genuine regret. They were good men, and he was sorry.

He folded his hands on the table in front of him. "Well," he said flatly, "I withdraw my previous objections. 'Total failure' *is* the proper phrase, after all. I apologize."

"We demolish the GW Interface-sharing program, then?"

He shook his head. "I'm not ready to answer that yet," he

told them. "This is all very new to me. I need to go run a set of extrapolations and compare them." *I need to go wash my mouth out with soap and spend an hour on my knees praying for my soiled lying soul!* "But you have my word—I'll go over the data, I'll reach an appropriate decision, and I'll advise all of you as quickly as possible. And if I need help, I'll call on you for input *before* I make the decision."

"Fair enough."

"Until next year, then, gentlemen."

"We don't disband this group?" Phong Lo Chen was clearly surprised.

"We don't disband this group," Heykus said firmly. "This is a group that will find a function—regardless of what my decision is regarding the Interfacing."

When they were gone, and he was left alone to stare down through the foolish floor at the dwindling tourists—some of whom were staring back—he reminded himself that this was all for the best, that it had been obvious from the beginning, and that all was as right with the world as was consistent with the human condition. If things had turned out differently, the problems of keeping every one of the lay linguists under adequate surveillance would have been a logistics nightmare. Even with the vast financial resources at Earth's disposal, it would have put a strain on his budget; there were better places for the money to be allocated.

But still . . . he had had that small hope. Foolish. Naive. Irrational, no question about it. *If* it had not turned out this way, and *if* whatever it was that motivated the linguists of the Lines had somehow transmitted itself, along with the languages, to the children outside the Lines—he would have been willing to take on the logistics. It would have been worth it, to have had all those new young men, each armed with the priceless treasure of an Alien tongue. And all of them under *his* direction, instead of the control of the Lines! If it *had* happened, he thought sorrowfully, if it had, he would have found a way, somehow, to pay for it.

CHAPTER 25

"The terms Lingoe *(for a linguist of the Lines),* wimpoe *(for an effeminate male individual), and* medicoe *(to refer to a physician), are coarse epithets, similar to ethnic slurs, and should be avoided. Educated people of good taste do not use them even in private conversation. (It should be noted in this context that the term* med-Sammy, *which entered popular usage subsequent to the publication of the much-anthologized Greddzohej essay titled "The American Medical Profession as a Samurai Class," is also to be avoided. It is not as vulgar as "medicoe," but is a slang term proper only for informal contexts and colloquial conversation. It should never be used in formal speech or writing.)"*

(from the Harbrace Handbook, *83rd edition, page 411)*

Heykus hated hospitals. *All* hospitals. They were almost always ugly, both inside and out, and this creaking old medical barn in the middle of Washington DC was one of the ugliest; the staff had not bothered even to take down the antique fluorescent light fixtures, although none had bulbs in them, praise be, to turn a person green and purple and bloated-looking like something left under water over a weekend. They were always clean, which was a point in their favor, and Washington General was no exception; its ugliness was a *scrubbed* ugliness.

But there were things about hospitals that bothered Heykus far more than their physical appearance did. There were the things that hospitals made him *think* of. That: with sufficient faith there would have been no need for hospitals or for any of their apparatus, because everyone who lay here being tended lay here for lack of sufficient faith in God and His Son. That: sickness

321

was a punishment for sin, so that a hospital was a kind of museum of collected sins, and no way to know what horrible secrets it might contain . . . there were no labels on the exhibits. (That offended Heykus; he felt that there ought to have been an orderly system, so that the sin of gluttony resulted only in gastrointestinal disorders, and the sin of pride only disorders of the genitourinary system, and so on.) That: there were people in hospitals who lay at the point of death, and many of those were headed straight for Hell and its eternal fires. None of this added to Heykus Clete's perception of hospitals anything but the internal equivalent of an all-pervasive stink; he did not think of healing when he came here, he thought of damnation. And he thought with shame of all the times he had resolved to find a few hours to come here and minister to those who would listen, and all the times he had found compelling excuses not to do so.

This visit was different. There was no excuse that would spare him this time. The man he was here to see had been a childhood friend; had been at Heykus' wedding; had been a deacon in Heykus' church before his incomprehensible conversion to Roman Catholicism in his early sixties; had been a business associate and a colleague; had been someone Heykus could always call on, always rely on in time of trouble. This was a man he loved, a man he had mourned over when the Romans ensnared him, and a man he would sorely miss when he was gone. It would have been a disgrace not to visit him as he lay here so desperately ill, and Heykus had known he *must* come. Philip Cendarianis had a right to expect him, and a right to expect him promptly; Heykus had come at once, as soon as he had heard that visitors would be allowed at all. But he still hated it. It was like visiting a cesspool.

In a more modern hospital there would have been a separate entrance, and separate elevators, to the private room where Philip was. But here at Washington General no amount of architectural ingenuity could have made that possible, not without tearing down the vast pile of brick and stone and starting over. (Which would have been an excellent idea, to Heykus' way of thinking, but was unlikely ever to happen; the building was on the list of historical sites.) And so the route to Philip's room led down a hallway past a public ward, where patients lay on beds with nothing to shield them except spotless bedspreads and blankets. It was indecent, and unkind; Heykus resented it on their behalf. The Supreme Court decision had been very clear and very precise: every American citizen, and any person visiting on American soil, was entitled by law to full medical care at the expense of the government of these United States, with no exceptions. But any such citizen not in critical condition was entitled to a medpod only if he or she chose to spend personal funds for it, not as an automatic part of that "full" medical care.

There was no excuse for that, Heykus thought. It was nothing more than the vindictive spleen of the ancient Justices, who had not had free medpods when *they* were young and therefore felt an obligation to get even. Earth had more than enough money to provide a free medpod for everyone who entered its hospitals; no one needed to lie in a plain bed with an ugly old healthy beside it clacking away day and night, *doing* things with its array of ingenious arms, in full view of anyone who chose to stroll past. *Disgusting*, he thought. And proof, as if any more proof were needed, that appointing Supreme Court judges for life in a time when "life" meant an average span of one hundred and thirty years had its serious drawbacks.

It was a relief to step into the elevator that led to the private wards. Heykus tried to compose himself as it swept him upward, and to put his frustration with the medical system out of his mind. Things had been much worse, as recently as the twenty-first century. There had been a time, impossible to conceive of but a matter of historical record, when the first thing required of a sick person entering a hospital had been proof that he had money of his own to pay for his care or had spent enough money of his own to oblige an insurance company to pay for it. There had been a time when hospitals turned sick people away for lack of money. There had been times of horrors, when the very term "health care system" had been synonymous with greed and degradation; it was during those times that the physicians had acquired the nickname "med-Sammys" that they still carried, although today their Samurai status was no longer quite so blatant. It was no longer possible for a physician to perform the equivalent of the beheading-by-whim, just by refusing to certify someone as near enough to death's door to require emergency care *regardless* of financial condition. Those awful times were past, relegated to the annals of barbarism, he reminded himself. When the heart attack had slammed its fist of pain into Philip Cendarianis' chest, he had not had to consider first whether he had money to pay for it before he called for help. And he would never have to lie, as people once had lain, in pain and in despair, unable to even begin to achieve the emotional peace that is as necessary to health as cleanliness, because he was frantic about the medical bills he would not be able to pay. No; things were better now. *Remember that, Heykus,* he told himself sternly, *and set yourself in order; try not to look like Death in person come to gather Philip Cendarianis to the Lord, or else go home and spare* him *this visit!* It was not likely that Philip needed to see a face that matched the grimness of the thoughts he was thinking at this moment.

The elevator sighed and brought him to a gentle halt only a short distance from Philip's door, high in a tower away from the noise of ground traffic and sufficiently well insulated to keep the air traffic noise to a constant hum rather than a roar. He shook himself, not just mentally but physically as well, not caring who might see him, to break the chain of thought the public wards had wrapped round his mind, and decided that he was fit to share the air of a sickroom at least briefly. Here the walls of the corridors were a pleasant soft blue, and the carpets were American Orientals—imitations, of course, but a lovely path of flowers and colors under his feet all the same—and the fluorescent fixtures had either been taken down or covered up. There were handsome framed prints and textured hangings to look at, and a holo fountain played at the end of the hallway. It was almost like any large public building of a certain age. He could feel himself beginning to relax, and that was an improvement; he went through the door into Philip's room with what he was reasonably sure was a pleasant expression on his face and a pleasant set to his body.

"May I help you, sir?"

The voice startled him; it was an astonishing voice, and it came from a tall woman in heavy black garments that marked her as a nun. He should have realized that there would be a nun here; he was fortunate there wasn't a priest as well. It had slipped his mind.

"My name is Heykus Joshua Clete, Sister," he said to her. "I'm a friend of Mr. Cendarianis—one of his oldest and closest friends. His doctor said I could visit him this morning."

If he had been a Catholic male he would have then told her that she had permission to speak, but he was decently Protestant and proud of it and he said nothing of the kind. Until he realized, as the silence dragged on, that she had no way of knowing that and was waiting for the ridiculous, hopelessly un-American line to come from his lips.

"I'm not Catholic, Sister," he told her, preferring that, hoping he didn't sound as repulsed as he felt; it wasn't the poor woman's fault that she was subject to a sociolinguistic constraint that made him queasy. "I'm Baptist . . . Protestant. You don't have to wait for my permission before you can talk. Is it all right if I come in and see Philip?''

She looked directly at him then, abandoning the lowered eyelids that went with the submission to silence, and smiled. "Of course," she said. "But please understand that you can't stay long—he's very weak. And I am ordered not to leave him; I'm sorry for the intrusion on your privacy."

That wonderful voice again! Heykus was charmed. To find such a voice, in such a place, and from such a source; he wondered how it had happened. Perhaps she had been a choir nun once, trained to sing those horrendously difficult Catholic substitutes for the wholesome Protestant hymns.

"I understand, Sister," he said, adding, "Please don't stand on my account."

She smiled again, and thanked him courteously, and he saw that although she wasn't young she was beautiful; but she remained standing at the head of the medpod where Philip lay. He supposed she must have been given orders to do that, too, poor thing.

"May I?" he asked, motioning toward the pod.

"Yes . . . for a very short time, please."

Heykus touched the small blue circle that made the pod transparent from the patient's waist to head, and braced himself for the worst, but it wasn't as bad as he had expected. Through the pod he could see that his friend was awake, and not in pain, and apparently not in emotional distress.

"Philip," he said, "you look well!"

"And you, Heykus, look surprised. What were you expecting?"

The voice was a little odd, coming through the pod's speakers, but it was strong and cheerful and amused.

"I don't know exactly," Heykus admitted. "I certainly wasn't expecting a man who looks and sounds ready to follow a plow."

"I'm only dying, Heykus. Not plowing. Death doesn't take much strength when you're tucked into a medpod. Plowing, now—that might be more than I could manage."

"I'm sorry this is happening, Philip," Heykus said, meaning it. "I wish I knew something to say that would be appropriate."

The man in the medpod chuckled softly. "Just don't pray over me," he said. "Anything but that."

"If—"

"I mean it, Heykus. No praying. You leave me to the pros."

To the priests. And to their blackgarbed handmaidens. Heykus glanced at the nun, but she had a nun's control of her face; she might have been carved of wood for all the sign she gave that she was hearing anything they said.

"Is there anything you *do* want, Philip?" Heykus asked, his voice rough with the very real affection he felt for this man, who had shared with him so much of his life but was clearly not going to share any more of his death than he absolutely had to. "Anything that I could get for you? Do for you?"

"Nothing at all. It's all been done. The lawyers are hovering, with the angels and the undertakers. As for me, I'm taken care of here as if I were a priceless treasure—you needn't worry."

"How about my keeping an eye on the hovering lawyers?"

"Why? I have three younger brothers. All sane; all capable."

Heykus made a mental note to keep an eye on the brothers, but he said nothing, and the nun cleared her throat softly in the stillness.

"Sister? Did you want to speak to me?" he asked, not certain that she could address him if he didn't ask.

"Only a few more seconds, please, Director," she answered, surprising him again. She knew who Heykus Joshua Clete was, then . . . that was odd. For all the power he had, his name was scarcely a household word.

"Philip?" He leaned over and touched the pod, near the sick man's shoulder. "The nurse says I must go now—I'm sorry. I'd hoped we could talk a while. But I'll be back tomorrow."

"I won't be here tomorrow," his friend said cheerfully. "I'll be in the arms of God or whatever. You stay in your office, where you can be of some use."

"Nonsense. I'll see you again in the morning. And every morning, for so long as the Almighty lets us keep you with us, Philip."

Cendarianis tried to smile, obviously very tired, and his eyes closed; Heykus stood a moment looking at him, memorizing the serene look of him, and then pressed the circle on the pod again to make it opaque and allow him privacy and rest. When it once again looked like the snow-white egg of a giant bird, and he was sure that Philip could not see him, he beckoned discreetly to the nun with one finger, hoping it was not too rude a gesture in these circumstances, asking her with his eyes to follow him to the door.

She nodded, and pressed a stud on her wrist computer, the long black sleeve falling away to show only more black fabric underneath; he supposed the stud must set the medpod's alarm system to signal her if anything at all changed while she was away from her post. She looked at him again, directly, and her eyes held him, somehow; he felt taller, and stronger, and wiser. He gestured to show that he would follow *her* from the room, but she shook her head to indicate that he must go first, and he turned his back on her and led the way, uneasy with this Catholic concept of manners. He could feel her behind him, even when he could not see her; he thought that if a man had to die, he could do worse than die in the presence of this woman. What was she doing here, a woman like this? In a place like this?

She let the door to the room iris shut behind her when they were in the corridor, but she did not move one step farther, and Heykus respected her vigilance.

"Thank you, Sister," he said. "I didn't want to speak in front of him."

"Yes, Director Clete," she said. "Quickly, then—what may I do for you?"

"I just wanted to know. . . . Are you allowed to talk about his condition?"

"You are not just a casual visitor, Director. What may I tell you?"

"Philip says he won't be here tomorrow. Is he right?"

"Oh, yes."

"He doesn't look that sick. He doesn't look that weak."

"The wonders of modern medicine," she observed.

"But it's only a heart attack, Sister."

"Nevertheless. There is multiple system failure, Director."

"And nothing can be done. He really will die, before tomorrow morning."

"Sometime during the night, yes," she said. "When the soul is most willing to leave and seek a respite."

"I beg your pardon, Sister?"

"Please forgive a foolish woman her maunderings," she said promptly, "for your friend's sake. And now I must go to him."

"He *will die* tonight?" Heykus knew how stupid he must sound, asking again, but it was so hard for him to believe. He was keeping her from her duties, perhaps obliging her to violate orders that she had been given; he would have to send her a note of thanks when he got back to the office.

"He will die," she stated firmly. "In peace, and without pain. Surrounded by love."

"I'll come back then, this evening," Heykus began, but she stopped him, almost touching his arm just at the wrist, a nurse's gesture and without offense.

"The ambulance will be flying him home in just a few hours," she said. "He chooses to be with his family."

"Oh. . . . I see." Heykus stood there struggling, not knowing what to say but unable to leave without saying it; he had the feeling that he must be opening and closing his mouth like a fish, but he didn't know what the words he needed were.

She knew, however, and she answered the questions he could not ask. "The pod will go along with him in the ambulance, Director. He won't have to be disturbed in any way—he'll hardly know that he's being moved, and there'll be no discomfort at all, I promise you. And I will go, also."

That caught Heykus' attention, and freed him from his temporary speech impediment. "Is that customary, Sister?" he asked. "For you to go with him, when he goes home to die?"

"He has asked me to go, and I am pleased to be of service to him. I won't disturb the family—they'll find me a corner of the house where I can wait, and pray. They won't even know I'm there."

"They *will* know," he heard himself objecting, "even if they leave you out in the street in front of the house."

Her lips twitched, the least fraction, and he felt privileged; he knew that she need not have let her control slip even that much, and that it was a compliment paid to him. And then she was gone, with a soft murmur about having to return to her patient, and he was staring at the closed door of the room and feeling like a fool.

A contented fool, he realized. A serene, contented fool.

Something . . . there was something here he didn't understand. Even through the closed door, through the solid wall, he was aware of her. Not as he was sometimes aware of women who for one reason or another brought lust stirring in his loins, annoying him mightily—at his age, and with great-grandchildren, and him a devout servant of the Lord, to still have that twitch of the devil about him!—but in quite a different way. *If I were dying,* he thought, *and she stood beside me, I would feel that a strong hand sheltered me. I would feel safe. Even standing here outside this door, in this hateful place, I feel. . . . What do I feel? Welcome? Comforted?* Both those things were part of it, but they were not all. There was something more, something that eluded him, that he couldn't put a name to. He closed his eyes, to shut out the visual data that might be interfering with his perceptions . . . what was that *feel*ing?

He recognized it then, suddenly, for what it was, and he backed away from the door as if it might blast him where he stood. What he felt, the warmth that was all around him like velvet against some unknown surface of his spirit, was the sensation of being *blessed*. He felt *blessed*.

By a woman. A Catholic, and a woman.

Heykus almost, not quite but almost, *ran* down the corridor to the elevator. Not even daring to look back.

His efforts to convince Philip's doctors that the nurse must be dismissed were useless, as he had suspected they would be. He had known that before he tried, but he had felt compelled to try nonetheless. It wasn't that he didn't have sufficient power to get her removed—he did, and he surely would—but this was not the way to go about it, and the ways that were adequate would not be quick enough.

"Sister Miriam Rose is one of our finest nurses," the med-Sammy said coldly. "The very idea of removing her is ridiculous."

"She should be removed at once," Heykus said back, far more coldly. He had forty years more practice speaking coldly than the arrogant young doctor. But he had no sensible reason to offer as support for his advice, and they wouldn't listen to him. As for the family, they were shocked and annoyed. They loved Sister Miriam, Philip loved Sister Miriam, in the few days they'd known her she had become one of the family, and was Heykus completely out of his mind, or what?

Stiffly, feeling the cold sweat on his upper lip, glad that there were no mechanisms analyzing *his* physical status, he insisted that he had good reasons for what he was saying but was not at liberty to make them specific.

"Nonsense," said one of the younger brothers. "What nonsense. At a time like this!" And he had hung up, leaving Heykus feeling old and weary and defeated. And more aware of Satan's awesome power than he had been in many years. But he had had to try.

To ease the weight of his helplessness, he looked Sister Miriam up in the databanks. She was there, with her Federal Identification number and her blood type, her height and eye color and allergies; because she was a nun—born at the convent, he noted, and illegitimate, parents unknown—she had no possessions and no record of any earnings. No titles, no distinctions. Her immunizations were there. Her mass-ed summary score. All those things that he could have read from the tattoos in her armpits if he'd wished to remove all that black fabric she was swathed in, but nothing else. No infractions of any kind; apparently she had no driver's or pilot's license, had never been to any school outside the convent, had never undergone even minor surgery. A thoroughly unremarkable life. The life of almost any nun, for all he knew.

He sat reviewing the brief entry, dissatisfied with it and not sure why; something about it bothered him. He knew it would come to him, whatever it was, and he waited patiently for the necessary neurons to kick in.

Ah! He knew what it was. *Parents unknown. Born at the Convent of St. Gertrude of the Lambs, parents unknown.* That was the problem. It should have read only "father unknown," if she had been born at the convent and not simply abandoned there. They would have had to know who the mother was, and the law required that it be reported. The nun he spoke to at St. Gertrude's agreed with him, and she apologized profusely. These things happen. Disgraceful. A clerical error, so long ago. A computer stumbling on a tiny chunk of data, so long ago. We are only women, we make errors. Such a shame. And so on and so on, until he knew it was a dead end and gave it up.

He considered it briefly, and filed it away. Come a time when he was not busy, should such a time ever appear on his horizon, he would bring it out again and pursue it, and he would find out what lay behind this convenient little gap in the data. But not right now. Right now he had too many other urgent matters to deal with, and no time to waste on one odd nursing nun, who had taken advantage of his distress about a dying friend and unbalanced him in some way. It had already taken all the time he could spare, and he had done all he could do, and none of it would be any use to Philip. He let it rest.

CHAPTER 26

It was not that we were unaware that all change comes about by resonance; we knew that very well. Our problem was that so large a number of men seemed immune even to the most fundamental frequencies.

(From "The Discourse of the Three Marys"— author unknown.)

There is a silence that follows reports of great tragedies of nature. Earthquakes and hurricanes; raging fires that swallow hundreds of thousands of acres of forests; volcanoes and avalanches. It was that sort of a silence, and Father Joseph sat within it waiting for someone to break it, thinking that when it was broken it would sound like ice breaking on a great northern lake. But the fearsome crack that split the air sounded nowhere except inside his throbbing head. The words, when they did come, were little more than a whisper.

The Cardinal spoke to him, calling him none of the things that Joseph had expected to be called, saying only, "Joseph, this is all very difficult for us to believe. You must understand that."

It echoed. How could a whisper echo? Perhaps you had to be a Cardinal, or perhaps it was this ancient cavernous room with its vaulted ceiling and its bare floors and uncurtained windows.

"I know that," Joseph mumbled through the weight of his misery. "I know that, Your Eminence. But I am saying—truly—what was said to me. And it is true, Your Eminence."

"It couldn't be a hoax? Or delirium—a dying woman's delirium? Surely, my son, it could be that."

He shook his head. "The Bishop did not think so," he said.

"And I don't think so. Your Eminence, I am familiar with deathbeds."

"Why did they send *you* to tell us?"

Still that eerie whisper, echoing, drifting up into the dimness of the ceilings high above; outside, a seagull screamed.

Joseph prepared himself to answer, thinking that until now "I'll never be a Cardinal" had been only something that modesty obligated him to say, not something he believed. Now it was a verdict passed on him; now it was a *fact*. Would they even let him continue to be a priest? He didn't know, and his Bishop had told him it would have to be decided at the Vatican; he hadn't known either.

"They sent me," he said, faltering, stumbling over huge consonants and vowels that stretched off into vast distances, the sounds that came from his mouth seeming to have nothing to do with him, "because things could not be any worse for me. No one else wanted to bring you such news. I didn't want to, either; the difference was that *they* had a choice."

The Cardinal was getting very old, but he was in no way frail; the color was coming back into his face as he adjusted to the shock, and the others around the room, his advisors and most trusted associates, were recovering as well. For a few moments they had been frozen, motionless; they had been the ice Joseph was waiting to hear break. How many of them were there? He didn't know, because he had not dared look. There might be hundreds, sitting back in corners and in alcoves, down stairwells, high on balconies. . . . No. Surely not. Surely only a handful would be allowed to know about this. He must keep his imagination under better rein; there was no one in the shadows. Except ghosts, perhaps. He could well imagine that there might be ghosts.

Now the Cardinal leaned forward in his chair; now, when he spoke, his voice was strong and deep and sure of where it went.

"My son," he said, "I want to hear it all again."

Joseph made a noise, not precisely a whimper, not precisely a moan. He said, "Your Eminence. Please. For the love of God."

"*For the love of God*, my son. Exactly. For the love of God, you will tell it all again. This time we will be prepared; we will not be so stunned that we can't hear you over our own foolish thoughts, roaring in our ears. You will begin again, Joseph."

"I have told it so many times." Joseph knew he sounded fretful, perhaps insolent; he did not care. It was hopeless. It no longer mattered what he did. He was a hopeless priest who had violated his most sacred vows, and it was a hopeless cruel exercise for him to sit here reciting it all again. He would do it because he was vowed to obedience, and because he was afraid to defy the Cardinal, and because he had no excuse to refuse. But it was awful. To say it all again. Horrible. Unbearable.

His mouth went on saying words, his tongue went on shaping them; the body simulated awareness. "There is a nun for whom I am—was—confessor. Her name was Maria. Sister Maria. I had been her confessor for more than ten years. She died two days ago . . . Wednesday, that would be, in the early evening. I was called to her to hear her final confession, and to perform the last rites." He could still see the agony that had been on Sister Maria's face when he had hurried into the room—he had turned in horror to the nurse standing in the door, to demand that something be given to still this pain, but she had assured him quietly that there was no *physical* pain. That had all been attended to. Whatever was troubling the nun cradled in the medpod, open now to give the priest access, it was not physical pain.

"Please go on, my son," instructed the Cardinal sharply. "We are waiting."

"Sister Maria was a humble woman, very ordinary. At least that's what I always *thought* she was. She worked in the convent office. Doing correspondence for the Abbess, keeping the databases in order, that sort of thing. Sometimes she worked in the convent library; she was good at little things. Details. She was dying— she sent for me." He drew a long breath, like a sob. "She told me that for nearly forty years she had been a kind of double agent. A kind of spy."

"Must you use such a melodramatic vocabulary, Joseph?" the Cardinal asked him, testy, but kind.

"Eminence, what *shall* I call her, if I don't? A liar? A traitor? A deceitful evil twisted fraud of a woman? Eminence, none of those is the right phrase, either. Eminence, she had posed forty years as a faithful ordinary little nun. And all that time, in every moment she could steal, what she was really doing. . . ."

His voice trailed off, and he saw that the Cardinal was no longer a real person. He was a flat cutout, garbed in red, perhaps braced by a stick in back. Joseph would have been afraid to look around behind him.

"Go on, my son. What she was really doing was?"

"She was making copies of the blasphemous King James translations prepared by the female perverts of the linguist families." Very quickly, he told the cutout that, so that it would be over.

"Copies of the *original* translations, you mean. Not the revisions that were done by order of Bishop Dorien."

"Yes, Eminence. And distributing those copies secretly to other sisters involved in the conspiracy."

"Double agents! Conspiracies! Joseph, these are only women. Only *nuns*. We are not talking of warrior chieftains on the Planet Gehenna, we are talking of *nuns!*" The Cardinal's voice thundered across the room toward him and Joseph crouched lower to be a less easy target for it.

"What do you want me to say?" he cried out, absurdly, panicked. "It's not my fault! There aren't any other words! What do you want me to say? *Tell* me, tell me and I will *say* it!"

The Cardinal stared at him; they would all be staring. You do not shout at a Prince of the Church.

You do not betray the sanctity of the confessional, either, and he had done that. You do not spend ten years hearing the innermost secrets of a woman rotted with perversion without ever suspecting, without ever noticing that help is desperately needed, either, and he had done that. His contempt for himself was greater, far greater, than his contempt for Sister Maria. He had failed her in life; and then he had failed her in death. How could he not have known? His Bishop had said, "I should think you would have been able to *smell* her!" He hadn't been; he hadn't guessed a thing; he had been her easy dupe, for more than ten years.

Wearily, he finished it. "She told me—Sister Maria told me—that the . . . that the *group* of nuns involved had been gathered together, recruited, by Sister Miriam of St. Gertrude's."

"The woman that Bishop Dorien put in charge of revising those translations so that they would be theologically pure," said the Cardinal wonderingly. "The same woman!"

"Yes, Your Eminence."

"How many copies? How many are involved? How many of our nuns have been corrupted by this Judas?"

This Judas, thought Father Joseph. It was apt, and it would be the first phrase on every priest's lips. The Cardinal had not known Sister Miriam, of course, had not experienced her commanding beauty nor the extraordinary presence that was like a garment she put on or took off, just as she chose. But Joseph's bishop had known her, and had known that her name was Miriam Rose, and had said a little more. He had called her "the Judas Rose." Judas for her treachery; Rose for her false perfection. Rose with a worm at its heart, a venomous worm; rose with poison tipping its thorns.

"She is the Judas Rose," he said aloud.

"I beg your pardon?"

"Bishop Paul said it. He said, 'We have all been betrayed by that Judas Rose of Dorien's.' "

"How *many?*" the Cardinal insisted, urgently, waving his hand with its heavy ring to indicate how little interest he had in Bishop Paul's flights of fancy. "We need numbers, my son."

"Your Eminence, I don't have any numbers to give you. Sister Maria died before I could question her properly. We tried the most powerful stimulants—I sent for a doctor—but she was gone, it was too late. I know only what I have already told you: Sister Maria said that the copies were sent to sisters 'all over the world.' "

"All over the world. It could be ten. Or a thousand."

"Surely not a thousand, Eminence! Each copy had to be made by hand—can you imagine that? By hand? Because of course the convents keep strict accounting of every hard copy from the comsets and the old copying machines that some of them still use. A sister can't just go run off a breviary for herself whenever the whim takes her, not on a poverty budget."

"Do you mean to say that 'made by hand' means *written by hand?* Actually written out in longhand script?"

"Yes, Your Eminence."

The Cardinal was nodding, his mind focused on the problem. He said nothing for a long time, and then he asked, "Did your Sister Maria tell you whether this blasphemy had been sent out into the colonies? To carry its evil *beyond* this world?"

"She did not say, and I had no time to ask. She said, 'For more than forty years I have been sending copies of the Láadan King James to other sisters, all over the world,' and then she died. She died almost at once, as soon as she had told me . . . I think she had just been waiting to tell me, Your Eminence."

"So!" The Cardinal folded his hands together before him. "So, Bishop Dorien's estimable Sister Miriam betrayed Holy Mother Church, then, and seduced others—perhaps many others— into joining her in that betrayal."

"Yes, Your Eminence."

"Joseph, I beg your pardon for my discourtesy. The term 'conspiracy' is indeed the precise term."

"Thank you, Your Eminence."

"Where is this woman now, Joseph?"

He swallowed hard; he had been dreading that question. "She died three years ago with her monstrous sins unconfessed, Your Eminence. She died alone, and no priest was called."

"No last words."

"None. She is gone, and all that she knew is gone with her."
She is gone to join the other Judas, at the very center of Hell,
Bishop Paul had said. *For all eternity.*

"I don't understand," declared the Cardinal's assistant, Father
Amos Stabledorn, his voice shaking. "How could such a thing
have gone on for so long, right under our noses?"

Joseph tried to answer . . . but he was tired. So tired.

"There wasn't any reason to suspect anything, Father Amos.
Sister Miriam personally supervised her staff of nuns in the
revising of the linguists' translations, to make certain that every
trace of heresy, every hint even of impropriety, was removed
from them. The materials were approved by her—the nuns who
worked under her complained often that she was overly severe,
that she was rigid to the point of exaggeration, that she was . . .
yes, they said that she was a *fanatic,* they used that word . . .
about stripping the translations of every conceivable taint. Things
the other nuns thought too trivial even to consider. When she
was at last satisfied, the materials were given her final personal
touches and then sent on to Bishop Dorien for his approval and
for storage in the databanks. I've heard the Bishop comment on
how very *bad* the revisions were as devotional materials; he
remarked a number of times on how extraordinary it was that a
woman so talented in other ways could have such a tin ear."

"We understand that now," said the Cardinal dryly.

"Yes, Your Eminence—it's obvious, now. Her intention was
to do just exactly what she did: to make the revised materials so
dreadful that they would be filed away and never used. To
destroy the Thursday Night Devotional movement by making it
so boring that it died of its own tedium."

"Which drove the practice back into the Womanhouses of the
Lines and isolated it there. That is—that is what it appeared to
do."

"Yes . . . plans within plans within plans, you see. We could
have discovered one level of deception, and never guessed that it
had still more within it. Thanks to my poor Sister Maria, we
have it all.'

"So," said the Cardinal again. "So, these revisions, deliberately distorted by Sister Miriam to be red herrings, went on to
Dorien's desk. Then what happened?"

"As I said, Your Eminence. They were filed away, and they
were willingly forgotten. And so far as any of us knew, the
originals—which I have never seen, but which I am told are utter
filth, evil beyond imagination—had been confined entirely to the

experience of the women of the Lines. Who can scarcely be considered normal women in any case, as you well know. There was no simple way to stamp them out among the linguist women, because not one of the Lines is Catholic, but we thought that this . . . this theological pornography . . . was in absolute quarantine.''

"And all that time, our Sister Judas was spreading the contagion secretly. Through women like Sister Maria."

"Yes, Your Eminence. And we never guessed. There was never a hint. Never!"

"She will burn in eternal fire, this Judas among nuns," the Cardinal said. He did not suggest that God have mercy on her soul.

"Assuredly, Your Eminence. So she will. But that doesn't help us now, on this Earth, in this galaxy."

The Cardinal frowned, and rubbed his hands together, palm to palm, thinking hard. "What else do we know, my son?" he asked. "What other facts do we have?"

"We have no facts," said Joseph dully, sagging in his chair. "We know nothing else. Nothing at all."

"Nonsense!"

"Uh . . . we know. . . ."

"You try our patience, Joseph." The Cardinal's voice was silky. "Tell us what is known, with no further hysteria."

"We know, I am trying to tell you, Your Eminence, we do know, that sixty years ago Father Dorien put Sister Miriam in charge of a project intended to put an end to the Láadan Heresy, also known at that time as the Langlish Heresy. We know that Sister Miriam served in that post for many years, seemingly with complete faithfulness, until she felt that it could continue without her supervision. At which point she requested and was granted transfer to Washington General Hospital, to finish her life as a public nurse. We know that unless Sister Maria lied, Sister Miriam was actually working against us all that time, or some substantial portion of that time. She was not trying to make the materials into something that would draw women to the Church, but that would be free of feminist contamination. She was deliberately sabotaging that plan. And at the same time she was—somehow, Your Eminence, we do not know how—recruiting nuns to *preserve* the heresy at the very heart of Holy Mother Church. She went to her death still honored for her work; she took the secret of her life of evil with her to the grave. And if it were not for poor Sister Maria's terror in the face of death, and her confession to me, we *still* would not know anything about it!"

"And that is *all* we know," he added defiantly.

"The sister named no other names, my son? No places, no times?"

"No, Your Eminence. She might have intended to, I suppose . . . she died before she could say anything else. With the most frightful suffering still on her face." The shudder that racked him was almost convulsive; he knew it was ugly to see.

"You absolved her, Joseph?"

"Of course!"

"Then put her death terrors and her pain out of your mind, my son. The Lord will have taken her to Him and banished both terror and pain, long since. Save your sympathy and your grief for Mother Church, who is sorely wounded; Sister Maria's problems are over now."

"Yes, Eminence."

"So! You heard her confession; you gave her the last rites; you saw to what needed to be done. And then?"

"And then I went home, and for the rest of that night I prayed. And when it was far enough into the morning to make it something like a decent hour, I went to Bishop Paul and I . . . I violated the confessional. I told the Bishop every word that Sister Maria had said to me."

"Look at me, Joseph." The old man's voice was powerful; it was the voice of one long accustomed to dominance. As were his eyes, when Joseph obeyed and met them straight on.

"My son, consider carefully," said the Cardinal. "If you had it to do over, would you do it again, just as you did this time? The truth now—do not lie to me, Joseph."

He wanted to look away from those eyes, but he found that he couldn't; he looked helplessly into them and said, "Yes! God forgive me, yes I would. I would do it again. I think I would do it even faster. I would wake the Bishop up instead of waiting for morning."

"Why?"

"To save the Holy Mother Church from this infamy!" He said it proudly; it was a comfort to be able to say something he could be proud of. "I would do it fifty times over, and if I must be condemned to Hell for that, then so be it. I will spend my term in Hell letting Sister Miriam know what she has done."

"You are quite sure, Joseph?"

"I am *absolutely* sure." There was no question about the sincerity of his words; he could hear it himself. Now, they knew it all. It was over. Whatever was going to happen would happen, the cardboard cutouts in their glorious robes would do whatever they were going to do, and he would live with it, and die with it.

He held his breath, and fought the gorge that rose in his throat, and his eyes clung to the Cardinal's.

"My dearest Joseph . . ."

He clung now to the words as well, glad that they were to be tempered with compassion, glad that there was not going to be *fierce* condemnation. The silky menace was gone from the Cardinal's voice.

"My son," the Cardinal went on, "if I had been in your place, I can only pray that I would have done just what you did." He smiled. "Except, as you pointed out, I hope I would have done it even more quickly."

Joseph was stunned. Shattered. He could not be hearing what he thought he was hearing. It was a delusion, born of his exhausted body and mind, pushed past its furthest limits. Surely it was a delusion. He stammered, hating himself for stammering, "I am not to be excommunicated?"

"No, of course not! Your penance will be long and it will be difficult and it will be wearing. But you are not to torment yourself with nonsense."

"I thought—"

"We all know what you must have thought. You thought you would be defrocked and excommunicated."

"Yes. At least."

"Joseph, when our Beloved Master took up a whip and went into the temple to lay it on the backs of the moneychangers and drive them out into the street, to stop them from defiling His Father's house, he could scarcely be said to be turning the other cheek. He broke His own commandments—he laid a scourge to the backs of those vermin, he did not offer them the kiss of peace. Jesus of Nazareth, that was! He could have gone in and reasoned with them; he could have compelled them peaceably by the force of his presence; he could have caused them to go blind; he could have done any number of things. He chose to go in and whip the bastards out of the Temple. He knew—as every one of us here knows—that there are times, very special times, when it is right to break even a good and a holy rule. The problem is that we are not Jesus the Christ, and we are terribly likely to be mistaken about what constitutes such a time. You are one of the fortunate ones, Joseph. You were *right*."

The relief flooded through him, poured through him, and he thought with horror that he was going to faint, like a woman, right here in the room with the Cardinal and all these dignitaries; he watched them dwindle to tiny figures at the end of a tunnel of swirling black specks and heard their voices fade away; it seemed to be taking an immensely long time. And then he felt the heel of the priest sitting nearest him come down on his own instep, *hard*. Hard enough to bruise; hard enough to hurt. The sudden blow shocked him out of the shameful swoon, and he was deeply grateful to the other man. On whose face there showed not the slightest trace of what had happened. He would thank him, later, if he had the opportunity.

"I am grateful, Your Eminence," he managed to say. He was.

"We are the ones who must be grateful," answered the Cardinal. "I don't know what we are to *do* now—but at least we know the rot is at our heart. At least we know it exists, and must be dealt with. God be praised, we are no longer ignorant of our peril."

Father Boris, a very tall man afflicted with protruding ears that would have been corrected long ago had he not been a priest and thus presumably indifferent to such things, spoke up then for the first time. "What *are* we going to do about this?" he asked. "Where do we begin?"

"I don't know," the Cardinal said. "I know what we *can't* do! We can't simply announce that every nun involved is ordered to turn herself in to us forthwith, and to bring the blasphemous materials with her to be destroyed. This episode must not become known to all and sundry, my friend. It must not become a matter of common knowledge that such a thing could go on within the Church for sixty years and more undiscovered, spreading no one knows how far. That would make what you quite accurately call a conspiracy look romantic, seductive, appealing, at the very least—and make us like fools. Our poor sisters would fight to become members of the secret cadre, all aquiver with the deliciousness of it . . . it would be the only topic of conversation during recreation." He made a face. "No, we can't do that. We'll have to find these women somehow, one at a time, ferret them out one at a time, compel them to give us other names when we *do* find them. This is going to take years and years—and how *many* years depends entirely on how many there are of the traitors."

"But I don't know where we would begin. I don't see *how* we would begin. Your Eminence, do you know either of those things?" It was Father Boris again, greatly distressed.

"Well . . . there are routine things we can do. We'll check the databanks, find out who Sister Maria sent correspondence to, communications to, over the years. Most of it will turn out to be legitimate convent business, because she will have seen to it that the records of what was not legitimate were destroyed. But there will be something there. She will have forgotten, now and then, to delete every trace. She will have been careless, now and then, as everyone is careless now and then. We can send priests to all the places that she was in contact with, explaining to them what they are to watch for. Any sign of nervousness, of guilt, of excessive strain, of secretiveness. A sister who is said to be a 'loner' or to suffer from hysteria. We can watch, and we can listen. For anything at all that is not ordinary. One of them will slip, eventually; it may take a long time, but one of them will slip. And when we have one, and we have the chance to convince her to tell us a few things, it will lead us to the next one."

"It will take forever."

"That is the advantage of being a church," the Cardinal said mildly. "We *have* forever. And it must be done, if it takes forever twice over. We must begin at once. You will go at once, each of you, and prepare a list for me. I need the names of priests you would trust with this task—men who can be relied on. Men who can be tactful. Men with the patience to let a cunning woman betray herself, and not move so soon that she is given time to alert the others. Men who can resist the temptation to flaunt their knowledge and administer punishment. Men with the sort of ear that hears the most minute taint, eyes that see the most nearly invisible contamination, even hidden away in the midst of what seems to be flawless devotion. Men who do not gossip, *ever*. Do you understand?"

"You aren't suggesting that they—" The Cardinal's assistant cleared his throat, and began again. "Your Eminence, are you suggesting that these women might be *practicing* their blasphemies?"

"It would be easy enough," the Cardinal responded. "Who pays attention to exactly what a silly nun's lips are mumbling when she is at prayer? Who would know if the words were just a little bit different from those that the other nuns were using? Certainly, it's quite possible that that *is* going on. And by this time, of course, those nuns will be feeling safe in their perversions; it's been such a long time, and no one has ever become suspicious in all these long years."

Joseph had not thought of this possibility; Bishop Paul had not suggested it. It made his skin crawl to think that in the convents where women spent their lives in perpetual devotion there might be those who spent their lives in perpetual blasphemy.

"Do you really think that could be happening?" he said, wonderingly. "Do you really—"

"They are fanatics, my son," the Cardinal interrupted, his voice grim and sorrowful. "You do not spend decades involved in a heretical conspiracy at the heart of the Roman Catholic Church, without ever being suspected by anyone, unless you are the most intense sort of fanatic. I do most certainly believe they may be introducing the heresy into their devotions; I believe there might be separate heretical services held in secret; I believe—since this is possible at *all*—that almost anything is possible. Satan has never lacked for ingenuity; let us not underestimate the possibilities."

"We'll need copies of the translations," noted the assistant. "The original ones. For every priest on the list."

"We have those," said the Cardinal.

"We do?" Father Joseph was surprised; he had supposed they would have to go begging for them to the linguists.

"Oh yes. Dorien always had the originals put into memory along with the revisions. I'll have copies put on chiplets this very day, enough for at least one hundred good priests. I'll need that hundred names from you, gentlemen. By tomorrow morning, at the latest." And then he stopped, and a strange expression crossed his face, and he looked almost amused. "Oh, dear Lord," he said softly. "I am such a foolish servant!"

"Your Eminence?"

"This has gone on sixty years or more. Think of it! Putting an end to it will surely take at least that long." He shook his head, ruefully; his amusement was for his own absurdity. "And here I sit saying 'do this today, do this this afternoon, do this at once,' as if a day or a week or even a month would matter, in all those years. I'm an old imbecile."

"It's quite natural, your Eminence," murmured the men around him.

"Yes. It is. But it's a natural tendency which we must prepare ourselves to resist. Any haste, any rush, any feeling that we must *hurry*, and we'll risk exactly what we must not let happen. Sister Miriam Rose, you will notice, knew better than to hurry—we must be no less canny. Ancient secrets, stretching into the future—*that* is what we are dealing with. And we must discipline ourselves to remember that. Or one of us—trying for efficiency and speed and all the rest of those modern virtues—will wreck the entire project. These women have hidden their work superbly, fiendishly well, for decades; let them have any warning that we're on to them, that we're searching them out, and they'll find a way to hide everything from us for another century! They will already have their networks of communication, their contingency plans. . . . We'll all be dead, and they'll still be at their filthy tricks. We *must* not give in to a feeling that we have to rush this, gentlemen! You must impress that on everyone we bring into the search, in the strongest terms. We will put an end to the heresy—in the Lord's good time— and no one will even know that it happened. That is how it must be done.''

"Your Eminence?" Joseph asked hesitantly, when he was sure that the Cardinal was through speaking for a moment. "Might I ask a question?"

"You may. Of course you may."

"I wonder if you have any idea . . . I wonder, where did this *start?*"

"I don't think I understand you, my son."

"How did it *begin,* Your Eminence? What could have started it off? I thought at first of the Lines, but that's absurd. They're not Catholic, they know nothing of nuns and convents and doctrine—those women wouldn't even known that what they were doing *is* heresy."

"I agree. The *men* of the Lines, however, are another matter entirely. And how they do love the game of power! This is just the sort of enormous joke—that is how they would see it, Joseph—that they would revel in playing on the Church. Perhaps it came from them."

Joseph was nodding, slowly; it was possible. "But how did they get to Sister Miriam? A *nun?* Even if it was them, *how?*"

"I don't know, Joseph. Sister Miriam is said to have known a number of languages, isn't that right? I'm sure I've heard Dorien remarking on that. Perhaps she had a linguist for a tutor, somewhere along the line? Perhaps she was allowed to correspond with linguists on points of grammar? I don't know how it could have happened, and undoubtedly it was those men, with their wicked mischief, who arranged for it. But I have said before, and I will say again: Satan has never lacked for ingenuity. And it was Satan who inspired Sister Miriam, I am very much afraid, no matter what the human tools used for the purpose. Inspired her to a kind of evil, a *scope* of evil, rarely seen. There is no source that precedes the Devil Himself, when it comes to evil."

"And I . . . what am I to do now?" *Always thinking of yourself, Joseph!* He could hear the Bishop now. The whole church threatened, and he was thinking only of himself. But he was too weary and too battered to care about the niceties.

"I will send instructions to Bishop Paul, my son," said the

Cardinal gently, "and he will see to all that. Put it out out your mind for now, and come with us, to have a good meal, and to share our good wines. It may be a very long time indeed before you have anything but bread and water again."

CHAPTER 27

"I have been asked now and then—usually by one of our nuns, sometimes by a young woman suffering her way through the necessary episode of Romantic Love that will protect her against the nasty stuff thereafter—if it isn't tragic that our men don't share the faith that sustains us. It's a good question, and a hard one, and over the years I've worked out an answer of sorts; but I keep longing for someone to provide a proper answer. Something that would be an improvement on my own verbal bumbling and blundering about; preferably something stunning in its absolute and glowing rightness! So that the questioner will say, "Oh, I see," instead of murmuring at me politely while thinking that I am a cold and cruel woman without compassion.

"We women provide the example, I always tell them. We haven't taken our faith and gone off with it into isolation and hugged it to ourselves like hidden treasure; we have never given in to that temptation. We have continued to serve as the data sources from which the men may work out for themselves the grammar of our theology; that sort of analysis and discovery is a task at which they are, after all, highly skilled. Theoretically— by the principle of resonance—if we were able to provide them a perfect example it would cause the same note to sound in them that sounds in us, and they would begin of their own free will to live according to those principles by which we live. That we women can be seen as heartless is an excellent measure of how far we miss the target of the Perfect Example; but that doesn't give us an excuse to abandon the effort.

"And then there comes the next question: why don't we simply tell them? Why don't we just explain? I am always grateful then if the questioner is a linguist, because I can turn that straight back and ask a question of my own: would they

*propose that an infant could learn to speak a language if someone
would simply have the kindness and the consideration to tell it
how?''*

(from the diaries of Nazareth Chornyak Adiness)

"There is *no end* to the wickedness of you women, *is* there?''
Jonathan Chornyak asked her, leaning back in his chair with his
arms folded across his chest, the delighted laughter in his eyes
serving more than adequately to cancel the stern tones of his
voice. "And as for your own particular personal wickedness,
what am I supposed to say? That the infinite nature of your
personal wickedness is even more infinite than the infinite nature
of the wickedness of all of you collectively? I do not intend to be
trapped into saying that, Nazareth, however superficially appealing it may be.''

Nazareth smiled at him, gently, leaning her chin on her cane,
and she waited. She didn't intend to be trapped into answering
the rhetorical questions, either, if she could help it.

"Nazareth,'' he chided her, "please. Help me. Don't just *lurk*
there like that. I didn't call you in here to admire your beauty.''

"I was never a beauty, my dear,'' she said. "Most of my life
I was quite frankly ugly, and no one minded telling me so. It's
only now that I'm so old, and nobody expects me to look like a
fairy princess any longer, that the matter even comes up.''

Jonathan was disgracefully fond of Nazareth, and much ashamed
of the fondness; to cover it up, he felt obligated to be stern with
her even when the two of them were alone. He spoke to her now
as he would have spoken to an obstreperous but much-loved
child.

"Nazareth,'' he said, "I'm serious. *Is* there no end to the
wickedness of you women, and the wickedness of you personally? Answer me, please.''

She pretended to think it over, and the corners of her mouth
twitched while her eyes stayed bland as any pond.

"There is no end to the wickedness of anything,'' she told
him gravely, after awhile. "Because it is a cyclic rather than a
linear phenomenon. To regret one's wickedness is to dwell on it,
which is wicked; not to regret one's wickedness is to ignore it,
which is wicked; to glory in one's wickedness is to perpetuate it,
which is wicked. There is no end to *wickedness*, Jonathan Asher,
at all. No matter whose you wish to specify.''

Jonathan chuckled; he loved it when the old lady played at

abstract thought and philosophizing. It was often very nearly poetry, the stuff she prattled, and when he wasn't busy he could listen to it endlessly, the way he would have listened to music.

"You're a holy terror, Aunt Natha," he said. "And this time, by god, you've outdone yourself. Do you know who came to see me today?"

She did know. She'd seen the ecclesiastical flyer arrive and the prelate flow over the lawn with minions scampering after him. But it is superfluous unkindness and discourtesy to spoil another person's tale-telling, and she only widened her eyes a bit and said, "No, Jonathan—*who?*"

"The Bishop of this diocese, that's who."

"My goodness!" Nazareth declared, her voice carefully pitched for just enough awe and a pinch of curiosity she didn't feel but was willing to fake. This boychild who sat here before her, Head of the Chornyak Line, and Head of all the Lines together, had never done her any personal harm other than through ignorance.

"Your goodness," Jonathan echoed. "Your goodness, indeed. We began this conversation by specifying that its topic was your wickedness, Nazareth Joanna Chornyak Adiness. Please keep that in mind."

Nazareth relaxed and let him tell her all about it, throwing in the occasional "Really?" and "Oh, dear!" and "Heavens!" and "Then what?" that he needed in order to organize his narrative. He was tickled to death, which was far better than Nazareth had dared hope. That he would find out someday had probably been inevitable; they'd been lucky an incredibly long time. She had hoped he would be only annoyed when it happened, rather than furious; that he was pleased was a wonderful and unanticipated event.

"It seems," he began, "that the Roman Catholic Church finds itself in a theological pickle of massive size and scope, Nazareth. It seems that some years ago a group of its nuns were invited to be guest speakers at a series of religious meetings held on Thursday nights around the country . . . I'm sure, Aunt Nazareth, that you will know to what series of meetings I refer. And it seems that the nuns were definitely shocked at what they heard at those meetings—shocked enough to go back and report to their male superiors that they felt something ought to be done. After all, the women who had started the meetings had managed somehow to interest large numbers of *nurses* in their so-called devotions, and the nurses were spreading the practice all over the country, and who knew what might not happen next?"

He stopped and grinned at her. "Nurses," he said softly.

"You clever little old females. . . . There you were with your silly 'woman's language,' all verbed up and no place to go. No way to get it out beyond the Lines. And then you remembered *nurses*—the only women who come and go freely between the Lines and the public, the only women who have the opportunity to talk to all sorts and kinds of people, and—coincidentally— women who had access to the hospital chapels. All you had to do was seduce the resident nurses from each of the Lines into your cozy little Thursday night meetings in the Womanhouses, and convince them that your Langlish twaddle was romantic and exotic and terribly terribly mysterious and exciting, and they would take it straight out into the world for you. And *damned* if they didn't fall for it!"

He threw back his head and laughed, while Nazareth waited patiently and watched the small golden fishes in the aquarium that was set into the wall behind him. He had added the aquarium because it distracted people talking to him; he had a screen he pulled over it when he didn't want them distracted. And when he looked at her again she was not looking at the fish but giving him her full courteous attention.

"It was all your idea, wasn't it?" he demanded.

"I'm sure I don't remember, my dear," she answered vaguely. "It's been such a long time ago. I suppose I may have had something to do with it."

He snorted. "You old fraud," he said.

"Thank you kindly, I'm sure, Jonathan."

"The priests were alarmed at what they heard," he went on, "and they seriously considered forbidding their women to take part in these shenanigans. But that would have meant passing up their golden opportunity, you perceive. Here were all these plump little round womanly souls, just waiting to be plucked and gathered in to the ample bosom of the church . . . it was much too good to pass up. So they set up an entire project, headed by a senior nun, to do nothing but fix up the Langlish Bible translations so they weren't offensive to Catholic sensibilities, and they churned the stuff out for *years*, Nazareth! All of it submitted in turn to a head honcho for approval, and certified squeaky-Catholic-clean, and authorized for use in church. And they sent their nuns back out into the cities and towns to spread the sanitized word across the land. . . ." He stopped and steepled his hands and peered at her over his fingertips. "Nazareth Chornyak—you wretched women had an entire *regiment* of innocent nuns employed in the furthering of your plan to spread Langlish beyond the lines. Or Láadan, if you prefer—the Bishop wasn't entirely clear on that, not that it matters. You have had working for you, for free, a crew of holy sisters and an actual Bishop! Nazareth, you perceive me before you *stunned*."

"Well," Nazareth murmured, "we tried, dear."

"You *tried!*" He pinned her in her chair with his eyes, and she looked startled, and let her tremor get just a tad worse. "You tried! You succeeded! How in the name of all the bleeding saints—especially appropriate in this instance—did you women pull that off? Nazareth, the Roman Catholic Church is not a little country chapel out on a frontier somewhere! We are talking of the Holy Roman Catholic *Church.* I understand why it had to be them . . . they were the only ones with women living all together in isolation from men, and they were the only ones with the necessary lines of communication. But damned if you didn't suck them in just as slick as smoke! God *damn,* Aunt Natha!"

"You're angry, Jonathan," Nazareth suggested, so that he could make his point.

"I certainly ought to be. Don't you think I ought to be?"

"Now how would I know that?" she objected. "I have never in all my life understood the workings of a man's mind, or what makes them angry, or what consumes them with bliss, for that matter. You are asking that question of the wrong person, Jonathan." And there had been a time when that was all true, and she had spent her life butting her head against the walls of maleness, tied to a husband she detested and subject to a houseful of other males she despised. But over the course of a hundred years she had learned a thing or two; she still understood very little about *why* men did things, but she had come to have a reasonable competence in predicting *what* they would do in response to a particular stimulus.

"Consider it as an abstract question, Nazareth," he said. "Shouldn't I be angry?"

"Well, are you?"

"No!" he declared, giving the old desk a brisk punch and sending files flying to the floor. "Never mind that I ought to be! The very idea of the women of the Lines suckering all those pious old potentates—how can I be angry?"

"We didn't ask if we could do it," she pointed out.

"No, you didn't. Because if you had asked, we would have said no, and you knew that."

"That's true."

"And so you did an end run around us—with the help of the nurses of America assembled, and the Catholic Church—and you wreaked glorious havoc! Bless your nefarious little hearts and whatever passes for your brains!''

Nazareth allowed herself a soft noise somewhere between a chuckle and a giggle, an old-woman sort of smothered noise, and Jonathan beamed at her, vastly satisfied. He had forgotten again about being stern.

"I would have said no," he repeated. "Damn right I would. I would have forbidden it absolutely, from the beginning. But since you didn't ask, and since I didn't say you couldn't do it, let me tell you that I think you women should get a medal for it."

"That's very kind of you, Jonathan," she said.

"Mmhmm. Hypocrite, as well as fraud. But Nazareth, old dear, it gets better. It gets *much* better. You've only heard the very beginning."

"Really?" Nazareth frowned, and bit her lip.

"Really."

"Why, what else could there be? I don't believe there could be more, my dear. Nor do I see why the bishop bothered to come talk to you, because that silly fad died out long long ago. Wasn't he a little late to be complaining?"

His eyes narrowed, and he ran one thumbnail back and forth across his lower lip, grinning at her, a narrow grin that matched the eyes. This was what he'd actually called her in for, she saw, but he had had it in mind to tease her awhile before he shared the news, whatever it was.

Nazareth had the privilege of great age; she had diapered this alpha male many many times. And of course, by comparison with her father and her brother, who'd been Heads before him, he was a very mild alpha male indeed. She leaned across the desk and patted his free hand.

"Don't tease now, Jonathan Asher," she admonished him. "I'm much too old for that. I'll forget what we're talking about and you'll have to start all over again from the beginning."

"Would you now?"

"I'm sure I would. In fact, I feel my memory failing me this very minute, Charles."

"You're faking," he said. "But you're right, I should get on with it. This is not a holiday, although I may declare it one yet, in honor of the triumph of the Lines over the ecclesiasticals. It's the way you women bamboozled the *priests* that warms my heart, you perceive."

"Oh? Really?"

"They're so damned irritating. They don't have the guts for being men, but they want the privileges, so they go hiding in the skirts of what they rightly call their 'Mother' Church, where you can't get at them. I suppose it's a good thing males like that have some respectable haven to flee *to*, but it rankles. You always want to dare them to come out and fight, but you can't do that because they're all dressed up in skirts. I can't tell you how much satisfaction it gives me that you women whipped that pack of—"

Nazareth clucked her tongue, and he stopped short.

"Well, they are."

"Some of them are rather nice," she said. "And think what a lot of good they do."

He glared at her, and she suggested that he tell her what had happened next.

"Oh, yes. Nazareth, what the Bishop came to tell me this morning is that the nun they had in charge of laundering your heresies—that's what he calls them, dear, 'heresies'—was actually in charge of a secret rebellion inside the convents. Can you believe that? All the time they thought she was doing nothing but following her orders and turning out authorized sanitized gibberish, she was in solemn truth recruiting nuns—who recruited nuns, who recruited nuns—to make handwritten copies of those very same heresies and distribute them in secret from one end of the world to the other. And they don't know how long that went on . . . they keep saying 'sixty years' but they don't really know . . . or how many nuns are involved, or how deep the Wicked Nun's tendrils are in the loam!"

Nazareth ignored the ache in her heart, and asked, cautiously, "What are they going to do to her, Jonathan?"

"To who?"

"To whoever it was that did this? The Wicked Nun? What will they do to her?"

"They can't do anything to her," he laughed, "except rejoice in what they confidently assume to be the warm place she inhabits in Hell; she died without their ever knowing what she'd been up to. And the nun that gave it all away only tattled on her deathbed; she's far beyond their reach as well. As for the ones she ratted on, only god knows what they will do to them—but she didn't name them, Natha, and the good fathers will have to *catch* them, first! And at this point—"

His face changed, and the sternness she saw there now was not feigned. "Nazareth," he said, "I gave the Bishop my word that what I am telling you will remain confidential, and I expect that promise to be honored. *You* may know—even the Bishop would agree that you're entitled to know, and whether he agreed or not, *I* would rule that you were. But you are not to tell anyone else. Do you understand?''

''Ah,'' she said, ''don't concern yourself; I won't speak of it to anyone at all.'' She did not add that she was safe as churches, but allowed him to make the joke and joined him in laughing at his wit.

''In confidence, then,'' he said. ''They have no information but the knowledge that the plot existed, and that it still exists. But so determined are they to 'stamp out the perversion' that they are sending one hundred priests—*one hundred*, Nazareth— to search out the terrible tawdry traitors and bring them in.''

Nazareth sat back and sighed, shaking her head in the amazement he would expect of her, her heart quieting on its own. It was all right; everything was all right. And she listened respectfully while Jonathan told her about the plan to post priests as observers to the convents until the guilty nuns betrayed themselves and then to bring them in one by one with no one else ever knowing, on trumped-up excuses. Finding and destroying the Láadan texts one by one as they went along, with no one else ever knowing. All very hush-hush and solemnly secret; it was clear that the priests were well aware that no more powerful instrument for change exists than language, for all that they weren't linguists, and that they took this matter absolutely seriously.

When he had finished telling her the last detail, and describing the discomfiture of the visiting bishop, and admiring the set of extraordinary coincidences the women of the Lines had managed to turn to their own purposes to make all this happen, and marveling over how many *points* all this meant for the Lines, he finally began to weary of the subject. He was vastly amused that one hundred priests were to go out and devote their lives to superstitious nonsense concocted by the linguist women and revised by nuns. And he most certainly would not, as the bishop had advised that he do, order the women of the Lines to give up the use of Langlish/Láadan forever.

''It will be a very cold day in hell,'' he noted grimly, ''theirs or ours, when we find it necessary to take instruction in the managing of our women from the Roman Catholic Church!''

''Such arrogance!'' Nazareth observed, looking shocked.

''So I informed him. And I gave him a thirty point blood

pressure boost by telling him that not only would I not forbid you women your Annual Central Caucus, as he said I 'must' do, but I intended to add an additional half-day to it to demonstrate what value I placed on his meddling.''

"My goodness.''

"I believe I made my feelings clear.''

"I'm sure you did. And well you should have. It's none of his business what we do.''

"I told him,'' Jonathan said, "that the women of the Lines have been speaking Láadan among themselves for decades, and that the result has been the antithesis of the corruption and cataclysms he predicts. The only effect the use of the language has had upon *our* women, I told His Exalted Whatsis, has been to make them ever more womanly.''

"Why, thank you, Jonathan! What a lovely thing to say!''

"It's no more than the simple truth,'' he told her kindly. "It has been good for you women, and for all of us. But, Nazareth—''

"Yes, my dear?'' She cocked her head and leaned toward him, her lips half-parted and her posture attentive.

"Nazareth, this must never happen again. I mean that.''

"I beg your pardon?''

"If you had come to me and explained what you wanted to do,'' he said, humoring her, and taking pleasure in the humoring, "I would have told you no. For many many reasons, not the least of which is that you women are far too busy to take on popularization projects of that kind. Not to mention that it was a disrespectful piece of mischief—the priests are poor excuses for men, but they are men nonetheless, and no doubt many of them, as you say, do a great deal of good. But Nazareth, most of all I would have told you no because the idea was a waste of time, with not a hairbreadth's chance of succeeding. I'm glad you weren't stopped, because it's tremendous that you women managed to lead a whole church round the barn like you did—but I would have stopped you if I'd known. I suppose you had some notion that if you could get other women to speak the language it would be helpful to them, didn't you? Yes . . . I see you did. That's very touching, and very generous and kind, and very romantic—but Aunt Natha, it's also ridiculous. Women outside the Lines aren't interested in languages! They are interested in their clothes and their houses and their clubs and their husbands and their children—period. *May*be—on a good day—they are interested in their gardens. Their heads are as empty of any other thought as an egg is empty of beefsteak. It was such a *hopeless* project, Nazareth! So foolish. . . . I am a little surprised that you encouraged it, frankly. Is it possible, Nazareth, that you really *are* getting old?''

She shook her head, and sighed again, and looked helpless and distracted, and he told her not to worry about it any more. Not to *ever* consider doing such a thing again, and not to let the details of the Church's current quandary go past this room—but not to worry about it. And she left him sitting there thinking what a dear old thing she was, and in a mood that meant a pleasant day for one and all.

In her bed, allegedly "taking a little nap," Nazareth carefully considered the status of the plan point by point and decided that she in fact did not *need* to worry, although her serenity of mind wasn't precisely what Jonathan had been envisioning. She was sorry that the dying nun had become frightened and talked, because it was a complication—and because she must have suffered over it. But it was bound to happen eventually, and Nazareth had expected it for years; it was astonishing that it hadn't happened sooner, in fact. And it wasn't serious, not now.

The tiny cells of Láadan within the convents were everywhere now, not only on this world but on colony worlds, and they were sheltered by women who knew how to nurture the language and who loved it enough to speak it and to teach it. For priests to be out searching for it, and with any luck finding it, thus putting themselves in the constant company of women who were being shaped by the language, was excellent. It was doing the men of the Lines enormous good, and it would be good for the priests as well. If they caught a nun or two, it would make no difference; the language had spread too far to root out. For all the technological marvels of this society, its men had not yet devised any way to put toothpaste back into its tube. Nazareth would in fact send out a message that a few sisters here and there might want to allow themselves to be "caught" at reasonable intervals of time. Just enough of them, and all of them too deeply repentant to bring down any punishment of consequence; it would lull the men of the Church and keep them from becoming excessive in their vigilance.

After all, hadn't it now been proved beyond all question that the language was no threat? It had been a *fad*, pushed by the forces of the media, waved in the public eye, taken up by the very best people, scholarly articles written about it by the most distinguished old puffballs—it had had everything going for it. And it had still failed dismally, no? Vanished! Evaporated! Who could be afraid of such a phantom as that?

Meanwhile, Láadan would spread; the tiny wild vine wreaths, unnoticed by anyone, would go up on wall after wall. It would continue to keep the women of the Lines, and all the women who knew it beyond, immune to the state of violence that the men struggled with so incessantly; it would continue to provide the women with the patience necessary to bring the men *out* of those endless loops of violence always begetting more violence. The day would come when they would have a war, and all of the men would look at each other and laugh and just go home.

Nazareth had no more intention of trying to explain to the other women how that would happen, or what the principle of resonance had to do with the price of eggs, than she had had all those many years ago of explaining to them what it meant to really *believe* that language can change reality. They would find out, in good time, long after she was gone; she was too tired to hurry that process or to wrangle with them about it, even if there were any reason to think that might be useful. They would have her diaries, full of casseroles and desserts and intricate soups and sauces ready for decoding; let them read about it there, with her safely out of range of all their argument.

In a while, Láadan would move out among Protestant and other women as well as Catholic, because the easing of the prejudice against the "Lingoes" was at last beginning to heal the split between them and the rest of the world. Soon women of the Lines and other women would be mingling freely again, whether the government approved of that or not; soon, there would be non-linguist women coming to the Womanhouses as friends, and bringing their children along with them to be friends, too. They would hear Láadan spoken there, not just in church services and set pieces, but as common everyday language. And the little ones, both boys and girls, would pick up the language as effortlessly as they picked up any other language, and use it among themselves.

Nazareth closed her eyes, thinking that after all she *might* sleep a little, and smiled at the ceiling. If she lived long enough, she would be so interested to see what they were going to be like—the first human men who had learned Láadan as infants and toddlers. It might make little difference, or no difference at all; on the other hand, it might make a difference worth rejoicing over, and the chances were good enough to make that the *likely* outcome.

We never dared teach our male children, she thought; it would have alerted the men to things they were better off not noticing. It was always "just for girls," and peer pressure has kept it that way without much effort on our part. But out in the world, and out in the colonies, it would be different. The little ones would be enchanted to have a "secret language" to play with and to share. Bless the children.

She wouldn't live long enough to see it all happen, but she didn't mind; it was enough to have lived to see it all begin. And so she drifted into sleep, at peace. No plan is one hundred percent successful; no woman expects any such thing. But this plan was moving along at a satisfying seventy-five percent, more than adequate for the purpose. A jog here, a jog there—the occasional dropped stitch that let you know it wasn't the work of a machine, and no harm done. She was more than willing to settle for that.

EPILOGUE

TO: The Council of the Consortium
FROM: XJH$_i$
SUBJECT: The problem of Earth

NOTE: This paper has been prepared in response to the COTC's annual resolution condemning the practice of perpetual surveillance over the planet Earth and its colonies, and to the annual proposal that XJH$_i$ at minimum begin reform of that practice by reducing the number of live observors in place within Earth's territorial boundaries. XHJ$_i$ must once again respond by requesting that the COTC decide upon an *alternative* solution to the Terran problem; until such an alternative is available, institution of reforms is not possible. XHJ$_i$ respectfully directs the attention of the Council to the attached position statement, which summarizes the situation and appeals—once again—for immediate action rather than a new series of delays. END NOTE.

The decision of the COTC to intervene in the evolutionary development of the planet Earth by providing aid on a limited basis was not made on impulse. It was based upon a set of alarming and inescapable facts. As follows:

1. It had become obvious that the Terrans were on the point of moving out into space whether we intervened or not, making it necessary that *some* action be taken.
2. Although Terran males remained at that stage of evolution in which violence is a primary drive of the organism, there were hopeful signs; a small but significant percentage of the males, although quite naturally unable simply to bypass this stage, had become aware that it was undesirable and were beginning to work toward the goal of going beyond it.

3. The majority of Terran females *had* moved beyond the stage of violence still gripping the males. (This is consistent with the general pattern of the species, in which development toward maturity proceeds somewhat more rapidly in females than in males, and was to be anticipated.)

4. Unfortunately, the result of #2 and #3 above was not, as might have been hoped, a stable cultural environment in which the evolutionary lead of the females spurred the males to close the gap. On the contrary. The male majority reacted to this gender difference *with* violence! Why this should have been the case is a matter of considerable controversy. The Terran males claim to have scientific evidence that the females are of an intelligence inferior to theirs; if they are correct, it is possible that this accounts at least in part for the failure of the females to function as effective models for the males. Whatever the explanation, however, by 11,302 one thing was certain: the females of Earth (together with the more advanced males viewed by their peers as effeminate and weak) were literally in danger from their male counterparts. The lack of developmental synchrony between the two genders of the species, which up to this time had been of no particular concern, now manifested itself as a difference so extreme that it placed a radical strain upon the entire Terran cultural fabric.

5. The weapons systems developed by the Terrans had reached a stage acutely dangerous not only to Earth but to its neighbors as well. Although we had ample measure for neutralizing the effects of these weapons systems when given advance warning of their use, a number of Consortium worlds would have been totally vulnerable to them if surveillance had not been maintained. (In this regard, XJH$_i$ would be most grateful if the Council members would explain how the safety of those endangered worlds could have been ensured *without* invading the privacy and violating the sovereignty of Earth!)

6. In 11,303 the problem was placed on the COTC agenda for formal discussion. The ensuing debate was characterized by what could almost be described as *earthly* vehemence, and resulted in a series of paradoxes that were not given the attention they deserved. Debate ended when it became clear that only three courses of action were open to us:

A. We could put an end to the matter once and for all by eliminating the planet, in its entirety, from the universe.

B. We could place Earth under complete quarantine, with

constant surveillance maintained to guarantee that its activities would have no effects beyond the borders of its own atmospheres, and leave it to work out its difficulties independently.

C. We could interfere in Terran evolution, minimally, in the hope that with our guidance Earth could be kept safe long enough for the males to reach the end of the violent stage and for balance to be restored.

Not one of these alternatives allowed the Consortium to maintain its own ethic of nonviolence—hence the paradoxes. Alternative A was not given serious consideration, although logic required that it be included in the debate. The focus of controversy, from the beginning, was on the choice between Alternatives B and C.

To implement B was, on the surface, ethically preferable; we would have left the Terrans to settle their own affairs, and would have confined our interference to that absolute minimum necessary to preserve the physical safety of our citizens. (That is, we would essentially have continued the policy we had been maintaining up to that point, without change.) But there were serious problems with that choice. For one thing, it meant abandoning the female population of Earth and some percentage of its males to an inevitable period of great suffering, the length of which we could not even estimate. This did not seem an admirable act on the part of the consortium of cultures allegedly more highly evolved than those of Earth. None of the logically accurate analogies drawn between this plan and the inevitable discomfort of necessary medical procedures lessened its obvious cruelty. There was also a strong feeling within the Council, especially on the part of the more conservative members, that Alternative B was nothing more than a disguised version of the unacceptable Alternative A; that is, it was highly probable that the violence of Terran males would result in the total destruction of the planet and its colonies long before the evolutinary gap between the genders could be resolved. (A number of moving speeches were made in which B was compared to standing fastidiously by while a child was devoured by some wild animal, for no other reason than the preservation of one's own ethical self-image.)

7. The final decision reached was to implement Alternative C, under the strictest possible controls. Interference would be confined to a carefully orchestrated introduction of technological advances in the guise of "interplanetary trade," together with a continuation of the self-defense measures

already mentioned. First contact was then initiated in early 11,304 under the supervision of the COTC, with XJH_i as the implementing agency; the existing surveillance systems were supplemented by the placement on site of live observers undetectable (with a single exception not relevant here) by the Terran population.

8. It is now shamefully clear that our choice *ought* to have been either Alternative A or B, repugnant as they both seemed at the time. THIS SAD CONCLUSION CANNOT BE AVOIDED, WHATEVER THE COST TO OUR SELF-RESPECT. We have not accelerated the evolution of the Terran males past the stage of violence in any way. On the contrary, we have *retarded* their progress! What we have managed to do by our inexcusable stupidity is make an endless expansion of that violence not only possible but *easy*. Those males whose violence requires overt physical expression are now exported to Terran colonies where their behavior is a threat only to the indigenous species of the colony world and to other such males. In the most extreme cases, when the degree of violence is viewed even by Terrans as inappropriate, these males are encouraged to relocate to the planet Gehenna, on which no law except brute force is allowed. Males in whom the trait has more subtle expression remain on the more developed worlds and devote themselves to the manipulation and control of this appalling empire. *In other worlds:* those who wish to slash and rape and disembowel go to the frontier to do so; the rest devote their lives to overseeing the slashing and raping and disemboweling from a safe distance and enjoying it vicariously. There is no sense in which this can be considered an improvement, although it is of course so perceived by the Terrans themselves.

If we had left Earth alone, one of two things would have had to happen. The Terrans would have destroyed their planets and all their peoples, thus putting a tidy end to the problem. Or, the imminent prospect of that destruction would have forced them to find some way past the evolutionary barrier, both genders would have advanced past the stage of violence, and eventually we would have been able to invite Earth into the Consortium like any other civilized planet. In hindsight, it is obvious that we should have stood by our principles and allowed Earth to find its own way to one of the other of these outcomes. THERE IS NO DISAGREEMENT ON THIS POINT—IN HINDSIGHT.

But it's far too late to do that now. We have now *widened* the
gulf between the genders on Earth. We have pushed the males
back farther into violence by making it easy, and convenient,
and without obvious penalty. We have further weakened the
females, because our meddling has enabled the males to reduce
them to a state of pampered ignorance and subjugation much like
that of domestic pets. We do not know if the original helplessness of the females in the face of the violence was really due to
inferior intelligence; if it was, we have probably made that worse
as well. We have now gone around our *own* evolutionary loop,
and we are back at the beginning. We are back at "square one,"
to use an apt Terran phrase, and the debate should once more be
before the Council—not for just one world, but for a swarm of
them. Now, instead of having to decide whether to cleanse the
universe of just one nasty little planet, or one nasty little planet
and a few nasty little colonies, we must consider the same
problem multiplied many times over by our bungling. And we
cannot evade our responsibilities forever by the stratagem of
annually issuing sets of documents deploring the situation and
demanding minor modifications of it from XJH_i.

What do we do now? That is the question that must be faced,
and formally asked, and formally answered.

Do we now put every last Terran world, from the largest
planet down to the tiniest inhabited asteroid, under strict quarantine, isolating all of them from us totally and leaving them to
find their own way to harmony or to annihilation? Now that we
have made their situation far worse than it was before we interfered? The prospect is not only horrible from the point of view of
morality, it is almost unimaginably complex from the point of
view of implementation. It could not be done secretly; we could
not just disappear like the deities in the ancient Terran myths and
legends, there one moment, gone the next in our flaming chari-
ots. We would have to separate ourselves from Earth and all its
territories as an open totalitarian act, with an impact on the
Terran populations that we cannot predict other than to say that it
would be destructive in the extreme. We would have to announce
that we had changed our minds, take back our technology by
force where that was possible and leave it to be misused where it
was not, and abandon the Terran peoples to deal with the messes
they could never have created without our help—messes that we
ourselves are unable to deal with effectively.

Alternatively, do we face the fact that we have now made the
problems of Earth so desperate that the only action consistent

with decency is for us to put the Terrans quickly out of their misery by destroying every one of their worlds and all of their populations? That is, have we made the unthinkable Alternative A not only thinkable but desirable? If so, we can only hope our own science is sufficiently sophisticated to predict what the consequences will be when that many planetary bodies are removed from space simultaneously. Or do we, to spare ourselves that last hazard, destroy every last vestige of the populations and leave the planets as empty monuments, to stand as a memorial to our genocide for all of time? If we resort to something so monstrous, can we stay sane?

It would be a fine and wondrous thing if we could reject both the plan of condemning the Terrans to a slow and miserable death and the plan of offering them a swift and painless one, and could instead attempt once again to guide them toward civilization. But we have *tried* interference already, and it has been proved beyond all doubt that we only make matters worse. We do not know enough—we do not understand the Terrans well enough. Their psychology is so alien to us that we have no foundation on which to *build* understanding. We have looked upon them as naughty children, but they do not have the minds or the hearts of *our* children. The analogy is not valid, and it never was valid; it simply eased our consciences.

We have made that mistake once; there can be no justification for making it again. XJH$_i$ hereby puts the Council formally on notice that it will fight any such suggestion with all the resources at its command.

The current policy of live and remote surveillance, which the Council each year condemns, is nothing more than a way of stalling while the inevitable choice is postponed over and over again. This is contemptible; it is cowardly; it cannot be allowed to continue. We must decide. We must make the choice, however difficult. Perhaps the females of Earth do have within them somewhere the resources to bring their runaway males under control? Perhaps the fact that we have provided them with ghettos for the most extreme manifestations of violence would be the slight edge they need to bring this about? Perhaps we should allow them the opportunity to try. Perhaps there are among the females some who have ways of creating real change—we have had reports from agents observing the families of Terran linguists, to offer just one example, suggesting that those women do understand the mechanisms of change and have the courage and resolve to set them in motion—although with a slowness that is not encouraging. Perhaps we should allow *them* to try.

And perhaps we should not. Perhaps that would only be still more cruelty. Perhaps they, and all the others, are entitled to our swift mercy.

But we *must* decide. Please do not insult the citizens of the Consortium with further evasions; we do not believe that they will be tolerated.

We look forward to hearing that this question has been placed upon the agenda for the current session of the Council.

XJH$_i$

Afterword
Gender, Technology, and Violence

The Judas Rose (1987) is the second book in Suzette Haden Elgin's
Native Tongue trilogy about the invention and social establishment
of a woman-centered language. The trilogy as a whole dramatizes two
themes: 1) the way languages work to structure perception and 2) how
we might understand and develop principles of nonviolence.¹ In the
trilogy's first book, *Native Tongue* (1984), we are introduced to a future
world where women have been returned to second-class status and
the economy is dependent on intergalactic trade. A small number of
superb women linguists secretly create a women's language that
not only introduces them to the *new* society of the Womanhouses—
a society radically altered by Láadan's impact on its speakers—but
also helps them to imagine and enact alternatives to the society of mas-
culinist violence in which they live. *The Judas Rose* follows the story
of that language, Láadan, as it is spread secretly and subversively to
link women worldwide and as the relationship between humans and
Aliens becomes more explicit. The concluding book of the trilogy,
Earthsong (1994), turns from the question of a gender-based language
to the broader question of alternate and nonviolent forms of nourishment,
as well as to the results of total economic collapse when the interplanetary
Consortium decides to leave Earth *en masse*.

The central strategy of the Native Tongue books is the invention
of a women's language, Láadan, in response to the idea that existing languages, reflecting and encoding patriarchal culture as they do,
often exclude and/or distort the experiences and perceptions of
women. The women of the Lines design Láadan to eliminate as many
such exclusions and distortions as possible. Elgin's basic tenet is that
language is power: "If speaking a language were like brain surgery,
learned only after many long years of difficult study and practiced
only by a handful of remarkable individuals at great expense, we would

view it with similar respect and awe. But because almost every human being knows and uses one or more languages, we have let that miracle be trivialized into 'only talk'" (*Language Imperative* 239). That Elgin draws a parallel between language and brain surgery is suggestive: as much as the two activities differ in their social reception, they are both interventions that can reshape the world. Like all technologies, language is reflexive: it both shapes us and is shaped by us. Because of this reflexivity, both brain surgery and language are technologies that have the power to change not only how we understand the world, but the world itself. Moreover, the comparison conveys Elgin's conviction that language, too, functions as a kind of technology, an extension of human capacities. Finally, linguistic knowledge can be a therapeutic response to violence, just as medical education is a therapeutic response to disease: "My position has been that the only nonviolent mechanism we have for reducing human violence is language, and that a major barrier to using that mechanism is public ignorance of linguistic science (just as public ignorance of hygiene was a major barrier to improving public health until very recently.)"[2] And it is precisely because language, as Elgin understands it, is material, technological, and curative that it is also charged with feminist significance. The language we use affects (and genders) our understanding of the world, our place in it, and our interactions with one another; changing our language can change for better or worse not only how we think, but the world in which that thinking occurs. The premise of the Native Tongue books is that a linguistic revolution is necessary, not only to challenge the linguistic foundation of patriarchy but to treat the society of violence that subtends it. As Elgin puts it, "patriarchy requires violence in the same way that human beings require oxygen" ("A Feminist Is a What?" 46).

Encoding women's perceptions, Láadan encodes nonviolence as well. Because the choices available for responding to conflict expand with the range of new alternatives imagined in the new women's language, for Elgin a woman-centered world is a peaceful one to be attained by a struggle both linguistic and therapeutic. While Elgin's vision here is essentialist in its notion that Láadan simply gives linguistic shape and power to the way women inherently *are,* it also contains the possibility of what might be termed a performative extrapolation from that essential nature. Láadan, in part, is developed around what the women of the Lines call Encodings, "the making of a name for a chunk of the world that so far as we know has never been chosen for naming before in any human language, and that has not just suddenly been made or found or dumped upon your culture. We mean naming a chunk that has been around a long time but has never before impressed anyone as sufficiently important to *deserve* its own name" (*Native*

Tongue 22). Creating the compilation of encodings that becomes Láadan, then, women are not simply creating new words. They are reordering the world: separating the significant from the insignificant, determining what will be perceived and what will go unperceived, and thus establishing a context for feminist experience and action.

The creative force of language is not only thematically central to what Elgin called the larger "thought experiment" of the Native Tongue books; it was actually the motivating force behind the series. Elgin wrote the books in order to test four hypotheses, not merely in fiction but in the *real world* context beyond the novels:

> 1) that the weak form of the linguistic relativity hypothesis is true [that is, that human languages structure human perceptions in significant ways]; 2) that Gödel's Theorem applies to language, so that there are changes you could not introduce into a language without destroying it and languages you could not introduce into a culture without destroying it; 3) that change in language brings about social change, rather than the contrary; and 4) that if women were offered a women's language one of two things would happen—they would welcome and nurture it, or it would at minimum motivate them to replace it with a better women's language of their own construction. ("Láadan")

Elgin admits that despite the success of the Native Tongue trilogy, her experiment did not produce the desired outcome beyond the world of literature. The fourth hypothesis was proven false when Láadan failed to be taken up in any meaningful way in society. But the broader questions of language, of gender, and of violence continue to resonate, both in fiction and beyond.

GENDER, LANGUAGE, AND VIOLENCE IN *THE JUDAS ROSE*

Because the action of *The Judas Rose* so closely depends on that which happens in *Native Tongue,* it is worth reviewing the plot of the first book so that we can see how the second builds upon it. There are three primary narrative strands in *Native Tongue,* though each overlaps with the others. The first narrative follows Nazareth Chornyak Adiness, a remarkably talented linguist whose difficult life demonstrates the need for a women's language as she leads the women of the Lines into using and teaching Láadan. The second narrative chronicles the long line of failures and disasters resulting from the U.S. government's attempts to Interface a non-humanoid Alien with a human infant. The third narrative connects the government Interfacing experiments to the work of the Lines by tracing the life of Michaela Landry, mother of an infant killed in an Interface who initially blames the Linguists for her child's death. While the conflict between Linguists and non-Linguists has led to two separate societies whose relations have been characterized by prejudice and isolation, the growth of Láadan brings women together, giving them a new, shared basis for social relations. *Native Tongue* dramatizes how changing a language can in fact change reality, as the spread of Láadan alters the very lives of the women of the Lines. No longer isolated from each other and subjected to the constant observation and supervision of their husbands and fathers, women now can work together for a society that is both fairer and less violent.

In *The Judas Rose*, the project of linguistic education for a general audience continues on both a Terran and galactic scale. Working with the unwitting assistance of both the Protestant and Roman Catholic churches, the women of the Lines find ways to send Láadan into the greater community in order to undermine the culture of violence the men have instituted. The women's project of expanding the reach of Láadan is a gentle echo of the Terran governments' project of colonizing space; while the former allows for greater communication among women, the latter reduces communication and connectivity as social deviants of all kinds are isolated each to their own designated asteroid. The Terran governments are less successful in attempts at linguistic expansion: the project of Interfacing non-humanoid Aliens with human infants (despite consistently horrific results) to extend the trade possibilities to those worlds as well as for linguistic exchange, also chronicled in *Native Tongue*, becomes less and less successful, and, ultimately, fails altogether—at least in producing the desired results. As the different projects of linguistic outreach continue (overtly and covertly), male members of the Lines are revealed to be linked to Alien objectives and monopolies, part of a coherent political power structure extending throughout the galaxy—a power structure undercut by the linguistic rebellion occurring secretly in their midst. Through these interwoven narratives and the lens of linguistics, Elgin deftly explores several issues that still have urgent relevance for us now, as the book is reissued, including the relation between gender and technology (both informational and biomedical) in the project of globalization (a project that is central to the new world order) and the possibilities for women to unite across boundaries of religion, class, nationality, race, and ethnicity.

Gender and Information Technology

In the simultaneously global and galactic context of *The Judas Rose*, language is presented as a potent technology for human communication, but one that can, paradoxically, be either enhanced or inhibited by information technology. This is nowhere so clearly represented as in the character of Selena Opal Hame. In *Native Tongue,* the infant Selena is fed a combination of hallucinogens before she is Interfaced with Beta-2, a non-humanoid whose worldview was so "alien" to the human mind that it had killed previous infants Interfaced with it. The hallucinogens did their work, in a sense: when Selena was Interfaced her tolerance for alternative realities was sufficiently great that she survived, while the Alien died. Yet one could argue that Selena's "survival" was minimal and carried with it an incalculable toll: she exits the Interface having not acquired a non-humanoid language, and, tragically, stripped of her own native tongue. The impact is devastating, forcing her to live in a non-linguistic world:

> I know that when their mouths move and noises come it is because they are sharing what is inside their heads. They can show each other, or they can do it when no other person is there. . . .
>
> I don't know what in me is the broken part. My ears work; my eyes work; my head works. My fingers are not broken; I can cut and sew and dig and stir and cook. All the doings. I can go where other persons go, I know it is not my legs. My mouth opens like their mouths, but it does not make any noise . . . perhaps it is my mouth that is the broken part. (202; 204)[3]

Selena's poignant linguistic dislocation and alienation emerges fully when the women of the Lines introduce her to a form of information technology: a small box with buttons on it that she can manipulate like a computerized voice synthesizer. Working with it, she is able for the first time to make complex, stable, layered sounds, which she learns to associate with objects and actions. In short, she learns to use language. For Selena, that breakthrough moment of communication seems elemental, miraculous: "When the magic came, it was like what the lightning does to the sky in the hot time! It was a great crashing and a tearing inside my head, and a great light flashing through me! I understood, oh I understood." (205)

While Selena struggles with a linguistic deficiency that is remedied by information technology, the woman known as the "Judas Rose" demonstrates a linguistic control and power that information technology is used to undermine, if only temporarily. Miriam Rose is a child of the Lines, raised from birth in the convent and placed at age thirteen in the Order of Saint Gertrude of the Lambs, where she grows up as Sister Miriam, part of Nazareth's scheme to extend Láadan beyond the Barren Houses of the Lines. Protected within the convent by sympathetic Sister Carapace and taught linguistics and Lines-quality bodyparl (though never defined by Elgin in the texts, context seems to suggest *bodyparl* is the use of gesture, movement, expression, tone of voice, and intonation to communicate nonverbally) by her mother in secret meetings, Miriam Rose grows up trained as a secret ally and weapon of the developing rebellion. Her notable linguistic mastery gives her access even to the Order's centers of power; soon, she is working intimately with the Abbot of Saint Gertrude's, Father Dorien. Although he prides himself on his ability to control the perceptions of others, even he finds himself under Sister Miriam's spell because of her tremendous linguistic ability:

> It was the woman's magnificent voice. A voice that Father Dorien was confident had been given to her by God, specifically to enable her to serve his purposes in this project. As he had anticipated, she had only had to speak one sentence to put an end to their objections. He had heard that voice many hundreds of times, because he was her confessor, but it never ceased to be something he marveled over. It was not just a voice, it was a musical instrument, and she was a virtuoso in its use. (178–79)

Her understanding of the power of language, both voiced and read, enables Miriam Rose to subvert the attempts of the Roman Catholic Church to reinscribe Láadan into the patriarchal hegemony. Only the deathbed confession of Sister Maria, the nun who had for more than forty years worked as a "kind of double agent" among the Roman Catholic clergy, alerts them to the existence of Láadan, the deeper layer hidden by the rebels beneath the clunky Langlish (335). As the person in charge of the seemingly impossible project to strip the Láadan Bible of any feminist influences—generated by the priests' demand for materials that would "draw women to the church, but that would be free of feminist contamination" or heterodox suggestion of a female deity—Sister Miriam Rose has final say on the form of the translated passages (337). This proves crucial, enabling her to subvert any attempts to render the translation in beautiful or moving language. As another nun laments, "Who would have suspected that Father Dorien's precious Sister Miriam Rose would have a terrible tin ear? It was shocking, the way she would take a properly defeminized section, with a lovely ring to it when you read it aloud, and fool around with it until it went clanking and stumbling over the tongue, completely ruined" (243). By changing the language to make it "clank and stumble," Sister Miriam Rose effectively prevents the "new" Láadan Bible from being a tool to convert even more women to the hierarchical, patriarchal religions. Father Dorien remarks on this effect when he muses, "It wasn't surprising that they kindled no religious fire in women; women were theologically illiterate, and they had to be attracted to the Lord by the rhythm and power of words and music well assembled. He had tried reading some of those recent bits aloud, and it had been like reading a comphone directory" (306). Such is her skill that almost no one even suspects deliberate intent on her part, even if they notice the discrepancies between her vocal and apparent written ability. Only Sister Gloria John glimpses part of the plan, when she mutters to the other nuns, "'Perhaps she does it on purpose,'... after one especially unpleasant sequence produced by Miriam's tinkering had been entered into storage as a final version..... 'Because ... the longer she can keep us at this, the longer she can avoid doing any real work herself. And when the Fathers read the garbage she has produced, they'll make her throw it all out and start over again from the beginning'" (243–44).

Sister Miriam Rose's power over influential men extends even to Heykus Joshua Clete, architect of planetary expansion and perhaps the most powerful religious man on the planet. When he meets her at a friend's deathbed, toward the end of the novel, he is surprised to find that he feels blessed "by a woman. A Catholic, and a woman" (329). Yet that initial frightening moment of trust seems dangerously seductive to Clete—emasculating, even infantilizing—and he turns to information technology to combat it. He counters the force of her presence with all of the technological skill at his command:

> To ease the weight of his helplessness, he looked Sister Miriam up in the databanks. She was there, with her Federal Identification number and her blood type, her height and eye color and allergies; because she was a nun—born at the convent ... and illegitimate, parents unknown—she had no possessions and no record of any earnings. No titles, no distinctions. ... A thoroughly unremarkable life. (329–30)

Yet if the databanks reassure Clete that Sister Miriam Rose is a nobody, the authority of that information extends only as far as the imagination interpreting the data. As the novel unfolds, the reader learns that she is far from the "thoroughly unremarkable" nun with "parents unknown" that the data entry summarizes. Indeed, the core significance of the novel emerges in the gap between the life documented in the databanks and the full account of the activities of the Judas Rose.

In the contrasting tales of Selena Opal Hame and Sister Miriam Rose, Elgin demonstrates that information technology, like other technologies, is not inherently gendered; whether its uses are emancipatory or repressive depends on who is wielding it, how skillfully, and to what ends. Though the databases are a form of information technology that enhances the power of the Terran government *over* women, both within and outside the families of the Lines, the 'thologies—another kind of information technology providing a National Public Radio–like narrative news programming—empowers Nazareth Chornyak Adiness, the leader of resistant women of the Lines, by giving her "a kind of grasp of events over the past hundred years. She felt a little less ignorant now, and that was the point" (82). Elgin demonstrates that the very form information technology takes—the extent to which we even *recognize* it as information technology—can also sometimes be gendered. To the databanks of the government, and the helpful 'thologies of Nazareth, we can add another form of information technology: the recipes of the women of the Lines, each replete with coded information accessible only to those who know how to access it, and stored in a recipe collection kept, "to the men's great amusement, on file cards" (73).

Gender and Biomedical Technology

The Judas Rose reveals that, like information technology, biomedical technology too has both dominant and subversive forms, uses that can be liberating or repressive. The medicalization of female resistance to male power is one such repressive use of biotechnology that the novel illustrates. Rebellious women are understood to be insane, and dealt with not through the legal but the medical system. Chapter six reveals this gendered use of biotechnology for social control when Heykus Clete receives Coast Guard Captain Frege's report that a group of women were discovered to have landed on an asteroid, murdered their male companions, and begun the work of establishing a women's settlement using only "antique hand tools and survival packs." Clete commends Captain Frege for making sure that the women have been carried "suitably tranquilized" to "the nearest institutional facility" by their Coast Guard captors, there to be administered with reversible procedures that would "clean out" their minds. But he reproaches Frege for calling the women "bitches" and viewing them as guilty of the murders they committed: "They are not responsible. . . . No woman becomes sick like that overnight. Where were their men all this time, while their minds were rotting away? Frege . . . could your wife, or your sister, or your mother, or any other woman in your care, reach a state of deterioration in which she would be capable of ending your life, without you ever noticing that she needed medical attention?" (90). Kekyus, who prides himself on knowing "everything there was to know about normal women," admits to himself that he is "baffled" by women who refuse the protective care offered them by the state. As he recalls asking such a subversive woman almost a decade earlier: "On earth, and on every colony of Earth, to the limit of our resources, . . . women are cherished. Treated tenderly. Indulged in every way. Looked after, deferred to, sheltered. . . . *Why* do you turn to this perversion? What more do you want?" (91). Yet Hekyus is certain that there is only one appropriate response to such behavior: "Such females should be given expert help immediately, at the first signs of their illness, not allowed to wander around in public with their pathetic condition on view to all the world" (93).

Biomedical technology, like information technology, is portrayed as variable and gender-specific in *The Judas Rose:* used by the U.S. government to put down female resistance but also by the Linguist women to subvert male dominance. In fact, Elgin portrays biomedical technology as a continuum, from the "healthies" of conventional high-tech medicine to the hands-on nursing practices and herbal remedies of the Linguist women. In the tale of Jo-Bethany Schrafft, who is sent by her brother-in-law to work as a nurse for the Linguists, we see the contrast between these two modes of biomedicine. Initially appalled by the primitive medical conditions in the Barren House, the Linguist facility for postmenopausal women, Jo-Bethany is even more surprised when she learns that this absence of high-tech medical care is *voluntary.* She had assumed that the absence of "healthies," servomechanisms that provide nursing and pharmaceutical care to the ill, reflects the age of the Barren House occupants and the relative poverty of the Linguists. In short, she assumes that faced with a need to provide health care that will be both costly and will yield no obvious social benefit (since the elderly linguist women are past reproductive age and unable to work any longer in the Interfaces) the Linguists have simply dumped their old women in the Barren House to die. But she is soon set right in her thinking:

> The [L]inguists didn't use healthies, they told her . . . because they were convinced that the touch of human hands, the nonverbal communication of live hands doing the tending, was absolutely essential to the care of the sick. . . . Only when there was no human being available to tend a patient, or when the only human being available would have been unkind or uncaring, did they consider healthies appropriate, and within the Lines those situations did not exist. They might have been wrong in their belief that the mechanical nursing was bad for the patient—certainly the physicians who had taught Jo's class at nursing school would have considered that not only scientifically incorrect but superstitious, and the evidence for the medical position was overwhelming. But the women of Chornyak Barren House were not without healthies because they were old, or because they were not loved. (117–18)

Yet if the Linguist women refuse the tools of high-tech medicine, their response is fueled not by abstract principle, but by what seems the most effective strategy for each situation. They reject the "normal" reliance on healthies in favor of more medically effective hands-on nursing, yet they also couple an extensive use of natural healing potions with a computerized tracking system for supply and applications: "the database on herbal medicine in the computers at Chornyak Barren House was awe-inspiring, and the women who put the potions together knew exactly what they were doing" (113). Moreover, if the Terran governments rely on biomedicine to maintain a galaxy-wide control over women, the Linguist women use biomedicine to extend their subversive networks fighting that massive system of control. This strategic work explains an event that greatly puzzles Father Dorien: the note from Sister Miriam Rose "saying only that she considered her usefulness in her present post at an end and humbly requested transfer to a nursing position in one of the large public hospitals in Washington. . . . Why [Father Dorien asks himself] would she want to trade [a] sweet sinecure for a hospital nursing post?" (303). Sister Miriam Rose wants to move into nursing because she understands that it offers the greatest access to the widest population, enabling the fastest diffusion of Láadan. As Jonathan Chornyak "explains" the women's plan to Nazareth:

> "There you were with your silly 'woman's language,' all verbed up and no place to go. No way to get it out beyond the Lines. And then you remembered nurses—the only women who come and go freely between the Lines and the public, the only women who have the opportunity to talk to all sorts and kinds of people, and—coincidentally—women who had access to the hospital chapels. All you had to do was seduce the resident nurses from each of the Lines into your cozy little Thursday night meetings in the Womanhouses, and convince them that your Langlish twaddle was romantic and exotic and terribly terribly mysterious and exciting, and they would take it straight out into the world for you." (348)

Clearly, Chornyak fails to understand the plan in its entirety, since he is unaware of the existence of Láadan. However, he has grasped the women's central strategy: the nesting circles of relations between women embodied in the symbol of the women's resistance, the wild vine wreaths.

WILD VINE WREATHS: WOMEN'S EMBEDDED CIRCLES OF RESISTANCE

In the image of the wild vine wreaths, *The Judas Rose* offers a structural alternative to the "endless loops of violence" that are the central problematic of Elgin's novel. While the resistant force of the wild vine wreaths is generated by women, it *must* extend beyond them if it is to succeed, and while the looping pattern of violence is generated and perpetuated by men, the diverse stories of such women as Selena Opal Hame, Jo-Bethany Schrafft, Nazareth Chornyak, and even of Benia, the young mother isolated as the only woman colonist on Polytrix, demonstrate how violence reaches beyond the male community into the lives of women and children. Elgin's use of multiple embedding strategies, imaged in the wild vine wreaths, articulates her understanding that feminist antiviolence work must proceed with an indirection, a circularity, and a capacity for diversion if it is to last long enough to have an effect. As Elgin explains:

> The women of the Linguist Lines hide their revolutionary mechanism—the woman-language Láadan—inside the silly fake woman-language Langlish. They hide their revolutionary messages inside their exchange of recipes; they hide their revolutionary communication inside their needlework circles and their caretaking of the elderly; they hide their dissemination of the real woman-language inside Thursday night religious services, which are in turn hidden inside hospital chapel ministries. They hide the real (womanist/feminist) translation of the King James Bible into Láadan inside the grotesquely-bad translation commissioned by the Roman Catholic Church and directed by the "mole" who is the Judas Rose—Sister Miriam Rose (herself physically hidden inside the R[oman] C[atholic] C[hurch] by the women of the Lines).[4]

Symbol of the intertwined circles of female resistance, the wild vine wreaths articulate another theme central not just to *The Judas Rose* but to contemporary society: the possibility that women can unite despite obstacles of race, religion, class, ethnicity, even galactic location. While even a decade ago this vision might have seemed too old-fashioned in its feminism to teach, from the perspective of the new millennium the trilogy has both a thematic and a historical interest. The very premise of Láadan itself, the notion of a women's language, is based on the idea, familiar to cultural feminism of the 1960s and 1970s, that women have a connection with other women that transcends differences of context and situation, a connection that can transcend other relationships. This principle is most evident among the women of the Lines, who already do have Láadan to connect them together. While the thirteen Households of the Lines span national and cultural boundaries (though most of the Households are in the United States), race is never mentioned. This omission—so striking to contemporary readers—both situates the trilogy in its own historical time by illustrating the unity among women argued in feminist thought just several decades earlier and serves as a vivid illustration of the theoretical and political lacunae that feminisms of the most recent two decades have critiqued. The women of the Lines demonstrate the kinds of connections that women can forge: through Láadan, through the recipe codes, and most importantly through the Barren Houses. The practices of speaking together, sharing recipes together, even living in old age in gender-segregated units, have a political effectiveness for the Linguist women that recalls theories of a unified women's culture in the era of cultural feminism. Significantly, Elgin's vision of this women's culture develops during the course of the trilogy. After the first book, women who are not barren live in Womanhouses; a barren woman could still live in one of the Womanhouses instead of a Barren House if that was her preference. Girl children move to the Womanhouse as soon as they begin to menstruate. Implicitly, then, they are united by their experience and essence as women, not by their new status as *cast-offs* of patriarchal culture.

Yet if the Linguist women, who live together, cook together, and talk together in a community that excludes men, find that their connection to each other flourishes, women outside the Lines have no such connections, even between women who are friends and whose backgrounds and lives are otherwise similar. At a dinner party, for instance, Cassie's husband suggests that the point of marital academies is to teach a female form of violence, one based on polite humiliation (259). The lack of a unified women's community provides opportunities for men to turn women against each other, generating verbal and social violence as another form of the generalized violence that keeps patriarchy in place. Cassie herself expresses disconnection when she thinks about losing her best friend to the colonies: "Cassie will be sorry to lose Brune, but maybe Doby will be kinder to her when they get out to the colonies; she hopes so. She doesn't like always having to feel sorry for Brune; it distracts her, and it makes her feel uneasy and insecure" (263). The women of the Lines pity other women for their alienation from women: "It did change your perspective about your own problems, remembering how much worse it was for most women . . . with no other woman to comfort her or help her or advise her. And the women of her family as ignorant as she was, even if they happened to be close by when she was miserable, by some accident" (298).

Connections between Linguist and non-Linguist women demonstrate both the possibility of alliance across differences and the difficulties of escaping context. When Jo-Bethany Schrafft first comes to Chornyak House, she is suspicious of the women, stunned by the accommodations, and horrified by the lack of bedside healthies (117). Although it takes the combined efforts of many women to settle her concerns, once the initial misunderstanding is gone, she does feel a connection. In *The Judas Rose,* Elgin implies that women are disconnected by the work of two major patriarchal instruments: the compartmentalization of women's lives in separate, male-headed households and the social structures that train women to be adversarial. As befitting its era, the novel suggests that if these factors could be overcome, if women could both regularly connect and learn to overcome their social training, women would have "natural" bonds together. Connection is possible, Elgin suggests in *The Judas Rose,* through women's invitation and women's effort. As the woman of the Lines at the dinner party says, "You're missing all the fun. My dears, won't you come play, too?" (270). Elgin's vision of this natural link between women depends on an essentialized vision of gender that to a contemporary reader has great historical interest precisely because of its distance from our current attention to gender as a category of performance rather than essence. In the Native Tongue trilogy, Linguist women are understood to have a special connection to things empathetic, earthly and spiritual, while men are conceptualized as aggressors; sexual intercourse between women and men of the Lines is portrayed overall as an unfulfilling and boring interaction offering little to the woman, and to the man only the assurance of his control of women. And though Elgin suggests that women can unite with effort, bonds with men are portrayed as inherently problematic. When Jo-Bethany Schrafft accuses the men of the Lines of being sexist for creating Womanhouses, the women respond:

> "Jo-Bethany, have you lived in a house with a man recently? Just one man?"
>
> "Yes. My brother-in-law. The man who sent me here."
>
> "Well, did you enjoy it?"
>
> She found herself looking straight into the other woman's eyes, and those eyes were dancing with amusement, as if Dorcas knew all about what it had been like to live with Ham Klander.
>
> "Oh . . ." she had said weakly. "No. No, not very much."
>
> "Then would you please try to imagine what it would be like

to live in a house with dozens of men? With fifty men, or more?"

The expression on her face must have been eloquent; and what she had said had been the perfect thing to say. She had heard her mother say it so many times. She had said, "A hill is to climb. A man is to pick up after." Talking to herself, really. And all of the other women had begun to laugh, laughing till there were tears in her eyes; laughing for her, not at her. (118–19)

The implicit assumption that relations with men provide no sexual or social benefits—since the violence integral to masculinity will inevitably express itself—means that women must work to connect with other women: the implication is that, in their world, women need to connect precisely because there are currently no healthy connections between women and men. But starting with connections between women can help enable the reeducation away from violence that will prevent the cataclysm that Elgin implies is impending, because it enables women to resist the violence men perpetuate as the galactic structure responds to the rising New World Order. (The resonances of Elgin's vision here seem as uncannily prescient as her portrait of a relatively peaceful womankind seems nostalgic.)

Through the complicated sets of relations it presents—Terran and Alien, Linguist and non-Linguist, male and female—*The Judas Rose* both articulates and critiques the New World Order that was beginning to develop when Elgin was writing the novel. It also speaks to our *new* New World Order, in which a patriotic nationalism claiming to support feminist emancipation is activated in the name of a transnational global culture whose economic order is indifferent, at best, to the well-being of women. From the Terran perspective from which the novel takes place, geopolitics is dominated by a race to the colonies between the U.S. and the Soviets. In reality, however, members of the inner circle of the Earth's governments understand that this "race" is in fact a manufactured one, tightly controlled by the Alien Consortium. The U.S. populace, on the other hand, in a continuation of the manifest destiny in which their political imaginary is rooted, believes that the endless expansion to new colonies is both a blessing and their rightful due. Although this race/expansion is understood religiously (Heykus Joshua Clete), evolutionarily (Aliens), and politically (Macabee Dow), the novel makes it clear that this only perpetuates and further solidifies the grossly unequal and violent status quo presented in the trilogy from the start. As Nazareth remarks, "Earth has been able to molder along undisturbed in its comfortable rut. Pressures that would have meant inevitable change before the colonization of space are siphoned off now—we just export them to the stars" (64).

Within the U.S. government of the twenty-third century, the New World Order is understood as a power struggle between the government and the Linguists, framed as the ability to control trade agreements with the Aliens. The Lines are described as "'control[ling] the fate of entire planets, and of whole alliances of planets'" (255). This is the thrust both of Macabee Dow's plan to Interface his son ["'The game, gentlemen, is *power;* there are no other games worth playing'" (104)] and the Roman Catholic Church's plan to convert the women who speak Láadan to proper Catholic worship ["'We wish to win those women—and through them, their men—and in the fullness of time, the Lines and all their power'" (183)]. Yet if the Terran battle is framed in terms of male or patriarchal power, by the novel's epilogue we learn that this violent race to power is futile: the Aliens control both the power and the alliances, and they understand the crucial problem facing Earth to be the human tendency toward violence. Even Alien intervention in Terran affairs—which, we learn, has taken place because humans were in danger of exterminating themselves—has failed to change the situation. The only alternative to extermination, as the Aliens perceive it, is to trust that the women will eventually change the world with Láadan. Thus the distance between the sexes poses a significant problem not only for female-male relations, but also for the future of the human species: it acts as an impediment to the only remaining solution to human violence, the possibility that women can influence men to renounce violence. As Nazareth explains,

> Meanwhile, Láadan would spread; the tiny wild vine wreaths, unnoticed by anyone, would go up on wall after wall. It would continue to keep the women of the Lines, and all the women who knew it beyond, immune to the state of violence that the men struggled with so incessantly; it would continue to provide the women with the patience necessary to bring the men *out* of those endless loops of violence always begetting more violence. The day would come when they would have a war, and all of the men would look at each other and laugh and just go home (355).

Despite Nazareth's optimistic vision, it is unclear that Láadan can spread fast enough to accomplish this immense transformation in human behavior. And in the novel's closing chapter, a paper prepared by XJH_i for the Council of the Consortium articulates the desperate choice facing those who wish to improve the Terran situation: Should women be allowed to continue their Láadan project, or should Aliens intervene, eradicating the world in "swift mercy"(363)? Whether the strategic embedding process central to the women's resistance—emblematically represented in the wild vine wreaths that head every chapter—will succeed or fail when the context has expanded from Terran to galactic-scale politics is the urgent question with which readers will turn to Elgin's final volume in the Native Tongue trilogy, *Earthsong.*

Susan M. Squier, Pennsylvania State University
Julie Vedder, West Virginia University
May 2002

NOTES

1. Please see the afterword to *Native Tongue,* "Encoding a Woman's Language," for discussions of how these themes can be explored through linguistic theory and feminist science fiction.

2. Suzette Haden Elgin, personal communication, 20 January 2002.

3. That any attempt to describe what it is like to be without language must itself be rendered in language is of course one of the ironies of Selena's situation.

4. Suzette Haden Elgin, personal communication, 20 January 2002.

WORKS CITED

Elgin, Suzette Haden. "A Feminist Is a What?" *Women and Language* 18.2 (1995): 46.

———. "Láadan." *http://www.sfwa.org/members/elgin/Láadan.html* (2000).

———. *The Language Imperative.* Cambridge, Mass.: Perseus Books, 2000.

CPSIA information can be obtained at www.ICGtesting.com
Printed in the USA
LVOW09s1915110215

426637LV00016B/562/P